how the **other** half
hamptons

how the **other** half
hamptons

Jasmin Rosemberg

NEW YORK   BOSTON

Copyright © 2008 by Jasmin Rosemberg

5 Spot
Hachette Book Group USA
237 Park Avenue
New York, NY 10017

Visit our Web site at www.5-spot.com.

5 Spot is an imprint of Grand Central Publishing.
The 5 Spot name and logo are trademarks of Hachette Book Group USA, Inc.

Printed in the United States of America

First Edition: June 2008
10 9 8 7 6 5 4 3 2 1

Library of Congress Cataloging-in-Publication Data

Rosemberg, Jasmin.
  How the other half Hamptons / Jasmin Rosemberg. —1st ed.
       p. cm.
  Summary: "LAGUNA BEACH grows up and moves to the East Coast in this chronicle of twentysomething excess"—Provided by publisher.
  ISBN-13: 978-0-446-19415-0
  ISBN-10: 0-446-19415-8
  1. Young women—New York (State)—Hamptons—Fiction. 2. Shared housing—Fiction. 3. Dating (Social customs)—Fiction. 4. Hamptons (N.Y.)—Fiction. 5. Chick lit. I. Title.
PS3618.O8H68 2008
813'.6—dc22   2007043731

Book design by Stratford Publishing Services, a TexTech Company

*To my parents, who guided me, encouraged me,
supported me, and never once stopped believing in me.*

Acknowledgments

I'm a bit of a writing cliché (or as luck should have it, a success story). After toiling away in a cubicle, I did what every aspiring novelist is told never to do: *I quit my day job.* I'd thus like to thank all the family, friends, and co-workers who stood by me when I moved home and set upon this journey—everyone who understood why I had to, everyone who truly believed I could do this. And to any aspiring novelists out there, I urge you, don't ever pay mind to the statistics.

In this business, I've learned that writing a novel and having the wrong agent is hardly different from not writing a novel at all. For this reason, I am utterly indebted to my writing's tireless champion, Paula Balzer, who saw something in me at the age of twenty-four, back before this book was even conceived. She is kind, candid, and available (not just because she set up shop near my parents' house), and has given me the greatest gift I ever could have hoped for—the chance to fulfill my dream.

I couldn't have envisioned having a better first publishing experience, and Grand Central Publishing has far surpassed my every expectation: My editor, Emily Griffin, is efficient, meticulous, and nothing short of an editorial superwoman; my publicist, Elly Weisenberg, so creative and enthusiastic, you'd have thought this novel her own. My sincerest thanks go out to them, to Caryn Karmatz Rudy, Tareth Mitch, Linda Cowen, Laura Jorstad, Miriam Parker, and the entire 5 Spot team.

I'm grateful to everyone at the *New York Post* (or formerly at the *New York Post*) who gave me the opportunity to write a column that would open more doors than they'd ever know: particularly, Faye Penn, John Lehmann, and Farrah Weinstein. I'd also like to thank Richard Johnson and Bill Hoffman at "Page Six," and Jared Shapiro at *Life&Style Weekly,* for their support.

I am fortunate to have such a loyal group of friends who've stuck with me through beach weather, ski weather, and every climate in between: Ali Jacobs, Ali Lasky, Alyssa Kessler, Amy Meyers, Betsy Rudnick, Blake Rose, Danielle Schwartz, Farah Goldstein, Jamie Dyce, Jessica Civitano, Katerina Zervas, Leslie Napach, Meri Strickon, Shari Mancher, Stacy Schwartz, Stephanie Baskin, and Tara Fougner. Also (while listing their names would double this book's length), thanks to the many share house members, nightclub affiliates, publicists, and friends who made my Hamptons experience worth writing about.

My younger sister, Kacey, was this novel's first reader, and is the person on the planet who knows me best (yet loves me anyway). Thanks for schlepping the uncondensed manuscript throughout Prague, for listening to endless book rhetoric, and for breaking up my monotonous routine with a story (or silly dance move). I know you will be a fantastic lawyer (and with any luck, a literary contracts one).

This book (or anything I've done in my life) would never have been possible without the guidance, encouragement, and generosity of my parents, who raised their daughter to believe that she could do anything. I bet they never imagined the girl who was so eager to leave home and embrace city life at seventeen would, years later, ask to return (and remain, for slightly longer than any of us ever anticipated). Thanks for giving up your dining room table, for rescuing me (when I was stranded in the Hamptons, and time and time again) and for never once, not even for a moment, doubting me. You are my role models, my support system (emotionally as much as financially), my entire world. You've given me more than any child deserves, more than I could ever repay, and I'll never stop wondering how I got so lucky.

how the **other** half
hamptons

Prologue

I t starts with a party, unlike any you've been to before. A party that goes something like this:

Just imagine you are riding in a crammed elevator.

Imagine you are doing so in a city as heavily populated as New York, where hundreds of people come in and out of your life on a daily basis and one space-squandering body is nearly interchangeable with the next.

Now imagine this same elevator has just slammed to a halt.

You let your eyes wander around, curious to see who is standing beside you. You wonder what it will be like once you're trapped with these individuals, and begin to scrutinize every detail of their appearance for signs of what to expect. You notice other people similarly scrutinizing your appearance, as is only fair, because you are suddenly in this together.

Then picture this group in a Manhattan bar, replace "involuntarily" with "voluntarily" trapped, and welcome to a Hamptons meet-and-greet party.

The time of choice: happy hour on a weeknight. The location of choice: a local dive in a neighborhood like Murray Hill, where 99 percent of the participants already coexist in adjacent doorman buildings. The crowd of choice: anyone willing to fork over upward of two grand for a single bed in a five-person bedroom on (alternating) summer weekends.

And, newcomers, beware: anything you say, do, drink,

dance on, or go home with will forever be held against you. Worse yet, it will *define* you.

But don't worry. Even though Memorial Day weekend is almost upon you, you will have anticipated this moment for weeks. The entire neighborhood will have been thinking the same, reflected by the growing crowds at New York Sports Clubs, Hollywood Tans, and the bathing suit section of Bloomingdale's. Preparing for a summer in the Hamptons is quite a daunting prospect.

Now, you're probably thinking: the *Hamptons*—private yachts, exclusive clambakes, Bridgehampton Polo Club matches, dinners at Nick and Toni's, and nauseatingly elitist company. Not even close.

What twentysomethings take part in each and every summer is an experience perhaps even unknown to Hamptons regulars. This underground practice is not only illegal but also cultivates a camp-like culture distinctly its own.

Prepare to enter the Share House.

The concept is surprisingly simple. One business-savvy individual—known as the "house manager"—rents a house for the summer, crams each room with as many beds as will (un)comfortably fit, and sells off individual shares for about a million times their aggregate value. (Think of buying an old car and selling off the parts—at, say, twenty-five hundred dollars per tire.) However, without this middleman cleverly partitioning the price, small groups of young professionals would never have access to such an illustrious vacation home.

Complete with pool, Jacuzzi, basketball court, volleyball court, and tennis court, by day this house is a playground for tanning, swimming, sports, and socializing. By night, nearly forty shareholders and their guests will compete to shower, primp, pre-drink, and eventually pass out in the confines of this ten-bedroom, five-bathroom abode. (You do the math.)

Of varying age, career path, and alcohol tolerance level, each of these mass-migrated Manhattanites is there under the pretense of meeting new people, getting a little color, and escaping the stresses of city life.

Each is also most likely to be single.

As a result, this share house will play host to drunken escapades, public nudity, hot tub hookups, hideous hangovers, explosive arguments, emotional bonding, and juvenile mischief.

And it will be the best time of your life.

Chapter One

J amie Kessler had never been one to play by the rules. Especially where guys were concerned.

She'd flirted with the teaching assistants who marked her exams in college. She'd kissed doormen to jump the line at coveted nightclubs. She'd hooked up with guys who hadn't even suggested taking her to dinner (in fact, she rather preferred it that way).

So there may have been only one cardinal rule at any Hamptons meet-and-greet party. Yet somehow, within the first five minutes, she was already contemplating breaking it.

"Well, why not?" she'd earlier challenged when her more conservative friend Rachel warned her to *not*, under any circumstance, go home with any guy from this party. Their disagreement was hardly a shock, as she and Rachel found themselves at odds about practically everything.

"Because then you have to spend the whole summer in the share house avoiding him," Rachel said, directing her words more at Jamie than their newly single friend Allison. "Or having every other guy avoid you, because you already hooked up with one of his friends. Is it really worth it?"

"I guess not," Jamie had agreed. And she really had been convinced. Until, of course, she spotted Jeff.

There may only be one cardinal rule—but there is also only one incontrovertibly hot guy at any Hamptons meet-and-greet party. And predictably, within the first five minutes, nearly every girl in the bar realizes it.

Not that any of these girls posed a particular challenge, Jamie thought, giving a cursory glance around the neighborhood watering hole DIP.

Three generic girls—with identical dark straightened hair, Seven jeans, Gucci purses, and scowls—nursed white wines in the corner. Holding court at the bar yet edging toward the dance floor was a perky pair of girls who were definitely not from New York, which was discernible as much from their enthusiasm as by their beverage choice: cosmos. And tucked into a booth all by herself was a pasty redhead who looked like she was awaiting a shot in a doctor's office.

Jamie smiled. She definitely had this one in the bag.

"I'll be right back," she told her friends, who were chatting with a pair of investment bankers (a ubiquitous type in Murray Hill, yet one she'd personally never found appealing).

Then in that fearless and haphazard way she had of approaching people, Jamie tossed back her tousled brown locks, abandoned her half-full vodka soda, and started toward the bar.

"So, are you doing this house?" she said to the most attractive guy she'd seen in…days. In doing so, she noticed but ignored the glares of the far less aggressive girls sipping wine in the corner. There were always girls glaring at her from the corner.

"If I wasn't, I am now," he said, shifting a pair of entrancing blue eyes to hers.

Managing to remain unfazed, Jamie evaluated the prospect before her. With a too-symmetrical face, cocky disposition, and looks he seemed much too aware of, he practically had ASSHOLE etched across his forehead. He was her type to a T.

"Seriously," she pressed, with a playful smile. "I'm not sure I'm sold yet."

But her companion apparently was sold. "Well, my buddy Mark runs this house," he began, his eyes dipping into her cleavage. "I'll make sure he puts us on the same weekends."

"Then I *definitely* won't do it," she joked, glad she'd worn the red shirt. She averted her eyes and looked longingly toward the bar.

"What are you drinking?" he asked, not missing a beat.

"Grey Goose and soda," she replied, even though her original soda had been mixed with well vodka.

"Done," he said, turning back toward the line. Satisfied, Jamie stepped a few feet away from the crowded bar, mostly to ensure that no one stepped on her brand-new peep-toe Louboutins.

She peered over at Rachel, who was conducting one of her marathon conversations with investment banker number one, and Allison, who seemed surprisingly entertained by investment banker number two. Allison was probably just being polite; after breaking up with her boyfriend of—four years? five years?—pretty much her entire existence, she wasn't easily entertained these days.

"Excuse me." Jamie felt a sudden tap on her shoulder.

"Are you here for the Hamptons party?" asked one of three guys in their late twenties standing behind her, his forwardness clearly fueled by alcohol. While none of the three was overwhelmingly attractive, each was appealing enough, with the boyish look and charm of a fraternity guy who had never grown up.

"What Hamptons party?" she said, then cracked a smile when she saw their expressions change. "No, I'm kidding. I'm Jamie."

"Good one." He chuckled a bit, noticeably relieved. "I'm Rob, and this is Brian and Dave."

"Nice to meet you," she said, giving each of the guys a could-I-possibly-hook-up-with-him once-over as she shook his hand. Rob was tall with a winning smile but thinning hair; Brian was jolly and teddy-bear-like; and Dave, the best looking of the bunch, was on the short side, with flirtatious eyes that Jamie didn't fully trust. "So," she continued. "Are you..."

"*Yes*. I'm the guy from that reality show," Rob confessed, tilting his head smugly.

Jamie looked at him questioningly. "I was going to say *Are you all friends from school?* But, um, what reality show?"

"You know, *The Apprentice*?" he said, his voice rising a notch. "Just don't let it get out. I don't want to be stalked by girls all summer."

"Oh, that's so funny," Jamie replied. *That's so funny* was what she said when she didn't really know what else to say.

"But yeah, we all went to Maryland together. Class of 2008," Brian joked, then abandoned the small talk completely. Though perhaps that's what happened when you got into your late twenties. In your late twenties, you tended to more immediate concerns. "Patrón?" he asked.

"Always," Jamie answered, never one to turn down free alcohol or undivided male attention. Maybe she'd been selling this share house idea short. "To a great summer," she toasted after he handed her a glass, then threw back the shot so fluidly she even surprised herself.

But the real surprise awaited her when she returned to the bar to dispose of her empty shot glass, and found her drink bearer standing not only with her Grey Goose and soda but also next to one of the wine sippers.

"Thanks," she replied, accepting the drink. Then she turned confrontationally toward the girl, whose features would actually be pretty if they weren't pursed so tightly. "I'm Jamie," she announced, in her sweetest too-late-he-bought-me-a-vodka-soda voice.

"Ilana," the girl mumbled before flipping her hair and slowly retreating.

Smart girl, Jamie thought. Once again in the clear, she picked up where they'd left off.

"So have you done this house before?" she asked, curious where a guy this catalog-worthy had been hiding.

"I've been out there the last five summers," he told her. Which made him—hopefully—under forty? "But we have a sick house this year, in Southampton. And we picked a much better-looking group of girls..."

"What do you mean, you *picked*?" she asked, though it was hardly inconceivable that a guy who looked like this could have his pick of whatever he wanted.

"We held interviews at Mercury Bar, to screen any groups that found out about it through the e-mails. But you must know Mark, then?" He gestured toward a tan, unshaven guy with longish hair, whose confidence alone indicated his position as house manager.

"My roommate's older sister knows him," Jamie said, her eyes lingering on Mark a moment longer. "They did a Quogue share together back in the day."

"Oh, Dune Road? That summer was a blast." A spark of recognition lit up his already iridescent eyes.

Okay, she had to ask. "So how old are you exactly?" Not that she'd ever discriminate...

"Twenty-nine," he said. "And you?"

"Twenty-three."

"Do you think twenty-nine is too old?" Those eyes found hers again.

"Too old to...talk? Not at all," she replied with a wink.

He took a deep breath. "So I guess you're going to want to know where I live, what I do, where I'm from, right?"

"Not particularly," she admitted, feeling the Patrón rushing to her head. She leaned closer and went in for the kill. "What if what I want doesn't involve talking?"

It took him a few seconds to digest her bluntness. "You're trouble," he said with a wicked grin, repeating the phrase many guys before him had used to describe her. Then, just as many guys had similarly done before him, he conceded.

"I live a few blocks away, Thirty-fifth and Lex," he suggested. He was standing so close to her now, she could smell the traces of that morning's cologne. "Why don't we just get out of here?"

I thought you'd never ask, Jamie said to herself.

Throwing back the remainder of her drink and pounding the empty glass down a bit harder than she'd intended, Jamie obediently followed her new friend. (Was it Mike? Jon? Had she even asked at all?)

And as she stumbled defiantly onto the Murray Hill street, she couldn't help but laugh at her friend's earlier forewarnings. Perhaps Rachel's stubborn rules applied if you were chasing a relationship. But if all you wanted from a summer was some innocent fun and a wild ride, it was like she always claimed...

Especially where guys are concerned, cardinal rules were made to be broken.

Chapter Two

Sinking back into an empty booth, Rachel Burstein allowed her aching feet a moment of rest. How she would ever survive an entire summer of this was beyond her.

Rachel hated long nights of partying at trendy nightspots; she hated public (well, perhaps even private) drunkenness; and most vehemently, she hated random hookups. Basically, she hated everything that characterized a share in the Hamptons.

But there was one thing Rachel hated more than all of these elements combined.

She hated being single.

And while there were no guarantees, a share was as good a way out as any.

She knew this, because it had been her sister's way out. Not that her sister had ever gone looking. For anything. Nearly two fated summers ago in former share house hot spot Quogue, her sister had been housemates with her now-fiancé, Gregg. It'd become a legendary tale, one Rachel had heard so many times she knew each nauseating word by heart. And while everyone was impressed when an engagement resulted from the summer fling, Rachel wasn't surprised that this share house romance stuck. Dana had been a legendary sister, a legendary student, and a legendary financial analyst, so Rachel expected nothing less than for Dana to be a legendary shareholder. Why, legendary things just seemed to come her way.

What Rachel was, on the other hand, was a legendary foot-step follower. Actually—merely a mediocre one.

All her life she'd strived to break into her sister's high school cheerleading squad, her sister's Ivy League university, her sister's bulge bracket investment bank, her sister's perfect world. All her life, Rachel had never quite matched these distinguished accomplishments (though she couldn't have imagined loving UPenn any more than Michigan, and believed the atmosphere much less brutal at Bear Stearns than at Goldman). However, far worse was her latest—this event-of-the-year wedding planned for late this summer. Rachel loved Dana, of course. But she dreaded the moment she'd have to watch her beautiful sister float down the aisle while she stood fittingly (and most predictably) on the sideline—unengaged, unattached, underappreciated, and alone.

But Rachel was intent not to let that happen.

Rising to her feet, she carefully reexamined the bar. Surely there was at least one guy here she could date. She'd had a promising conversation with Aaron, an investment banker, earlier (how she'd kill to wind up with an investment banker). Though he'd excused himself to find a restroom, and she'd lost track of him...nearly an hour ago.

Still, there was a swarm of suits by the bar, a few stragglers in the booths, and—

"And then there were two," Allison sang, interrupting her thoughts.

"What?" Rachel asked.

But Allison needed only to hold her Motorola RAZR phone up to Rachel's face for Rachel to understand.

Her eyes scanned the words, though she already knew what they'd say—especially since they were text-messaged to the friend least likely to reprimand her.

From: Jamie
Left the bar, C U 2morrow ;)
                Wed, May 25, 9:33 pm

"Wow, can you believe it? That had to have been record time!" Allison exclaimed. Allison had been absent from the singles scene for the last five years (and the four preceding those...so for pretty much ever) and was just now learning the extent of Jamie's forthright ways.

"Can I believe it or do I approve of it?" Rachel replied, then let out a long sigh. "She's just never going to learn. Drunken hookups never lead to relationships."

"Maybe she doesn't want a relationship," Allison suggested, recalling Jamie's frequent claim.

"Every girl wants a relationship," Rachel stated matter-of-factly. And by *every girl,* she most of all meant herself.

Though it wasn't like she hadn't been trying, endlessly, with that same determination with which she attacked everything in her life. She'd resorted to Facebook, Friendster, MySpace, and even enlisted the help of any willing friend to set her up with potential Mr. Rights. And on that count, she had succeeded, for Rachel had almost as many dates as there were nights in the week. In the way that Allison was a serial girlfriend, and Jamie a serial one-night stand, she was a serial dater. Still, all the first dates in the world did not a husband make. But just as she was about to suggest throwing in the towel in favor of a Pizza 33 stop...

"So are you here for the Hamptons party?" asked a voice behind them.

Turning, Rachel found herself face-to-face with one of three guys. He was oozing with personality and clenching two shot glasses. Giving each the could-he-possibly-be-my-husband once-over, she immediately assessed them as being on the older side, yet not the type of guys who seemed in any rush to settle down. Hoping she was wrong, she proceeded to introduce herself, as she'd never been one to discriminate.

"Yup, we're in the house. I'm Rachel," she offered, putting out her hand aggressively. "And this is Allison," she added, feeling the need to assist her more reserved wingman.

"Rob, Brian, Dave," he said, pointing to himself, then to his friends as he spoke.

"Hey," Allison said, turning toward Rob, "weren't you—"

"Yes," Rob proclaimed, raising an eyebrow. "That *was* me on *The Apprentice*."

"Wait, what?" Allison replied, pushing a piece of her short brown hair behind her ear. "I was going to say *Weren't you talking to our friend Jamie before?*" She flashed him a shy smile.

"Oh...yeah." He recovered, glancing around. "Where'd she go?"

Why, to get ass, of course! Rachel thought.

"She had to get up early, I think," Allison said. Allison was always the compassionate one. But since they'd be housemates for the entire summer, Rachel imagined they'd figure Jamie out soon enough. She decided to change the subject.

"You were on *The Apprentice*? Ohmigod, I totally recognize you," Rachel exclaimed. Everyone knew the way to a guy's heart was through his ego.

"Yup," Rob responded, quite eager to elaborate. "Season Two. I was only on one episode because—"

"Patrón?" Brian cut in, offering them each a shot glass.

"I can't do tequila on a Wednesday," Rachel excused, omitting the fact that she couldn't do tequila ever.

"You look like a tequila-on-a-Wednesday kind of girl," Brian entreated Allison, handing her a glass. And to Rachel's surprise, she agreed. Allison may have been shy, but she didn't have a single mean bone in her body. That, and she was always eager to please, making her a prime girlfriend candidate. Why, she'd been single for less than fourteen days, yet Rachel would bet money she'd be snapped up again before the weekend.

Which reminded Rachel to get down to business. "So where do you guys live, what do you do, where are you from?" No sense in postponing the interrogation.

She soon learned Reality Star Rob doubled as a pharmaceutical sales rep; Brian was a portfolio manager (with a penchant for Patrón); and Dave, the best looking of the bunch but at least two heads shorter, dabbled in real estate. Yet there was something about his eyes that made Rachel nervous, like he was dying to rip off either her clothes or Allison's clothes or both their clothes at the same time.

"What about you? Were you girls in the same sorority?" Dave asked. Guys always assumed girls knew each other from their sorority.

And on many occasions, they were right. "Well, Jamie and I, yes—we went to Michigan together, and Allison is our best friend from camp. Although she's from New Jersey and I'm from Long Island—"

"Where on Long Island?" Dave asked, indicating he was as well.

Rachel smiled. "Plainview?" she responded, as if simultaneously probing *Who do you know?* But she was a pro at Long Island geography, and always welcomed someone throwing out a name.

"Do you have an older sister named Dana?" he followed.

Rachel froze. Any name but that one.

"Yes…"

Before she knew it, Dave was turning around and calling out to three high-maintenance-looking girls who were sipping wine in the corner. "Ilana, you were right."

Peering up from their private powwow, one of the girls, nearly interchangeable with her friends in jeans and a black shirt, rose to her feet.

"I knew it!" the girl responded, her heels staccatoing as she approached them. Instantly the iciness on her face melted away. "Your sister was president of my sorority at Penn. We only overlapped for one year, but I *love* Dana! What's she up to?"

"She's...great," Rachel replied, desperately wishing they could talk about someone else's sister. Just as she suspected, though, she was out of luck.

"Hey, Mark," the girl beckoned in a whiny tone to a lean, scruffy-looking guy a few feet away. Growing impatient, she flipped her hair with her hand. "Come here! You know who this is? This is *Dana Burstein's* sister."

"So you're the one she e-mailed me about," he said, studying her as if, when he looked hard enough, he might find Dana underneath. "No way. I never would have guessed."

No one usually did, for which Rachel had grown to be monumentally grateful—even though her sister was positively breathtaking and such a statement could only imply her to be the opposite. For Dana was three crucial inches taller and naturally thinner, despite the fact that Rachel worked out and watched her weight obsessively. And while they both had similar blond-streaked hair and light eyes, Rachel had heard Dana's features described as "softer" and "more delicate." Plus, in contrast to her own preference for plain black clothing, her older sister had a sick sense of style and was effortlessly cool in every way, shape, and form. She was the kind of cool that made people stop and stare. The kind of cool that, as hard as she tried, Rachel knew she'd never be.

"Wait—Dana Burstein from the Dune Road house?" someone else shouted. And before Rachel knew it, a small crowd had gathered.

"How is Dana? That girl was a blast!"

"She's engaged, right? I saw the announcement in the *Penn Gazette*."

"Have you seriously not heard? Dana's a *share house success story*. But her sister probably knows all the details."

Overwhelmed by the fan club multiplying around her, Rachel pounded back the remainder of her drink. *Figures*. It was just like her sister to dominate a party she wasn't even at. But Rachel tried to be kind, since showing any malevolence toward a girl the entire room (the entire *world*) loved would have only made her look silly. Silly, or what she actually was, which was undeniably jealous.

So Rachel answered every question and retold every tale, keeping a smile plastered across her face the whole time. But the question lurking in her own mind—perhaps now more than ever—was why she had even done it, why she always felt compelled to follow her sister. Why hadn't she just found her own share house (run by someone other than Dana's friend), her own hobbies, her own social scene, her own path?

Still, in the course of the action, Rachel hadn't even noticed that Aaron, the investment banker she'd met with his friend Steve earlier, had once again surfaced among the crowd. And after the commotion finally died down, he made his way over to her.

"Where'd you disappear to?" he asked, his tone noticeably more animated than before.

Not that Rachel was complaining. True, he was on the dorky side—a bit too thin, with wire-rimmed glasses and a bone structure so refined it was almost effeminate. But such was consistent with Rachel's honed preferences, as she believed superhot guys never made for good boyfriends. In fact, she'd come to prefer that down-to-earth, subtle attractiveness.

"I've pretty much been here the whole time," she said, confused, but not dismissively so.

He decided to move on. "So are you girls out there Memorial Day weekend?"

"That's the plan," she responded, hoping this wouldn't preclude his taking her phone number.

"Well, why don't you give me your number, just in case," he said, flipping open his phone, thus reading her mind.

Beaming, Rachel recited the digits clearly, and for one sole moment she was thrilled. Until she leaned over and caught sight of the name he'd keyed in to precede them.

Quicker than you could say *Patrón,* Rachel felt like she'd done that tequila shot after all. For she hated high heels, she hated swapping pickup lines, and she hated leaving alone.

But there was one thing Rachel hated more than all of these elements combined. What Rachel Burstein hated most was being: DANA B SIS

Chapter Three

Allison Stern had far too much baggage.

But more important, she desperately needed to pack for the Hamptons. The only problem was, as she rummaged through her closet in attempt to select her weekend attire, traces of her failed relationship seemed to linger everywhere.

It was bad enough that they lingered in her head. And so, just last week, she'd rid her studio of all the obvious offenders—his toothbrush, pictures she'd framed, each piece of Tiffany jewelry he'd given her for each anniversary (there'd been five in total). Yet there was one vital place that had escaped this thorough purge.

Her wardrobe.

Painfully unprepared, Allison unleashed the memories all at once. And all at once they struck her, taking the tangible form of her favorite garments. There was the black three-quarter shirt she'd worn on their first dinner date at Cornell. The red silk sleeveless top that spent more time on the floor than on her body. The white lacy number that witnessed his first "I love you." And worst of all, the baby-blue tank she'd worn just fifteen days ago, when she'd told him it was over.

Josh hadn't done anything wrong per se, though it'd been a while since he'd done anything *right*. Since it *felt* right. Still, she cared about him more than anyone in the world, and he was undeniably her closest friend. But the more time passed (oh, how quickly it passed), the more Allison realized that "a friend" was pretty much all he was—or would ever be. And when the last of her sexual desire eventually vanished, even her body was telling her it was time to get out.

Though how shocked he'd been when he'd come over that Wednesday to watch their favorite show, *Lost*. And, fielding his *lost* expressions, she'd nearly changed her mind, until sadistically he changed his tune.

"I think you're right," he'd said, trying to save face. He always did care too much about what other people thought. "We've been together practically forever," he'd continued. "We should probably try being *single*."

In the manner he knew it would, in the manner he'd intended it to, that word rattled her every nerve. For in her head, it'd sounded right. In theory, it'd sounded necessary. But now coming from his lips that night, it sounded frightening. It sounded hasty. It sounded irreversibly wrong.

Dismissing these thoughts, as she regularly had to do, Allison exhaled one long, cleansing breath. This was just silly, she told herself, turning back toward her closet with new momentum. Everyone has baggage, she thought. The trick was not to take it with you to the Hamptons.

But even trickier is what you actually *should* take when you've never really been in the Hamptons scene. When you've never really been in the *singles* scene. When you're barely ready to be seen at all.

It'd been two weeks since she'd been anointed with the scarlet letter *S,* and Allison for the life of her couldn't remember how to be single. How to sleep in a bed unaccompanied. How to drift off without that last good night. How to hear one of their private jokes and not jump to dial him on her phone. How to flirt like a girl on the hunt. But not only did Allison not remember these things, she didn't want to relearn them.

And what good were clothes? she wondered, touching each item listlessly. Without a guy, she felt naked.

Reaching for the phone, Allison dialed Rachel and Jamie's number. No matter how much time elapsed, she could never imagine becoming like her friends—she just wasn't the type to look for dates, introduce herself to strangers, or conduct endless small talk with people she hardly knew. On the contrary, she was the reserved type, the loyal type, the girlfriend type. And if she said so herself, she had come to be pretty damn good at it.

"I'm not really having much luck here," she confessed when Rachel immediately picked up the phone. Rachel always answered her and Jamie's apartment phone after one ring, as she kept it by her side religiously. "I know Jamie said to bring going-out clothes...but skirts, tank tops, dresses—what exactly are we talking about?"

"Oh, don't stress about it. I'm sure whatever you feel like wearing is fine," Rachel said. This was kind but hardly helpful. And while Rachel always looked appropriate and trendy enough, her clothes were muted (usually black) and rarely memorable. Fortunately, Jamie—who would sooner feed her Dolce & Gabbana obsession than feed herself—grabbed the phone from Rachel.

"So what's the question? What should you bring?"

"Yeah," Allison admitted, feeling suddenly silly. "I've just never really been to the Hamptons."

"Well, I've only been to my premieres and stuff," Jamie said, her PR job having offered her a few choice excursions to the East End. "But here, I'll run you through it—"

Allison grabbed the nearest pen, hoping her friend would expound on every delightfully superficial, unspoken detail. And thankfully, Jamie didn't disappoint.

"Okay, so for the daytime, think second floor of Bloom-ingdale's—Juicy, Ella Moss—or those Calypso types of cover-ups...Bring a different bathing suit for each day we're there—repeating is like the biggest faux pas—and sunglasses you'll wear twenty-four/seven, obviously..." *Obviously.* "Take shoes you don't care about ruining in dirt—although isn't that what the shoe man is for? Jeans, dresses, tank tops—nothing that wrinkles—and a jacket 'cause it's not really summer yet, but bring one really nice skirt or dress just in case...." *In case of what? An emergency charity event?*

But just as Allison felt that knot in her stomach beginning to resurface, Rachel grabbed the phone back.

"Don't listen to her—she doesn't know a thing about share houses. It's not like we're staying at The Estate." After some brief squabbling in the background, Rachel added, "Oh, but she was right about the shoes. Only bring one nicer pair and one going-out bag, to minimize losses. And on that note, don't bring any-thing you'd cry if you lost, like really nice jewelry or anything."

Allison paused. "I thought the Hamptons was like a fash-ion show, and everyone wore their money out there."

"Some people do...just not the same people who are doing share houses," Rachel explained.

This was somewhat reassuring. "Anything else?"

"Yeah, don't forget blankets and pillows and stuff—they're not provided—and take two towels in colors you'll remember, one to shower with and one to use at the pool...Also, bring a sweatshirt in case the house is freezing at night...And your phone charger, 'cause not having that would just be annoy-ing...And we're bringing all the weird stuff."

"Weird stuff?" *This should be good,* Allison thought.

"Yeah...you're going to think I'm neurotic."

"I already do," Allison assured her.

"Okay, I'll read you the list my sister gave me. A full-length mirror—so you can get ready even if the bathrooms are occupied—big bottles of water for when you wake up in the morning and feel like crap, aspirin, hair powder, nail glue, magazines, pretzels, that Hamptons directory *Jodi's Shortcuts,* the *Intermix BlackBook* nightlife guide, and...hey!"

"One more thing." Jamie's voice burst over the line again.

"Sounds like you guys already have everything covered," Allison said.

"Wear only sexy underwear, even to sleep."

Allison waited for the *just kidding* that never came. "Are we still on rules for the Hamptons, or have we progressed to your rules of sexual enlightenment?"

"Ha. Anyway, stop worrying. If worse comes to worse, I can always lend you something," Jamie offered, although Allison could think of nothing *worse* than donning the kind of ostentatious stuff Jamie wore. Then she added, "I'll pick you up as soon as Rachel gets out of work tomorrow, figure like five." Jamie's PR office had summer Fridays, so she got out at three, and Allison was teaching summer school on the Upper East Side and finished at that time normally. "Get excited!" Jamie sang as she hung up the phone.

And maybe Allison would have been excited if her thoughts weren't now so preoccupied by baggage (as in, the kind she was bringing to the Hamptons).

At promptly five twenty (Allison had learned to add an extra twenty minutes onto any estimate Jamie ever gave), Jamie screeched her mother's white Lexus SUV to a halt on the corner of Thirty-fourth and Third. At least Allison thought it was Jamie. She could barely spot her friend's head among all of the luggage.

"Are you moving?" Allison asked when Jamie got out of the car to give her a hand.

Jamie flashed her a guilty grin. "I know, I'm a really bad overpacker. I have a bag this size that's my makeup alone," she said, demonstrating with her arms. Allison knew this, though, from having once taken a ski trip with Jamie to Hunter Mountain. Jamie was probably MAC Cosmetics' single biggest source of revenue, and never went anywhere without her entire collection. So much for minimizing losses...

Popping open the trunk, Jamie threw what Allison had moments ago believed was a reasonable-size rolling suitcase on top of her twenty or so items and Rachel's large, patterned Vera Bradley duffel. Then she slammed the door. It didn't shut.

Then she tried again.

After about ten minutes of rearranging (all the while holding up northbound Third Avenue traffic), a nearby doorman surrendered his post to help them negotiate it all in. And then they were off.

And on. And off. And on, and then back off again. Which is pretty much the sensation Allison felt each time Jamie slammed on the brakes, then accelerated at exaggerated speed.

"I thought you said you'd gotten better," Rachel remarked.

Jamie spun around, sending her dark mane flying, and Allison only hoped she still had an eye on the road. "What's that? You want to be dropped back off at the apartment?" Because she was from New York City, Jamie was the only one who had a car readily accessible. Which, as Allison was learning, didn't mean that she knew how to drive it.

"I am *never* raising my kids in the city," Rachel remarked as Jamie flew down Thirty-sixth Street. The statement was unnecessary. Everyone in the car knew Rachel intended to raise her children in the exact Long Island town in which she'd grown up.

"So do you think we should try the LIE?" Jamie asked, ignoring the dig. "It's going to be the biggest nightmare, but it's the only way I know how to go."

"No, here. My sister told me about a shortcut," Rachel said, pulling out a printout. This was unsurprising: She never did anything spontaneously. Or without first conferring with her sister. "Get on here…slow, *slow!*…and take the Midtown Tunnel to the Northern State," she directed.

It was the only time Allison had ever seen Jamie listen to Rachel—or anyone else, for that matter.

"So now that we have some time to kill, care to elaborate on what happened to you Wednesday night?" Rachel asked Jamie once they were safely on a highway.

"It was fun," Jamie said. "He was pretty cute, right? Oh, and don't worry, we didn't have sex," she added, turning to Rachel.

"I didn't say anything about…what you did," Rachel replied. Rachel hated talking about sex. Mostly because she believed sex was something only to be shared with a boyfriend, and, well, it'd been a while since she had a boyfriend.

"I just hope he doesn't get attached to me," Jamie continued, twirling a lock of hair around her finger. "These guys nearing thirty always have total commitment issues." Jamie was the only person Allison knew who defined *commitment issue* as actually wanting one.

"The problems you have," Rachel teased.

"So what happened with that guy you were talking to, the *investment banker*?" Jamie mocked.

"Nothing," Rachel said. "Well, he text-messaged me last night at like two AM, but I ignored it. I mean, granted, it was a Thursday, but you know how I feel about late-night *text messages,*" she exclaimed, pronouncing the words with distaste.

"Plus, he said he used to work at Goldman with my sister, and I can just tell...I can just tell he's a tool."

"I could have told you that," Jamie said. Then she glanced through the mirror at Allison, sitting quietly in the back, who often preferred to be a listener rather than a talker. "I think Allison should just hook up with anyone tonight, to get the ball rolling," she proposed with a wink. But what began rolling was the car, nearly into the next lane.

"I think you should focus your attention on the road," Allison replied.

"Fine," she huffed, scrolling through the radio stations. "Rach, you're going to have to help me with everyone's names today. Really, don't assume I remember anything."

"Sure...You know, in this day and age of technology, you are the only person I know who still listens to the radio," Rachel said.

Jamie laughed so hard she threw her head back. (*Is it too much to watch the road?* Allison thought.) "Radio will become the most obsolete thing in the world, and I'll still listen to it."

"Why?" asked Allison, who was never without her iPod.

Jamie's eyes met hers in the mirror once again. "Because I don't like knowing what's going to come next."

Funny, because at that moment Allison would have killed to. In fact, all she wanted was a crystal ball to tell her when her life would return to normal (and by *normal,* she meant *not* single). Why, not even a month ago, her biggest idea of adventure was sampling a restaurant not listed in *Zagat,* and here she was doing a share with forty or so strangers in the Hamptons.

When she happened upon "Livin' on a Prayer," Jamie turned the dial up full-blast, and the three of them began shouting each word with exhilaration. It was a most unexpected morale booster; the energy in the car quickly rose. Feeling her adrenaline soar, Allison decided this ride was a perfect analogy for how she felt: excited, anxious, not fully trusting, and slightly nervous she wasn't going to make it.

After switching highways what felt like a gazillion times (Allison knew little about the interworkings of Long Island roads), they finally found themselves on infamous Route 27. Creeping east along the one road that spanned the entire Hamptons, they passed through Westhampton, Quogue, and Hampton Bays, in turn. That's where the traffic hit, though, as 27 merged into one inadequate lane—which was frustrating, but according to their directions was a sign that they were practically there. Realizing this, her friends grew giddy with excitement, but as they turned off the highway at the indicated Texaco, what Allison grew was desperate to prolong this state of limbo. The car had become her comfort zone, and more than anything she didn't want to get out.

After making a few swift turns and veering down a few interminable winding roads, they eventually came upon the last step in their directions. (How they didn't get lost was a mystery to Allison, as they'd been following obscure instructions like "make a right at the white picket fence," and, well, *Jamie* had been driving.)

"There it is!" Jamie squealed, after inching so slowly along the highway that she'd received half a dozen honks ("better I piss them off than hit something," she'd argued). "Ten Eighty-eight Montauk Highway!"

Jamie crunched on pebbles as she swerved into the extended stone driveway, then threw everyone forward as she jerked to a halt. And despite any previous apprehension, when Jamie silenced the ignition what Allison felt most was relief.

"It's beautiful!" Jamie exclaimed of the grand two-level white house.

Timidly stepping out onto the pebbled path, Allison peered around, struggling to orient herself. She noticed a handful of other cars parked in the driveway (all shiny new two-seaters and SUVs, of course), and heard a flurry of voices that simultaneously hushed.

"Let's take all our stuff in now," Jamie decided, unloading the trunk. Since Allison had half as much as her friends, she found herself unintentionally taking the lead. Lugging her things up the steps, she then turned to discover her friends still a good distance away.

She really didn't want to go in first. But since people were already watching her through the windows, she realized she had no choice. And so, grabbing her luggage, she bravely pried open the door, inched warily inside, and found herself face-to-face with...her other baggage.

Chapter
Four

Sun Tzu believed "The art of war is of vital importance to the state." But what Rachel believed most important to the share house was the art of conversation.

Which, at the moment, was lacking. For when you find yourself in a house with forty or so strangers, and your only common ground is the hefty deposit you've all paid, you become increasingly desperate for an icebreaker.

Naturally, Rachel and her friends (along with everyone else who first walked in) had already exhausted the obvious course of action.

They took a tour and raved over how *amazing* the house was (having never seen another share house, they knew it might not have been, but for two grand they would certainly convince themselves it was).

They dumped their stuff into the room they were assigned, which was indicated by a sheet of loose-leaf paper tacked to the door (and sneaked glances at the names written on each neighboring door). They then casually observed how every other room had a closer bathroom/more mirrors/stronger air-conditioning and was in some way preferable to theirs. They didn't put their sheets on the beds just yet, but would later realize they should have, as stuff is easily displaced by tired drunken bedless people (a category that was never lacking, according to Rachel's sister).

Finally, they regrouped in the main room to watch as

others filtered in, feeling highly relieved to be the ones sitting on the couch rather than the ones entering—as in *The Real World*—to instantly become the subject of collective scrutiny.

At first glance Rachel recognized a lot of the shareholders from their profiles on Friendster, MySpace, and Facebook, which she perused daily, and also from seeing them out and about in Murray Hill. Though of course she didn't say anything—no one ever said anything. Still, she wondered how many people were simultaneously recognizing her. But any recognition, at least among the girls, was instantly dwarfed in the face of competition. And here's where the art came in.

Carefully compare the opposing army with your own, so that you may know where strength is superabundant and where it is deficient. (Sun Tzu, *The Art of War,* Section 6.24)

Almost immediately (and in many cases, unconsciously) the girls sized one another up, assessing how they ranked aesthetically. In fact, even Ilana, the girl who had earlier been gushing about Rachel's sister, seemed to have resumed her unfriendly persona, perhaps because of her dislike of Jamie. Jamie was often a girl other girls initially disliked. She didn't seem to notice, though—or if she did, didn't pay it any mind—and proceeded to assert her gregarious personality, which irritated the girls even more. Watching Ilana whisper to her two dark-haired friends (who were all, coincidentally, wearing black Juicy velour and Gucci sunglasses functioning indoors as headbands), Rachel could sense a full-fledged war in the making. Or at the very least an uncomfortable summer. But having grown up with Ilanas her entire life, she knew exactly how to handle them.

Standing on the defensive indicates insufficient strength; attacking, a superabundance of strength. (*The Art of War,* Section 4.6)

"Hey, how are you?" Rachel asked, boldly approaching the huddled clan, thereby disrupting their Juicy-Gucci homogeneity.

"Oh...hey," Ilana said, smiling perhaps because Rachel's friendliness surprised her. Or because Rachel was Dana's sister. Funny, even though Rachel was standing right there, Ilana's eyes were fixed on Jamie.

"My sister wanted me to tell you she says hi," Rachel began, smiling sweetly.

Ilana finally surrendered her attention. "Oh, that's so nice," she said, with about as much emotion as Jamie's *That's so funny.*

Rachel chose to ignore it. "Did you go to Penn, too?" she asked, turning to address the clones. Who told her that no, they went to Florida, but had, in fact, both grown up with Ilana in Great Neck, and, who would have thought, lived next door to a guy Rachel had taken to her sorority formal.

"Have you guys done this house before?" Rachel asked, inching closer to them.

They all looked at one another silently before one of the clones responded. "Well, it wasn't this *exact* house, but we all did shares with Mark last year."

"What was it like?" Rachel said. "Was that the Quogue—"

"I miss our old house!" Ilana whined.

Rachel disregarded the fact that she'd just been interrupted. "Was it nicer than this one?"

"Well...no," Ilana admitted, flipping her hair. "We just had, like, a really good group."

"Yeah, I don't even know any of these people," a clone complained, more to her friends than to Rachel.

"There are, like, no guys here," the second added. "I don't see *one* person I'm attracted to."

Ilana did a quick survey of the room. *"Seriously,"* she said, though Rachel couldn't help but notice her eyes wander back to Jamie.

Satisfied she'd exchanged just enough small talk to break down any silent boundaries (which, in a share house, can prove more vicious than words), Rachel excused herself and eagerly retreated.

What she returned to surprised her. The blob of awkward people in the common room had quadrupled in size, just as a bar goes from being empty to packed with no stage in between. At least once every five minutes as new shareholders surfaced, everyone went around and attempted to introduce themselves (an activity that was pointless at best, as everyone promptly forgot each of the forty new names as soon as it was offered). Still, it proved remarkably easy to retain the name of the one person who struck your fancy (Rachel had her eye on Dan, a guy with a buzzed haircut and an NYU LAW shirt in the corner), or in Allison's case, the one person who's fancy you'd already stricken.

In a horrid stroke of misfortune, Allison had walked in to discover her ex-boyfriend Josh and his best friend, Rich, among the guys who'd signed on at the last minute to do the share. Apparently Rich knew the house manager Mark from home, yada yada. And while she imagined inside it was killing her, Rachel believed Allison had handled everything quite well. For after the original shock of seeing Josh had set in, she'd taken to avoiding him completely.

"So how was your ride out here?" she overheard Allison ask Brian the moment they arrived, striking up a conversation with very un-Allison-like assertion. Though she was far from flirting, Allison looked relieved to have spotted one of the few familiar faces they recognized from the meet and greet.

Which Rachel was glad they attended, even if they'd only met what now seemed a mere fraction of the people occupying the living room. She hadn't thought to factor in those who decided to sign on last-minute, those who deemed themselves too cool for a cheesy party, and those who were there, yet had fallen under the radar (and would all too soon fall under it again).

"Are you quarter or half share?" was the question everyone asked, and "*Whose* guests are you?" was the one that often followed. For, according to Rachel's sister, there was a second factor rendering many of these introductions unnecessary. As new shareholders would quickly learn, you'd never see the exact same people on any given weekend, and you might never see some of these people ever again. This was due to the variety of shareholder categories: half shareholders (who only came out on alternating A weekends or B weekends—or any off-weekend they wanted, though they weren't guaranteed a bed), quarter shareholders (who were assigned four weekends in total—A1, A2, B1, or B2), guests of shareholders (who paid seventy-five dollars a night to sleep on the floor, and were supposedly allotted two visits max—yet were rarely refused, especially when the house manager was trying to recoup financial losses), weekend swappers (due to weddings, vacations, and personal scheduling conflicts), or freeloaders (people from neighboring houses or no house at all, who came merely to hang by the pool and take up a lounge chair or pre-game before going out and to deplete the vodka supply). In short, only those people you saw more than once had names worth committing to memory.

Still, harder than remembering everyone's names was gauging everyone's sincerity, which can only really be revealed with time...though alcohol can certainly speed things along. And so, deciding only her immediate friends could be trusted, Rachel assumed each smile a front until proven otherwise.

All warfare is based on deception. (*The Art of War,* Section 1.18)

"It is *so* nice to meet you!" "I *love* your shirt!" "You live in Murray Hill? *Me* too!"

Even those who originally looked Rachel up and down now attempted to be outgoing—or tried their hardest to fake it. It was sort of like the first day of classes when you didn't yet know whose notes you'd need to copy. (Or, in this case, who was from your town, who lived in your building, who worked at that company you were dying to score an interview with, or who was BFF with your ex-boyfriend.) The only exception was the two girls from the Midwest—squeaky little Jill and tall muscular Robin—who were genuinely friendly, and consequently sure to get eaten alive.

"You're from New York, right?" Robin asked her, reaching out and touching her arm.

"Yes," Rachel answered. "How did you know?"

"*Everyone* here's from New York. Also, I could tell from your accent."

Rachel smiled, finding it funny that this Midwesterner thought *she* was the one with an accent. "Where are you from?"

"Minnesota," the two girls replied together.

"So how'd you end up doing this house?" Rachel asked, as inoffensively as she could.

"A girl I work with forwarded me the e-mail," Jill said. "We just moved here, and we thought it would be a good way to meet some people. Fortunately everyone seems so nice."

"*So* nice," Rachel repeated, but quickly fled when she saw a brunette approaching Dan.

It was unfortunate, though merely how the game was played: from the moment you walked through the door, all bets were off, all whistles blown, and the first twenty-four hours were by far the most crucial.

And as Rachel had learned through sorority life, *Don't think she won't do it.* Don't think the girl with the pleasant demeanor and the shy smile wouldn't think twice about moving in on your turf—or rather, your crush. So while Rachel hadn't taken her eyes off Dan, not even for a moment, she suspected others hadn't as well. Still, she was waiting for a prime opportunity to advance, one when he wasn't so fully surrounded; her first attempt had been prematurely intercepted.

"This is such a great house!" she'd exclaimed, then looked to him for approval. When he nodded, she'd added, "What's your name?"

Only no sooner had he answered "Dan" than his friends had come over and sat between them on the couch.

The two-second exchange served to put her on the map, but her words had been bland and brief, and he really hadn't gotten a sense of her at all. And she wished more than anything that Aaron would leave her alone. Once his false intentions and disgraceful phone etiquette had been revealed, Rachel no longer considered him a strategic use of her time.

"So how come you didn't text me back?" Aaron asked, inching away from his friend Steve and closer to her, giving others the impression that there might be something between them.

Instinctively, Rachel took a step back, yet found herself momentarily distracted by his face. Even with his glasses on, he was the perfect mix of intellectual-meets-boy-next-door. So much so, Rachel had to remind herself of the words he'd texted her obscenely late the other night: "Hey it's Aaron from DIP. What's going on?"

In Rachel's opinion, a text (an appropriate one, at that!) was a lame excuse for a phone call...it ranked even lower than an e-mail, because you had to take the time to type out each silly little letter. And maybe she would have otherwise given him the benefit of the doubt, had he not already had such a significant strike against him. Like the rest of the world, he was clearly only interested in her because of her sister.

"I never got a text from you," she claimed. Which was pretty much the biggest lie in technology history. Then she said, "Excuse me," and promptly slipped away.

There was no need for Rachel to expend any energy on guys interested in her only because she was the next best thing to Dana. Or even worse, guys who were trying to snag an invite to Dana's wedding. Especially when there were tons of other guys there, ones whose interests were a lot less superficial (perhaps they were merely trying to get ass). Taking another look at Dan on the far end of the couch, Rachel decided it was time to make her move—even if it meant intruding on a male congregation.

The control of a large force is the same principle as the control of a few men: it is merely a question of dividing up their numbers. (The Art of War, Section 5.1)

Zeroing in on her target, Rachel determinedly approached, then balanced herself uncomfortably on the couch's bony arm.

"So, I don't remember seeing any of you at the meet and greet the other night," she said to the group, though she concentrated her gaze on Dan. She then decided that *Were any of you at the meet and greet* might have been the slightly less hungry approach, but it was too late.

"No, I had to work," he said. His light eyes wandered the room as he spoke, and Rachel guessed he was reluctant to commit to a girl so early in the game. Everyone knew first nights were critical in dictating romance patterns for the rest of the summer.

But Rachel wasn't dismayed.

When he keeps aloof…he is anxious for the other side to advance. (The Art of War, Section 9.19)

"So what do you do?" she asked, lunging forward on the narrow arm and accidentally toppling over a bit before making a quick recovery.

"I'm a lawyer," he stated, with an air of pride. Rachel immediately picked up on it.

Pretend to be weak, that he may grow arrogant. (The Art of War, Section 1.22)

"Oh wow. A lawyer? What kind?"

"Corporate." Still no love.

"Which firm do you work at?" she tried again, pleased she had remembered to call it a firm and not a company.

"Willkie?" he replied, mentioning one of the more prestigious law firms in the city as if it were a question, clearly presuming a girl like her couldn't possibly be familiar with such an exclusive field. *Ha.*

Attack him where he is unprepared, appear where you are not expected. (The Art of War, Section 1.24)

"Oh, so you work in the Midtown office?" she asked, rather nonchalantly. Thanks to her widespread dating, Rachel had yet to meet a guy whose field she was unfamiliar with. "Because my friend is a summer associate in that building. Matt Sherman?" In truth, she only minimally knew Matt, having once gone for drinks with him at the W months earlier, but really that wasn't the point.

"Of course," he said, looking up from the television screen and growing noticeably more interested. "I went to NYU Law with him, but he's a Two-L."

"Really?" Rachel exclaimed, even though she'd totally known that's where Matt had gone.

"What'd you say your name was?" he asked, making real eye contact with her for the first time.

"Rachel," she repeated. And that's how the game was played.

And how it continued, for a good hour. But after each introduction had been made, each six-degrees-of-separation connection established, and Rob had again made everyone aware that he'd been on *The Apprentice,* silence once again overtook the awkward assemblage. And no one knew what to do next.

They looked for assistance to the house manager, who was pretty much the only direct connection among everyone. Yet Mark was running around addressing the urgent dilemmas that, ironically enough, all stemmed from the girls in the house. (From "the air-conditioning is too high" to "someone else's stuff is on my bed" to "there's no toilet paper in the bathroom" to, most disturbingly, "everything smells like mildew.")

This left anything else under the jurisdiction of Craig, a husky guy whose bark was far worse than his bite, and who bore the title of assistant house manager. Upon first meeting Craig, Rachel found two things immediately apparent: (a) Craig took his job way too seriously, and (b) *assistant house manager* was code for "resident nagger."

"I need your money" were the first words out of his mouth. "Anyone with an extra car needs to park at the train station" were the next. Clearly, Mark had hired Craig to be the bad guy. And a bad guy was certainly necessary, since share houses were technically illegal per the outmoded "brothel laws" of New York State—only a certain number of unrelated people could legally live under one roof. Therefore, Craig told them, anything remotely resembling a share house was under close watch by the cops, subject to raids at any time of day, and handed fines for practically anything. (For instance, only eleven cars were permitted in the driveway overnight, and while the first fine would be only, say, a hundred dollars, Craig swore additional ones could go up by ludicrous increments.) Still, at the moment no one minded being hassled by Craig. At least it provided activity.

Slouching back into the couch seat she knew she'd lose if she got up, Rachel lifted her wrist to look at her watch, then stopped herself and put it down again. As her last hundred glances had revealed, it was some weird disorienting time like 8 PM—too late to eat dinner, too early to get ready (besides, everyone had already showered at home, as the thought of getting ready in a share house was still disconcerting), and too dark to venture out anywhere. Leaving nothing to do but sit around sluggishly, even though the last thing Rachel possibly felt was sluggish.

The movie *Anchorman* was blaring across the large television screen, but not only had Rachel already seen it, she hadn't particularly cared for it the first time around. Still, she attempted to feign interest, mostly because everyone else was. In fact, from the looks of things, you would have thought it was the most thrilling movie anyone had ever seen. Noticing that day's *Post* on the coffee table, she picked it up and casually flipped through the pages, which she'd already read thoroughly this morning. Next to her, she watched as Jamie bummed a cigarette from Dave, even though her roommate hadn't smoked since her junior year abroad.

Rachel began to think that the ease of conversation was inversely proportional to the number of people in the room.

Despite forty or so bodies, the comments were few and far between, and even the extroverted people filtered what they put out there. Still, she laughed at any jokes, agreed with any remarks, and thought long and hard for something to interject, but dismissed everything as *retarded* after first running it through her head.

And just like with her watch, she kept feeling the urge to glance at her phone, though of course not a single person would have called.

Was this share worth it? Rachel wondered, her eyes moving from Dan to the rest of the room and carefully weighing the issue. Was it worth subjecting herself to all this weirdness? Not to mention the opportunity cost of this past hour of thumb twiddling. She always complained how she didn't have enough time as it was, yet somehow all she'd done since she'd arrived here was sit around and waste it. Perhaps it wasn't too late to get their money back, drive back to the city, and endure boredom in the privacy of her own apartment.

Then, just when she'd reached the brink of discomfort (not to mention frustration), there came the icebreaker in the form of a guy named—

"Hiscock?" Ilana shrieked, stampeding downstairs with the clones at her heels. A gazillion eyes turned to face her all at once. "Very funny. Who wrote that name on one of the doors?"

"I did," Rob and Brian said at the same time, calling both their bluffs.

"I did," Mark responded, glaring at the guys and eagerly taking a brief hiatus from his calls of duty. "But that's really his name. I promise you it's not a joke."

"You honestly expect us to believe John *Hiscock* is someone's name?" Ilana challenged, resting her hand on her bony hip in confrontation.

"Swear to God!" Mark attested, his pupils dancing as he jumped from his seat in defense. "There's a group of Australians doing a quarter share. I met up with them last week, they're totally normal." Seeing everyone still unconvinced, he added, "And apparently *Hiscock* is a pretty common last name in Australia."

"So then...where is *Hiscock*?" Ilana asked, giving rise to torrents of laughter. Taken aback at first, Ilana eventually grinned, and catching her eye, Rachel offered her a smile back. At least for the moment, any ill will between the two groups of girls had subsided.

"That's a good question," Mark answered, turning to Craig. "Wasn't Hiscock supposed to be out this weekend?" Which summoned even harder laughter. "Oh, come on. Be adults about this," Mark scolded playfully.

But that was all anyone needed to hear. After that, it was a free-for-all.

"Is *Hiscock* coming?"

"Have you seen *Hiscock*?"

"Leave *Hiscock* alone!"

Not even a group of ten-year-olds would have found the word any more amusing than this assembly of repressed twentysomethings. Instantly each became abundantly grateful not just for the name *Hiscock,* but for the fact that someone had discovered it at that particular moment. And before Rachel knew it, tears were rolling down her cheeks, and she found herself hiccupping uncontrollable laughter. Its contagion spread to nearly everyone around her, people who just moments ago were utter strangers, but with whom she'd now bonded by virtue of *Hiscock.* And after that, the conversation flowed effortlessly. Because after you've yelled *Hiscock* at the top of your lungs, you feel significantly less guarded about anything else you say.

And Rachel was shocked at exactly how many jokes could emanate from one name. They kept coming and coming, and just when she thought they were over, out popped another. Wiping her eyes, Rachel once again glanced around the room, noticing the merriment on not just the male faces, but everyone's. True, the potential for meeting someone may have been what lured her here, but she now realized a guy wasn't the only reason she should stick it out this summer; perhaps not even the most important one. It was suddenly apparent that this share house was a means to share in wildly unpredictable and memorable new experiences. So it wasn't Dan but, rather, *Hiscock* that had shown Rachel exactly why this was worth it in the first place.

Perhaps the only person who didn't find *Hiscock* ridiculously entertaining was Allison, who'd lost her sense of humor when she'd discovered Josh in the house. Still, Rachel imagined, screaming *Hiscock* in front of a guy whose anatomy you'd seen regularly was about as comfortable as watching a sex scene with your parents. And for the first time ever, Jamie was in a room with guys whose anatomy she hadn't yet uncovered, a source of entertainment in itself. Even if she had been continually looking around—presumably for Jeff, the guy she worried would be stuck on *her.*

Craig finally put an end to the *Hiscock* jokes. "I don't know how much time you guys need to get ready, but we have to leave by eleven."

This was enough to set each girl into a frenzy. Glancing at her watch, Rachel discovered—much to her delight—that it was way later than she'd thought. Joining the stampede up the steps, the group scurried off in a million directions to get ready.

Back upstairs in the room, Rachel dug swiftly through her duffel, though a smile lingered on her face.

For Rachel still believed that the art of conversation was of vital importance to the share house. But apparently not as important as the existence of this particular shareholder.

So at the end of the day, it didn't even matter that *Hiscock* never came at all.

Chapter
Five

F *lip* went the cup as Rob, one of the many showered-but-half-dressed people gathered around the dining room picnic table, succeeded in overturning an all-important plastic prop.

Flip went Jamie's mood, as she realized her Friday night now revolved around watching this.

Spurred on by loud chants and a banging on the table that reverberated through the house, Rob triumphantly downed the cup of beer while Jamie threw back the remainder of the vodka she'd served herself. She hadn't poured nearly enough.

Resting her empty cup on the coffee table, which was littered with cigarette stubs and trash, she leaned her designer-clad body back and sank farther and farther into the beer-drenched sofa. If the LIE hadn't been enough of a clue, it was now painfully obvious to Jamie that she wasn't in Manhattan anymore.

In fact, with her four-inch stilettos, loud designer mini dress, and artfully made-up face, against a backdrop of people playing a drinking game that warranted ratty old T-shirts, Jamie looked like the answer to a what-doesn't-belong-here puzzle. Worse yet, she felt like it.

"No flip cup?" Dave asked, scurrying by her, but not without first giving her the obligatory checkout, to her satisfaction.

Too pained to speak, Jamie merely shook her head. Then she buried it in her perfectly manicured hands. Oh, where in the world was she?

Or rather, where in the Hamptons was she? Jamie prided herself on knowing everything there was to know about the Hamptons, and what she hadn't known, she'd researched. She'd watched *Single in the Hamptons, Murder in the Hamptons,* Barbara Kopple's Hamptons documentary...She'd read countless issues of *Hamptons Magazine, Dan's Papers,* and "Hamptons Diary" in the *New York Post*...For an added kick, she'd even spiced up her French manicure with East Hampton Cottage (a dazzling shade of pearl pink from the Essie summer nail polish line). But much to her chagrin, Jamie had just uncovered a part of the Hamptons she'd never known existed.

This wasn't the *fabulous* celebrity mecca where regulars like Kelly Ripa, Star Jones, or Alec Baldwin roamed freely. The party haven where the Hilton sisters, the Olsen twins, or the Hearst girls caroused famously. The photo op that Patrick McMullan, Rob Rich, or WireImage longed to capture.

This was the utter antithesis of fabulous. This was where fabulous came to die (or, should it wish, play flip cup). This was a camp-like, beer-drenched, post-college purgatory.

This was Frat-Hamptons. And like it or not, Jamie was discovering the secret life of shareholders.

True, she'd seen how the *other half* Hamptoned before... for like a minute. But—judging from that one time she'd stopped by a co-worker's share house—the houses appeared livable enough, at the very least a means to an end. Besides, she thought it might actually be fun to have people around her all the time (and by *people,* she of course meant guys). Although none of the ones here seemed to impress her all that much, and the girls were beyond irritating, and, well, she'd escaped flip cup in college the first time around.

And where in the world was *he*? Not that her misery was entirely due to the fact that Jeff wasn't here...though she'd be lying if she denied that his presence might have made things somewhat more interesting.

In fact, hearing Justin Timberlake's "Summer Love" erupt from someone's iPod speakers a full flight away, Jamie decided anything might have been more interesting than killing the nine-to-eleven pre-going-out time slot with a plastic cup and a disturbing amount of beer. Why, Jamie didn't even like beer. And she certainly didn't like any game that monopolized every guy's attention.

Plus, if she'd known any better, she wouldn't have rushed to get ready at such lightning-quick speed. A nightmare of a process to begin with, further complicated by the fact that the full-length mirror they'd so wisely brought along had gone missing.

Now, a compact mirror might have been misplaced. But a seven-foot-tall, flower-trimmed object? Not a chance. When Jamie discovered this, something in her just snapped, setting her off on a small rampage.

She'd knocked on nearly every door in the course of her investigation, all the while picturing exactly how it'd gone down. She imagined that some girls doing a routine tour just happened upon the large mirror, and joyfully abducted it in conspiracy. Jamie couldn't be too angry about it; she herself would probably have done the same. But upon her polite inquiry, each group hastily told her no (Ilana even did so with a smirk) before eagerly resuming elaborate grooming procedures. And as she stumbled across each set of open luggage bags and straightening irons and stray heels on her way out, Jamie grew increasingly frustrated. However, when it became apparent she wasn't making even the slightest bit of progress, she had no choice but to abandon the search for the moment. True, recovering the mirror would prove no easy feat, though neither would be getting ready in such a limited time frame.

Their delayed start didn't help matters: After devoting so much time to ransacking the house, Jamie and her friends had lost out on any available bathrooms. Strategizing, Allison stationed herself in front of one downstairs (which she didn't expect to free up any time soon, as it was occupied by nothing short of a small female army), while Rachel camped out at one close to their room upstairs (similarly unpromising, and frighteningly coed). In the meantime, Jamie began applying her makeup at a tiny mirror she discovered in the kitchen (acceptable only because it took her the longest to get ready by far).

Even so, she wasn't having much luck. Though she'd never considered herself shy, she'd also never applied makeup in front of such a captive male audience. And who would have guessed guys found makeup application so fascinating? Why, she'd only just begun when she observed a growing group (assembled early to pre-game) following her every brush-stroke in amazement.

Fortunately, Rachel soon signaled from upstairs that the bathroom was free. Barging in with all their toiletries and clothes in hand, the three of them slammed the door and frantically locked themselves inside the four-foot-square cube.

At this point it was every woman for herself. Because no one else is going to care if you smudge your mascara, leave a kink in your otherwise-straightened hair, throw on overpowering earrings with an equally bold necklace, or wear something unflattering due to lack of a full-length view (even by standing on the toilet seat). And though the lighting was dim, the space confined, and the pressure mounting, it became all about the treasured mirror, which they divvied up as follows: Jamie, squatting, took to applying eyeliner from the corner right; above her and nearest to the outlet, Rachel used an iron on her hair in the corner left; and from the distance,

Allison modeled shirts and made the others halt entirely every five minutes to let her sneak a glance. Complicating matters, Jamie's makeup brushes kept rolling into the dampened sink, Allison kept tripping over everyone's stuff, and Rachel's iron upped the temperature in the room by at least a million degrees. Intermittently someone left something of necessity back in the room (which was as good as leaving it back in the city), someone wasn't happy with the way her makeup/clothes/hair was coming out, and someone from the outside pounded relentlessly upon the door.

They were dying to open the door, if only for a second, to let some cool air in. But that was a risk no one was willing to take: one moment of weakness could allow a hostile takeover. And so each worked in grave silence until Rachel's stomach interjected with a loud growl.

"You guys, I'm *starving*," she said, clipping back a section of straightened hair.

"Me too!" Allison and Jamie cried in unison. Come to think of it, Jamie hadn't eaten anything since early that morning, assuming they'd have plenty of time to stop once they arrived here (only they didn't).

"Oh well," Jamie dismissed, eager to finish her eye contour. "If we drink on empty stomachs, we'll get drunk faster."

"We'll throw up faster," Allison countered, and Rachel nodded.

"I can't not eat, my stomach is growling so loud it's embarrassing," Rachel said. She paused in thought, then proposed, "What about the pretzels? You brought them in from the car, right?"

Jamie considered this as she twisted open her mascara. "Yeah, but if we open the door someone is totally busting in."

"Not if we hold it really hard," Rachel offered, with an air of desperation.

Jamie tore her eyes away from the mirror for a moment, her mascara wand in midair. "Well, I'm not about to run out there in boxer shorts with only half my makeup on. But they're in my red bag, so be my guest."

Before Rachel could protest—her hair was divided into a million different sections secured by assorted clips and scrunchies—Allison stepped up.

"I'll go," she said. "I only need a minute to get ready, and I have to wait for the mirror anyway."

And so they opened the door just enough for Allison to squeeze herself through; then they slammed it behind her as she scurried across the wooden floor. In a matter of milliseconds she returned, clutching the prized Rold Gold Honey Wheat godsends. Tearing open the bag, which was disappointingly smaller than she'd remembered, Jamie grabbed a handful of pretzels and shoved them into her mouth. Though she was probably biased because of her hunger, they were the best pretzels she had ever tasted. Attempting not to think of the socialites currently dining at Jean Luc while she subsisted solely on convenience-store fare, she inhaled a few more handfuls. But she had no sooner resumed applying her blush than Allison hit them with a time bomb.

"So I sort of told Brian he could shower in a few minutes."

Like nothing preceding it, this succeeded in summoning everyone's undivided attention. *"What?"* Jamie and Rachel cried, confronting their selfless friend.

"Well, what was I supposed to say? We've been in here almost half an hour, and he needs to *shower*." It was an unfortunate though unspoken protocol that showering took priority to anything else.

"Can't he wait, I'll be done in like *two* minutes," Jamie lied, her motions quickening.

"He said there's a mirror in his room we can use, above his

dresser," she said, and as if on cue they were startled by an encroaching knock.

"Ladies," Brian called, the familiarity of his voice softening them. "If you let me in, I promise I'll be out in five minutes. Starting...now!"

Jamie sighed. *"Fine."* Picking up all their stuff—now unpacked, it was almost impossible to carry—they reluctantly opened the door.

"Thank you," Brian said, coming in with nothing but a towel and watching in awe as they hauled out a small truck-load of things. "Downstairs, second door on the right," he directed.

They decamped downstairs, a brigade of girls with partial makeup, nonsensically clipped hair, and sorority-logo boxer shorts. Frustrated, Jamie couldn't help but scowl as they trudged past Mark's room, for really, that's where she'd wanted to get ready...

In a house where people were packed like sardines four to six to a room, Mark had his own fully furnished master bed-room—complete with king-size bed, large-screen TV, walk-in closet (stocked with every brand of liquor imaginable), and one of the biggest bathrooms Jamie had seen anywhere short of the Ritz. It was pure paradise, a vision of sparkling white tile, wall-to-wall mirroring, and flattering fluorescent light-ing. As if that weren't enough to make a shareholder envious, there was not just one, but two adjacent sectioned-off toilets, a huge marble whirlpool, and a shower so massive you could fit like four people in it. Made solely of glass, it was entirely see-through and had already been dubbed "the sex shower." But while guys would be drawn immediately to the shower, girls were in awe of the wall-to-wall mirrors. Girls *put out* for the wall-to-wall mirrors. Heck, in the absence of any game, that room alone made Mark the biggest pimp in Southampton.

However, Mark, like a majority of guys, saw showering and getting ready as the only time of day he couldn't be drinking or eating or hooking up or doing nothing. So it was a chore to be executed in record time, which gave Jamie the brilliant idea to ask Mark from the moment they laid eyes on his bathroom if they could use it that night to get ready.

He couldn't have cared less, but unfortunately he'd already promised that privilege to Ilana, who had inserted herself up his ass from the moment they'd walked through the door. Ilana and her friends Tara and Jocelyn (or was it Jocelyn and Tara?) had all done Mark's house for the past two summers and thought themselves highly superior for it—and seemingly, highly superior regardless. Jamie was appalled, but decided it was in her best interest to pick her battles.

Now parading past those already dressed and drinking, they finally arrived at Brian's room. And knocked. And knocked harder. When no one answered, Jamie boldly pushed it open, revealing Rob with nothing but a towel around his waist and a joint in his hand. Rather than recede in embarrassment, though, he promptly about-faced and jokingly flashed what little was left to the imagination.

Jamie didn't know it then, but he was only the first of the many naked people they'd see on any given weekend.

"Brian said we could use your mirror," she stated.

"Knock yourself out," he volunteered, re-covering himself (and his surprisingly defined physique) with the towel.

Jamie didn't think it possible, but this mirror was smaller and more poorly lit than the one upstairs. Their efforts were further hindered by Rob, who, in a most surprising diversion, kept interrupting them.

"Do you like this shirt?" he asked. And, flattered he trusted their judgment, they were happy to voice their consent. Until he repeated the procedure with about six other shirts. Then he came over and asked to "sneak a peek" in the mirror, which was technically his. But he considered a "peek" to mean running his hand though his hair, flicking it every which way, and continuing to do so for an inordinately long time. Did he not realize it wasn't going anywhere? Jamie wondered. Then, just when they thought he was finally through, he turned to them and asked, "Anyone have any hair stuff?"

"Uh, what kind of stuff?" Jamie replied, offering him her fortress of hair products and wondering whether he in fact used *stuff* on a daily basis or simply wanted to make the most of the situation.

Faced with his choice of gels, mousses, and laminates, Rob examined each product, scientifically inhaled a teeny whiff, then tested it out on but a few strands of hair. The girls, all the while waiting their turn, sighed in frustration and made impatient suggestions to help him along.

Shortly, in strolled Brian, in what now appeared to be the house uniform of a towel. Without any hesitation, the girls promptly charged back upstairs, banging their bags behind them. Predictably, the bathroom was already taken, but luckily only by some random guy using it to emit foul-smelling excrements, evident the instant he opened the door. "You might want to wait a minute," he warned them, but they didn't listen, as a minute was all it took to lose the room again.

Holding their noses, they reentered the bathroom, now a complete sauna from Brian's hardly abbreviated shower. Absorbing the steam, their roots began to recurl, the color melted down their faces, and they went from feeling ready to go out to ready to hit the shower themselves. Fortunately, the only thing Jamie needed to do was physically change her clothes; to her relief she was finally finished. Just as she was about to ask her friends if they were ready to escape the humidity, though, Allison turned to her.

The lowest-maintenance of the bunch, Allison had applied some barely discernible makeup, run a brush through her naturally straight light brown hair, and remained quiet throughout the remainder of the ordeal.

"Jamie?" Allison asked, her voice foreign with trepidation. "Um, I was thinking…"

"Oh, don't worry about it," Jamie assured her friend, who'd looked positively miserable since the onset of the evening. "Just forget he's here. You're doing great." Peering back into the mirror, she scrunched her hair again.

"Actually, I was wondering if I could borrow a shirt."

"Really?" she asked, whipping around in total shock. Allison looked just as she normally did, wearing a simple J. Crew tank top and jeans. Her basic style had always suited her fine.

"Yeah, I don't really like anything I brought," she said, barely looking in Jamie's direction. "And, um, since we're here, do you think you can do my makeup?"

This was enough to shock both Rachel and Jamie. In the entire time they'd known Allison, they'd only seen her wear makeup (well, visible makeup) for weddings, formals, and Halloween. And even though each minute in the sweaty bathroom felt like an hour, Jamie knew she had to do her friend this small favor.

Rifling through her extensive luggage, Jamie produced a tight metallic Nicole Miller top and—to her surprise—Allison didn't object. Then she did Allison's makeup, instantly transforming her in the way you can only transform if you never wear makeup. Jamie had never seen her friend look better, but she knew that on the inside Allison had rarely felt worse.

When they finally emerged from the bathroom, in full going-out attire and arms packed comically full of luggage, the girls clattered across the floor in heels and a potent cloud of perfume (an odd amalgamation of three separate scents).

And that's when they discovered the raging flip cup tournament in progress. Since people wanted to get as drunk as possible before going out, especially the guys—most girls got ready up until the moment they departed—a large game was organized every night from as early as nine till whenever everyone left for the clubs.

As they entered the dining room, Rob entreated the girls—clearly out of politeness—to join in the game, and Allison shockingly said yes. Jamie spotted Allison's ex Josh on the other side of the room, so it was easy for her to guess why, but Jamie would never have allowed a guy *she'd* dumped to have such a pronounced effect on her. Accepting the tattered T-shirt Mark produced from his mother of all closets, Allison quickly changed out of the gold top and took a seat next to the other girls ballsy enough to attempt a sloppy drinking game (coincidentally, only the two who weren't from New York).

Less shockingly, Rachel abandoned Jamie to watch the game next to Dan the lawyer, whom Jamie found dull at best, trying to win him over with conversation. Left to her lonesome, Jamie retreated to the couch—far from the juvenile proceedings (and from the bleacher seats that were frequently splashed on).

Though she was relieved she wouldn't have to think about getting ready again until...tomorrow, her spirits were far from high. And now her friends had deserted her. As she watched the tournament drag on, Jamie feared it might never be over.

Eager to pass some time, she pulled out her phone. "Hey!" she said the moment her co-worker answered. "Are you out east?"

"Sorry, I can barely hear you," shouted a voice amid loud commotion. "I'm at dinner at Savanna's, but everyone's going to Dune later. See you over there?"

Jamie started to fume all over again. Over the past two weeks her inbox had been flooded with invites—Memorial Day weekend being that notorious occasion when nightclubs battled it out for supremacy with celebrity guests, newly renovated spaces, and world-renowned DJs. What a nightmare it'd been to choose! Especially for someone who regarded party selection as nothing short of an art form—one to be evaluated by PR backing, venue choice, and anticipated guest list. Still, as Jamie quickly learned, in a share house this decision is made for you. So even though Dune (new from the owners of Marquee nightclub) promised to be hosting one of the hotter parties, followed closely by Stereo with DJ AM, Mark was "running a list" at Pink Elephant that evening—where the entire house would thus migrate. "Can't. I sort of have to go to Pink Elephant."

"What? Oh, well, I'm sure that'll be good, too. Listen, I have to go—"

"Wait! Can you get someone to put me plus two on the list there? There is no way I'm paying to go to Pink Elephant *just* because it's where our house manager wants to take us."

Jamie whispered this last part, but it was no secret that each share house manager doubled as a nightclub promoter; the majority actually were nightclub promoters who'd decided to run a share house. For delivering up cover-paying heads at set parties each week, Mark walked away with a small percentage of the profit (say, seven bucks each time anyone dropped his name at the door). It was usually a win-win situation: His list entitled partygoers to pay a reduced admission price (maybe twenty bucks instead of twenty-five), assume a no-hassle group plan (making a decision like this among forty people would be impossible), and receive preferential treatment upon arrival—like bypassing the line. To people like Jamie, however—who not only never paid cover due to her myriad PR connections but also came equipped with her own "it" party agenda—not having input threatened continual conflict.

But tonight, she'd decided to suck it up. Her friends were right: straying from the house the very first night wouldn't be very social, and more important, they had absolutely no idea how to transport themselves anywhere. And so, once her co-worker confirmed they were on the list at Pink Elephant, Jamie vowed to dismiss the matter entirely.

This left her thoughts wide open to return to Jeff, the only guy she could recall who hadn't asked for her phone number afterward. The whole thing just didn't make any sense. Why, she'd put on one hell of a show, if she said so herself. And she hadn't even burdened him by staying the night. Of course, he clearly assumed he'd see her this weekend...a mystery unto itself. She couldn't help wondering where he could possibly be at this moment, and—if he *had* been here—how he would have factored into everything. Would he have made the getting-ready process somehow less irritating (and given her somewhat more of an incentive)? Would he be keeping her company at this very moment? Or would he have instead opted to join in the flip cup game (which, to Jamie's delight, finally appeared to be dissipating)?

When the last *"Ohh!"* had been shouted, the last drop of beer guzzled, and the last person with a dry T-shirt drenched, the cups were abandoned so everyone could change their tops.

And just as Jamie slipped away to reapply her lipstick for a final time (in the bathroom that was becoming like her second home), she heard a most unusual battle cry from the outside.

"Everyone to the front! The *party vans* are here!"

Hurrying out of the bathroom, she found the formerly tame

pack running amok in a million directions, buttoning shirts, hunting down purses, downing shots, and pouring that final drink that would hopefully last them an entire car ride.

"The what?" Jamie asked, alarmed at the sudden pandemonium and scanning the room hastily for her friends.

Craig halted between bellows. "The party vans."

Jamie looked at him like he had six heads. "What," she reluctantly asked, "is a party van?"

"Go outside and find out," he said, ushering her along with the rest of the stragglers.

To her horror, a "party van" was exactly as frightening as it sounded. Stepping outside, Jamie discovered two mini school-bus-looking things consuming their entire driveway, with people flocking to board like an airplane. *Perfect,* she thought, cynically observing the scene. Rather than arrive via chauffeured car, or at the very least in a cab, she'd be showing up at a nightclub doorstep looking like a member of a traveling circus act. This night was getting better by the minute.

Allison reached out and yanked her down the front steps just in time for the mass announcement.

"*Hello*, Ten Eighty-eight Montauk!" sang the driver, whom Jamie could only hope was sober.

"*Chuck!* How'd the winter treat you?" Mark saluted, slapping him five. Then he addressed the crowd. "Everyone, this is Chuck, the best cabdriver in all of the Hamptons."

Carefully wading through the pebbles in her stilettos (which cost more than a night in this sharehouse, pro-rated), Jamie stopped before him. "Why is that?" she challenged, half sarcastically, and half because challenging guys was an unconscious reflex. Though unlike any guy she normally challenged, Chuck (or "Fingers," as he was later called) had huge arms protruding from the T-shirt he wore (despite the brisk night temperatures), a head of gray-tinged hair straying off in different directions, and only four fingers on his right hand (Jamie counted twice). She didn't know exactly what had happened to create a stump of his fifth, but since the injury could have been incurred in the line of duty, she preferred to be ignorant.

"You kiddin'? I've been driving Ten Eighty-eight Montauk since before yous was born," he said, from which Jamie gathered he was a local. And while everyone she knew wanted to have a house in the Hamptons, she'd never actually met anyone who was *from* the Hamptons. It was oddly unnerving. "Best rates around," he continued. "Seven bucks a head to Pink Elephant, ten to Star Room. You try and beat that! Here, take a card," he said, distributing them.

It was a cabdrivers' conspiracy that group fares in the Hamptons were calculated on a per-head basis, rather than the flat rate found in the city. In the latter case, more people splitting a cab amounted to a cheaper fare all around; here large parties were penalized. Penalized, and smushed.

"How many are you?" Chuck asked, attempting a head count.

Mark beat him to it. "Forty-six." Jamie had no idea how they'd grown so exponentially in a few hours' time, but attributed it to the many friends of friends (of friends) who'd come over to pre-game.

"Two should do it," Chuck radioed over some dilapidated walkie-talkie. Then he turned to the group. "Squeeze in as many as you can to a row, and girls need to sit on guys' laps," he instructed.

Jamie's jaw dropped. "Is he serious?" she muttered aloud, failing to believe a registered driver could order such a dangerous-sounding thing. Why, in the city, sitting on people's laps was illegal. Not to mention that if you had any more than the four-person-per-cab limit, you were immediately kicked to the curb. However, it was now abundantly clear exactly how Chuck managed to offer the best rates in the Hamptons.

"Don't worry, you can sit on my lap," Dave volunteered with a devious gleam in his eye. Which was all well and good, but Jamie didn't *feel* like sitting on anyone's lap. And she certainly didn't feel like doing so inside a *party van.* Before she could object, though, Dave climbed in and pulled her after him. Sitting down so she was barely resting any weight on him, she adjusted her new Diane von Furstenberg dress, hoping he could balance both her and his beer cup. That, and that he wasn't deriving a single ounce of sexual pleasure from this.

Behind her, Rachel pounced on top of Dan, who looked less than thrilled, and Allison sat beside her on Brian's lap while he whispered something in her ear. Nevertheless, Jamie caught a twinge of discomfort on her friend's face upon discovering Ilana's friend Tara—or was it Jocelyn?—sitting on Josh's lap two rows back. Ilana of course sat perfectly comfortably up in the front with Mark—whom Jamie couldn't help but feel annoyed at for initiating this whole outing with its ridiculous means of transport.

No sooner did everyone pile in than concentrations of ice-cold air burst from the vents and an eruption of foreign techno music blared from the speakers. Still, it paled in comparison with the people screaming (coming off a flip cup high), the buzz of conversation, and the animated storytelling of Chuck—who, given such a captive audience, could clearly talk for days.

Staring out the window into the utter blackness, Jamie held on tightly to the seat in front of her as they bumped along, swerving down winding roads and through forests as if they'd entered some alternate universe—one devoid of streetlights and seat belts and manners precluding guys' hands from inching up your thigh. Fortunately, she knew the journey couldn't last too long, as Pink Elephant was fairly close by in South-ampton (of course, so was Dune—not that she was dwell-ing on it). But even an abbreviated trip provided Dave ample opportunities to assert himself.

"Want some?" he asked, offering her his cup in a grand gesture that would similarly gauge her fear of his saliva. "You seem too sober."

You can say that again, Jamie thought. Glaring at the beer (a substance she'd renounced right after freshman-year frat parties), but deciding it was better than arriving asleep, she put out her hand. At that opportune moment Chuck hit a bump, causing the contents of the cup to spill straight down her chest.

"My dress!" she squealed.

"My beer!" Dave countered, equally (if not more) upset.

Now that they were thoroughly soaked, they couldn't arrive at the undesirable destination fast enough. As soon as they did, it was evident from the obscene crowd of cars and cops and clubgoers canvassing the outside that sitting in a party van wasn't so horrible an alternative.

"This is insane," Jamie gasped, her eyes peeled to the nightmarish scene at the door, with a line extending from the big blowup pink elephant at the entrance all the way through the parking lot.

"It's Memorial Day weekend," Mark reminded her. "But don't worry, I've got it covered."

I should hope you do—it's your party, Jamie thought.

"Here we are," Chuck announced unnecessarily, halting directly in front of the entrance, and entreating all to debark. Which they did, with all the subtlety of an arriving jetliner.

They'd calculated the van money beforehand, but in the midst of the commotion they were now a good deal short anyway. And after everyone was asked a hundred times over

"Did you pay?" "Did you pay?" the mathematicians in the front realized they'd forgotten to add on a tip.

Pushed around by the mobs, people scattered every which way, but Mark quickly took control. He gestured for his party to follow him, and though Jamie felt absolutely ridiculous arriving somewhere with forty people, given all the confusion she followed suit. The Pied Piper led them straight up to the doorman—a stylishly dressed guy with a shaved head, who seemed unnecessarily harsh yet still overwhelmed—who greeted Mark tersely and asked him to gather everyone off to the side. Again, Jamie obliged. And a few minutes later, as promised, the doorman lifted up the rope so Mark could wave in the colossal group, handing everyone a tiny orange movie-theater-style ticket that entitled them to pay the "reduced" price (he handed Ilana a blue one, which Jamie supposed was a comp).

When their turn approached, she rejected Mark's offer of a ticket (at which he raised an eyebrow) and spoke directly to the door guy.

"Hi, Alex? We should be on the comp list. Jamie Kessler plus two," she stated, addressing him by the name she'd been given.

Alex's hardened face moved from Jamie, to Mark and the share house crew, then back to Jamie. "There's no comp list tonight, it's a holiday," he said sternly, not even consulting the list. Apparently he wasn't impressed in the slightest that Jamie addressed him by name, but the crowd assembled before him now happily ingested this new piece of information, as cries of "Alex" ricocheted from the line. "I can give you reduced," he declared to Jamie, with an air of finality, then turned his back.

And in that moment, she could hear it. The sound of her world going *flip.*

Jamie sighed. Though she'd never expected this, she imagined it was probably easy to be hassled out here. Unlike in
the city, where at the slightest list problem you could simply walk a few blocks to a new destination, this doorman
knew well that no one who'd just traveled half an hour to the
middle of nowhere would hop in a cab, pay twice as much,
and travel to possibly a different town to go to a different
club—especially when there were no guarantees the same
thing wouldn't happen all over again.

But Jamie wasn't easily bullied. Waiting until he lifted the
rope for two girls too tall to be anything but models (with
a suddenly accommodating attitude, she thought), Jamie
tried again. "I *am* on the list. I work for Spotlight PR and my
co-worker just put us on Rocco's list."

Her impatience (not to mention her self-righteousness) only
made him more adamant. "Look, Rocco's an owner. *Everyone's* on Rocco's list. If you're not going to take the reduced,
then please move aside." His eyes at that point dismissed
her; even though she remained physically in front of him, he
looked right through her.

Not for long, though, as she was soon accosted by the
clichéd security guard dressed all in black, who looked so
inflated you could pop him with a pin. "Please move off the
line," he ordered, extending his arm.

Jamie satisfied him minimally by taking a few steps back,
retreating once again into the throngs of people pushing
every which way, who probably would have paid generously
for the opportunity to go in without waiting. She pulled out
her cell phone, then realized it was after midnight, and there
was no one to call. But above all else, she refused to make
eye contact with Mark, whom she knew was lingering just
beyond the doorman.

"Look, twenty dollars isn't that much," Rachel offered,

aware of her roommate's headstrong personality, and also that they didn't have much choice in the matter.

"Yeah, let's just go in," Allison agreed. She turned to Jamie. "If you don't have enough money I can lend you."

"That's not the point," huffed Jamie, a girl who'd happily drop two hundred on a shirt yet not a dime on cover, if only out of pride. Jamie glared back at that jerk of a doorman. Didn't he realize who she was? She didn't wait on lines, she didn't fight through crowds, and she most certainly didn't pay cover (no comp list, her ass!). And a part of her believed this wouldn't have even happened had they not arrived via the circusmobile and instead been three hot girls stepping out of a cab like they usually were. In the city Jamie always knew the door people, she always was on the list, and she always got her way. But of course she wasn't in the city anymore. She—along with forty negotiable composites—was in the Hamptons. Frat-Hamptons.

And she was hating every minute of it.

Opening her wallet, which usually functioned solely as an accessory when she went out, Jamie realized this was going to be one hell of an expensive summer. (Just not for Mark, whom she saw tell Alex to tally them as in his group.)

Trudging through the crowd, Jamie discovered on the inside exactly what you'd expect from a club that looked like that on the outside: an overwhelming, sweaty, chaotic mess. Sure, the recent million-dollar renovations the venue had undergone looked great, if only there had been two hundred fewer people in there enjoying them. Add to the mix assaultingly loud hip-hop, hordes of gyrating bodies, and public displays of intoxication, and Jamie was ready to make a run for it. As her feet were pounded upon, she directed what no longer felt like her body behind the conga line formed by their share house, deeper and deeper through the masses. To

Jamie's dismay, the group migrated to a section buried far in the back, way past the VIP tables (where she spotted Jamie-Lynn Sigler, Tinsley Mortimer, Rachel Hunter, and a slew of socialites in dresses—she knew they were socialites, because only socialites wore couture dresses to nightclubs). In the city Jamie always knew someone (who knew someone) who invited them to join one of these tables—exactly the opposite of tonight, where she not only did *not* get the VIP treatment but barely made it inside the club at all. Why, Jamie hadn't felt this subpar since those rare occasions she'd been negged with a fake ID before she turned twenty-one. And like those nights, she wanted desperately to leave. She wanted to go home.

And just when she thought it couldn't get worse, the darnedest thing happened.

It didn't.

The host (Jamie hadn't even noticed they'd been following anyone) led them to a huge round table, apparently comped for Mark because he was "running a list." Instantly a busboy produced a giant tin of ice, dozens of glasses, and carafes of tonic, orange juice, cranberry juice, and soda. Taking a seat on the rim of the booth, Mark entreated them to follow his lead, so Jamie and her friends climbed up next to him. When the waitress returned with a bottle of Grey Goose, Jamie hardly objected when Mark offered to mix her a drink. And three strongly poured concoctions later, that twenty-dollar cover seemed an insignificant (and quickly recovered) loss.

And in that moment, she could hear it. The sound of her night going *flip.*

From her new vantage point, Jamie could actually enjoy the club. Listening to the sounds of the skillful DJ, their entire group was soon moved to dance. Like actually dance. Like not just bop to the music or sit around and sway, but get-down-and-sweaty dance. Like she hadn't done since spring break in Cancun. And it wasn't cheesy or out of place. And Jamie remembered how much she liked it.

Surprisingly, in addition to being an adept spiller, Dave was actually a really fun dancer. And willing to get right up there on the booth with her were the two girls (delightfully) lacking New York–bred inhibitions. And while Ilana and her friends tried, they couldn't seem to hold a beat, which Jamie found secretly amusing. But most amusing of all were the guys, who were quickly becoming their best friends. Dave kept pulling her out on the dance floor, everything out of Rob's mouth was totally hysterical, and Brian tended to them like a brother, continually refilling their drinks. And continually ordering up rounds of tequila shots, which added to the mood nicely.

Why, Jamie had to admit, she'd wildly underestimated this party. When you go somewhere with forty people, though, you pretty much are the party. For it's impossible to do a lap or walk anywhere without running into someone you know— which Jamie was actually now finding preferable to being a few girls inside a VIP section where they hardly knew anyone. Besides, she could sit around and look cool anytime. Tonight she was enjoying dancing with her friends and looking ridiculous. So as the night wore on, every song the DJ played was her "favorite song ever," everyone sang and clapped to the lyrics, and the energy in the group grew stronger by the minute. In fact, Jamie paused only to use the restroom, at which point she was in awe of how fast the hours flew.

When the clock struck two, she recalled, inebriated, that she'd usually be picking her target now. She could tell Dave liked her, and suspected a number of other willing participants if she so chose.

But for the first time in a long time, it wasn't about being at the hot spot, or sighting celebrities, or being photographed, or even about consummating a night out with a guy. Tonight had been about bonding with the group and spending time with her friends, with nothing more to be desired. And for that matter, they could have been absolutely anywhere. (Well, maybe not Whitehouse or 21 Water, but pretty much anywhere else.) And Jamie only wished the night could slow down.

But around three (the early group had departed around one thirty), Craig rallied the remaining people together to get a van. Mark had disappeared ages ago.

"Already?" Jamie asked, feeling like a five-year-old being told to go to sleep. But satisfied with the turn the night had taken, she obediently followed.

Funneling out of the club into the abyss of darkness, Jamie didn't even notice Kevin Connolly standing outside as she strolled out. And she didn't even complain about the sardine effect as she piled behind twenty people into one of the waiting vans.

"Ten Eighty-one Montauk!" a distant voice directed the driver.

"No, it's Ten Eighty-eight!" another argued.

"Can we stop at 7-Eleven?" voiced a third.

But Brian had other ideas. "Anyone thirsty?" entreated his voice from the back.

"Where'd you get that?" everyone cried, whipping around as he unveiled a half-full bottle of Grey Goose from underneath his shirt.

"At five hundred dollars a bottle, I couldn't just leave it on the table," he said. Reaching in front of him and grabbing Jamie's head, he motioned like he was going to pour it in her mouth.

Shocking everyone, most of all herself, she tilted her head back, opened wide, and allowed him to do so.

The vodka burned her throat as it trickled down, but made her feel wild and alive and uninhibited. And most of all, happy.

Throwing her head up and wiping the spillage off her face, she turned to her friends. "You guys, I had so much fun. This was one of the best nights I've had in a long time."

From next to her, Dave turned to look her in the eye. "Oh, the night is young," he said, much to Jamie's delight, as the last thing she felt like doing was going to sleep. He then smiled mischievously. "Four AM in a share house is when the party first begins."

Reveling not as much in her vodka shot as in the anticipation of it, Jamie shot him a smile back.

And as they pulled away from the club, Jamie gazed out at the maze of loiterers smoking cigarettes, engaging in PDA, puking curbside, and evading the numerous cop cars ready to pounce. She shook her head. Oh, where in the world was she?

Perhaps this was unlike anywhere she'd ever been, anything she'd ever done, anyplace she'd wanted to be. Perhaps her glamorous Friday nights had taken a total 180-degree flip.

But be it East Hampton, Southampton, or indeed, Frat-Hampton—she was loving every minute of it.

Chapter
Six

When you're done going out, there is the going-out aftermath.

Not that Allison didn't believe the night (the weekend...the year) had already been enough of a roller-coaster ride.

Still, from the moment they decamped from the club, that aftermath began.

Aftermath in a share house started with food. Though, since most things outside Manhattan (notwithstanding its residents) do not operate nocturnally, people had only four choices: pit-stopping at McDonald's (if you think emaciated girls who refused to touch a carb all day wouldn't rifle down fries at 4 AM, you are clearly mistaken); pit-stopping at 7-Eleven (what inebriated men in their late twenties wouldn't do for a blue Slurpee!); ordering from the only open eatery, the Hampton Bays Diner (speed-dialing during the van ride home proved most time-efficient); or, for the more culinarily inclined, throwing anything lying around that was remotely edible onto the barbecue grill (and hopefully remembering to turn it off again).

Now, while any of the above options may seem in itself sufficient, over the course of one night Allison saw each one exhausted.

And that was just for starters. Once everyone was properly nourished, that was when the throwing commenced. (Oh yes, the throwing.) In a take-no-prisoners manner, *everything* was thrown: furniture into the pool, clothes onto the floor, food into your face. The share house mantra? *If it's lying out, consider it thrown.* And if you stood too close to the pool, well...consider yourself warned.

Unfortunately, Tara (Jocelyn?) came to establish this rule when Rob shockingly pushed her in and inspired (nearly) everyone's pity. Now, Allison wasn't a sadistic person, but she was an observant one—and all too aware that said target had occupied Josh's lap the entirety of the van ride, and was also the willing recipient of his drink offers. So Allison didn't entirely mind when Tara/Jocelyn hit the water, complete with clothes and cell phone and jewelry. Until Tara/Jocelyn relayed that she'd yesterday had her hair chemically straightened—a process that not only took five hours but cost her nearly five hundred dollars (a figure at which the damage finally resonated). Following this process, she wasn't allowed to wash her hair the entire weekend so as not to upset the chemicals, something the chlorine most certainly succeeded in doing. And while her friends tried to reassure her that her hair wouldn't fall out, Rob atoned for his guilt by offering to lend her Brian's hat.

Needless to say, she was the last girl he attempted to throw in the pool. That evening.

It wasn't, however, the last of Rob's practical jokes. When the let's-think-of-something-to-do stage of the aftermath ensued, and mundane amusements such as Truth or Dare or I Never were proposed, Rob voiced a more creative suggestion.

"I know," he said. "Let's play Find the Mirror."

It took a moment for his hoax to register. *"Hey!"* Jamie shrieked, going over and pounding him playfully with her fist. "Where is it?"

Smiling, he responded with only one word. *"Cold."*

Allison suspected that Jamie might have been furious

had his answer not been so creative (and memories of their dreadful getting-ready experience not so far behind them). Obligingly, her friend took a dramatic step to the left, which garnered her a prized "Warmer."

Pretty soon the entire room was enraptured in a convoluted game of Hot and Cold, which led them fruitlessly in and out of each room, and finally to the mirror's hiding place in the closet.

Then, after everything hidden had been unearthed and everything throwable had taken flight, the group's late-night personalities were revealed. And up until now, Allison had been an impartial observer, with a mission merely to understand the ways of drunken single people. But witnessing oddities she'd never before encountered, she found the colorful cast of characters before her to be altogether immature, unnerving, and endlessly shocking:

- The WWF (Wasted Wrestling Fools): This was the group of guys (presumably members of that destructive fraternity that was always on probation in college) who couldn't drink without taking on Rocky's fighting mentality. With them, any ill-considered comment escalated into an argument, and every inadvertent tap into a full-blown wrestling match. In short, to drink was to become belligerent (and consequently, to break something).

- The Male-Attention Whore: There was always one whiny girl (who is made considerably whinier with intoxication) who stopped at nothing to be the center of all male attention. She would not be satisfied unless she was the orchestrator of every joke, narrator of every story, and focus of every eye. And if she wasn't, she'd employ any degree of shrieking, flirting, and ridiculing to capture this status.

- The Stripped Tees: The naked drinkers, the guys whose after-hours activities seemed to always involve losing their shirts. They did so in an only partially disguised effort to expose their gym-honed physique (something the next day at the pool could have similarly accomplished).

- The Mutes: The omnipresent people who hung around not saying a word or doing a thing, but continued to linger slumpishly into the AM anyway. They didn't take any value away from a room, but (aside from sheer volume) certainly didn't add to it, either. And for that matter, they might as well have gone to sleep hours ago.

- The Eccentric Eater: He or she concocted the weirdest combinations of food imaginable, less for shock value than for gastronomic pleasure. This was not to be confused with the Oral Fixator, who shoveled into his or her mouth anything and everything in sight.

- The Marathon Puker: The overindulger who left the bathroom off-limits for the entire evening—who seemed utterly repulsive, until it became you.

- The Leaning Tower of Tequila: This was the guy who drank so much, he could barely hold himself up, and for whom the night became an unending quest for balance. Pushing him back into an upright position required a frequent and collective effort.

- The Hot Tub Christener: The person who continually suggested hitting the hot tub—merely because he or she thought it the cool thing to do, and wanted to be known as the one who made use of the hot tub. Unsurprisingly, this was invariably the person who was *least* cool, and least inclined to get any action sans steam.

Allison noticed that missing from this ragtag bunch were the house managers—even though the dearth of supervision left the house open to implosion. Mark had disappeared from the club extremely early in the evening, and though no one had seen him even speaking to anyone, everyone assumed there was a girl with him behind his closed door. And while Craig had upheld his surrogate duties by waiting out the night at Pink Elephant, he hit his bed the moment they returned to the share house...proving him either a heavy sleeper or prescription-friendly.

He wasn't the only one in such lackluster pursuit. As many people as there were who wanted desperately to break dawn with the biggest ruckus possible, there were others who craved only enough tranquility to fall asleep. But hearing outside distractions while lying in a *bed* was quite the desirable predicament, given how many others couldn't share in the luxury and had to stake claims on any available couches; while others were assigned beds only to find them prematurely occupied.

Last but not least (in fact, undeniably most important), intertwined among all of the above were the ass seekers—more imperative on the first night than on any subsequent night. And while girls mostly sat around and looked available, Allison found it quite amusing to study the guys in their approach. She determined their tactics to be less calculated, more impulsive, and subject to countless revision: First they'd set their targets high, on whomever they'd earlier deemed the hottest girl in the house (usually overlapping with other guys in this estimation). Should their efforts be refused (not so much previously in the day as at this pivotal moment), they'd instead zero in on a second girl—one they were still attracted to, but perhaps not initially their first choice. Should this girl seem unlikely to oblige them, they'd move farther and farther down the ladder. And so the pattern continued until they'd finally identify a girl whom they perhaps barely found attractive, but whose appearance was secondary to her obvious willingness.

Similarly amusing, as the hours wore on, the testosterone-driven tactics grew increasingly immature and increasingly transparent. The guy who began by drumming up polite conversation might progress to poking fun, then to pushing and shoving, and finally to nailing his target with french fries.

Allison couldn't decide who was the more culpable party: the guys who resorted to fast-food throwing or the girls who succumbed to this romantic gesture.

Holding their own in the bastion of sexual tension were Allison's friends, whom she believed to be faring pretty well.

Despite his initial indifference, Rachel had made remarkable headway with Dan. She'd spent the bulk of the night huddled in the booth in conversation with him, to which the nightclub was hardly conducive. Still, she advanced and advanced and advanced until she finally got her way. Or what one might perceive to be her way.

For, Hamptons or not, Rachel wasn't one to compromise her strongly practiced convictions. (Those convictions being to not practice at all.) So Dan, thinking he'd at the very least secured a kissing buddy, was in for quite the surprise when they got back to the house.

"My room or yours?" Allison overheard him whisper, firmly clutching Rachel's hand.

"Oh," she remarked, taking a reflexive step back. "I think you have the wrong idea." Then, seeing the bewilderment on his face, added, "I mean, I don't see why we should rush into anything. We should go for dinner this week."

Upon mention of the D word, Dan did the only thing a hormone-raging (and time-handicapped) guy at 4 AM in a share house possibly could do. He released her hand (so quickly you'd suspect it was stricken with disease) and hastily set off to find a less moral target.

Fully distraught, Rachel joined the large group that had congregated around the living room sofa. And she stayed there, until Aaron and Steve came over. Allison wouldn't have minded talking to Steve again—at the meet and greet he'd seemed incredibly polite—but Rachel clearly didn't want to give Aaron a second of her time. Further aggravated by his presence, she declared it "insanely late" and decided to call it a night.

Jamie was a different story, though Allison had long ago quit trying to track her capricious friend's love life. And while she noticed Jamie's ears fine-tune to a conversation confirming the absence of her recent conquest ("Jeff was so pissed he couldn't make it out this weekend," someone had mentioned), it didn't seem to take her long to recover.

Dave had taken an obvious liking to her from the start, and while Allison initially thought his height would put him out of the running, she noticed Jamie's growing interest in him. Allison imagined he'd won her over with his unexpected dance skills, mischievous smile, or the one thing that Jamie was helpless against—constant attention. During the course of their flirty interactions, Brian had kindly kept Allison entertained, but when Jamie stepped into their bedroom to change for the night (not before giving her friend an encouraging nod), Allison saw Dave sneak in after her. (Pretty much the whole house did.) She subsequently heard a loud bang, but didn't see him scurry out again.

And she didn't know what to do next.

New to this problem—she'd always had a serious boyfriend to whose apartment she could easily retreat—her instincts told her not to rush back in. Brian offered momentary relief, and, though distracted, Allison talked with him rather effortlessly. Really, anyone could have, as Brian was one of those guys it was hard not to like (though she couldn't yet tell if he was also that one every girl laughed with, yet none took seriously). His humor wasn't of the loud, obnoxious, attention-seeking sort, as Rob's was; he was instead witty and subtle and quick. You had to really pay attention or you'd miss his sharp interjections. Unlike most of the serious guys Allison knew, Brian used this humor to deflect the gravity of nearly every situation, and almost got away with it. However, his eyes gave away his vulnerable, sensitive side—the guy who just wanted to be loved, and in return would treat a girl like gold.

Still, despite Brian's efforts and the fact that the room was packed and buzzing, Allison now felt strangely foreign in it without her friends—only now fully appreciating the comfort of their presence.

In the midst of the unfamiliar, Allison was drawn to the familiar. She found these urges to be altogether immature, unnerving, and endlessly shocking.

But when you're done going out, there is the going-out aftermath.

Aftermath among exes starts with surveillance. And Allison honestly intended Brian no disrespect. But from the other side of the room, she now felt herself extremely conscious of Josh—whom she'd resolved to ignore (for the most part succeeding) from the moment she discovered him.

This proved to be a whole lot easier in theory. And so, she'd allowed herself to steal intermittent glances, finding it impossible to keep her eyes from the one place she knew she shouldn't look.

Phase two of her game was the I'm-over-you facade. After most satisfyingly detecting Josh's eyes on her, Allison acted the part—that of a person who was fully self-sufficient, fully capable of thriving in a boisterous share house environment, and who'd fully and unmistakably moved on. Allison and said counterpart bore no similarities. Still, she flirted like each guy was full of potential, laughed like each joke was the funniest thing she'd ever heard, and danced like no one was watching. But only when he was.

Believing in this facade was an entirely different matter. Though she'd spent the whole night at Pink Elephant trying to look like she was having the time of her life, all she'd been able to think about was the guy sitting opposite her. The one who knew more about her than anyone else in the world. The one with whom she'd shared nearly every moment of five years. The one she could bar from her vision but never her memory.

Not that Josh hadn't been pretending-to-have-moved-on back, and a hundred times more viciously, as guys often do. He'd made obvious his interest in Tara/Jocelyn (whichever one had suffered the chlorine mishap), who was the type of girl Allison knew always tempted him. Someone high-maintenance and fashionable, snooty to other girls and thus to guys a desirable conquest. The type of girl who couldn't have been any farther from herself. Of course, Josh had always denied it, but she'd always suspected he was disappointed that she didn't know one designer from the next, was the last to catch on to the Murray Hill trends, preferred flats and casual, nonrevealing clothing, and didn't turn guys' heads when she walked down the street.

That she'd never been any of these things had never bothered her in the least. Until she realized Tara/Jocelyn embodied all of them.

What's worse, Allison had been forced to watch them from across the communal table the group had shared. And though she'd kept busy dancing, Rob had kept them laughing, and

Brian (often the ventriloquist to Rob's dummy) had supplied a generous stream of tequila, she'd found herself yielding to what she couldn't deny:

Doubt.

Otherwise known as the remorse portion of the aftermath. And as each Patrón shot hit, she'd grown more and more gripped by it, more and more uncertain. Uncertain about their breakup, but certain she was missing him. Watching him entertain Tara/Jocelyn, giving off that smoothness he so naturally projected, Allison fondly recalled the days when she'd been the recipient of it. It felt like a lifetime ago. How she longed to hear the compliments that had made her blush, to feel his arm around her waist in the manner she'd always claimed was too tight, to summon the jovial grin that lit up his face in a way she'd always thought so goofy. Though she feared she no longer had access to these things, she'd realized she needed to try.

So last but not least (in fact, undeniably most important) came the relapse. Seizing the brief hiatus Tara/Jocelyn had taken from Josh's side, Allison now excused herself from Brian and bravely moved in.

"Hey," she said, timidly approaching the couch, then seating herself in the empty spot beside him. She felt her pulse begin to race; she was quite unsure how he'd react.

"Hey," he answered, with a hint of surprise, seemingly unsure himself. He studied her, fixing his eyes on her disconcerted face. So she left hers on his as well.

It was odd. For Allison had always found him attractive, but it was as if she was suddenly seeing him through different eyes: namely, Tara/Jocelyn's. And while Allison knew it was horribly immature, through them his own deep brown ones seemed more endearing, his bone structure more defined, the sole dimple he couldn't frown away more charming. Undeniably, this stranger before her was entirely more attractive, more desirable, and more perfect a catch. Like everything that was no longer within her reach.

"So you know me now," he said sarcastically.

Immediately Allison apologized, as was always her first instinct in the face of conflict. "I'm sorry. But what could I possibly do? This isn't easy for me, either." She glanced worriedly around to ensure they had no audience.

"It sure looks pretty easy," he said, less concerned with concealing their history than with making his case. (Little did he know what effort "looking easy" had taken.)

"Well, it doesn't seem like you had such a hard time tonight," she said, more to vindicate herself than put him on the defensive, and unconsciously turning toward the door Tara/Jocelyn had exited. To this he had no answer. Or perhaps no incentive to argue.

They sat in silence a few interminable minutes (she'd resisted getting up twice) before he spoke again. "So why are you doing this? House," he made sure to clarify.

She took a deep breath. To be honest, she'd been asking herself that same question all night. *Because I'm single now,* she wanted to say. *Because I need to move on, and this seemed an ideal way.* But instead she answered, "Why not?"—something a professor had once said was the quintessential answer to the question *why.*

Josh was hardly satisfied. So she added, "Jamie and Rachel wanted a third person to do a share with them." Having then earned the right, she readily returned the question. "Why are *you* doing this?"

It was an inquiry he should have anticipated, yet he looked wholly unprepared for it. "Well, Rich grew up in Scarsdale with Mark, the guy who's running the house, and he does it every year," he stammered. Which made them pretty much even, if not equally clueless. Piercing her with his eyes, Josh took his interrogation a step farther. "Why'd you look so disgusted to see me?"

Allison had no idea she'd looked that way upon seeing him, but she had no desire to relive their first encounter of the evening. "I wasn't disgusted. I was just...well, surprised. You never told me you liked the Hamptons."

"You never told me you weren't happy." He looked up at her earnestly, finally asking her for the answers she even now couldn't give. At once the anger fled from his face, the defensive lines in his forehead softened. And for the first time all day, for the first time since their breakup, Josh let his guard down.

"I *was* happy," she said, not lying, not wanting anything but to appease him. With every word she spoke, she knew she was regressing. But looking around at the random house filled with random people all on a frivolous and hormone-driven mission, there was no one with whom she'd rather be. No one who even came close.

"You look really beautiful tonight," he told her, this one comment making all of Jamie's efforts worthwhile. Unlike her friend, she didn't need to dress up for a nightclub of posers; she dressed up for the people that mattered. And she was beginning to revisit the possibility that Josh mattered.

"Thanks," she said, blushing as she often did when put in the spotlight, then looking around at the people lingering awake to pair off. "This is so random," she whispered, *random* being the only word she knew to describe it. "I would love to be back in the city, back in my apartment right now."

"On the couch, eating grilled cheese and catching up on DVR," he said, describing their weekly routine. "By the way, did you see *Lost* this week?" Then, as if there hadn't been a two-week interruption, they reverted to the kind of conversation they always had—the kind of conversation that satisfied her like a favorite meal when she hadn't eaten in a week. She'd been starved for this kind of trivial comfort.

"You'll never guess what happened with my kids the other day," she began, and relayed the story she'd been holding in. The one no one else could appreciate. And it felt reassuring. Comforting. Tempting.

And so, waiting until most of the room had dispersed (her friends weren't near ready for this), Josh leaned over and kissed her. Allison couldn't remember the last time they'd both been up at five in the morning. And she couldn't remember the last time he'd kissed her like that. Like he appreciated every ounce of her.

Quietly slipping into Josh's room (where there were about three other guys dead passed out), they attacked each other with a hunger neither had felt nor expressed in a long time. A hunger that possibly had never existed in the first place. "I forgot how great it was to be with you," he said, wrapping tightly around her waist that arm she had craved. And convincing her that nothing that felt this good could be so entirely wrong.

Paralyzed by pleasure, Allison hardly knew what was right anymore. Despite her hasty desire for reconciliation, she still thought in the long run this might not work out. But helping him remove her clothing and yanking off his in return, she didn't want to think beyond the moment. She didn't want to think at all.

His hands expertly roamed her body, navigating in the way he knew she'd be receptive to. It felt good, to not be ignoring him. It'd been a long time, since they'd connected so deeply. Their every breath seemed amplified against the dark eerie room, uniting them against the share house, them against the unfamiliar. Just like it had always been. Just like it always could be.

Did Allison really want that? she wondered. Tomorrow, she imagined, once again she wouldn't be sure.

But on this roller-coaster ride of a night (a weekend...a year), if only for a moment, it felt nice to get off.

Chapter Seven

Deductive Reasoning: The process of drawing valid conclusions from a given set of premises. (V. Goel and R. J. Dolan, "Explaining Modulation of Reasoning by Belief")

Waking up in a Hamptons share house is much like solving a mathematical equation. It's all about deducing the unknown.

Lifting her head from her pillow that morning, Rachel had no idea where she was, or who she was with.

But once she came to, only one of these things was resolved.

"Jame," she whispered, peering cautiously around the room, able to identify only her one friend sleeping beside her. The blinds were pulled completely shut, barring any trace of sunlight that might offer orientation; it could be 7 AM or 2 PM. Rachel imagined it couldn't have been too late, since everyone else was still sleeping. Then again, everyone else had gone to sleep after her (who knew how much after), and, well, stranger things had happened in the Hamptons.

She tapped Jamie gently, but not a sound emanated from the one person in the room Rachel did recognize. The unidentified individual enjoying blissful slumber across from her, however, continued to snore at leisure.

"Jame!" she whispered.

At this, Jamie finally rolled over, but showed no other signs of life. "What time is it?" she slurred.

Rachel couldn't answer that, so she stated her more imme-diate query. "Who is *that*?" Rising to her feet, she pointed to the lump of covers she now saw was too large to be a girl. She turned toward Jamie again. "And where is *Allison*?"

"What? Oh, I don't know." Satisfied it was nothing urgent, she rolled right over again.

But Rachel was far from satisfied. *"Ew!"* she shrieked. "He's sleeping on her sheets!" she exclaimed to no one at all. Tiptoeing over, she noticed a chunky metal watch (clearly belonging to a guy) abandoned on the nightstand, as well as a silver sequiny shirt atop a pile of clothing on the floor. That's when she realized there wasn't just one intruder. There were two.

That's also when she realized that while she'd been sound asleep, horny, inconsiderate shareholders had been ripping each other's clothes off mere feet from her. Repulsed (yet slightly grateful they had co-opted Allison's bed and not her own), Rachel peered over, more determined than ever to catch a glimpse of the culprits.

She made one of them out to be Dave (whom she vaguely recalled trying to climb into bed with her, before she pushed him off...or had she merely been dreaming?). The other was a girl Rachel had never seen before (or that was the conclu-sion she drew from the mop of blond hair).

Who this girl was and how the two of them wound up in a room alongside her was really quite a mystery. But the bigger one, in Rachel's eyes, was what had become of Allison.

Did she get up early and slip out to the pool? Rachel won-dered. Had she fled back to the city in the middle of the night? Rachel's mind drifted back to the last image of her friend that she could recall. *Wait a minute,* Rachel thought, vividly pic-turing the late-night scene. She couldn't possibly have hooked up with...*Brian?*

No way, she decided, bending down to dig through her luggage. She knew full well that Allison wasn't ready to enter the field again. Why, she'd even said so herself! (Besides, the last thing Rachel wanted to entertain in the wake of her romantic rebuff was the idea of someone else's success.) And so, pulling out a bathing suit, towel, and toiletries, Rachel deduced that Allison must have gotten a head start at the pool—at which point these people had eagerly commandeered her bed. It made perfect sense, for Rachel had no idea how anyone could sleep long in these conditions.

What a wretched night it had been, what with the door opening and closing every five minutes, the sounds of screaming and banging bursting through it, and—lo and behold—an X-rated display at arm's length. It was a wonder she'd slept at all!

Growing strangely dizzy, Rachel sank back down on her bed again. She hadn't noticed it before, but the air in the room was palpably warm and oppressive, and she was suddenly overcome by a fit of nausea—no doubt from everything she'd drunk the night before. (What *had* she drunk the night before?) For unlike in the city, where drinks are twelve dollars a pop and your wallet naturally inhibits your alcohol intake, Rachel could barely count the number of drinks she'd had from Mark's bottles. In truth, she stopped *trying* to count when she realized that number surpassed three. Stumbling toward the door, she could only imagine how her friends would feel—they'd drunk twice the vodka she had, not to mention an indeterminate number of Patrón shots. This, without downing the precautionary bottle of Poland Spring she always gulped down after drinking. Which reminded her, she really had to get to a bathroom.

Cracking open the door and creaking out onto the wooden floor, Rachel couldn't believe the sight that greeted her. Now she felt nauseous not only from the amount she'd drunk, but also from the vile state of her surroundings.

Sun (O blessed sun!) fought through the glass door leading to the patio, but its cheerfulness cast a depressing gleam on the disastrous condition of the share house, which barely resembled the house they'd arrived at yesterday. Leftover food, wrappers, and garbage polluted every inch of the living room, some organic yellow liquid had dried to the floor with sticky resilience, and there were enough beer bottles hidden in obscure places to make finding them a new game. Balancing awkwardly on the balls of her feet in her flip-flops (to make contact with as little floor area as possible), Rachel patiently negotiated the mess obstructing her path and wandered the upstairs.

Comically, in addition to food and alcohol and garbage, there were also people littered everywhere. Camouflaged by their environment, it took Rachel a few minutes to discover the three figures compressed on one futon, the girl nestled inside a sleeping bag on the floor, and the dozing couple whose interlocking limbs draped over the side of the sofa.

So maybe they'd ignored the noise. Maybe they'd shut their eyes to the garbage. But she found it absurd that they could overlook the worst hurdle of all: the smell. The distinct, pungent odor of fraternity-party-in-the-morning. The entire sticky, stuffy pigsty reeked of stale beer and rotting meat and bodies roasting in the morning sun, sweat and tequila seeping from their pores. Rachel had barely been awake ten minutes, and already she could have vomited three times over. And when she retreated to the bathroom, it looked like someone already had. Without bothering to close the door, she rushed (skeptically) to the downstairs bathroom. Stepping in, her feet encountered a layer of water coating the floor, but she nevertheless barricaded herself inside. The lock didn't appear to be working—it now seemed too much to ask for there to be anything functional in this house—so she slid on her bathing suit and sarong at record-breaking speed (all the while picturing someone barging in on her). Then, clearing the sink of partially full cups of beer, she quickly washed her face and brushed her teeth. There was no towel with which to dry her hands or face (good thing she'd brought her beach towel), and no toilet paper. Searching the house and deeming it a lost cause, she settled on grabbing the roll of paper towels from the kitchen and leaving them in the downstairs bathroom as a courtesy.

After that, you couldn't have kept her inside that house another minute, not for anything. And so, returning to her room just long enough to replace her toiletries and grab some things (no one had moved an inch), she closed the door and hurried back out to the pool.

Sliding open the heavy glass door, she allowed the cool morning breeze to hit her, inhaling air as if for the very first time. Though it wasn't quite summer yet, the sun shone with promise and immediately brightened her mood. Rachel wasn't even alarmed when Allison wasn't outside as she'd expected. What *was* there, however, was a similar array of cups and wrappers and residue, and a number of pieces of deck furniture had found their way into the water. If Rachel hadn't known better, she might have suspected a small tornado had hit the property while they slept inside.

Outside, too. Rachel froze as she noted a handful of bodies sprawled out on lounge chairs. Still, she was developing a buffer to the house's absurdities, so she simply dragged a lounge chair to the pool's edge and angled it toward the sun.

Laying out her pink towel (coordinated to match her brand-new swimsuit, natch), she smothered herself with SPF 45 (no need to risk burning this early in the summer...or wrinkling this early in her lifetime). While Jamie was the darkest of the bunch, believing *too tan* just as silly a term as *too rich,* and Allison's skin assumed a healthy outdoor glow, Rachel preferred to maintain the porcelain quality of her own—to the point that her friends teased her that she'd never really been sunburned just like she'd never really been drunk. (Just like she'd never really been...ravaged.) Though she disagreed on all three counts, Rachel nevertheless couldn't prove them wrong.

Soaking up the calm, Rachel decided that this was the perfect time of morning. The sun was strong enough to keep her warm, yet mild enough that it didn't threaten to overheat. A quick glance at her cell phone revealed that it wasn't yet nine thirty, but Rachel had never been a late sleeper. She'd never been much of a sleeper at all. Because of this, she religiously went to the gym every morning at five thirty before arriving at work at nine, so even on the weekends her body was inclined to wake up. Now a blessing, this had posed quite the problem in her childhood days, when she'd always been the first to pop up in her sleeping bag at slumber parties, and would pretend to be sleeping for hours until the other girls awoke. Funny, she felt as ostracized being the early bird now as she had back then.

Still, even in the eerie solitude, she closed her eyes and attempted to enjoy the blissful peace.

She didn't get very far. Within minutes, she heard the recognizable swishing of the glass door sliding open. Curious to see who'd gotten up as insanely early as she had, she turned and spotted a girl dressed in a trendy outfit that last night was probably hot, but in the morning light looked ridiculous: tight low-slung jeans, pointy pumps, and, wouldn't you know it, that silver sequiny top (one of those items that looked a lot better on a hanger—or, as opportunity had provided, on their bedroom floor—than on a body). But Rachel regretted these insensitive thoughts when she realized the girl had been crying.

"Are you all right?" Rachel asked, leaning over the lounge chair and calling out to the figure frozen on the patio.

"Yeah," the girl sniffled, hardly looking all right, and hardly looking in Rachel's direction. She paced back and forth almost in a trance before approaching Rachel's chair. Sinking lugubriously into the seat opposite, she eventually decided to elaborate. "My cell phone was stolen last night. I'm so upset."

"Are you kidding?" Rachel asked, pulling herself upright. Rachel didn't think she was kidding, but didn't really know what else to say.

The girl merely shook her head, setting her blond mane flying. Last night's mascara stained black her entire eye area but couldn't mask the pretty blue eyes buried beneath, and there was something about her bed-set locks that looked very modelesque—the overall effect of which inspired sympathy. "Can I use your phone for a minute?" she asked after an overdrawn pause, and after eyeing Rachel's phone beside her.

"Uh…sure," Rachel replied, suddenly imagining the girl using up all her minutes, or calling out of country, or accidentally dropping it in the pool. But she had no choice.

Trying not to appear anxious as the girl pounded authoritatively on the dial pad, making one call after another, Rachel couldn't distinguish the words she muffled softly and privately until the girl addressed her directly. "What's the address here?"

Rachel drew a blank. Fortunately, the number she'd drilled repeatedly into her head (in the event she was lost, abducted, or assaulted) resurfaced. "Ten Eighty-eight Montauk Highway."

The girl repeated this verbatim. "A cab's coming to get me," she announced a few minutes later, then handed Rachel back her phone.

Casually accepting it, Rachel resumed her normal breathing. "That's good," she said. Then, since the girl still lingered beside her, she added, "So...I guess you're not in this house?"

Staring into space, the girl seemed to still be thinking about her phone, but then surprised Rachel by responding. "No. My friend hit it off with some guy at Pink Elephant last night, so she begged me to come back to this house with her."

"Wow, that was really...nice of you," Rachel exclaimed, imagining she'd never have done anything of the sort.

"Stupid is more like it," the girl acknowledged, rummaging through her bag and emerging with a pack of Marlboro Lights. "Because they started hooking up, so I just found a bed and went to sleep, and God knows where they are now." Rachel noticed she'd left out the part about hooking up herself, but saw no need to point it out. The girl sighed, depression visibly washing over her again. "I just want to get the hell out of here and try to find my phone," she said, lighting the cigarette she dangled from her mouth. "Want one?"

"No, thanks," Rachel said, feeling too sorry for the girl to ask her to please smoke in a different direction. A few minutes later Rachel's phone rang, and the girl immediately grabbed at it. (*So now she's getting calls on my phone?* Rachel thought.) But after speaking for only a moment, the girl returned it and rose to her feet. "My cab's here. Thanks for your help," she called as she ran off, a blaze of smoke and sequins.

"Sure," Rachel said, with considerable relief. And so she settled back into her chair again, alone with the silence that, a few minutes later, seemed to have never left.

Her mind instantly began to wander—replaying the details of the night before, freezing on the part she didn't care to think about. The part that was Dan.

She'd been so hopeful about him—of course, that was before he tried to capitalize on their chemistry. Before she'd realized that what to some was "chemistry" was to others "anticipated ass." It was a shame, too, because really he had everything going for him that she usually looked for, every element of the equation. What a devastating (and time-consuming) blow this had been! But she knew as well as any that some equations have no real solutions.

As the minutes drew on, more and more girls began to spring up and scatter themselves among the lounge chairs (where had they come from?). At first Rachel tried to be friendly, but either these girls weren't morning people or they had serious sticks up their nonexistent asses. And so they all coexisted awkwardly, with their identical pink iPods and *Us Weekly*s and chick-lit novels…their hot little swimsuits (boasting New York Sports Club–sculpted and carb-starved bodies), dark straightened hair (tied back to deter frizz), and thick designer shades (this season's Chanel, Gucci, or Marc Jacobs)…and with the dismissive attitude they had mastered—conveying bored yet arrogant in perfect proportion. But beneath it all raged insecurities and a desire to just blend in. In irritating New York intonation, they yammered on their cell phones (the smallest, newest flip-top models), disclosing minute details of the night before (which Rachel found especially ironic, as everyone in the house had pretty much had the same night—all that differed were the names each whiny voice dropped). The voices started off hushed but took on volume, and while everyone around the pool pretended not to eavesdrop, each word of each frivolous conversation became universal (if inconsequential) knowledge.

Once the guys started filtering outside, things became a tad more interesting. But just a tad. Like a boy-girl party from fifth grade, the guys and girls instinctively divided themselves to opposite sides, barely acknowledging each other. This separation wasn't difficult to maintain, since the girls preferred to bask on lounge chairs (filling up quickly) while the pool became the guys' safe haven. No girl, in the name of vanity, ever fully went in.

Still, in the midst of all this, Rachel was quick to notice something appearing before her. Something of which she was so desperately in need.

A new variable.

When you can barely distinguish one person from the next, as is often the case the first full day in a share house, people assume identities based solely on their swimsuits. And so, awakening to the splash of a body she had certainly never before seen hit the water, Rachel came to monitor that pair of yellow trunks. Equally, she monitored the face attached to them—a rugged unshaven face with dark features, longish hair, and a happy-go-lucky smile. True, he wasn't the tallest guy there, but he compensated with both an evident gym commitment and deliberate placement of his broad shoulders to exaggerate their effect. Plus, he was tan. Not just red-enough-not-to-be-white tan, but dark-incapable-of-burning tan—which people are in May only if they make a concerted effort.

This wasn't the only effort he made. "Hey," he said, lunging over the pool's edge and flashing her a smile so personable she wondered if she knew him. "Do you have any sunscreen?"

She did, of course, right next to her. Though she found the remark funny, because from her experience sunscreen ranked so low on guys' lists of priorities that not only did they never bring it, but they applied it only when they reached the brink of lobster red that prompted everyone to continually ask "Are you wearing sunscreen?"

Happily accepting it as a conversation starter, Rachel knelt beside the pool's edge and handed it over.

"Forty-five, huh?" he said, in a way that made her blush. "Guess they were out of sixty," he joked, then squeezed some out with that indiscreet blurping noise. He thanked her, again flashing an exaggerated smile.

"Did we meet last night?" Rachel finally asked, alarmed at the prospect she had forgotten a face (and silently vowing to ditch the embarrassingly strong sunscreen).

"Probably not, but I thought I'd play it safe," he said in an effortlessly charming manner. "We came late and went straight to the club. Brett," he added, a wave of water splashing her as he put out his hand.

"Rachel," she said, leaning over to shake and paying the water absolutely no mind (so long as it didn't go anywhere near her hair). To be safe, she sat back down again. "So you're up early," she said, realizing he could say the same to her. And leaving it open for him to do so.

He waded a bit closer. "I have to be at work at six thirty every day, so I always wake up early on the weekends." A man after her own heart!

"What do you do?" she asked, as nonchalantly as she could. But not quite nonchalantly enough.

"I'm a trader," he said, which made sense given his slick persona. "You?"

"Analyst," she answered, before steering the conversation back to him again. "Do you work on Wall Street?" she continued, hungry for details.

"No. Lehman, in Midtown." He gazed away and closed his eyes for a moment, as if concentrating on tanning would maximize the effect.

"Ohmigod, I work right around there. At Bear," she said, lunging forward on her seat. This was just getting good. "So what do you trade? Stocks, bonds, derivatives?"

There was something utterly out of place about hearing the word *derivative* poolside. He picked up on it as well.

"Fixed income, institutional side." Just as she was about to bombard him with a dose of names, he added, "But I try not to think about work on the weekends." That said, he changed the topic. "So where'd you go last night?" It was the question uppermost on everyone's minds in the morning, used to ascertain whether or not they had missed a better time elsewhere.

"Pink Elephant," she said. "And you?"

"Yeah, I was at the Pink Elephant." It irked her when people added *the* on to the names of clubs, but it bothered her less once he pulled himself out of the pool and positioned himself on the edge of her chair, somewhat presumptuously. "What'd you think?"

"I had a lot of fun," she said. Which she would have claimed even if she hadn't, for it was her policy to act like everything in life happened the way she intended. "What about you?"

"I was so drunk I couldn't tell you," he said, half complaining, half boasting. As if suddenly recalling his hangover, he hung his head back like it weighed a hundred pounds. The spot where he was sitting on her towel had developed a huge wet splotch, but Rachel considered it a small price for this intimacy. She'd never known a guy to act so casual around a stranger—like they were already well acquainted. "So I don't know about you, but I'm starving," he said, straightening up. "Do you want to take a ride to the bagel store?"

Stunned, she looked at him like he had just proposed marriage instead of a food run. "Do you...have a car?" she finally responded.

"Yeah, it's in the driveway. Come on," he said, standing up and gesturing with his hand for her to follow.

Rachel had absolutely no desire to eat a bagel, and even less to leave the house before connecting with her friends. (Where *were* her friends?) Flattered by the impromptu invitation, though, she accepted. Agreeing to meet him in front of the house in five, she dashed up to her room, threw a brightly colored Juicy skirt and wifebeater over her bathing suit, and had just pulled the door shut behind her when it reopened.

Out stepped Dave, wearing nothing but boxers and rubbing his eyes groggily.

"Listen," he began. "About last night…" A decently attractive guy, he now looked like he was seeing daylight for the first time in months. His light hair was standing up in a way she would have thought impossible without ultrastrength mousse, and he peered lazily at her through half-shut eyes.

Confused, she waited for him to elaborate, though he seemed to be having trouble finding the words. That, and commanding his vision. "What are you talking about?" she asked, hating to keep Brett waiting.

His eyes widened, fully unsquinting as if he'd instantly come sober. "Oh, we didn't…last night?"

"No!" she shrieked. Perhaps her reaction was a bit harsh, but she was more appalled by the act he was insinuating than the possibility it'd been with him.

He seemed only for a minute insulted. But looking hastily at her again, he then whispered, "Do you have any idea who, then?"

Rachel stared at him in awe, unsure whether to laugh or reprimand him. As time was ticking, she decided it wasn't her place to do either. "Didn't you wake up next to her?" she asked, straining to bar any judgment from her tone.

"Nooo," he sang, as if that answer was obvious. "There's no one in the room now but Jamie, and I only saw someone's back before." He inspected Rachel again. "Are you sure? I came into your room with Jamie, and I got into bed with someone."

"Yeah, that part I remember. I pushed you off onto the floor," she told him, flashing him a scolding look. "But here's what I don't get," she proceeded, now quite invested in the mystery. "I went to bed first. And you're saying you came into the room with Jamie?"

"Yeah."

"And there was a girl sleeping in Allison's bed?"

"There were people in both beds." He shrugged.

Rachel digested this. "So then why didn't Jamie make her get up?"

Oddly, this Dave could answer. "Maybe because that other girl you came with was hooking up. Jamie said she was going to."

"What?" Rachel exclaimed, her eyes bulging. She wasn't sure what shocked her more—that Allison had done what she'd least expected, or the extent of Jamie's manipulation. "Who did Allison hook up with last night?"

"Hey! Can we first figure out who I hooked up with?" he shouted, though at the same time smiling.

Rachel sighed, and for a moment contemplated making him sweat. "I hate to break it to you, but she ran out of here early this morning."

She expected Dave to look distraught, but instead discovered him overwhelmingly relieved. "Who was she?" he finally asked.

"I have no idea, some random. Her friend's hooking up with a guy here," she replied, though Dave was no longer listening. Instead, he was covering his mouth as he let out a loud yawn.

Seeing that her work here was done, and having wasted far too much time already, Rachel about-faced. But Dave blocked her with his arm, posing one final question before she could hurry away.

"Last thing...was she cute at least?" The mischievous gleam returned to his eyes.

Rachel smiled, once again embracing the opportunity to

make him sweat. "She looked as hot as you possibly could wearing club clothes at nine in the morning."

With that, she pounded down the stairs.

Running outside to greet Brett, she found him leaning idly against his car and talking into his cell phone, hardly seeming like the same person. He'd thrown on a bright white T-shirt (which served to illuminate his tan) and shiny square sunglasses that hid much of his face. In fact, they hardly seemed the same two people who'd been lounging hungrily beside the pool ten minutes ago. As a mere layer of clothing had afforded, he was now a guy, and she was a girl, and that was a 2008 silver Porsche whose door he was holding open for her.

At that moment, Rachel grew suddenly shy. Going for bagels. This was a date...sort of?

She examined the evidence:

If she and Brett were going for food (a = b)
And going for food is considered a date (b = c)
Then she and Brett were going on a date. (a = c)

And there you had it. Proof by deduction.

Chapter
Eight

When you come to a crossroads, there isn't always a clear-cut choice.

But there they were, the very last night of the very first weekend, and Jamie was determined to have her way at least once.

So far she'd sucked it up rather heroically and followed Mark to each of his respective clubs. They'd accompanied the share house to Pink Elephant on Friday and Star Room on Saturday; they were supposed to return with them to Star Room tonight for the final evening of the holiday weekend. But after the three girls had packed up from the pool and retreated to their room that afternoon, Jamie decided the time was right to propose her alternative.

And it wasn't that she'd been having a bad time at these places. On the contrary, she'd been bonding with her housemates, letting her hair down, and having a refreshingly unpretentious, great time. Still, she couldn't ignore the fact that each party (and partygoer) had been disappointingly...ordinary, and she craved a small taste of the glamour for which the Hamptons was known. And—more important—the guys said glamour enticed.

There was no arguing that guys who flocked to "the scene"— to quote her friends—weren't the type of guys looking to settle down. Well, actually, there was a lot of arguing about it. Incessant arguing, as a matter of fact. For Rachel (and perhaps Allison, too, though Rachel was far more vocal about it), any guy who was so infatuated with frequenting the "in" party, running with the right crowd, and being the focus of beautiful girls (plural) wasn't the type of guy who deserved any of her time. Especially not when there were perfectly decent, spotlight-shunning investment bankers waiting in the wings elsewhere (*elsewhere* being the slightly less exclusive venues). There you would find countless guys who spent their time raking in dough rather than obsessing over party schedules and promoters and everything else Rachel equated with misdirection. Guys who, come the weekend, looked to the Marks of the world to direct them to a place they could trade in their credit cards for bottles—a place whose name they would quickly forget but would temporarily provide a normal-enough crowd, ego-stroking girls, and free-flowing booze.

This, for Jamie, was not enough.

Unlike her friends, Jamie herself resembled the scene-seeking playboys. When she went out she did so to let loose, to see and be seen, and to mingle with tons of people (the more, the better) rather than to weed out the one guy who could potentially be her husband. And it wasn't so much about the attention (though naturally, the attention always did follow). It was about the liberation, the defying of convention, and, for better or worse, the glamour. And it suited her just fine.

Deep down she hated that her friends saw this as a sign of immaturity, some rebellious phase she would eventually outgrow. Yet if maturity was synonymous with monotony and monogamy, Jamie hardly saw herself reaching that point in the near future. This wasn't to say she couldn't appreciate a guy with a solid education and a promising career who was from a world that closely mirrored her own. And she certainly wouldn't undervalue any good-looking ones (namely

Jeff, whom she was beginning to think was a figment of her imagination). But she soon discovered that talking to one Mike/David/Jon who worked in finance/law/medicine and was from Long Island/New Jersey/upstate was the same as talking to ten others. And after two nights of doing exactly that, she tired of these hordes of homogeneous cookie-cutter people—who were of course all that filled the clubs on three-day weekends. Finding a trendy nightclub scene in the Hamptons on a holiday appeared no more feasible than finding one in Manhattan on a weekend (when any ounce of weekday trendiness was lost to the masses desperate to go somewhere and willing to pay good money to do so). Lacking as a result was any flair, any flavor—and most of all any space to move around. Jamie saw tonight as a final opportunity to take hold of the wheel and steer her reluctant friends into uncharted territory: the private party. She had a feeling it wouldn't go over well.

"So, the *Hamptons Magazine* party at Hampton Hall tonight is, like, the kick-off to the summer," Jamie began, more fervor slipping into her tone than she intended. As time had taught her, her friends were inherently suspicious of anything she wanted too badly. "My whole firm is going to be there . . . basically *everyone* is going to be there," she added, flopping onto her bed and attempting not to sound like she cared too much.

Unfortunately, it didn't work. "That sounds way too complicated," Rachel said, shooting her down immediately. "It would cost us a million dollars in cabs, and no one even knows how to get anywhere." Jamie wondered how much her friend was being swayed by that guy Brett she'd met yesterday. Clearly she was in no rush to separate from him.

Allison at least entertained the idea. "I thought we decided it would look bad if we split from everyone the first weekend?"

she pointed out while neatly repacking her pool stuff. Now that she'd reunited with Josh, Allison had thankfully returned to her good-natured self.

Jamie was prepared for this rebuttal as well. More so, she'd been counting on it. "We can still meet up with them at Star Room after. This is an *early* party, it starts at *nine*," she explained, emphasizing the key to her argument.

No one spoke for a moment.

"Oh," Allison finally said. "I guess we don't usually do anything during that time anyway?" And it was true. The ideal time slot for getting ready in a share house—four to seven PM—was unofficially naptime.

Seeing she was quickly losing out, Rachel hurried to intervene. "So how would we even get anywhere?" she asked, wriggling upright on her bed.

Jamie grinned, conscious that Rachel was slowly conceding. "Okay, so here's my plan. I would drive us to the *Hamptons Magazine* party at Hampton Hall and leave my car parked there overnight. Then we can take a cab from there to Star Room, where we'll meet up with everyone, and someone can drive us to Hampton Hall to get the car tomorrow morning." She relayed the details as slowly as possible, though any way you put it, it was a mouthful.

"Do you even know how to get to Hampton Hall?" Rachel fired off.

"I'll get directions. How hard can it be? The Hamptons is only one road," Jamie assured her. Sensing her friend's lingering doubt, she added, "Besides, we're not even going that far. Hampton Hall is right here in Southampton, on Elm Street." Jamie neglected to add that she'd never even heard of Elm Street; she figured this argument needed no further obstacles.

Pausing only to regroup, Rachel went at her again. "How do you know you can park overnight?"

Jamie rolled her eyes. "I did it every time I came out last year." (Which really meant once.) "These places totally *expect* people to do that, because everyone gets so drunk they can't drive home." This part involved some speculation, but it sounded feasible enough.

Rachel addressed Allison. "What do you want to do?"

Allison's indifference was predictable. "I'll do whatever."

Turning back toward Jamie, whose resolute look suggested she'd forever hold a grudge otherwise, Rachel finally agreed. "Okay, let's do it."

Which was fortunate, because Jamie already held her cell phone in hand and had prematurely begun to dial.

Once this plan was sealed, though, it actually made the getting-ready process that night monumentally easier. Because they weren't leaving for the *Hamptons Magazine* party till eight thirty, for the first time all weekend they could actually get ready with ease, hours before anyone else would be vying for showers or mirrors.

Plus, they were finally afforded the prized opportunity to take over Mark's spacious bathroom—a privilege he'd quickly conferred on them before running out to grab food at a place known only as "the Pork Store."

After they'd filed into the spa-like enclave, Jamie closed the door behind them, opened her arms, and took a few blissful spins. It was the only bathroom in the house remotely spinnable.

This space also instantly transformed the girls' moods. After setting up Allison's iPod speakers and blasting music, they started their own little party. However, no sooner had they showered, blow-dried, and taken to simultaneously applying makeup along the never-ending countertop than someone broke it up.

"Oh," Ilana said, walking in and seeming startled to find

them. But then her tiny features tightened. "I need to shower," she whined, clutching her towel and things restlessly.

"Don't let us stop you," Jamie said, continuing to work on her eyes while gesturing to the transparent shower. And wondering how she possibly could have forgotten to lock the door.

Ilana grimaced, flinging her towel over her shoulder angrily. "Does Mark even know you're in here?" she spurt, color rushing to her face.

"Yes," Jamie replied, touching gold MAC shadow to the crease of her eye ever so gently. "He gave us the bathroom because we need to get ready for the *Hamptons Magazine party,*" she pronounced, insinuating not just that their time was more important, but that their social connections were superior. Driving in the knife, Jamie added, "We'll be done at nine"—even though she expected to finish a whole half hour beforehand. Then she presumptuously gripped the doorknob, waiting until Ilana took the cue to leave before closing it again. And this time locking it.

"Jame, she's a friend of my sister's," Rachel protested. Rachel preferred to be on good terms with everyone she'd ever met in her life, because she never knew who had a friend who had a friend with whom she could possibly be set up.

"I can't see why," Jamie answered, returning to her makeup and giving Ilana's hostility no further thought.

It was almost nine by the time they finally all got their acts together—or rather, that Jamie did. She really intended to be ready on time, but always seemed to encounter some last-minute problem. After bursting out the front door (and having to bend down and physically yank her heels out of the cracks in the wood as they hurried across the deck), all of a sudden, Jamie stopped short.

Heading directly toward them, still twenty feet away but

in her direct line of vision, was a familiar form that looked entirely out of place here—that in fact might have looked entirely out of place anywhere short of an Abercrombie catalog. Noticing this as well, her friends continued on into the darkness and waited some paces ahead.

As he drew closer, Jamie worried he'd think she was staring, so she began unnecessarily digging through her bag until moments after his footsteps should have given him away. Then, in a dead giveaway that she'd seen him, when he was a few feet from her she looked up and straight into his face.

"Hey?" she said, as much a question as a greeting. His striking blue eyes studied her with the innocence of a child, and she realized that as he was checking her out, it hit him that it wasn't for the first time.

"Oh...hey," Jeff said, forging a massive save. He bent over and air-kissed her on the cheek, a bit too methodically for her taste.

"Getting a late start to the weekend?" she asked. She'd heard several times that he wasn't going to be here.

"Yeah, I was so bummed," he said, his eyes still locked with hers in a manner that made it difficult for her to process his words. But then he quickly moved them off her, as if aware of their effect and opting to use it sparingly. "I thought I'd be out on Friday, but I got assigned to a deal at the last minute."

Now, if she'd ever had any interest in knowing what he did, she might have asked him to elaborate. But to Jamie, details surrounding the guys who came in and out of her life like seasonal runway fashions always seemed superfluous. "How'd you get here?" she asked instead, bending forward to peer behind him and finding it a bit odd that he should appear off a highway.

"I just finished, so I caught a train two hours ago. The stop is like a block away," he explained, waving behind him to the empty space. "Figured I could salvage what was left of the weekend," he added with a shrug, shifting his duffel bag from one side to the other, as well as his gaze from her to the windows. Lingering silently, Jamie was hoping he might drop some casual comment about her, or about them...or, well, about her. Only "Is Mark in there?" were the next words out of his mouth.

Jamie nodded, wondering how her party attire might have managed to escape him. Just then, as if reading her mind, he turned back and reexamined her, this time seeming to register that she was dressed up and heading out somewhere. That, and every bit as alluring as other guys made her believe.

"Where are you going?" he asked, those eyes doing a scan of her body in a way she didn't exactly mind, except that they landed on every inch of her besides her face. Again, something about his mannerisms reminded her of a child—one capable of entertaining only one notion at a time, who wore his desires on his sleeve and saw no need to filter them with adult-like discretion.

"To a party," she said, soaking up every bit of this attention—no matter how indiscreet. "But we're going to meet up with everyone later," she made sure to add.

"Well, you look great," he said, which was perhaps the most frustrating male comment of all time. Not because she didn't want him to think she looked great, but because the fact that he did proved inconsistent with his actions. See, girls whom guys thought "looked great" usually received a phone call. Jamie, on the other hand, had not. "See you later," he then called over his shoulder, instantly dismissing her as he concentrated all his effort on lugging his stuff up the stairs.

Hearing the door slam with finality behind him, Jamie ran to catch up with her friends. As she struggled to regain her composure, she felt like she'd just been visited by an apparition, and worried that her face reflected this. It was ironic, though, that she'd spent the entire weekend wondering what it would have been like if he were here…and now that he finally was, she was (literally) running away from him. Plus, was it the lighting, or did he look way better than she'd remembered? Though it was perhaps the kind of "way better" most guys looked in light of not having called.

Shaking off the encounter so as not to appear weak (harping on guys was the epitome of female weakness), Jamie directed her attention toward her more obvious shortcoming—driving.

"Whoa, it's dark," she muttered under her breath as she stabbed the pebbled grounds with heels she could barely walk in, much less drive. Approaching the car, she rummaged through her Marc Jacobs bag for the keys she'd just minutes ago placed there (which took a remarkably long time, considering the small size of her bag and the fact she could barely fit anything in it). After much anticipation, she located the Tiffany heart key chain and clicked the alarm, jumping back at the startling noise. Then, pausing momentarily and staring around, she couldn't help but exclaim again, this time louder, "You guys, it's like totally pitch-black!"

This wouldn't alarm a future passenger in the least.

"Let's not do this," Rachel immediately said, putting her back to the vehicle as if proof she was ready to turn right around and forget it.

But the thought of walking back inside and admitting defeat when everyone (namely, Jeff) knew they were going out was something Jamie refused to entertain. Fear or no fear, when Jamie set about doing something, very little could stop her. "Don't be silly," she said, climbing awkwardly into the front seat with new momentum, and gesturing for her friends to follow her.

After they reluctantly obeyed and slammed shut the doors

that sealed them tightly inside the dark vehicle (for better or worse), nervous apprehension seemed to fill the car.

Taking a deep breath, Jamie started up the ignition, which emitted a loud scary rumbling like a beast she wasn't sure she could tame. After she adjusted the mirror and was reaching for the gear, she shut it all back off again and spun abruptly around. "You guys, I don't think I can do this. It's just *really* dark." *And I'm scared out of my mind,* she thought.

"Look, do you want me to drive?" Allison offered from behind. "The dark doesn't bother me. I'm used to driving in this."

"Yes!" she cried without a moment's hesitation. Rachel hated driving, but this was something Jamie hadn't even considered! "I'll sit shotgun so I can direct you," she offered, sliding over and feeling as if a huge weight had been lifted off her chest. Before long the three of them had swapped seats and set off. Not only did you need the right people in your life and in your car—you also needed them in the right seats.

In much better (safer) spirits, they creaked down the driveway, and Jamie got her personality back. Watching Allison maneuver the car so expertly (and with so little apprehension), she realized she had in no way been ready for the challenge at hand. This was especially evident when they started off down the road and Allison clicked on the brights (Jamie had never used brights in her life—nor driven anywhere that had warranted them).

And she had to hand it to Allison: So far they were doing okay. Three days had hardly acquainted them with the area (they'd moved the car around the driveway a great deal, but taken it no farther than the bagel store or the 7-Eleven), so Jamie did her best to follow the directions.

"So was that weird, back there?" Rachel eventually asked, referring to Jamie's encounter with Jeff.

"No, not at all," Jamie said. But then she turned her whole body around. "Why, did it look weird?"

Rachel quickly shook her head. However, now that Jamie no longer held their lives in her hands, her thoughts were free to roam back to the house's newest arrival. She hated to be doing so, but she wondered what he might be doing, where he might be going, and why she even cared. She wondered when they'd get to this silly party already, but only so they could turn around and meet up with the rest of the house. And most of all, she wondered how Allison could see a darn thing.

Damn was it dark. True, Jamie had heard it said that when driving, you often can't see any farther ahead than your headlights—but that's really all you need to get through the journey.

Unfortunately, it wasn't.

Out of nowhere, they came upon a point in the road that their directions hadn't mentioned—or that maybe, in her distraction, Jamie had overlooked. Either way, they just weren't prepared for that sudden split, that T-shaped junction that forced them to pick one way or the other. And really, there wasn't a clear-cut choice.

"Do I go left or right?" Allison asked, her voice remaining remarkably calm as her head turned from one side to the other.

Leaving it to Jamie to furnish the necessary melodrama. "Um, I'm not really sure!" she cried, panic in her voice. She whirled around to Rachel, tapping her hand impatiently a few times on the seat. "Left or right?"

Predictably, Rachel was engulfed in her own world of daydreaming. To her, not being able to drive justified not paying attention. "What? Oh, I have no idea," she sputtered. And then, catching on a moment too late, "Are we lost?"

Hitting the brakes, Allison approached the junction as

slowly as she could. But the cars behind her honked furiously, forcing her to make a choice. Jamie stammered, "Uh, I would say left but—"

"Right!" Rachel screamed, so resolutely that Allison took the hard turn.

"Hey, are you sure?" Jamie asked, glancing back at her friend once the turn had been made, and they were starting down a road no less dark or desolate than any other.

Rachel looked back at her and merely shook her head. "No, not really. But since we were guessing randomly, I've noticed things are usually the opposite of what you think."

Jamie swung her studded bag in Rachel's direction, but then laughed, realizing her friend was probably right.

Thus they started down the dark little road—if you could call a barely defined sequence of bumps and quick turns and no lights a road. It was only one lane, and there was an impatient Range Rover bullying them from behind, so they dutifully turned corners and rounded turns and kept up a reasonable speed (and a reasonable confidence level). Still, no sooner had they circumvented some massive body of water (a lake? river? ocean?) and entered an unfamiliar residential terrain than Allison voiced what everyone had been thinking. "You guys, do we think this is wrong?"

Each nodded silent consent, although *wrong* was clearly an understatement. They had far surpassed wrong—why, they'd left it back at the crossroads twenty minutes ago. Wrong was straying from the share house, appointing Jamie navigator, attempting this ill-conceived journey in the first place. Now they were entering the vicinity of *stupid*.

"Yeah, maybe turn around at the next opportunity," Jamie said, trying to be helpful. But that opportunity just didn't come, and that car kept pressing from behind, and minutes later the road split again. And they passed more strange water and more foreign houses and more disorienting sights. Finally Allison veered off onto some grassy nonroad and pulled a desperate U-turn (something Jamie would never have been able to do in one motion). Then, battling the poor visibility and the fact that what they could see all looked the same, they rationally tried to retrace their steps. But it's hard to remain rational when you're working at it, and they must have taken a wrong turn somewhere...because before you knew it (and I imagine you did), they were lost.

Like, insanely lost. Like not just made-a-wrong-turn-and-need-to-turn-around lost. No, wholly and irreversibly lost, in an abyss of black darkness, following one long twisting road that never seemed to end. Lost to the point you couldn't even remember what it felt like not to be lost lost. It was a two-minute mistake that became a ten-minute one that became a whole-hour one, and that seemed more and more hopeless with each passing minute.

Not to mention the party had started an hour ago. So not only were they lost, but they were also late. Staring out the window and praying for some sign of civilization, Jamie (mostly) focused on the former.

"Well, look on the bright side," she said, attempting to lighten the gloom for which she was solely responsible. "We may be lost, but if I'd been driving, we'd have been lost *and* we'd probably have hit something." No one so much as smiled. Instead, they panicked.

"We're like a hundred miles out of the way now!" Rachel cried, as if she'd actually been paying attention for more than two seconds. "We're going to miss the party!"

"We're not going to miss it," Jamie said, herself only 50 percent sure. "But I'm *so* sorry I suggested doing this. I thought it would be really simple!" She knew full well she'd lost any planning leverage for the remainder of the summer.

What happened next must really have involved some miracle. For out of all the roads, in all the towns, they somehow stumbled on the right one.

"Wait a minute!" Allison cried. "Is this Elm Street? I think that sign just said Elm Street!"

"Are you serious?" Jamie shrieked. And indeed it was. And before they knew it, they came upon a crowd of dressed-up people hovering around a grand wooden clubhouse, with a sign announcing HAMPTON HALL. And it was the sweetest sight Jamie had ever beheld.

"We made it!" she shouted, unable to recall the last time she'd felt so relieved to arrive at a party. This, despite the fact that they'd missed nearly half of it, as it only lasted till twelve (more important, so did the open bar).

Pulling up in front of the crowd, Allison handed over the keys to Jamie, who thrust them at the valet like they were some kind of explosive. Never was she so eager to get rid of a car, or so in need of a drink.

"To the bar!" Jamie ordered the moment they walked in, immediately embracing the party's vibe. The historic wooden ballroom was packed, but not in a fear-for-your-shoes way, and certainly not in a nightclub way. There were food stations and cameras flashing and just enough attractive (or at least well dressed) people to make it all interesting. And while even the right elements don't always create the desired effect, the colored lights were enlivening, the sounds of the DJ electrifying, and the energy contagious.

Still, they could have been at a dive bar for all Jamie cared: Her mission right now was alcohol. Lots of it. And so she proceeded to order one after another of the colorful promotional martinis (complete with glow-in-the-dark keepsake floating inside, of which she quickly collected an impressive number). She double-fisted the entire time—something she'd normally think was tacky—and later on, even downed a few shots with the bartender (after all, they were leaving the car here and cabbing it from this point on).

Once satiated by just enough top-shelf liquor to forget the last hour's trauma entirely, Jamie surveyed the room more closely. A typical *Hamptons Magazine* event, the party was a welcome relief from the nightclub scene, which lacked sophistication and class. What's more, it seemed as if the usual New York crowd had hopped a Jitney en masse and transported themselves over here: prominent figures at the magazine were doing their laps, the requisite socialites and heiresses dropped by to make colorful cameos, and this month's cover model Beth Ostrosky (Howard Stern's girlfriend) was posing endlessly for the paparazzi (most notably Rob Rich, Hampton photographer extraordinaire, who snapped party pics of the famous and unidentifiable alike).

But while the atmosphere was fun, Jamie had to admit, it wasn't the be-all and end-all of parties. Upon closer inspection, it was like that clothing store you walked into loving the look of everything, but not finding a single shirt you wanted to try on. Mostly she enjoyed getting out of the share house, occupying a room of normal density, and feeling like an individual again rather than a member of a kindergarten class. Though even if she hadn't been enjoying it, she would have darn well pretended to. After all, it'd been her idea.

Despite this fact (and she would never in a million years admit it), all Jamie could think about was meeting up with the share house. Well, meeting up with Jeff. And so most inconspicuously, she kept eyeing her watch, having mentally decided they should leave no later than eleven. Only that's when the alcohol finally kicked in, and the music switched from atmosphere to hip-hop, and the guys got just drunk enough to strike up conversations (though Rachel had tried to engage a good many before this). So upon discovering it almost eleven-thirty, Jamie proposed they make a beeline to Star Room.

Of course, Rachel wouldn't leave before using the bathroom, which was pretty much the same thing as all three of them waiting to use the bathroom. And so to the coed bathroom they went, and on the stagnant line they waited, and down the sole functioning toilet flushed another twenty minutes.

After grabbing their gift bags and hurrying outside, they realized they couldn't have timed things any worse. For the party was just wrapping up, and they found themselves mixed in with the mob all leaving simultaneously. There wasn't a single cab in sight—just hundreds of people all in pursuit of one. It was an absolute nightmare. (Actually, what it was, was Memorial Day weekend.)

"Wait, I have an idea," Allison suggested after they'd been shivering in the cold for twenty minutes. Digging through her wallet, she produced Chuck's business card, which she'd wisely held on to. Jamie eagerly dialed his number.

"Hampton Cabs," barked a voice that belonged to a cab dispatcher rather than Fingers himself.

"Hi, I'm at Hampton Hall and I'd like a cab to Star Room," Jamie nonetheless said. There was a long pause, and she feared she'd been disconnected.

"How many people?" the voice then demanded.

"Just three. We don't need a van or anything," she made sure to add.

There was another indefinite pause, after which the voice mechanically concluded, "South to East, that'll be seventy dollars."

"What?" she shrieked, wondering if she'd misheard a quote of seventeen. "It was ten dollars a head the other night!"

"Not for three people it wasn't." The dispatcher sighed, obviously impatient at the constant stream of calls she fielded, very few of which resulted in cab orders. "Do you want it or not?"

Jamie glanced from the hungry horde of cab seekers to her agitated friends, and realized there was nothing to debate. "Okay, fine."

"You're looking at about forty minutes," the dispatcher said.

"No way," Jamie decided, hanging up in disgust. Moved by desperation, she stepped a few feet out into the street, flailing her hand frantically at any vehicle passing by. And wondering if she preferred being stranded or being lost.

She didn't stop any cabs, but she did succeed in garnering enough honks to make a prostitute proud, as well as generous offers of rides from random men (which she came *this* close to accepting).

About forty minutes had passed when a long black stretch limo pulled up to the curb. Once it was apparent no one was getting out, the window creaked slowly down, and the driver asked them, "Where you going?" in a shady whisper.

"Star Room," Jamie burst out, approaching the vehicle.

"Flirt," cried the girl next to her, approaching as well.

"I can take all six of you," he said quickly, averting any competition. "Wainscott is on the way to East Hampton. Twenty-five each," he added, in a way he almost challenged them to oppose. And any other night they might have.

"Fine!" came a resounding chorus. Everyone eagerly piled inside the car's spacious interior. Jamie had only been in a stretch limo a handful of times, for proms and funerals; this occasion was highly unlike either.

As one of the other trio blared the radio, Jamie couldn't believe that in a five-minute time span she'd gone from freezing her ass off on a deserted highway to dancing in a limo to

Kelly Clarkson (whose lyrics everyone knew, though it took an occasion like this for them to admit it).

Having as much fun singing inside the limo as she'd had at the magazine party (perhaps she was a tad drunker than she'd realized), it wasn't long before she recognized the prominent red star outside Star Room. That, and the ubiquitous mass of people that wouldn't let you forget for a second it was a holiday weekend. Wondering what kind of nightmare they'd encounter trying to get home from this place—it was already practically one—Jamie almost wished they'd asked to be taken back to the house instead. But after paying the driver and climbing outside, she confronted the next hole in her plan. The line.

Courageous (or rather, inebriated) enough to tackle this, she shoved her way to the front, her friends timidly following the path her body carved. She overheard one guy gripe to his friend, "I've never wanted to hit a girl before," but she didn't let it deter her.

Fortunately, the door was being manned by a guy named Pete whom Jamie knew from the city. She only sort of knew him, but this slight recognition coupled with the fact they were carrying gift bags from the *Hamptons Magazine* event was enough to persuade him to lower the ropes. Pushing through the throng of highly concentrated (and highly intoxicated) revelers clotting Star Room's expansive patio, Jamie was grateful for the one thing that night that hadn't presented a problem.

And walked straight into another.

Even before she pieced together the scattering of familiar faces from the house, stationed around an outdoor table juxtaposing the club's two main rooms, she saw Jeff. Then she saw Ilana. Then she felt the martinis resurfacing.

It wasn't so much that they were touching, as the invisible

energy pulling them toward each other, signifying that they were about to. The kind of energy that is perhaps more identifiable to onlookers than to even the subjects themselves. Refusing to acknowledge it, Jamie silently trailed her friends.

Joining the group, and oblivious to the Jeff–Ilana development, Allison ran straight to Josh; Rachel, to her new friend Brett. This served to alert Jeff to Jamie's arrival, and he looked slightly taken aback. In what she took as a good sign, he visibly backed away from Ilana, but Jamie wondered if she was already too late.

Finding herself up against him as she floated around saying hello, she was pleased when he took the initiative to speak to her directly. Until she heard his words.

"So I hear you had fun Friday night," he said with a wink.

"Yeah, it was fun," she said, but from the gleam in his eye she gathered that wasn't his implication. "Why, what did you hear?"

He gave her a nudge like she was one of the guys—though unlike one of the guys she was wearing heels and nearly toppled over. "You. And Dave," he added.

Jamie laughed uproariously, like he'd just paired her with Osama bin Laden. "Where did you hear that?"

He pinned her with his eyes, and she heard the name *Ilana* in her head even before he answered. Though to her surprise, his answer was "Dave."

"What? Well, that's ridiculous. Dave has no idea who he hooked up with that night. I mean, he slept in our room, but..."

"He slept in your room?" Jeff raised a suggestive eyebrow.

"Yeah. He tried to hook up with me, then with Rachel, but we both refused. So then he got into Allison's bed, and hooked up with the girl who was sleeping there."

"Which girl?" he asked, this piece of information new to him.

Jamie paused. "I have no idea. Some girl whose friend was

hooking up in our house. But she left really early in the morning, and no one saw her but Rachel."

The words lay out there a minute before they registered. "So the only person who can confirm this story is your best friend?" he concluded, with a derisive laugh. "Look, I don't care if you hooked up with Dave. Whatever happened the other night...happened. I'm not exactly looking for a girl-friend this summer."

Jamie didn't know what riled her more: that he'd said this out loud, or that he wanted to curtail a desire she didn't even have. "Well, I'm not looking for a boyfriend," she said, grow-ing instantly defensive. "And I'm not lying about Dave, but you can believe what you want."

"I believe you," he said, though he hardly seemed to mean it. "Now you'll just have to work on the rest of the house." His eyes lingered long after his words, conveying just enough sexual interest to belie any claim he'd made to the contrary.

Jamie smiled. "I couldn't care less what anybody thinks," she said, though she found herself suddenly caring what he did.

Then an impatient Ilana reached over and grabbed Jeff's arm as if Jamie weren't even standing in front of her. Watching her whisper something into his ear (something of such importance it couldn't wait another moment), Jamie's revulsion was momentarily eclipsed by the knot in her stomach.

Try me, she thought, watching them, waiting for the bomb to explode. Once it did, she didn't plan to go anywhere near it. Lucky for him—and against all her expectations—it didn't. As close as they got, their lips never met. And so right then and there, Jamie called the race with Ilana on.

Back at the house, at first opportunity, Jamie yanked Dave aside. "What are you telling people?" she demanded.

Even in his inebriated state, he knew what she was alluding to and recited his preconfigured defense. "I'm not telling people anything. What they assume is their own business."

"So why don't you correct them? We did *not* hook up!"

"Maybe we did," he said with a smug grin.

"No we didn't!" she shouted, hoping she wouldn't further incriminate herself if people presumed they were having a lovers' quarrel.

To this, he spelled out the way he'd conveniently rewritten history in his mind. "There were three girls in your room, and I hooked up with one of them. So—there's a one-in-three chance it was you."

Jamie couldn't believe they were having this conversation. "There is a *none*-in-three chance, because you know it didn't happen!" she bellowed. Screw who was listening. "And if you tell one more person we hooked up, I'm going to spread something *so much* worse about you!"

"Fine," he said, with a wicked grin, looking like he was enjoying every minute of her reprimand. "But next time I sleep in your room, you have to promise to keep your hands off me."

In her mind, the matter was dismissed. But in his, this confrontation was merely the evidence he'd been waiting for that she, in fact, really wanted him. And so he annoyingly clung to her side the whole time the crew—including a still-platonic Jeff and Ilana—hung around the living room late-night. People lingered until exhaustion took hold and they began to peel off to go to bed. Allison went to go sleep in Josh's room; Rachel retreated early, bummed that Brett had brought back a girl (bummed most of all when it turned out to be his girlfriend).

Then what had started as a race evolved into a waiting game. Eventually the only people left bullshitting on the couch were Ilana, Jamie, Jeff, and Dave. It went something like this: Ilana and Jamie both wanted to hook up with Jeff, Dave clearly wanted to hook up with Jamie (but would probably settle for Ilana), and no one was really sure what Jeff wanted. This game became ridiculous—none of them had any real desire to be chatting aimlessly at five in the morning, though no one wanted to be the first to fold and cede the competition. Basically, it was a four-way cock-block.

As the minutes passed, Jamie grew increasingly tired (and felt increasingly retarded). But it was like waiting on a line. The longer you've stood there, the less you can justify turning around.

Eventually, their peripheral conversation came to a standstill and the sun peeked obnoxiously through the uncurtained windows.

"I'm just so not tired yet," Ilana said, yawning.

"Me neither," Jamie answered, promising a sprint to the finish line.

"Hot tub anyone?" Dave chimed in, throwing back his umpteenth beer. When no one moved to second that, Jeff rose to his feet.

Throughout the last half hour, he'd maintained a questioning look on his face, and Jamie wondered what he was thinking. She wondered why, if he really wanted to hook up with her, he hadn't yet tried. She wondered why Jamie-versus-Ilana was even up for debate. And most of all, she wondered how it came to be that she'd given up the driver's seat.

But this wondering didn't persist much longer.

"I think I'm going to hit the sack," Jeff said, leaving all three of them stunned.

At least for the night, it was decided. Not only did he see no clear-cut choice, but no junction of any kind.

Still, the moment the light threatened red was always the point at which Jamie decided to speed up.

Chapter
Nine

Tequila—unlike any other drink—has a delayed reaction. It doesn't enter your bloodstream immediately, but rather stores up in some organ or another before smacking you in the brain all at once. And in that single moment, you feel the belated effects of your previous actions.

Waking up next to Josh that morning, Allison's actions—or rather, the delayed *re*actions she'd previously set into motion—hit her all at once.

What had she possibly been thinking? It had taken her weeks to build up enough courage to finally end things, and in one weekend of weakness (one weekend of tequila-inspired vulnerability) she'd completely undone everything. And as she lay there, after being awoken by the snort-like snoring that had prematurely awoken her for five years running, Allison vowed to leave this house today exactly as she entered it. Single.

Rolling over in the bed, which was barely big enough to contain a child, she freed herself from the arm that hung lifelessly over her waist, only to feel it reach around and grip her even more tightly. His grip threatened her like a noose—and not only had she succumbed to it, she'd lowered her head and hung it around her neck herself.

Right then and there, she knew she needed to get out.

"Where are you going?" Josh whispered as she thrust his arm off her and struggled to her feet.

"I'm going to sleep in my own bed. I'm just not...comfortable here," she said, aware that this was a notion he wouldn't understand. One that all the tequila, all the loneliness, all the unfamiliar share houses in the world would never fully suppress. So it was with overwhelming relief that she tiptoed out of his room that final morning and ever so resolutely closed the door.

Making her way back to her room (through the house that looked exactly as demolished as you'd expect on the last day of a three-day weekend), she knew that in just a few short hours their first weekend would be over and they'd finally be heading home. However, when she crept into bed and sought the sleep her body so desperately craved, she found herself unable to attain it.

Just when she'd reached the brink of frustration, sure that the morning light precluded any possibility of sleep, she drifted off. When she awoke with a start, the two beds across from her were empty, their sheets cast sloppily aside.

She hurried out to find her friends, though what she found instead was tension. Watching hungover groups (whose sole aim over the past three days had been peak inebriation) hauling out luggage with renewed responsibility, Allison could feel the start of the workweek upon them.

Fortunately, not everyone felt this way. Last days in the Hamptons were split down the middle: like a movie-theater crowd, half the people made a run for it before the credits started to roll (hoping to beat the rush), while the other half lingered in their seats passively, clearly in no rush to get anywhere.

Thinking her friends were in the latter category, Allison was just about to reach for the sliding door leading to the pool when someone whooshed it open from the other side.

"Hey," Josh said warmly, assuming her delayed appearance

to be proof she'd really sought sleep and not escape from him. And foiling her plan to avoid him completely. "We called in an order at Goldberg's. Take a ride with me?" Calling in group orders was one of the first tricks they'd learned that weekend. By doing so, you wouldn't have to wait on the insanely long line once you got there (or risk having the town's sole bagel store run out of bagels—something conceivable only in the Hamptons).

"I should probably see what the girls are up to," she said, afraid her disconcerted expression might give something away.

"They're just lying out, we'll be back in five minutes," he said, tugging at her arm. When she still hesitated, he added, "I got you a toasted poppy seed with that vegetable cream cheese you like." And with that, Allison supposed she was going to the bagel store.

They could have made it halfway to Manhattan, though, in the amount of time the short ride back took. The trip there had been fine, but heading west, single-laned Route 27 was clogged with luxury vehicles all attempting a mass exodus. Josh had his air going full-blast, but the sunlight beat relentlessly through his windows in way that made Allison unable to stop sweating. And though she knew that there was never a good time to be stuck in standstill traffic, this time felt less ideal than most. To pass the minutes, Josh began talking idly, while Allison's sweat was dripping, and the noose tightening.

"So what are you doing on Wednesday?" he asked, peering back at the traffic through his mirror.

"Um, working?" she answered, though he'd clearly meant Wednesday night.

He flashed her a look. "No, I mean after. Because you're not going to believe who's in town from Chicago."

Allison wiped the sweat from her forehead. "Who?" she asked, even though she was nearly certain it would be—

"Leslie and David."

"Oh, wow. Leslie and David?" Allison *hated* Leslie and David.

"Yeah, I was thinking we should do sushi this time, maybe by my apartment so we can watch *Lost* after."

Glancing away, Allison felt the noose tick another notch tighter. "Well, maybe—"

"I know, we usually order in sushi on Sunday. But if we leave here by three to drop the car with my parents, we can have dinner with them on Long Island and catch an eight fourteen back to the city."

"Tonight?" The sweat was practically seeping through her shirt.

"Yeah, why? Did you want to get back earlier? Because maybe there's a seven thirty-four we can take. Or else—"

"Josh?"

"Also a six fifty-two. Let me just call my parents to make sure—"

"Wait."

Unaccustomed to hearing her raise her voice, he turned and stared at her—although now that she actually had his attention, she didn't know what to say. Finally, glancing out at the traffic that wasn't going anywhere, beside a guy with whom her future was similarly stagnant, Allison opted not to wait for a crowded share house to face her looming tasks.

"I just don't think...this is such a good idea," she said. She spit this out as fast she could, as uneloquently as she feared. The moment she did, though, the moment his deep brown eyes showed confusion rather than warmth, she wished she'd waited. Not because he reacted with rage, but because he failed to react at all. Because his silence instead suggested a delayed reaction—one she dreaded might build with time.

When he still didn't answer, she turned to him gravely.

"I know, this weekend was totally my fault. It was so weird seeing you in the house, and I honestly still care about you. But—"

"*Fuck,* Allison." He pounded the dashboard hard with both fists. For a moment she feared he was going to blow up, but he seemed too flustered to even find the words. "You know what, I don't want to hear it. Just do me a favor and stay the hell away from me."

From that point onward, it became the longest, most intense car ride ever. "So sushi on Wednesday?" she longed to interject, if only to bring back the amicable vibe. Instead, Josh turned up the radio, at a volume high enough to preclude all conversation. And though the music exploded from speakers near their ears, neither of them could hear it.

When Josh finally pulled back into the driveway (jerking Allison forward with unnecessary roughness), she more or less made a run for it. Josh, on the other hand, merely delivered the huge bag of bagels (a small reward for an hour's worth of driving) before he and his friend Rich grabbed their things and took off. Upset and dismayed, Allison was hoping she could soon do the same.

However, hurrying up to the pool, she discovered Jamie—whose skin had darkened about five shades since Friday—on a mission to suck up as much sun from the weekend as she possibly could.

Rachel (whom Allison was surprised to see keeping up with Jamie—given her tendency to burn) sat beside her, looking rather flushed and flipping through a thrice-recycled copy of the *New York Post*. (One that one house resident had purchased, but had gradually made its rounds all over the pool—mostly so everyone could confirm via "Page Six" that it *was* actually Jessica Simpson who'd been partying beside them at Pink Elephant. Only, in later retellings, someone like Rob would claim she was dancing topless, on guys' laps, and had tried to take home his friend.)

Allison glanced around and found the scarcely populated pool area stricken of its stick-thin figures and daunting air, a quiet peace taking its place. Perhaps because the overabundance of bodies—all vying for lounge chairs and the attention of the opposite sex—had dwindled, or perhaps because the tumultuous weekend had finally taken its physical toll.

"Hey! Where've you been? You're missing such good sun!" Jamie greeted her, retying the bathing suit straps she'd undone to avoid tan lines. Carefully sitting up, she peered over at Rachel. "Rach, you're looking kind of red. Maybe you should switch back to your *own* sunscreen?"

Rachel shook her head disobediently. But both quit joking when Allison sank solemnly onto the end of Rachel's chair. "What happened?" Rachel asked.

"I went to the bagel store and broke things off with Josh," Allison answered, all in one breath, as if both events were of equal importance.

"What?" Jamie and Rachel gasped, staring back at her in shock. Then Jamie added, not trying to be funny but coming across that way, "Again?"

At that very moment Craig burst out onto the patio in a small frenzy. They might have been alarmed if Craig didn't do everything in his life at breakneck speed. "Jamie!" he barked. "If you want a ride to get your car, I have to take you now." Craig was the type of guy who would bark "I love you" to his girlfriend. Assuming, first, that he had one.

"Oh, I do!" Jamie said, jumping to her feet. She tied her matching sarong around her waist and slipped her feet into her impractical Prada flip-flops. "Let me just get my keys and I'll meet you out front."

Jamie hated to be torn from the sun the way a starving

person might from a sandwich. But she was aware that Mark had disappeared and Craig was individually responsible for getting everyone out of there, so she hardly wanted to cause a problem. "As soon as I get back, we'll make a plan," she assured her friends, scurrying off.

Taking over Jamie's chair, Allison stared at her poppy seed bagel (toasted, with that vegetable cream cheese she liked), but couldn't bring herself to take a single bite. It was just as well, for Jamie rejoined them at the pool in a matter of ten minutes. Which wasn't just quick—it was too quick. As in, she hadn't left yet. "Wanna hear something weird?" she called out even before she had fully approached them. "I can't find my keys." She paused dramatically for effect before inquiring, "Was anyone else holding them?"

Allison and Rachel both looked at each other with alarm.

"I'm almost positive you didn't give them back to me," Allison said, vividly picturing the Tiffany heart key chain. "But I'll go in and check my bag," she offered, jumping to her feet.

The three of them charged up the stairs, and Jamie didn't even flinch when they bumped right into Jeff, luggage in hand—to whom she breezily said good-bye. But time was of the essence since Craig (who was pretty much the last person on earth you'd want to hold up) was waiting in front, and, well, they had much bigger problems to worry about.

"Nope," Allison concluded, after a quick search confirmed what she already suspected. She looked inquisitively at Jamie. Then she had a scary thought. One so scary she knew it had to be true the second it came to mind. "You did get them back from the valet, right?"

Jamie's eyes popped out of their sockets. *"Shit!"* she yelped. And in a single moment, the repercussions of her earlier mistake hit her all at once.

Actually, they hit them all.

"Are you serious?" Rachel exclaimed. "You left your keys with the valet?" she added, shrieking as if Jamie had confessed to having murdered the valet.

"Well, none of you reminded me!" Jamie attested, throwing down her evening bag since searching it was now pointless. "I'm not a driver, I don't think of these things!"

"But see, you were the driver, and it was your job to think of these things!" Frustrated, Rachel placed a hand to her cheek, which had turned a glowing shade of red. "How does a girl who remembers to bring her full-length mirror forget about her *car keys*?"

"Please, I was so happy to get there I never wanted to see those keys again!" Jamie argued, immediately defensive. "And we were *all* wasted by the time we left…and I guess I just wasn't thinking."

"Well, now what?" Rachel asked, panicking the way her mother might (Rachel's mother feared for her daughter's life if it was scheduled to rain too hard). "What do we do if we can't get them? I have my sister's dress fitting tomorrow!"

"Look, getting upset isn't going to do us any good," Allison cut in, almost relieved to have a distraction. "Let's just have Craig take us to Hampton Hall and see if anyone's there first."

Once that was decided, the three of them hurried to the front and found an impatient Craig glowering behind the wheel. "What took you so long?" he barked, even harsher because he actually had a real reason to be annoyed.

They looked from one to the other, as if silently debating who was "it."

Of course, Jamie finally described the dilemma—which was so ridiculous, you couldn't have made it up if you tried. And boy, did Allison wish they had.

"You forgot your keys!" Craig roared, half in amusement, half rebuke. Comical or not, he was now a party to dealing with it. "How could you forget your keys?" he announced again. "Well, come on, get in."

After they all hopped into Craig's car (which was a bit like submitting themselves to Craig's dictatorial rule) Allison endured the *second* longest ride of her life—the first, coincidentally, had occurred that morning. Thankfully, this time Craig expertly navigated the back roads, and Allison realized it actually wasn't that far away. During the ride, no one said so much as a word, all equally anxious (and engaged in silent prayer).

As they pulled into the vacant lot across from Hampton Hall, their worst nightmare was pretty much realized. For starters, Allison had a hard time believing that this desolate building had been up and running in the last month, not to mention the site of last night's lively party. Gone from the towering edifice were the festive decorations and the glistening lights and the press line of paparazzi, leaving nothing behind but a haunted-house-like monstrosity blanketed by a thin layer of dust.

Getting out and peering around the parking lot, Allison expected to see numerous cars likewise abandoned in the name of partying. Instead, it was almost painful to spot Jamie's mother's (filthy) white SUV all by itself, and even more painful when they tried, fruitlessly, to open the doors. However, all was not lost (or vandalized or towed); it was merely locked.

Running up Hampton Hall's vast steps and approaching the grand doorway, they at first knocked optimistically. Then they pounded. Then they yelled.

This isn't looking good, Allison thought as she leaned sullenly against one of the tall white columns. Taking the lead, Craig then motioned for them to follow him as he circumnavigated the building, glaring in every window, inspecting every inch. In fact, he knocked harder and yelled louder than all three of them combined (finally, a constructive channel for his abundant intensity). But all the yelling in the world won't do any good if there is no one there to hear it. Which there wasn't.

"Goddammit!" Jamie yelled, kicking the dirt (and then dusting off her flip-flops).

They all lingered another moment in silence, and Allison was shocked that Craig hadn't complained yet. Surprisingly, something about this scenario made him oddly sympathetic. "Come on, there's nothing else we can do here," he said, in what was clearly not a bark. "You might as well try to call from the house." And so, just as empty-handed as they'd started, they mournfully headed back. No one said much during this ride, either, though their anger had shifted to disappointment, their anxiety to fear.

"Sorry," Craig said while they emptied from his car, as if this misfortune was something that had befallen them instead of something they'd foolishly incurred.

"No, thanks for your help," Jamie said, and the other girls echoed her. But back in their room, all hell broke loose.

"We're *stranded*!" Rachel screamed, her words all the more emphatic coming from a flaming-red face. "How are we going to get home?"

"How could I have been so stupid?" Jamie shrieked, pacing wildly.

"How could we have *let* you be so stupid?" Then Rachel stole a glance in the full-length mirror, the delayed reaction to her own mistake staring her in the face. "How did I get so sunburned?"

"How did I *forget the keys*!" Jamie bellowed. And to that, there was no argument.

Each comment they shouted upped the previous one in

desperation and volume, prompting Brian to warily poke his head in from the hallway.

"Why are you so quiet in here?" he asked, looking roused from the dead. Though it was almost one in the afternoon, he was one of those guys who was more than capable of sleeping the day away.

"I left my car keys with the valet!" Jamie cried at the same time Rachel burst out, "We're stranded in the Hamptons!"

This chaos was clearly too much for someone just meeting the day. "What?" he asked, rubbing his eyes and looking to Allison for clarification.

"You guys, we're not stranded," she said, taking the opportunity to set the facts straight. And thinking that Brian looked charmingly boyish in his Maryland basketball shorts. "Worst-case scenario, we can try to get a ride, or we could always take the Jitney back."

"No one's stranded, you'll come with me," Brian stated, shooing the idea with his hand like an invisible fly, even before he fully understood the situation.

"Well, we still haven't tried everything," Jamie said, calm for perhaps the first time all morning. "I'm going to call everyone at my firm and see if we can track down someone who can help."

And that's what they did, for the next hour or so, Brian's lingering presence calming them. They tried every owner, every manager, and every contact. Unfortunately, most calls went straight to voice mail, and most people's mailboxes were so full they couldn't even record a message. And all the while, the share house continued to clear out.

As the girls watched group after group pile into cars, they couldn't believe they were so envious of the others for simply being able to leave. Thoughtfully, numerous people poked in their heads to offer assistance (or to confirm the rumor that they'd *actually* left the keys with the valet). Just as he promised, Brian shipped his previous passengers Rob and Dave off elsewhere, making good on his pledge to stick it out with them till the end.

Allison felt somewhat guilty that he was hanging around, since he'd already gone above and beyond the call of duty. But something about his presence was particularly comforting. Maybe it was the fact that he was taking control of things and keeping them calm. Maybe it was the fact that he was thirty, and could offer physical and financial support beyond that of guys their age. Or maybe it was the fact that Allison felt like she was starting to like him.

When Jamie—suspecting this—slipped away to apply aloe to Rachel's face, Allison found herself suddenly uncomfortable being left alone with him.

She shouldn't have been, for both outwardly and inwardly Brian reminded her of a teddy bear. Outwardly, because he was a larger guy with a more generous build—neither muscle nor flab, but something seemingly pokeable, like the Pillsbury Doughboy. And inwardly, because contrary to his size was his propensity for emotion, a sensitivity he streamlined into hazel-colored eyes. When Allison looked into them, it felt like she was looking straight into his heart.

Like now.

"You don't have to stay, you know," she said for, like, the zillionth time over.

"I know," he answered, focusing his enamored gaze on her. He was sitting pretty close to her now, and she instantly became conscious of this. "So, where's your boyfriend?" he asked, the intent pause that followed belying any attempt to appear casual.

"He's not my boyfriend," she said, like it was a ridiculous claim that might never have been true, least of all this morning. She quickly changed the subject. "So what do you think we should do?" she asked, relieved to confide her worry in someone it wouldn't serve to upset further.

"Get comfortable." Seeing that his joke didn't help matters, he added, "No, seriously, any time you want to leave I'll give you guys a ride." As he said this, his gaze didn't falter once, and if they were having a staring contest, he certainly would have won.

"Thanks," she said, averting her eyes and smiling tensely.

"Relax," Brian said, reaching forward to jokingly massage her shoulders—which actually inspired the opposite effect.

And when Jamie and Rachel reappeared, Allison immediately sprang to action.

"Anything?" she asked, gesturing hopefully to Jamie's phone.

Jamie shook her head. "I guess I have to call my mother and tell her what happened. She's going to love that I left her car parked at a lot overnight."

The room hushed as Jamie made the call, though her mother's yelling would've been perfectly audible even if they hadn't lowered their voices. But eventually the yelling gave way to Jamie's compliant stream of *okay*s.

"You're not going to believe this," Jamie said, hanging up.

They all simply stared at her, no one eager to elicit an additional surprise that day. "What?" Rachel finally asked, the word sounding as painful as the burn on her face.

"My mom's driving here."

"Where?" all three cried, in disharmonic pitch.

"To the Hamptons."

"Your *mom* is driving to the *Hamptons*?" Rachel said, digesting the sheer absurdity of it all. And perhaps the reality that they'd have to wait it out until she arrived.

"Yeah, she's leaving this minute. But wow, is she pissed!" No one said anything for a moment, perhaps because no one knew what to make of the situation. It was undeniably a better resolution than returning the following day, but in a way it felt like all of their parents were coming here to call them out on their mistake. "Watch her take away my share house privileges!" Jamie exclaimed, not kidding in the least.

Brian regarded this in a wholly different light. "Your mother," he got out, between spurts of laughter, "is coming to this share house?" To someone with car keys this proved resoundingly amusing.

"Stop laughing," Jamie said, smacking him with a pillow.

"It's not funny. It's just really...nice," he said, swallowing his chuckle. It *would* be funny...just not until many months later.

Jamie's mother soon called again from her car for directions, and then at two-minute intervals for clarifications. In the meanwhile, they really had nothing to do but sit around and watch *Anchorman*—which was playing for like the fourth time that weekend, but no one cared enough at that moment to get up and change it. Once Craig was satisfied things were taken care of and he took off, they officially became the only people left in the share house (well, aside from the cleaning lady—whom they sheepishly watched undoing the mess it had taken three days and four dozen people to produce). To Allison it felt like the Twilight Zone. Lingering alone in this gargantuan, noiseless abode was like lingering in a nightclub after someone had turned off the music and emptied out the crowd. And while they'd been too preoccupied to notice before, they were now ravenously hungry.

They made it through the remainder of the Rold Gold pretzels (now properly deemed "Hamptons pretzels," and now the largest component of Allison's weekend diet)—along with Klondike chocolates discovered in the cabinets, and two episodes of *Entourage* on HBO on Demand—when Mrs. Kessler finally called from Route 27. Running out to the porch, the group awaited her arrival as formally as that of the president.

No less than twenty minutes later, Jamie's mother pulled cautiously up to the share house (in Jamie's father's sports car rather than the SUV they'd abducted, and in that careful controlled manner characteristic of a mom). As she opened the door and placed her kitten heels on the dirt, this petite older woman (clad in neither beach gear nor club clothes) looked comically out of place. Sort of like when your parents visit your high school on open school night. Approaching the welcoming party with none of the screaming or chastising they'd feared, she politely greeted the group. However, her clamped jaw and tense body language revealed the fury inside.

"Mom, you're in the *Hamptons*!" Jamie shrieked, running forward to offer her a hug and simultaneously gauge the degree of her anger. "Do you want a tour?"

"I want you to take me to my car," she replied coldly, unreceptive to her daughter's embrace. So, loading their luggage, to the car they went, finally leaving 1088 Montauk behind.

Setting off down the road, they formed a slow-moving caravan led by Brian and the girls in his car, with Mrs. Kessler following behind (no one dared ride with Jamie's furious mother, least of all Jamie herself). Jamie and Rachel had scrambled into the backseat, so Allison was forced to sit shotgun next to Brian. It took her aback at first; climbing in, she felt like she was joining her boyfriend. But perhaps her friends assumed she was the closest to him out of everybody. Or perhaps they could see something she was far too shy to admit.

When they returned to Hampton Hall, the building looked exactly as uninviting and desolate as it had hours earlier. Which was probably just as well, because it would have been even more upsetting to arrive and discover someone sitting there with the keys.

"Yay!" they all cheered when Jamie's mother produced the prized object and easily unlocked the door. For a moment, even Mrs. Kessler looked relieved.

"Thanks, Mom!" Jamie said, giving her a less unwelcome hug. She agreed to lead her mother back to Sunrise Highway and hurried to transfer her luggage from Brian's trunk to hers. Rachel followed suit, but when Allison reached for her bags, Brian touched her arm.

"Ride with me," he said softly. And though she worried it might be awkward, and that she'd run out of things to say, she had to admit she'd seen it coming—and had wanted it to.

As they took off from Hampton Hall with the speed he'd suppressed in the procession there, Allison's stomach soared with excitement. Gliding swiftly onto the highway, she found herself strangely disappointed that there wasn't a bit of traffic. True, she was worn out from the weekend, and hated to think about working summer school the following day, but at this moment she felt fully at ease. Maybe it was the fact that they'd resolved their car dilemma. Maybe it was relief from cutting Josh out of her life. Or maybe it was the comfort of having Brian beside her. Either way, there was no more sweating; there was no more noose. Josh had been abrasive (both on the road and off), but Brian had an easy laxness about him. You could see it in the way he drove with one arm draped leisurely around the wheel, the way he struck up conversations like he wasn't under any pressure to, the way he conducted himself naturally in the company of girls (perhaps he'd had experience dealing with them in the seven years he had on her).

Only before she knew it, the ride was over—at which point things happened very quickly. Or, more problematically, they didn't happen. Much to her chagrin, when he braked abruptly in front of her building, he didn't make a single advance. He didn't ask her for her number; he didn't attempt to see her again. Instead he merely handed over her luggage, gave her a timid peck on the cheek, and rejoined the sea of red lights blazing up along Third Avenue.

Tossing in bed that night, Allison replayed it all in her head. Of course, there was little to hold against him, for he couldn't have been more of a gentleman. But was that it? Had she been foolish enough to mistake his kindness for romantic interest? She didn't think so. Still, recalling their flirty exchanges, she couldn't help but feel disappointed.

Then, to her delight, an e-mail showed up in her inbox at school the very next day.

```
Tuesday, May 31, 2008 10:44 am

Hi there -

I got your e-mail from Mark, hope you don't
mind. Don't worry I haven't sold it to any-
one just yet. ☺

Some weekend - You guys didn't by any chance
find my hat or any one of the other thirty
things I lost in the house this weekend did
you?

Also - what are you up to this week?

Brian
```

Allison smiled. True, it was a bit of a delayed reaction. But the euphoria smacked her in the brain all at once.

Chapter
Ten

After only one weekend in the Hamptons, Rachel had been burned—both inside and out.

Of course her failure to meet a guy was far less evident than her failure to protect her face. And when she greeted her mother and sister outside Vera Wang that Tuesday, the pair promptly exploded.

"Ohmigod *her skin*!" Dana shrieked, discerning the damage even as Rachel approached. Her sister had an irritating habit of referring to Rachel like she wasn't in the room, and instead merely a wedding prop like the cake or the flowers.

Rachel's mother proved more sensitive, though equally horrified.

"Sweetheart, what happened?" her mother exclaimed, anxiously inspecting her daughter's face as if it were covered with incurable green dots. "What did you do to your skin?"

"I guess I overdid it with the sun." Rachel shrugged, saying hello to her aunt and the rest of Dana's bridal party, who had gathered for the bridesmaids' dress fitting. And wishing—however unsuccessfully—to curtail her family's overreaction.

"Susan, have you *ever* seen a burn like that? Do you think it will scar?" her mother asked, gripping her daughter's face between her hands and presenting it to her aunt for a second opinion.

Leaning over, her aunt brought her face just a bit closer to Rachel's than was otherwise comfortable. "Does it hurt?"

she asked, pressing a cautious finger to Rachel's cheek and observing the color change, as if her face were one of those Hypercolor shirts everyone had in the 1980s.

"Not really," Rachel lied, glancing away.

Dana, on the other hand, was practically having a heart attack, visibly assessing the implications of her sister's sunburn on *her* life. "Why weren't you more *careful*?" she cried, with a hand gesture she'd only begun to employ since its four-carat enhancement. "Do you realize how long it can take for sunburns to fade? We have wedding pictures in two months!" Why, the nerve of Rachel to invite this burn in the wake of impending wedding pictures!

"I'm going to call Dr. Goldenberger," her mother declared, unclasping her quilted Chanel tote.

"Mom, I don't need to see a dermatologist!" Rachel attested. This was worse than she'd expected. "It's a *sunburn*. People get them all the time," she said, repeating verbatim what Jamie had told her.

Shaking her monthly blond dye job, her mother hardly looked convinced. "One week," she decided, refastening her purse. "If it's not significantly better in *one week*, you'll come home for a visit."

Rachel rolled her eyes, and as they rode the elevator up to the designer's showroom (complete with elegant, price-inflated dresses and the snooty Louis Vuitton set who inflated them), for once she was happy to let her sister resume the spotlight. After that, no one said another word about her tomato-red face, even though Rachel knew they were still thinking about it every time they looked at her. Instead, it became the elephant in the room.

Rachel also *felt* like an elephant—the largest land mammal in existence—as she tried on her bridesmaid gown beside an abnormally size zero bridal party.

Of course, Rachel knew she wasn't fat, and God knows she
certainly worked out enough (New York Sports Club was her
second home a minimum of five mornings a week). But even
though her size six figure would, by most standards, be considered exceptionally thin, it hardly looked that way alongside this unlikely cross section of teeny, little-girl-like bodies.
Discovering she was the largest of all of them was like scoring a hard-earned B on an exam, only to discover the rest of
the class had received A's. And it certainly didn't help matters
that the dress they'd ordered months ago, tailored to their
exact measurements, fit a bit too snugly in the bustline. Sucking in her stomach, Rachel imagined her new diet of alcohol,
fast food, and Rold Gold pretzels might have had something
to do with it.

"You guys look so beautiful!" Dana squealed, happily making the rounds to examine her carefully selected bridal party,
each member modeling the (even *more* carefully selected)
black silk strapless gown. As she did, she exuded a pride that
might not have been equaled if she'd mothered the girls herself. Until she got to Rachel.

"Her boobs are popping out!" Dana exclaimed to their
mother. This comment simultaneously alerted each of the size
zeros swimming in gowns beside her, as well as every other
nosy New York woman cohabiting the fitting room. Upon the
upheaval, their Vera Wang seamstress instantly rushed over,
asking Rachel to hop up on the central pedestal for assistance
(that, and even more public perusal).

Rachel felt herself blush, though—proving surprisingly
useful—her sunburn covered it up nicely. What ensued was a
blur of fabric tugging and alteration clipping and schizophrenic
instructions to raise, then lower, her arms so many times Rachel
could nearly have taken flight. And had she a magic feather (or

exceedingly large ears), she most certainly would have. But after all the fussing, they were still faced with the inevitable reality that the one thing this wizard of a seamstress couldn't do was snap her fingers and make more material appear.

"It's not *that* bad," her mother commented, still noticeably perplexed at how the measurement taken just last fall could now be so off.

"Not bad? I think Rachel looks stunning," her aunt Susan intervened. Rachel flashed her a grateful smile in the gargantuan three-way mirror.

"Are you kidding? That's embarrassingly tight!" Dana complained, seething as if Rachel had purposely tried to foil her festivities. As Dana glanced frenziedly around the room, Rachel half expected her to pick another maid of honor on the spot.

"I think she can definitely get away with it," the Vera Wang girl added helpfully. "But if you want"—*you* being directed at Dana, her aunt, and her mother—"we can try to put in a rush order for a larger size. Although, two months *is* cutting it close..."

"Oh, don't bother," her mother said. "It's just water weight. She'll drop that by August," she declared, more a command than a statement. Once Rachel stepped down from the pedestal, her mother leaned in closely to her boob-popping, water-inflated, sunburn-scarred daughter. "Sweetheart," she began in a poorly executed whisper, "are you getting your period?"

She wasn't, but now she was getting a complex.

It was only exacerbated when they went to eat afterward at nearby Atlantic Grill, phase two of this "bridesmaids' outing" that had warranted begging her boss for an extended lunch hour.

To Rachel's surprise, as soon as they were seated at a large round table right near the front of the colorful restaurant, the first question Dana directed to her had nothing to do with the wedding.

"So how was your first weekend in the Hamptons?" Dana asked, opening her menu but locking eyes with Rachel.

Rachel was shocked her sister had remembered, and even more shocked that she cared. Still, she would wholeheartedly welcome any reprieve from the incessant wedding talk, even if disclosing a piece of gossip to this table full of girls involved only slightly less exposure than publishing it in "Page Six."

"It was really fun," Rachel said, scouring the menu. Or rather, scouring the salad listings. She tried to come up with a tidbit that would be adequate for Dana, settling on "The house is gorgeous."

"That's it?" her sister asked, far from satisfied. Looking up at her friends, she raised a perfectly sculpted eyebrow suggestively. "She's doing Mark's house."

"Mark's house?" Each of the five zeros (who lacked personality as well as body fat) let out an ear-piercing shriek.

Then they all started talking at once.

"How *is* Mark? That summer in Quogue was, like, the *best* time of my life!"

"Do you remember our first night at Jet? That was the *best* night ever!"

"It was the *best* weekend ever!"

If there had been any doubt, it was now painfully obvious to all they had mastered the art of the superlative.

"That's the weekend I met Gregg," her sister added, unconsciously fingering her engagement ring. Staring off into space, she brushed her long blond hair back with her hand. "Do you remember how he hit on me so hard-core at first, but I wouldn't give him the time of day?"

"You guys were totally getting together," a zero claimed, a dreamy look in her eye.

"I knew from the second you met," another added. "Where was it again? By the pool?"

Here we go, Rachel thought. Though, just as she was praying her sister wouldn't launch into "the story" for the thousandth time, her mother cut in with an even more objectionable topic.

"Honey, did *you* meet any boys?" she asked Rachel, looking up from her menu and intervening for the first time in this conversation. But not for the first time in Rachel's love life.

"Sure, I met a bunch," Rachel said, opting not to elaborate on all the weekend's near misses—which she was trying her hardest to move past.

First there'd been Dan, the lawyer at Willkie who didn't apply the same gravity to his social life as he did to his professional one. That'd been a shame. Though Rachel had been far more disappointed to discover that Brett, the trader whose office was within lunch-dating distance of hers, had a girlfriend. Rachel knew this because, well, she'd met her personally.

"Heather's not my girlfriend. It's...complicated," he'd claimed, and being as he was one of the hottest guys to ever show interest in her, she'd been tempted to believe him. But Rachel had learned to interpret that pervasive catchphrase as "I have someone I'm probably going to marry, but we're taking a break so we can screw around this summer." Rachel wanted no part in that. Bringing her grand total of summer prospects down to...

A zero was watching her from every which way.

"So you didn't meet anyone?" her sister asked more pointedly. Rachel looked up at the six gaunt, heavily made-up faces eagerly awaiting her answer (and staring at her sunburn—or was that merely her imagination?).

"Not really," Rachel said, pretending to be studying the menu she could by now nearly recite, and considering rehashing the Dana–Gregg meeting story herself.

Fortunately the waiter came to take their order (which, who would have guessed, consisted of salads all around). But even though Rachel was hoping his departure might inspire a change of subject, Dana picked up right where they left off.

"So what clubs is Mark promoting?" she said, awaiting the answer as if she'd just asked *What's the meaning of life?* Rachel was long accustomed to her mother's probing, but her sister's interest in anything besides herself was novel. Why, if Rachel hadn't known any better, she might have suspected Dana was the tiniest bit jealous.

"Pink Elephant on Friday and Star Room on Saturday."

"Star Room!" the zeros shrieked, exchanging enamored glances as if Rachel had just conjured up some long-lost memory.

"We also went to a *Hamptons Magazine* party at Hampton Hall," Rachel added, neglecting to elaborate on the drama that resulted from this. Although just as she was about to mention the celebrities she'd seen...

"So is there anyone in the house I'd know?" her sister asked, which Rachel construed as, *Back to me.*

"Probably not," she lied. "But I mean, it's not like we sit around talking about you or anything."

Dana didn't buy this for a minute. "What about Ilana Friedman? She e-mailed me and said that she met you at DIP the other night."

"Oh, yeah. She's doing the house with two girls."

"Girls from Penn?"

Because that would validate their existence? "I have no idea,"

Rachel said. Although glancing up at Dana and her friends, they suddenly struck her as spanking images of exactly how Ilana and the Tara/Jocelyns might look three years from now: harder faces, more shrunken bodies, fussier personalities, and clad in much more expensive designers.

Dana paused only to regroup. "Well, what did you think of Mark?"

"Mark!" erupted the group. Looking down, Rachel was beginning to feel sorry for the diners at the tables beside them.

"Did you tell him you're my sister?" she said, plunging forward.

"Oh no, I forgot," Rachel fibbed, purely to ruffle Dana's feathers.

Dana looked noticeably disappointed. *"Definitely* tell him next time. Isn't he adorable?"

Rachel hadn't really thought of Mark that way; she and her friends had spent the entire weekend debating whether his aloofness was due to the fact he wanted to maintain his authority, or because he was lacking in the personality department. Perhaps annoyed over the club debacle, Jamie contended it was the latter. "He's a good-looking guy, I guess. A little distant, but he's so wrapped up in the house."

"It is *so funny* he's running a share house!"

"He was, like, the baby of *our* house!"

"It's crazy how things change."

Jerking her head back and forth, Rachel could barely follow the babble. Or the gazillion names being fired off in rapid succession.

"Do you guys remember 'Fingers' Chuck? I'm getting chills!"

"And ADD Craig? But he threw one hell of a White Party!"

"What about Jeff Grossman? What a waste of a face."

Could this be Jamie's Jeff?

"Actually, there was another guy who knew you," Rachel

suddenly recalled, reluctant to introduce the name of a guy who'd snubbed her, but curious for some backstory.

"Who?" Dana pried, her eyes blazing.

"Aaron."

Instead of a scream, his name garnered a tableful of blank expressions.

"Aaron who?" Dana asked, scrunching her perfect (cosmetically corrected) nose.

"Not sure. He's cute, though," Rachel admitted. "Said he used to work with you."

"At Goldman? Oh, Aaron Nash? He's a total dork."

"I think he used to like you or something," Rachel said, neglecting to mention it took asking for *her* number to realize this. "At least it seemed that way."

"Doubtful," Dana said. "We actually never used to get along." She shuddered, as if physically repulsed by the idea of him. "Anyone else?" she asked greedily.

Rachel shook her head. "No, that just about sums it all up." It was merely her wishful thinking.

But shortly the waiter brought over their salads. All had personalized them with some ingredient omission ("no bacon" or "no cheese") that was hardly enough to distinguish themselves.

"I miss the Hamptons," one of Dana's friends said, sighing as she placed her bony elbows on the table. Rachel could always tell a zero by the way she preferred conversation to food. But only in public. "I mean, I wouldn't still want to be doing a share. But it was a blast while it lasted. Like college."

"You couldn't *pay* me to spend a night in a share house and split a bathroom with forty people again," Dana declared, delicately placing a forkful of lettuce into her mouth. "Besides, I think it's so pathetic that these thirty-year-old guys are still running around share houses hooking up with twenty-one-year-olds."

"If I remember correctly," her friend retorted, "when you were twenty-one you liked the thirty-year-olds best!"

Dana shot the zero a wicked grin, and they (finally) progressed to talking about something of greater significance: the delicate art of table seating.

After the waiter cleared away the abundant leftovers and presented them with the bill, Rachel's mother and aunt resurfaced from their own conversation.

"So when is your next trip to the Hamptons?" Rachel's aunt asked her from across the table.

"Not this weekend, the weekend after," Rachel said. "We have a half share, so technically we could go on off-weekends without a bed, but—"

"Where would you sleep, if not a bed?" her aunt asked. The specifics of share houses sounded so silly when conveyed to adults. Or really, to anyone unfamiliar with the inane customs.

"Um, in empty ones. Or on the couch, or sleeping bags on the floor." Or with other people, Rachel thought, not that she'd ever do anything of the sort...

"On the floor? How much are you paying to sleep on the floor all summer?"

"Like two thousand."

The pain of this number seemed to revisit her mother all over again. "Two grand and there's not a single guy in that whole house you're interested in? At least for Dana it was an investment in her future," her mother joked, though Rachel wondered how much of the comment was truly in jest.

"Mom, we only *just* met everyone. Plus, it's really hard to meet people when you're out at nightclubs and stuff." Which

Rachel regretted the moment she mentioned it, for she knew what was coming next.

"Can you believe these girls go out as much as they do and *never* meet anyone?" her mother exclaimed, expressing to her aunt something Rachel had heard many times before. "Young, smart, beautiful..."

"Well, maybe Rachel will meet some eligible guy at the wedding," her aunt suggested with a wink.

"Actually, I don't really have that many single friends," Dana said, her brow furrowing. "That's why we invited all the single people with dates."

"Oh," her aunt said. This was news to Rachel as well. "Is Rachel bringing a date?" Aunt Susan innocently asked—and a hush came over the entire table.

For just like that, she'd mentioned it. The even bigger elephant in the room.

At once all eyes were on Rachel—the girl burned in the romantic arena now just as visibly as the physical one. And again, she was glad her face was *already* red.

"No," her mother responded for her. "Unless...honey, did you want to bring a date?" As if it had just now occurred to her, she asked what they'd awkwardly been tiptoeing around for months.

"That's just silly," Dana butted in before Rachel could answer. "She's not even dating anyone. Who would she possibly bring?"

"There are *plenty* of people I could bring," Rachel said. Who did they think she was, the Elephant Man?

"People you want us to pay two hundred dollars for and introduce to every family member?"

Rachel paused. As usual, Dana was on-point with her social perceptiveness.

"Well, the wedding is three months away. A lot can happen

in three months," her aunt said, giving Rachel a hopeful nod. Though from the dubious looks of everyone else at the table, no one imagined anything would change in the next three months.

This disparagement didn't bother Rachel much, for its persistence over the years had forced her to develop thick skin— at least on the inside. And as she followed her family out of the restaurant, she banished their pessimism wholly from her mind.

But an elephant never forgets.

Chapter
Eleven

A white-frosted cake was front and center in Jamie's eye line when she stepped into the share house their next assigned weekend. But as she greeted everyone (one particular male face standing out among the twenty or so others), front and center on her mind was her desire to *take* the cake.

Though with Ilana continually attempting to steal the show, she imagined it wouldn't be easy.

"What is *that*?" Ilana demanded the moment she pranced in. She extended a French-manicured finger dramatically, as if not only had she never seen a cake before in her life but the sight of one fully repulsed her.

"It's a cake," Rob answered. "You know, food? Some people eat it?"

Ilana flashed him a reproachful look before flipping her hair, and turning to Jeff to giggle girlishly. "Obviously. But how did it get there?"

"I brought it for Jill's birthday," Mark answered, referring to one of the perky pair of girls not from New York. His face quickly reddened, though, when this summoned a chorus of the *Awwww*s girls typically reserve for babies or pets. "Oh, don't be too impressed. They sell these at the Associated Supermarket by my apartment," he justified, smiling shyly.

Catching his eye, Jamie grinned back. Perhaps he was more decent a guy than she'd originally thought...

"So what's this I hear about your mother coming to the share house?"

Then again, perhaps not.

"Who, *my* mother?" she returned, hoping she wouldn't have to answer. But the rumor had propagated at rapid speed, and the house demanded answers.

"Did the valet really refuse to give you your keys 'cause you were drunk?" someone asked.

"Wait, I thought you lost them in a club?" came another voice.

"If your mother wanted to do a share, she should have just paid like the rest of us." (That was Rob.)

Jamie hated being interrogated on this subject, but apparently hating it even more was Ilana. For she quickly tried to refocus the attention back on herself.

"That's nothing. Once, I mixed up the address and we went to the *wrong house!*" she interjected, attempting to one-up Jamie just as Jeff said, "So how did your mother even get here?"

And in the name of taking the cake, Jamie happily took the abuse.

Which wasn't all that bad, because even though it was only their second weekend out there, Jamie felt like she'd known this group for ages. Sort of the way that, when you live on the same hall as people freshman year, one week in college time translates to four or so normal weeks. Of course there was a sprinkling of new faces, but enough of the core group was present to erase any of the awkwardness of the first weekend. And as they gathered to sing happy birthday to Jill that night before heading out to Pink Elephant, a close-knit family appeared in the making.

Few of them touched the cake, though. In an unsurprising turn, no one was eager to waste calories on what was known to be a supermarket concoction. Not that Jill minded, or even expected anything to the contrary. In bikini season, it was two entirely separate matters to have a cake and to eat it, too.

And apparently, a third altogether to exhaust energy in putting it away.

Thus, out it sat on the table all night, a disfiguring blob of gooey frosting. And out it remained all the following day, while the house fielded the muggy eighty-degree heat poolside. In the worthy company of food leftovers and garbage and cigarette stubs, the cake soon became a kitchen table fixture, a landmark they'd pass en route to the pool or numbering their trips to the bathroom. After a while its unsanitary presence was no longer questioned, but rather expected. And after a longer while, the birthday token was pretty much forgotten.

Until everyone all poured in from the sun around 5 PM—post-pool, pre-barbecue—and piled sluggishly around the long wooden table.

It was like the cake was staring at them.

"I'm hungry," Ilana whined, triggered perhaps by the smell of liquefying frosting. The Tara/Jocelyns loyally agreed.

"Are you going to barbecue?" Mark nudged Craig, who took pride in his position as resident Saturday chef.

Craig's eyes lingered on the dessert sitting in front of them before rising to his feet. "Oh, let them eat cake," he scowled before retreating. Which was pretty mocking, because most of them wouldn't even eat bread.

Rob, now eyeing the uneaten baked goods suggestively, suddenly proposed an idea, almost as if he thought the reality-show cameras were still rolling.

"So how hungry *are* you?" he asked Ilana, picking up the melted heap of sugar and presenting it to her as a waiter might.

"That is so disgusting," said Ilana, to whom a twenty-four-hour-old cake was only marginally more disgusting than a freshly baked one.

"What if I pay you to eat it," Rob offered, the fraternity boy in him resurfacing. "A hundred dollars says you can't even finish half."

"I'm in on that," Dave and Brian added immediately.

Seeing all eyes on her, Ilana actually debated it for a second. Though naturally she refused, so Rob assumed the wager on her behalf. For nothing short of a hundred bucks and a half-used MetroCard, he bet he could consume the entire cake in one sitting. And pretty much for lack of a better activity, everyone in the house gathered around to watch.

He dove in headfirst, shoveling cake into his mouth at an impressive (if horrific) pace, and Jamie had a difficult time watching. Which she was still doing, however, fifteen minutes later, when he reluctantly admitted defeat. About a third of the cake remained when everyone headed outside for Craig's barbecue (everyone except for Rob, who presumably headed to the bathroom). But that's not all that got regurgitated.

When Ilana later rehashed his defeat to any eager listeners at Star Room that night (the way she normally rehashed every inkling of house gossip unrelated to herself), it didn't seem to bother Rob much—until it scared away each of the potential conquests he'd lured to the table. And then it bothered him immensely.

"Could you shut up with that story already?" he said after the latest round of reality-show groupies departed "in search of a bathroom," yet in the direction of the dance floor.

"You're the one who tried to eat a whole cake," Ilana said with a shrug, reminding him of, well, the *reality* of the situation.

Rob pounded his fist into his palm in frustration. Taking a deep breath, he tried to approach this rationally. "You're embarrassing me in front of my fans."

"Fans?" Ilana let out a roar of laughter. "You were on a cheesy reality show for, like, two seconds. No one even knows who you are!"

Rob's face flushed with anger. And though he began to utter a retort, he apparently changed his mind and turned dismissively away. Needless to say, he and Ilana were fiercely at odds throughout the remainder of the evening.

Not at odds, however, were Jamie and Jeff. With Ilana otherwise engaged (and emerging more as the house enemy with each passing moment), Jamie felt "the cake" increasingly within her reach. She'd felt that way from the start of the weekend, as if Jeff had come away from the last one having had time to reflect on what he really wanted, and having identified her as his target. And no doubt regretting his previous lapse in judgment. Jamie still didn't like it, but she was willing to overlook his initial hesitance. Not that ambivalence was a quality with which Jamie was well acquainted. For when she wanted something, she went for it. Like now.

As she danced by the booth with Rachel (Allison and Brian had been attached at the hip, spending every minute of the past off-weekend together), Jamie could feel Jeff's eyes on her. And though she sensed his cocky resolve, she had to admit she was all too eager to oblige. But it was like those occasions she went into a store with a specific (however sizable) agenda in mind. If she knew she was going to finish the sale, what reason was there to make the sales guy work for it?

So even though there was a bottle of vodka on their table, when Jeff came over and asked if she wanted to get a drink from the bar, she easily followed him.

As they pushed through the crowd, he didn't really say much. Though in Jamie's opinion, anyone who looked like that didn't really need to. Still, she noticed numerous girls attempting to get his attention with come-hither looks that faded into disappointment once they spotted Jamie trailing him.

When they got to the bar, he ordered something dark and scary like Jack. Jeff then pointed to her, and Jamie smiled at the bartender as she requested white wine. Even though she religiously drank vodka sodas (whose ingredients were stocked in bulk back at their table), when something is too readily accessible to you, you begin to lose interest.

"Thanks," she said, accepting the drink from Jeff with a flirtatious smile. "I'll have to get you back later."

Then along with the drinks, he ordered two shots of tequila. The bartender gave him a telling smile when he handed the drinks over, some male-to-male gesture acknowledging the female at his side. Jamie pretended not to notice. This move nevertheless emboldened Jeff, and he surrendered his attention to her after throwing back the shot.

"So what's going on?" he said, disarming her with his clear blue eyes.

As if she were watching a movie and suddenly placed an actor, Jamie just then recognized something very Jordan Catalano about him. The slow, simplistic way he spoke, the distant pauses where his mind drifted noticeably elsewhere—as if life itself was a bit over his head. Also like Jared Leto's famed *My So-Called Life* character, he'd learned to say as much with his eyes as others could with their words, exuding a vulnerable charm to which girls found themselves helpless.

"Just hanging out," she said, grinning playfully as she sipped her drink.

"So how are things going with Dave?" he asked. It was a joke, she presumed, but one he pronounced just as even-temperedly as everything else.

"Ha," Jamie said. "You don't still seriously believe that?"

If he did, he seemed to move past it quickly.

"That's a hot dress," he said after a brief pause, looking at her clothing so intently Jamie feared he could see through it. Not that it was much of a mystery to him what lay beneath.

"Thanks," she said, opting not to correct the fact it was a skirt and not a dress (two items whose names most guys found near indistinguishable).

"All the guys in the house were talking about it," he said.

"Who?" she asked, allowing her curiosity to get the better of her.

"I don't know, Mark, Craig, Dave." He downed nearly half his drink in one sip, and Jamie wondered if his sudden reinterest arose from competition.

Just then, his eyes followed the motions of a blonde towering above Jamie's head, reminding her she was one of many contenders for his attention. Why Jamie forgave this was beyond her, for normally if a guy wasn't fully into her, she'd instantly dismiss him. Well, she liked to think she would. Because normally when a guy was talking to her, she was the one whose eyes were habitually inclined to wander.

Still, standing passively beside Jeff, Jamie didn't like this role reversal one bit. She didn't like the insecurity, the second-guessing, the constant desire to prove herself. But above and beyond these feelings, she didn't like the fact that she submitted to them.

"So...why didn't you call me the last time?" she heard herself saying. She hated these words the second they came out, for they hardly sounded like her own. But she really wanted to know—really thought there'd be an answer.

He shrugged. "Because I knew I'd see you here. Come on, let's do another shot," he suggested. At the moment, this seemed like the ideal solution.

Afterward, claiming he wanted to dance, he pulled her

toward the back of the Hip Hop room—an unlikely move on three accounts. First, because their group (and comfort zone) was all stationed outside. Second, because Star Room's Hip Hop room at two in the morning transformed into a hazardous sandwich of people, much the way Cinderella's coach turned into a pumpkin at midnight. And third, because this wasn't like a wedding where two people just stood up to go dance together. Dancing at nightclubs was pretty much a collective and impromptu event.

Still, perhaps because he was gripping her hand, in a gesture that seemed both intimate and deal-sealing, Jamie followed him. The dirty floor was flooded with an inch-thick puddle of alcohol, and the oppressive heat generated by gyrating bodies seemed to intensify the farther they ventured into it. Ever conscious of appearance, Jamie hardly wanted to assimilate into this random crowd of people, what with the humidity and body odor. And her motto *Always look available* was difficult to uphold front and center at a grope-fest. But glancing around (once, or twice, or twenty times), she fortunately didn't see anyone she recognized.

She wasn't shocked to learn that Jeff couldn't really dance—no doubt another skill he'd never had to develop, because his looks more than compensated. So it was more like they were swaying together, pressed up against each other for the sole purpose of enjoying publicly sanctioned affection. It felt a little ridiculous because it was a fast song, and Jamie actually *did* dance. But she went with it. And before long he was sweaty and she was sweaty and the two of them were sweaty together. And Jamie stopped caring who was in the room with them.

Then they got another drink. And did another shot. And after that, it was all a bit blurry...

"I am so drunk," Jamie said at one point, clasping her head

with her hands as if she could manually steady the rocking sensation.

"Yeah, me too," Jeff said, which—she often noticed—is something a guy always seconds after a girl professes it first.

After that, the time all blended together, a blur of dancing and drinking and words that flowed effortlessly, but that Jamie knew she'd barely remember. When they finally went outside in search of the group, their share house crew was nowhere to be found. In fact, few people remained on the patio at all, as if the venue had been officially evacuated by a police or fire alarm.

Jamie stared around at the drunken stragglers, alarmed to be mixed up with the sort of people who linger at clubs latenight. Pulling out her phone, she discovered a series of missed calls and text messages from her friends, who had supposedly "searched the entire place for her" and departed with the group hours ago. She knew this, because the last call came in around two something, and it was now somehow almost four in the morning.

Jeff led her to one of the waiting vans, which were scrounging up latecomers to deposit at various houses in various towns. The two of them took up the whole last row of seats, sitting unnecessarily close to each other, finding means to occupy their hands.

When they finally made it back to 1088 Montauk, the house was strangely empty, even though the group often stayed up much later. Throwing down her purse, Jamie flopped onto the sofa, and unsurprisingly, Jeff flopped down next to her. Jamie had a feeling where this was heading, but it was one of those things you couldn't consider a given until they actually happened. And the prospect of it happening right here in the open was rather invigorating, almost like bringing a guy back to her parents' house when she knew any minute her mother could walk in.

Which wasn't exactly out of the question, as Jamie's mother and this share house were hardly mutually exclusive. Still, Jamie found this unprecedented privacy a bit discomforting.

"How can everyone all be sleeping?" she asked a little too loudly, looking again at her watch (but instantly forgetting the numbers).

"I'm not complaining," Jeff said, pulling her toward him. And just like that, it happened. One second, they were merely sitting there, and the next they were going at it. It was all a bit surreal, and in her plastered state Jamie felt like a robot able to register only her motions. Expertly he lifted her shirt (dress? tomato, to-mah-to!) over her head and unclasped her bra. And before she knew it, Jamie was sitting on the couch where anyone could walk in at any second, topless. And then it got even better.

In one gallant motion he scooped her up as if they were honeymooners crossing a threshold and carried her in the direction of the deck. To be polite, Jamie asked if she was heavy, but he put her quickly at ease by assuring her she weighed "like nothing" (she loved when guys said that).

Swishing the door closed behind them, he placed her down beside the hot tub. At once, they stripped themselves of any remaining clothing and climbed inside. Oddly, Jamie had never been skinny-dipping before, and had never hooked up in a hot tub either (she associated such simulated romantic environments with shows like *The Bachelor*). But she found herself warming to the idea—despite the fact Rachel warned them hot tubs were a breeding ground for disease, and even despite the looming possibility they could be interrupted at any moment. Actually, Jamie was enjoying it *because* of these dangers.

Of course Jeff had something to do with it, too. While uttering how she had a "sick body," he glided his hands over it in a fluid way only water could enable. In a way she'd craved since the last time, when she hadn't really taken it seriously. It was a little scary that every inch of her was exposed in early-morning daylight (especially since she was inclined to hook up with the lights off), though Jamie had never been one to feel embarrassed by nakedness. Never been one to step back from the spotlight.

"You are so beautiful," he whispered, touching her face like if he pressed too hard, it might break.

This was a compliment Jamie was accustomed to hearing, almost to the point that she wondered if it was something guys learned to say in Hooking Up 101. Though hearing it at that moment, from this guy, was pretty much the icing on the cake.

In fact, with the sun peeking through in the background, at the disorienting hour that is just past night but not quite morning, it was pretty much the perfect moment.

Until Jamie spotted the face.

For a minute she thought she might have been imagining things. But Jamie was certainly not that drunk, and her subconscious not that cruel, and well, she would have recognized that face anywhere. The face, and the shrill voice that came from it.

"Eeeeew!"

Instantly Jamie clasped her hands over her chest in a feeble attempt to cover herself and flew to the other side of the hot tub. But the voice from the window didn't stop.

"They're *naked* in the *hot tub*! Everyone look outside!" In her typical whiny, attention-seeking tone, Ilana did her best to awaken the entire house. (Which, if you're ever trying to do, is easily accomplished by throwing around a few key words. Like those.)

Getting caught naked in the hot tub had pretty much the same sobering effect as seeing your parents when you were drunk, and what progressed next felt like a nightmare. Chivalrously, Jeff tried to shield Jamie behind his back, but there was no avoiding the gawking and the whistling and the window pounding and the camera flashing. *What are they, five years old?* Jamie thought. And though it was soon over just as quickly as it started, the damage had been done. Practically half of the house had just seen her naked, and those who hadn't could certainly catch up by way of Ofoto. Though once the X-rated entertainment had finally grown old, Ilana's was the last image Jamie saw retreating from the glass.

Aghast, the two of them just stood there staring up at the window—like that moment when the villain in a movie has just been shot, but you're not quite sure he's dead yet. Finally stepping out of the tub, Jamie slinked her clothing over her sopping wet body (silently mourning the ruined fabric). Still in shock, she crossed her arms protectively over her chest, not wanting to remain outside topless, but in no hurry to rush back in, either.

"How immature are they?" she at last exploded, growing as enraged as she was embarrassed. Though she had to wonder, did the blame lie with the people who ran to witness a colorful exhibit, or the people foolish enough to exhibit themselves in a notoriously nocturnal house?

Definitely, it lay with the person who publicized the exhibit! Picturing Ilana's smug face at the window, Jamie vowed to make her regret this in the immediate future.

But as angry as Jamie was, Jeff was angrier. "I can't believe that bitch!" he fumed, kicking the hot tub with his foot.

"Waking up the whole house up at five AM. She's, like, sick or something!"

Jamie had known this all along, of course.

She retreated to her room alone, to sleep alongside Rachel and Allison (and Brian). Only a few hours later, though, she awoke to piercing shrieks that not only ricocheted throughout the entire thin-walled house, but probably served as an alarm clock for the entire town of Southampton.

"Eeeeew!" sounded the high-pitched cry—the same one that had summoned the house to the hot tub site hours earlier.

"I've been caked!" it rang out again, from a predicted two rooms away.

Caked?

That's when the door to the girls' room burst open.

"You did this!" bellowed the drama queen, lunging decisively toward Jamie's bed. Refusing to acknowledge her, Jamie buried her face back into her barely dented pillow. But she couldn't help first sneaking a peek.

Just as she expected, there stood Ilana. Her eye mask was hinged on the top of her limp brown locks, and she wore the same frilly pink Victoria's Secret short set she usually slept in. But unlike other mornings, she now stood before them decorated head to toe in...cake?

Clots of sticky brown paste clung to her hair, patterned her pajamas, and stuck to her face in unnatural brown splotches.

And it was completely hysterical.

Jamie couldn't have planned it any better if she'd been the avenger herself. (Which, despite her denial, many believed she was, and had this not occurred, she very well might have been.)

From what Jamie later learned, it was mostly Jeff's doing, though Rob had been all too eager to assist him. Ransacking the house for a torture device, Jeff had happened upon one staring him right in the face. And so they'd patiently waited until nearly 6 AM before grabbing handfuls of Jill's recyclable birthday cake and mauling Ilana in her sleep.

Jamie had no pity, of course, not one single dollop. Though long after they'd rid their room of Ilana, mental images of her frosting-doused foe made it difficult for Jamie to return to sleep. No matter. Revenge was sweet . . . and a whole lot easier than she'd originally anticipated.

Now that Ilana was covered in more calories than she had probably consumed in weeks, justice was finally served.

It was a piece of cake.

Chapter Twelve

A black swan is an outlier, an event that lies beyond the realm of normal expectations. Most people expect all swans to be white because that's what their experience tells them; a black swan is by definition a surprise. (Nassim Nicholas Taleb, *Learning to Expect the Unexpected*)

Newcomers quickly learn that the only way to survive in a share house is to expect the unexpected.

If *you* aren't asleep in your bed, expect that someone else soon will be. If you're standing in the vicinity of the pool, expect you're going to be thrown in. And if you fail to lock the door before changing, expect your body to be put on public display.

Even equipped with this information, Allison and Brian discovered something neither expected.

From the moment she had received his e-mail and met him at Mizu for sushi the following night, Allison and Brian became "that couple." The couple who united the very first weekend and were subsequently attached at the hip for the rest of the summer. The couple who spoiled the debaucherous atmosphere for everyone else; who looked as pained to be in a party house as your grandparents might—and for that matter, wouldn't be, if not for the unrecoupable fee they'd paid.

On these grounds alone, their newfound romance met with considerable resentment.

Don't you think you're rushing into this? Allison's acquaintances would urge. *Do you really like Brian, or do you just want to be back in a relationship?* It was the same argument she'd always had to defend against when she moved on from each short-lived period of singlehood.

Couldn't everyone see that having feelings again so soon was as much a surprise to Allison as to anyone else? *Why, of course I like Brian,* she'd argue. And it wasn't so much that this happened quickly, as that it happened in reverse. *We saw each other in pajamas even before we exchanged five sentences!* was the catchphrase she'd say.

But there was one thing she didn't say. One thing she'd never say, much less own up to. That, as their sushi date turned into a sleepover, turned into additional dinner dates, turned into takeout and TiVo...the tiniest part of her felt relieved to retreat from the Hamptons' cutthroat singles scene.

Which is perhaps why Allison had always been sympathetic to Sara.

While otherwise unremarkable, Sara had done something unprecedented in share house history: taken a share by herself. Really, it'd come as quite the surprise when Mark received an e-mail from her, claiming she'd heard about his house from a friend of a friend (traceable to any of the thousand e-mail addresses he'd swiped off forwards in composing his—highly indiscriminate—promoting distribution list). But despite the rumors (that her parents had laid out the money for a quarter share and forced their socially inept daughter to attend), Mark hadn't minded one bit. Twelve hundred fifty dollars was $1,250, no matter how eccentric the source.

Only fast-forward to Memorial Day weekend. And enter Sara.

Allison easily identified Sara as the lone shareholder she'd heard about, on account of the girl's appearance alone. A pasty redhead in her late twenties, Sara looked so rattled each time she opened her mouth, she made Allison nervous by association. Still, when she passed the entire first day huddled inside with a book rather than outside at the pool with the masses, everyone merely supposed she was shy. But when she opted to crawl into bed rather than accompany the house to Pink Elephant that evening, everyone knew she was done. With the Hamptons, that is.

"I don't want to do this anymore," she'd pleaded to Mark after her first (and only) weekend at the house.

Mark wasn't exactly surprised. But as he later relayed, he *was* faced with a quandary he'd never encountered in his many years of share house managing. On the one hand, he certainly couldn't refund her money. She *had* reserved one of the limited spots he might have sold elsewhere, and he needed to maintain some authority, after all. But allowing his compassion to get the better of him, he decided to cut her a deal.

Rather than lose the money she'd paid, he welcomed her to find someone else to take her place.

She thankfully obliged, informing Mark to expect her friend at the share house her next assigned weekend.

And if Sara was the black sheep, her replacement was a black swan.

Allison was almost grateful she and Brian had gotten to the house early that Friday in mid-June, to witness the colorful entrance. They were all lounging around on the couch, in typical just-arrived fashion, when they heard an atypical knock at the door. This was highly unusual, since share houses were diligently left unlocked at all times, and everyone simply barged in. Everyone except Sara's startling substitute.

At barely five feet tall, swimming in a tank top and cargo shorts, and clutching only a knapsack, he pointed to his chest and introduced himself as "Jim." Then, lingering awkwardly in the doorway, Jim timidly took in his surroundings.

"Can I help you?" Mark asked, convinced this interloper had stumbled upon their house by mistake.

"Jim," he insisted again, to the cluster of bewildered faces. "I pay...," he continued, frustratingly searching for the English words he hadn't yet mastered.

"Buddy, do you know the address you're looking for?" Rob chimed in, taking a break from the sandwich he was devouring on the couch.

Flapping his arms, Jim grew even more flustered. "No, no! Ten-eight-eight Montauk. I pay...Sara?"

Mark was about to usher him out when this registered. "Wait...you're taking Sara's share?"

As if Mark had just uttered the correct answer in charades, Jim nodded his head emphatically. Mark's face remained frozen in disbelief.

Catching on, Allison shot Brian a disconcerted look, as if they'd just been informed that a murderer would be sharing the house with them. This was sure to go over well! However, leave it to Rob to find the humor in any situation. "Jimmy, my man, come on in!" he called out. Placing down his sandwich, he smacked the couch seat next to him. "Take a load off."

Removing his backpack, Jim positioned himself upright on the edge of the couch and flashed the kind of smile that made you forget there was anything wrong in the world—that made Allison regret her premature judgment. And in a manner less mocking than eager for amusement, Rob continued to engage him.

"Jimmy, you hungry?" Rob gestured to the humongous hero he'd picked up from the Pork Store on his way.

Jim shook his head out of obligation. "No, no..."

Sensing this, Rob ripped off half the sandwich and graciously handed it over anyway.

"Thank you," Jim said, bowing his head in gratitude.

As they watched Jim digging in, deriving from this sandwich the kind of all-encompassing satisfaction twentysomethings barely derive from anything, it was clear that Jim would be staying in the share house.

Only through excessive probing did they unearth that Jim, new to both New York and the Hamptons, was a student at NYU's Stern Business School. (That, and an avid peruser of Craigslist, where they later learned he'd happened upon Sara's quarter-share listing.)

Oddly content sitting around and observing the arrivals, Jim didn't exactly know what to do in a share house. Which was just as well, because Mark didn't exactly know what to do with him.

Perhaps it had been a little presumptuous of Mark to assume that Sara's spot-filler would be a girl similar to herself. And, eager to accommodate her, he hadn't inquired into the specifics. But as the individual responsible, he quickly made the necessary adjustments.

Instead of sleeping in Sara's assigned room with the Midwesterners, Jill and Robin, he told Jim to take the empty bed in the room with Josh and Rich.

Josh, who'd been adapting to his breakup with Allison by visibly blocking out her existence, projected a resultant hostility onto everything share-house-related. This considered, his outburst was unexpected, even from him. "No way! If you put that random who just walked in off the street in *our* room, I want my money back."

Everyone (including the random) turned to face him.

Allison was aghast. Was this the "sensitive" guy she'd spent five years of her life with? Forget the intimate vacations, the year of practically cohabitating, the four previous ones that were college...Sometimes it took a non-English-speaking, five-foot-tall...well, random to unveil someone's true personality.

But before Mark could react, Brian spoke up.

"Dave's away at a wedding this weekend. He can stay in the room with us," he offered of the room he shared with Rob and Dave.

"You hear that, Jimmy? The party's in our room tonight!" Rob roared, raising a triumphant fist.

Allison—who'd taken to sleeping with Brian in his room—was, um, thrilled.

Still, as far as anyone could tell, the Jim problem was solved. And no sooner had everyone make a mad dash for the bathrooms—to simultaneously primp for the evening's festivities—than was Jim utterly forgotten. So it was only upon reconvening for the flip cup/pre-gaming process that the even greater problem was revealed.

Jamie, whom Allison had filled in on the Jim situation the moment she and Rachel arrived, was the first to take notice.

"He can't wear that," she stated, referring to the wifebeater and shorts cloaking his teeny frame. Everyone looked at her as if she'd just insulted the style sense of a five-year-old. "No, not because there's anything wrong with it!" she clarified. "It's just, they'll never let him in."

They'd all totally overlooked this, instead perceiving his clothes as simply part of the oddity that was Jim himself. But it was now apparent Jamie was right.

"Dude, you can't wear shorts or tank tops to nightclubs," Rob tried to explain. He patted the knapsack Jim had once again fastened to his back. "What else you got in there?"

Unzipping it, Jim began digging through a mess of papers and books that flooded over the sides. Funny, it looked almost as if—on a last-minute whim—Jim had decided to hop a Jitney after finishing his final class. But the fact remained that Jim didn't have a single thing to wear to a swanky, dress-code-enforcing nightclub. Nor did anyone imagine he'd ever been to one.

"Does he even want to go?" Josh snarled from across the room. Aware he wouldn't so much as acknowledge her, Allison shot him a dirty look.

"Well, we can't just leave him here," Mark said, his intonation going up at the end as if he was tempted to make it a question.

But Allison, whose compassion was what had driven her to become a teacher, spoke in Jim's defense. "Can't someone lend him something?"

Every male in the room looked away. Apparently it was two entirely separate matters to give a stranger half a sandwich, and to entrust said stranger with your favorite pair of two-hundred-dollar designer jeans.

Lucky for them, as they peered uncomfortably around at one another, it became clear that every guy in the house that weekend was over six feet tall.

"I think he stands a better shot being underdressed than wearing clothes that are ten times too big for him," Rob reasoned.

"Okay, then you be the one who takes him home when the door people start shouting 'No tank tops, no shorts,'" Mark countered. "Why should we give them a reason to neg him?"

Jim, who'd been standing around sullenly while the room debated his fate, seemed more capable of cognition than anyone gave him credit for. Sensing this, Allison gave Brian her most sympathetic pout.

"All right, Jimmy, come with me," he finally agreed. "Let's see what we can do."

Jim's face lit up, though not half as brightly as Allison's.

And, with naive optimism, the three of them headed back to Brian's room.

Rifling through his duffel, Brian handed over to Jim a pair of distressed Diesels. After being rolled up about five times at the cuff, and kept from falling to his feet with a thick leather belt…well, they still looked ridiculous. Even more ridiculous was how he looked in Brian's oversize dress shirts, so—rummaging through Mark's closet—Allison was pleased to come upon a child-size green T-shirt boasting I LOVE SOUTHAMPTON.

"Maybe we really should just let him go in his own clothes?" Mark said after viewing the (hardly improved) result. But even if that had been a better option, the vans outside soon honked their arrival. So, ugly duckling or beautiful swan, Jim would have to go as is.

A nervous energy filled the share house residents on the van ride there, as if they were trying to sneak their own food into a movie theater. But once they debarked, their plan was executed flawlessly.

Basically, Jim stayed hidden from view behind the taller guys (read: all the guys) while Mark collected the group's reduced-price tickets. Then, when Alex waved them in, Mark kept him occupied with small talk so the group encircling Jim could mass-migrate inside, garb unnoticed. Score one for 1088 Montauk.

Once they were within Pink Elephant's gates, everyone rejoiced as fervently as if they'd just sneaked their underage sibling inside the club. As if they needed a reason, this called for some serious celebrating.

"Patrón, Jimmy?" Brian offered.

Jim refused to touch a drop of alcohol, but this was hardly evident from his behavior. The energy in the club had produced its own high, and, embracing the beats that pulsated so hard you could feel them in the floor, Jim appeared to be having a fabulous time.

His delight was contagious. That night the group all seemed to be experiencing the club through a newcomer's eyes.

Except for those using their eyes to project their hatred.

Of course, Allison hadn't expected Josh to be overjoyed at her developing relationship with Brian. And up until this point, she'd been surprised not to have sparked any type of reaction from him. But never in a million years did she expect him to react so spitefully. Or to do what he did next.

It started innocently enough. Taking the hand of Tara/Jocelyn (whose interest in him Allison had detected since Day One), Josh made a prominent show of pulling her out to dance in the aisles—being careful to glance back at Allison every so often. Naturally, she tried to ignore this, though it was an eerie feeling to look up and meet his concentrated gaze.

"You guys, he's giving me death stares," Allison whispered to her friends, wondering if she'd invented a good part of this.

"I know!" Rachel said without turning around.

"Ignore it," advised Jamie (who, by choosing to bypass her usual frolicking to sit in a booth with Jeff, was exhibiting some shocking behavior of her own).

But despite her previous success at indifference, as much as Allison tried she simply couldn't ignore Josh's feature perfor-mance. Really, no one at the club could. For, at just the right moment, when he was certain he'd captured an audience, he leaned over and began making out with Tara/Jocelyn. Right there on the dance floor. In *public*.

"Whatever! That is so immature," Rachel said, dismissively turning her back to it.

In a less discreet response, Jamie forged a gagging gesture.

"What is he, like eighteen?" she shrieked. "That's the most disgusting thing ever!"

Still, disgusting or not, it was like that bloody scene in a movie that made Allison instinctively cover her eyes...but she couldn't help peeking at it through the cracks of her fingers anyway.

Sure, she expected him to move on! Sure, she knew watching it would never be easy! But even more disturbing to her was the emergence of so many awful qualities she'd never before seen. This viciousness, this cruelty, this spite! Where had it all come from? So sure, it shocked Allison to watch Josh making out with another girl. But, coming from someone she had loved so genuinely then, and had honestly believed she always might, was to Allison the most piercing surprise of all.

Thank goodness for Brian.

Sensing now hurt she was, he protectively reached out and grabbed hold of her hand, sandwiching it tightly between both of his. Almost as if she were a child who'd just fallen and skinned her knee and in a minute she'd let the hysteria fly.

"I have an idea," Brian whispered, pushing her hair behind her ear. "Want to head back to the house? We'll have my room to ourselves for a while."

They'd been alone every consecutive day of the last few weeks—but because each minute she watched Josh somehow negated all this, Allison jumped at this opportunity.

Little did she know, she would soon jump again.

They caught a cab back to the share house, and as they stepped inside Allison embraced its vast emptiness. Not even pausing to put down their things, they scurried downstairs to Brian's room and threw open the door.

And again, Allison and Brian discovered something neither expected.

To their absolute horror, there was a full-grown man asleep in Brian's bed.

Opening the door wider, they revealed a woman's figure buried beneath the sheets in Rob's bed. And finally, there was good ol' Jim, still sporting his borrowed jeans and Hamptons T-shirt, sprawled across Dave's bed. (At least *he'd* gotten the sleeping assignments right.)

"Ahhhh!" shrieked Allison, instantly startling the sleeping people.

"Ahhhh!" echoed Jim, jumping alarmingly to his feet. In a desperate plea, he ran over to them. "These my parents!" he shouted, his eyes dilated in fear. "They visit from Canada and have no place to stay."

Glancing from the grave gray-haired couple back to each other, Allison and Brian were too stunned to speak. Settling on reshutting the door, they attempted to contain all the strangeness in that one room and went upstairs until the rest of the house returned.

Conveying the story to a skeptical Mark (who believed it was a prank up until the moment he personally bore witness), they interrupted the family's slumber just once more—to inform Jim that his parents could stay on the living room sofa.

And so they laid their heads that night in the same place where many a beer had been spilled, and many a sexual escapade had been implemented. Though come the next morning, any trace of Jim and his parents had vanished from sight (with the exception of Brian's jeans, length restored, and laid out thoughtfully).

It was the most unexpected of all surprises, and afterward, those Allison told of the Jim fiasco never quite believed it. Though following that weekend's episodes, anyone who set foot in the share house came to expect the black swan. Or rather, the swan(s).

Chapter
Thirteen

Rachel believed life was a zero-sum game. To get one, you had to give one. +1 for −1. Total gains equals total losses. In other words, no one got something for nothing.

This translated effectively into the romantic arena as well, thus inspiring her to develop a finely tuned dating platform. A set of uncompromisable rules of etiquette, if you will, that she adhered to like a religion. And while inarguably conservative, this mutual system of give-and-take had always served her just fine.

Case in point: If a guy wanted to hook up with a girl, he needed to take her out to dinner. If he wanted oral gratification, he needed to (satisfactorily) deliver it up first. And if he wanted to pass go, you'd better believe that the *relationship* title needed to be adequately established.

A bit on the technical side? Perhaps. But dealing with dating game theory, where payoffs depended on the choices of two people, Rachel determined this an effective means to optimize both interests. To establish a long-run equilibrium.

That following Saturday, however, the guys in the share house were forced to acknowledge a different zero-sum principle: to get into the club, they had to first buy bottles.

While this was hardly novel in the world of New York nightclubs, the house had managed to avoid this huge expenditure by frequenting the places Mark promoted. Leading the pack like the Pied Piper, he could escort in a gargantuan group for a minimal cover charge—highly advantageous to guys, whose presence was about as coveted as fruit flies around alcohol bottles. So come that third weekend, when Jamie fought over comps with Mark and convinced a sizable chunk of the share house to split off to the new hot spot Dune, their vanload discharged to a less-than-warm welcome.

"Excuse me?" attempted several members of their group, striving to seize the attention of the oblivious gatekeepers.

They'd have had similar luck with a bullhorn. Even though they'd arrived at the insanely early hour of ten thirty (at which time there wasn't the slightest semblance of a line), they were left to fester outside for a good fifteen minutes—purely for show. During this lengthy interlude, the intimidating bald man overseeing the door (whom Jamie quietly identified as "Rich Thomas, from Marquee") stood silently beside security and ignored their entreaties the way a celebrity might whistles from paparazzi.

When he was good and ready, he looked up.

"How many?" asked a voice already sounding annoyed. Under his discerning stare, Rachel began to think they had had a better shot of getting in before he granted them eye contact.

Dave, by virtue of being the nearest person to him (for better or worse), did a quick head count. "I think we're just twelve," he said, aware that *just twelve* sounded as much an oxymoron as *jumbo shrimp.*

"Two tables," he pronounced without so much as a flinch. That settled, he raised a challenging eyebrow and began to reach for the rope.

"Wait…two bottles?" Dave asked, while various exclamations of shock mounted from the group behind him.

"Two *tables,*" he repeated, rolling his eyes and looking past Dave to the hordes of imaginary people coming at him from all ends. "Two-bottle minimum each."

"What?" gasped several of the bottle-service novices. *"No way!"*

On cue, security then informed them to please move aside if they weren't going in, so as not to hold up the "line" (of which they were currently the entirety).

Outraged by the prospect of being bullied into bottles, Ilana and posse decided to simply cab it over to Star Room (where a twenty-dollar cover was seeming more and more insignificant). And then there were nine.

"Do we really want to go in here?" Dave asked, feeling obliged to step up after being unofficially appointed ringleader. Which Rachel found amusing in itself, because in the short time she'd known him, Dave had proven to be much more the mooch than the spender. If pressed, he'd state his occupation under the ambiguous umbrella of "real estate," though he often seemed to lack any disposable income—and what he lacked most of all was any sort of ambition. Given his decent looks, girls were eager enough to overlook this, but from rides to food to alcohol, his friends continually picked up the slack for him.

"What do you girls think?" Brian said, turning it over to the ladies.

Rachel glanced around at her friends. Now remaining in the group were six guys (Dave, Brian, Rob, Jeff, Aaron—who'd been trying to atone for his 2 AM faux pas with uncanny niceness—and Aaron's investment banker buddy Steve) and three girls (Allison, Jamie, and herself). Personally, Rachel could have lived without ever setting foot inside this bottle-service trap (plus, she had qualms about being the only girl not paired off), but she was all too certain what Jamie would think.

"Well, it's like the hottest club in the Hamptons right now," her friend stated. Looking longingly back at the door, she whispered to Rachel, "And if we were by ourselves, we'd be inside already."

Just then, as if planted by the club for occasions like these, three girls made a grand show of exiting from a cab directly in front. It was impossible not to watch as they climbed out one by one, each more eye catching and glitzed out than the last.

In an ostentatious blaze of sequins and bold color and arresting perfume, they frolicked right up to the door, where Rich, smiling widely, was waiting with open arms (and lowered rope). After a series of air kisses, they started inside (but not before holding their hands out to be stamped for free admission).

Rachel observed this from the sidelines, where they were awkwardly standing around in limbo. More important, Dave observed this, and it instantly overturned any reservations he might have had.

"Let's just do this," he said. He counted the group up once again, this time with growing resolve. "Now there's only nine of us, so maybe we can get by with one table. And even if the bottles cost eight hundred dollars, that's less than a hundred each..."

"The girls aren't paying," Brian argued (just as Jamie was about to open her mouth in protest).

Dave sighed. "Fine. That's still six of us. Let's just go in already," he urged, as if doing it quickly would make the overall effect less painful. Like ripping off a Band-Aid.

And so it was decided. Six of the guys would go in on the bottles, Rich willingly agreed to wave in the girls...now someone just needed to put down a credit card. At that, Dave's enthusiasm to be the ringleader instantly waned.

"Does anyone else have one? I'd do it, but I just charged a shitload this month."

Brian went to reach for his back pocket, but Aaron was quicker.

"Thanks, Nash," echoed the group.

"No problem," he answered, smiling at Rachel as he handed his card over.

In truth, Rachel had been warming to Aaron over the course of the last two weeks—though this did nothing to reverse her opinion that they were romantically incompatible. Sure, he was attractive, but a young, attractive, financially sound guy who was "loving life" could be found at any bar, any night of the week (and a truckload at sports dives on Sundays). Quite frankly, Rachel had been down this road too many times with too many guys, and was acutely aware of the warning signs. Thus, a drunken text message at an inappropriate hour wasn't just a text message: It was a rude, disrespectful, premature booty call. It was a tip of the scale, an uneven exchange, a brazen attempt to get something for nothing. It was a dismissal of rules, of courtship conventions, of courtesy, of etiquette.

But that was no reason they couldn't be friends.

Following the bottle host to their table, Rachel was shocked to find the spacious room practically empty (and totally freezing). Why, Dune should have been paying *them* to come inside, not vice versa! And, sneaking a glance at the liquor menu the guys were poring over, she learned that this privilege didn't come cheap. It was probably the only menu Rachel had ever seen where each item's price was listed in hundred-dollar denominations.

Once the order had been placed, and they sat themselves along the interconnected strip of banquettes, there was nothing left to do but peer around observantly.

It's an odd moment when you find yourself at a club before anyone else. Time is seemingly at a standstill, you feel a little too lame and a lot too sober, and no stretch of the imagination enables you to picture the empty expanse packed with people.

Getting drunk thus warranted their undivided attention—it being second to sleep as a vehicle to accelerate time. In pursuit of this, an ice bucket and mixers (inclusive of the Red Bull cans Dave insisted on, at an additional cost) were promptly delivered to their table. Though the true party only began upon the arrival of their esteemed vodka bottles.

Of course the same labels were available in a liquor store for a painful fifty dollars—the monetary discrepancy owing to the rental of prime banquette real estate. That, and an unspoken, less tangible transaction. One to which no guy could ever accurately attach a price. Namely, that other, uglier, manifestation of the zero-sum principle: to get ass, guys gave out free alcohol.

And to save money, more girls than you'd think readily accepted.

Girls highly unlike Rachel, who begged to differ on this account. Of course, she was quite familiar with Jamie's line of thinking: that being offered a free drink was like spotting a twenty-dollar bill on the floor; you'd have to be a fool to not take advantage of it. To Rachel, taking a drink from a guy was more like indulging in a hot fudge sundae: the eventual repercussions far outweighed the momentary benefits. So maybe that drink seemed a blessing at first, but in the uncomfortable moments that followed, it would leave her feeling like she owed a guy something—be it sexual or as trivial as her conversation. And Rachel would prostitute her time no sooner than she would her body. Especially to someone like Aaron.

"Want a drink?" he predictably asked her during those first crucial moments when vodka is worth its weight in...well, vodka.

"No, that's okay," Rachel said after a brief moment of debate. Debate only because in this instance, the bottle wasn't entirely his. But accepting *his* drink offer would be owing *him* gratitude, which would disrupt that precious equilibrium. And so, excusing herself to use the restroom, she stopped afterward at the bar to buy herself a glass of wine.

As she lingered over the counter while the bartender poured her drink, she spotted the three girls who'd preceded them into the club now standing around sullenly. The ebullience was zapped from their faces, their hands were empty (save for designer bags), and their gazes appeared fixated on the display of top-shelf alcohol...as if mentally trying to will it toward them.

"So, do you guys want to just buy a drink?" Rachel overheard one propose. This suggestion was contemplated with the gravity it deserved.

"Nah, I'm going to wait a bit," another decided, her friends dutifully following suit. And the dark cloud of sobriety settled over the group once again.

Chuckling as she returned to the table, Rachel knew what they were waiting for, of course. They were waiting for the "giving hour"—the point when guys got just drunk enough that their inebriation took a charitable turn.

She just hadn't expected the generosity to come from her own.

Rachel wasn't exactly sure when it happened, for all at once the time had slipped from eleven to one and the room transformed from dreary to overflowing—as if someone had manually flipped a switch. A switch that likewise ignited an energy Rachel hadn't found before in the Hamptons. As she was quickly discovering, there was much to be said for having a table at a communal venue like this, where groups bled (and sweated) together in the large nautical-themed room, standing on booths and shaking to the pulsating hip-hop sounds. What's more, it was the kind of sceney place where if you didn't have a table or know a group, it was easy to feel like an outcast.

Sort of like those girls, whom Rachel had noticed making lap after predatory lap, summoning the indiscreet glances of countless male onlookers with each. The trio danced around playfully, weaving themselves in and out of tables while air-kissing some guys but ignoring most others. All the while they laughed overzealously and shook their bodies with a reckless abandon that only the observant might realize wasn't fueled by alcohol, but rather faked in pursuit of it.

Tiring of their show, Rachel soon tuned them out—until she saw them halt alongside Dave at her table. After a mere two seconds of conversing, he proudly gestured to the bottle and uttered those words every guy loves to say, and every girl loves to hear. "Want a drink?"

What happened next could rival Pamplona. Quicker than you could say *stampede,* the girls charged at the bottle. It was a collective effort—one girl doled out glasses, another shoveled in a strategically minimal amount of ice, and a third generously dispensed the vodka supply.

Rachel was stunned. She shot an appalled look at her friends, but both were too preoccupied with their respective male distractions to register this outrageous event.

"Have a seat" were the next words out of Dave's mouth, and their entire group slid over and smushed together. After a moment of consideration, the girls sat down.

Surely he must have seen the pause? Rachel wondered. That brief hesitation implying that the last thing these girls wanted was to be stuck at this table with these guys. But then it dawned on her. Pause or no pause, guys liked having pretty girls at their table. This was more even an exchange than she'd thought.

"So what are your names?" Aaron asked, practically drooling. Though he was a smart guy, he seemed totally oblivious to his role as a vodka-dispensing target. Before long, one swindler had entranced Aaron in conversation, another Dave, and the third was chatting up both Rob and Steve. Finding this extremely irritating, Rachel pretended not to eavesdrop as she nursed her white wine.

Funny, after five minutes and one superstrong vodka cranberry, one of the girls was visibly itching to rise to her feet. Her friend next to her tactfully thwarted these efforts, tugging downward at her arm and shaking her head *not yet*.

And so the conversations continued, with varying degrees of enthusiasm among the participants. One girl gushed with overbearing energy, another was perfectly polite but introverted, and that restless third looked like she'd rather be having a Pap smear. She was the one who suddenly reached over and seized the gigantic bottle with one hand. "This isn't strong enough," she declared, emptying more vodka into her *second* vodka cranberry.

Eagerly, her energetic friend held out her glass as well, and the first refilled it till it flooded over the brim.

Now *this,* someone would surely put a stop to, Rachel was certain. But if anyone minded, they masked their disapproval brilliantly. On the contrary, Aaron appeared fully content with his present company. Actually, more than content. Having captured the attention of the quiet fashionista, with curly hair, cat-like green eyes, and skin so flawless she could have passed as a Noxzema girl, Aaron looked perfectly enamored. Just as Rachel was beginning to wonder if this girl might actually be interested in him, the timer went off.

Shooting to her feet at the ten-minute mark, his companion announced (with unnatural volume), "I think I'm going to the bathroom."

What a shock! Rachel thought. And so surprising that her friends all insisted on accompanying her! Off they danced, looking as spirited as animals that had just been uncaged.

The second their flashy outfits blended back into the crowd, Rachel flew from her seat over to Jamie. "Did you see those girls?"

"Ugh, I can't stand them," Jamie said. It comforted Rachel to know that her friend wasn't blind. "I see them *everywhere.* They think they're socialites or something."

"Did you see how much vodka they were stealing? I was dying when that girl refilled all their glasses! And I can't believe Aaron was just egging them on!"

For some reason, this last statement was the only one Jamie seemed to register. "So I'm confused…I thought you liked this guy at DIP?"

Had they *not* been through this?

"Um, that was before he drunk-texted me at two in the morning!" Rachel said defensively, aware she was entering into territory Jamie would never understand. Jamie, who was currently hooking up with a guy in a situation that had yet to translate outside the Hamptons. "It's just, I have a certain way of doing things. When it comes to dating, I think there's a certain…etiquette."

"Are you serious? No guy cares about etiquette! It's the summer, loosen up!" Jamie said, taking a hearty swig of four-hundred-dollar vodka she hadn't paid for. "Life's not that cut-and-dried. Personally, I like to live outside the box. I don't believe in rules."

And apparently neither did a second group of girls, who had migrated to their table while Rachel was talking to Jamie. One, with a particularly arrogant air, professed to be Steve's "girlfriend" (he later denied this) and took to pouring drinks for herself, her friend, and her cousin visiting from Miami (to whom Rob immediately took a liking). And Rachel began to wonder if Jamie was right after all.

Thus, noticing Aaron unoccupied, she went over to him,

with the intention of looking beyond his drunken offense. He didn't make this very easy.

"So how's Dana doing?" he asked not even a minute into the conversation.

"Fine." Rachel's eyes drifted down to her drink.

"Are you guys doing a lot of wedding stuff?"

"Tons," she said. Fueled in equal part by irritation and sobriety, she decided to just put it out there. "Why do you always talk about my sister?"

"I don't know," he said, growing embarrassed. "I guess...you remind me of her."

"We don't really look alike," she shot back.

He considered this. "It's more like your mannerisms."

"Oh." Rachel brushed her blond hair back with her hand. "Do you know her well?"

"Pretty well. I mean, we worked together." He paused momentarily, as if searching for words. "She's a hard girl to not notice..."

"Yup," Rachel said, throwing back the remainder of her wine in one gulp, then glancing around dismissively. If she wanted to talk about her sister's numerous fine attributes, she could have just phoned Bridezilla herself.

Though, instead of going on about Dana, what Aaron said next took Rachel by surprise.

"Why do you hate me?" he said, looking at her intently through his thin wire frames.

"I don't hate you," she replied, mostly out of reflex. *I just hate guys like you,* she thought. Seeing as she'd captured his attention, she contemplated broaching the whole text-message topic, but ultimately decided against it. "I can just tell we're different types of people."

"How so?" he challenged in a way she should have anticipated.

Various nods to courtesy and etiquette (and utter lack thereof) ran through her head, but—recalling Jamie's words—she simply shrugged the matter off.

"You're almost done with that," he said, pointing to her empty wineglass. "Can I make you a drink now?"

Eyeing the bottle (which a lot less deserving girls had less guiltily reaped the benefits of), Rachel decided to finally give in. "Sure," she answered, prompting that smile from Aaron that had always appealed to her in a guy-next-door way. And with that vodka cranberry she took one tiny step away from her rules, and in the direction of faith.

Yet one giant leap en route to intoxication. Thanks to its composition of 90 percent vodka and 10 percent juice (something she'd noticed, but seemed to underestimate the effect of), the drink soon numbed her to everything except their conversation, which became one of those exchanges where everything the other person says seems handcrafted for your ears. Though just as Rachel was supposing the green-eyed girl's loss was her own gain, the pseudo-socialites chose to resurface.

"Hey!" said girl called out to Aaron, fingering her (predictably) empty glass as the three of them approached.

"I'll be back," Rachel said, deciding it an ideal time to excuse herself. Joining the single-file bathroom line that moved barely an inch per song, Rachel's buzz had fully evaporated by the time she returned. And at that point—twenty or so minutes later—the only people she recognized at the table were Aaron and the three freeloaders. Rachel immediately reached for her phone, but to her dismay, she had no service. Though just as she was about to interrupt Aaron...

"Have you seen any of the guys?" he asked, a worried expression on his face.

"No," she said. "Do you know where my friends went?"

He shook his head. "But I wasn't really paying attention."

I wonder why! Rachel thought. Upset now, she wasn't exactly sure how she'd wound up in this situation, but she knew she wanted to get out of it. Glancing back at Aaron and the D-listers, she decided that, worst-case scenario, she could always take a cab to the house by herself. Whatever the cost. But the far greater cost appeared to have fallen on Aaron.

"Well, they just brought over the bill and I can't find anyone," he said. In his drunken stupor, he tried to think. "Do me a favor—stay here and watch the table for a sec?"

"Sure," Rachel agreed. Because nothing would make her happier than being left alone with these three! Though once he ran off, she couldn't help but sneak a glance at the table's abandoned bill (and had to do a double take upon discovering it to be around nine hundred dollars).

Fortunately, that's when she spotted Dave.

"Oh, hey!" she called out to him, grabbing his arm through the crowd. "Aaron's looking for you. They just brought over the bill, and we can't find anyone!"

"Yeah, okay, thanks," he said. He turned (unbiasedly) to all three girls, who were busy sucking dry every last drop of remaining vodka. "So, what do you girls say? Want to move the party back to our house?"

The girls exchanged anxious glances. Then one of them exclaimed, on a falsely high note, "This is such a great party! Why would you want to leave?"

"Oh," Dave said, a bit befuddled. Warming to the idea, he added, "Yeah, we can stick around."

But no sooner did security come over—informing them that if they didn't want another bottle, they should pay and clear the table—than the girls departed. They slid a whole two tables over to a group of suits with an unopened Belvedere, passing out flutes of champagne.

It was just one of life's inequalities that girls *could* get away with something for nothing.

And it was a spiteful move for Dave to attempt to as well. Watching him, Rachel could almost see the spokes in his mind turning as he grappled with the (non-zero-sum) game that is prisoner's dilemma. If he cooperated, he and Aaron would split the bottles and put in $450 each. If he betrayed, he'd pay nothing while Aaron was left with the whole nine hundred. And if Aaron betrayed, well, Dave would be held responsible for the entire sum himself. So the solution to this self-serving game was that no matter what Aaron did, Dave was better off defecting.

"Tell Nash I'll be right back," he uttered, slipping away. That was the last Rachel saw of him that night.

Half an hour later Rachel and Aaron shared a cab home. After ransacking every inch of the club and calling every phone number they had, Aaron was forced to charge the entire bill on his Amex. He was justifiably furious, even after being enlightened as to the drunken aftermath: Jamie had stepped on glass and flipped out because her foot was bleeding; Allison, Brian, and Jeff had escorted her home; Steve and Rob went back to some other house with Steve's "girlfriend" and her Floridian cousin; and Dave insisted that he couldn't find anyone and had to leave the club alone.

Regardless, Rachel continued to feel sorry for Aaron, who was a decent guy and didn't deserve this. Though Aaron didn't allow his friends to get away with something for nothing for long.

On Monday morning he sent out an e-mail to the entire share house. It was titled "Bottle-Service Etiquette":

1. If you enter the club for free with the people getting the table, you contribute.

2. If your friends already have a table, and you want to just hang out, let several table members know you are *not* drinking, and just want to use the precious seating space.
3. If you walk in and want "just one drink" from the table, put in twenty-five dollars immediately to the head of the table, or the one of us who is least drunk.
4. If you are paying for the bottle, that does *not* mean you can offer your girlfriend, and her friends, and their cousins visiting from Miami, a drink. Every *one* person who pays can host *one* other person. (Dave—just because you are trying to sleep with three women that night, does not mean all three can drink from our bottle. Pick a girl and stick with her.)
5. Do *not* leave the table until the check is paid and the person who put the credit card down is content. (Dave, Brian, Rob, Jeff, and Steve—I'll expect cash or check in the amount of $150 each.)

And that was how Nash established a house equilibrium.

Chapter Fourteen

The first time she was dissatisfied with the way Mark was running things, Jamie decided to bite her tongue.

But as the summer wore on and her list of share house grievances grew exponentially, Jamie began to bite his head off.

"How can you expect us to go to your clubs every weekend and not give us a *single* comp?" she'd argue. Accustomed as she was to waltzing in for free anyplace she chose, by virtue of contacts she knew far less intimately, Mark's stinginess week after week continued to astonish her. She'd tried to inform him of this. "Do you realize I have friends who'll take care of me any other place I go?"

No matter how convincing her pleas (which most people found pretty damn convincing), Mark would show her no leniency. "I just can't comp some people and not others," he'd say.

Which made her that much more adamant about the issue of weekend swapping.

"I have the premiere for the new George Clooney film this Friday," she'd explained, in a way any reasonable person would understand. "Do you care if we come up next weekend instead of this one?"

"Sorry, next weekend's rough," he'd replied, even though every weekend Jamie had been there so far was decidedly "rough," and she couldn't imagine the subsequent one being any less so. When she'd pointed this out (ever so politely), he failed to budge, merely repeating, "You know the rules."

And *you know* exactly where Jamie wanted to shove them!

But, looking back, those were comparatively minor conflicts. The final straw came when Jamie brought up Fourth of July weekend.

"What do you mean, our friends can't come out? Everyone's friends are coming!" Jamie cried to Mark over the phone just a few days prior.

"Can't do it. The house is already packed," he stated, his tone frustratingly stoic.

"But they'll even sleep in our beds with us, and pay your obscene holiday guest fees!" Jamie shouted. *What* was his problem?

At this, Mark was silent for a moment, and Jamie wondered if she'd convinced him. She didn't wonder for long. "Why don't they come a different weekend?"

"Why are you such an asshole?" she blurted out.

"Listen," he said with a sigh, not letting her rile him one bit. "If I didn't have rules, the entire share house would fall apart. There wouldn't even be a share house to begin with." He chuckled a bit at his own supposition—a pompous, self-indulgent chuckle. "I know you think I have it in for you, but this is just how I run my business."

"Well, don't worry," she snapped. "You've made it quite clear to everyone your interests are purely monetary."

Seething as she hung up the phone, Jamie decided then and there that she was done biting the bullet. This was war.

"I hate him!" she shrieked to her friends, pounding her fist on the steering wheel during their trafficky drive to the house that weekend. "Have you ever met anyone so insensitive? Maybe he'd actually make some friends if he stopped trying to steal everyone's money!"

"Apparently not everyone thinks so," Rachel reminded them. "I've never seen a guy get that much ass! He leaves the clubs practically the minute we get there to bring girls back to his room."

"I know! He's not even *that* cute," Jamie said, picturing his beach-bum-browned unshaven face and hating to acknowledge that he wasn't utterly repulsive. "It cracks me up how these girls flock to him like he's a celebrity, when all he does is run a cheesy share house! And run it horribly, I might add."

Breaking her silence thus far, Allison once again proved to be the sympathetic one. "Well, it must be hard to make everyone happy," she piped in from the back, only to be met by Jamie's and Rachel's death stares. "Imagine you were the one running the share house. No one likes to be the bad guy."

"First of all, I would *never* run a share house. And second—haven't you noticed, he's only the bad guy to *us*!" Jamie bellowed. "Practically every other group is bringing out friends this weekend! Do you really think two more people would make the house any less of a mob scene?"

"Ugh," Rachel moaned, her face overtaken by disgust. "I'm dreading what the clubs are going to be like."

"That's another thing!" Jamie continued (since complaints were like cocktails—why stop after one?). "If we go where *he* wants—which we're going to want to do, so we can be with the group—we'll have to pay those atrocious cover prices. I am so sick of this!" Throwing her head back in surrender, she pummeled the wheel once more for effect.

But that's when Jamie had an idea.

"What if we get the whole house to go somewhere else tonight?" she said, the rebellious plan taking shape in her head. "That would certainly show him—if he lost, like, forty people's worth of cover!"

Rachel's eyes perked, and then dropped. "Yeah, but there's no way to guarantee twenty guys will get in *anywhere* Fourth of July weekend without buying bottles...and you remember what happened at Dune." Mulling it over some more, she shook her head conclusively. "They won't want to do it."

"Maybe they will," Jamie argued.

They didn't. And understandably so, for when they walked in, the house was flooded with so many new faces, it was almost like being at a party already. Why, there was barely a need to go out at all, much less any impetus to deviate from a situation that—from vans to venue choice to line skipping—was so neatly worked out for them. Though, as an endless stream of unapproved guests continued to file in, Jamie felt less inclined to celebrate the American Revolution as to lead a revolution of her own.

Infuriating her even more was the fact that Ilana and her friends had spawned a crew of clone-like counterparts, all equally self-righteous and even more obnoxious than the originals. Seizing control of the central couch, their positioning enabled them to drive the room's activity like the nucleus of a cell. Jamie thought that this would never have been possible had she been permitted to bring her own friends...which actually *would* have been possible, if not for the Grinch who stole her Independence Day.

Just for that, Jamie refused to so much as look in Mark's direction the entire time they were downstairs, and she resolved not to for the remainder of the summer.

Once she was upstairs getting ready for the evening, though, Jamie could suppress her anger no longer. "Screw it. Let's just us three go somewhere else tonight."

Predictably, Rachel and Allison exchanged dubious glances.

"Because that worked out so well the last time?" Rachel asked.

"We only had a problem because we tried to drive. This time we'll just take cabs," Jamie reasoned, having learned never to bite off more than she could chew. But her friends had learned a different lesson: never again to follow her lead.

"Let's not try this," Allison suggested, as firmly as she ever said anything. "Besides, all the guys are going to Pink Elephant. Brian—"

"Oh, you can leave Brian for one night," Jamie teased, aware her scheme would entail leaving Jeff as well. But there was little Jamie wouldn't give up in this endeavor, as it was now a matter of pride. "I just *refuse* to give that guy any more of my money. Please? I'll work out all the details."

So after much pleading (followed by even more pleading), she eventually did. A quick text message to Mike Satsky—who was an owner of Stereo by the Shore in Southampton—and they were on the list for the Victoria's Secret party that night. See how simple this could be? And, just as Jamie was picturing the look on Mark's face (upon discovering they were straying off somewhere else, somewhere *better*), she was afforded a glimpse of that very face a bit sooner than she'd planned.

"Jamie," Mark called from outside their room, his voice laden with authority. Knocking sternly, he opened the door they'd left slightly ajar.

Still wearing an oversize T-shirt and the horrific plaid boxer shorts she'd gotten as a sorority favor, Jamie was busy doing (what else) her makeup at their full-length mirror. Not bothering to turn around, she merely gazed back at the reflection of the last possible person she wanted to see.

"Sorry to do this to you," he said—the last possible words anyone wants to hear—"but I need you to move your car to the train station."

"What do you mean?" she shrieked, whipping around defensively. "It's *our* weekend, and that's the *one* car for our group."

"I know," he continued unapologetically. "It's just, Fourth

of July is a joint weekend for A and B people, so there are too many shareholders' cars to begin with. We're asking people to move them on a first-come, first-served basis."

This last part silenced her, as she was about to demand *Why me?* But, desperate to be rid of him, she quickly muttered her assent. Only he didn't go anywhere.

"Actually, Craig's waiting out in front. He's leading a whole group of people to the station now, so he can drive everyone back all at once."

It took Jamie a moment for this to register. "Wait, you want me to move it *now*?" she repeated. "No way, I'm not even dressed." (That, and she looked like a ghost in the transition stages of blending her eye makeup.)

Mark sighed. "There's going to be no one to take you later once we all leave for Pink Elephant—"

"*We're* not going to Pink Elephant," Jamie practically sang.

"Well, unless you're taking your car *with* you, I think you should just go with Craig now," Mark cautioned, paying her admission no mind. When Jamie didn't exactly jump, he added, "Please don't fight me on this—you know we can only have eleven cars in the driveway overnight. And trust me, the cops are looking to give people a hard time this weekend."

Like one car is really going to make a difference? she thought. But in the interest of time (and to the detriment of her eye makeup), Jamie chose compliance. "Fine," she sputtered, hatred for him seeping out of her ears like smoke. And as she pulled on a pair of jeans, she couldn't believe he'd found yet another way to spoil her weekend.

Scary ghost makeup aside, Jamie probably looked possessed as she flew out into the pitch blackness, hopping madly into her car amid the awaiting congregation. She was just as unnerved operating a vehicle on the dark rural roads now as she always had been (if not significantly more so, as even *she* would never live down publicly smashing another shareholder's car). But blasting up the music (and deciding that, in the event of an accident, Mark would simply be the scapegoat), her anger somehow inspired courage.

And off they went, a lineup of cars not unlike a funeral procession. As Jamie followed each unmemorable turn, she couldn't help but think what a pain in the ass it was that the train station was almost twenty minutes away. (Was Mark *trying* to make her late?)

However, she spotted train tracks before she knew it. Parking in the spot Craig directed her into like an airplane, she breathed a sigh of relief that the life-endangering portion of the evening had concluded.

"Do you have your keys?" Craig demanded, less a joke than a credible inquiry. And after flashing him a look, Jamie nodded (but then checked).

Now here's the part she hated to confess: the ride back to the share house was actually a relatively good time. Forgetting for a moment about her haphazard appearance (even forgetting that, in all the chaos, she'd *forgotten* to put on a bra), Jamie basked in the attention of six new guys she hadn't met before. As the only girl in the group, this was quite the responsibility. But no sooner did she reenter the house and storm past Mark than she reapplied the scowl this fruitless errand had deserved.

Though as it happened, that scowl was the last time she frowned all night. By nothing short of a miracle, everything else went exactly according to plan.

First, the cab they'd pre-ordered pulled up to the house at eleven on the dot. (Jamie felt entirely no remorse as she sauntered past the flip cup station.) Mike Satsky was stationed conveniently out front when they approached the crowd at Stereo, and waved them inside (past notoriously selective Butter doorman Binn) effortlessly. But best of all, beyond the mobbed exterior, the party inside was thriving.

This indoor-outdoor venue—complete with tropical decor and the vigorous sounds of DJ AM—was filled with energy. Sure, there were Victoria's Secret models and a sprinkling of celebrities (Haylie and Hilary Duff were currently in her eye line), but not in that see-and-be-seen way; it was more of a just-want-to-dance-and-let-loose thing. So that's exactly what they did.

They were thrilled to see different faces, to hear the impromptu performance given by drop-in guest Lily Allen, and most of all to *not* be at Pink Elephant. Which Jamie resolved could be only fractionally as fun, during her many mental comparisons. Why she bothered was beyond her, for really there was nothing to compare: Mark was a cheap ass-hole who treated them like walking wallets, while Mike had invited them to join his table, introduced them to his colleagues, and treated them as his guests.

And as the time ticked on, and the music grew infectious, and the benches became any dancer's game, Jamie didn't want the night to end at all.

When they finally severed themselves (leaving a less successful Alessandra Ambrosio still in motion on the dance floor), Jamie felt extremely satisfied. See, they didn't need Mark to have a good time, she thought. In fact, they didn't need Mark at all.

What's more, throughout the cab ride back Jamie considered what a loss it would have been had they missed this night entirely. Only stepping into the share house, what they'd apparently missed was plenty.

"Holy shit!" Jamie shrieked, walking in to discover more people crammed in the common room than she would have thought existed in all of the Hamptons. It reminded her of back when they used to smush as many bodies as they could into a phone booth, only this hardly seemed intentional. Jamie and her friends gazed around in astonishment.

There were people on the couch. There were people by the grouch.

There were people on the ground. There were people sleeping sound.

There were people here and there.

There were people everywhere.

Which, in share house world, could only mean one thing…

"Two Oh Eight North Sea Road just got raided!" a redhead snuggled beneath a sleeping bag shouted, as she'd apparently been doing every five minutes for new arrivals.

"Ohmigod!" Allison gasped, lunging toward Brian (whom Jamie could now recognize huddled around the coffee table with faces she'd actually seen before). But, frozen in alarm, Jamie cautiously took in her surroundings.

"What do you mean, *raided*?" she asked, taking a timid step forward (yet being careful to mind the wall-to-wall human obstacles).

While she imagined the drama had already been rehashed a good dozen times, several strangers spoke up with undimmed enthusiasm.

"The cops busted in at, like, three in the morning!"

"My car got a ticket for two hundred dollars!"

"Two hundred dollars? Now that the house is shut, we've all lost thousands!"

Just as Jamie was struggling to get the facts straight, a guy with squinty eyes and a mop of brown hair (who appeared so high, this all seemed amusing to him rather than frightening) stepped forward. "Basically, the cops came and woke everyone up about an hour ago," he said as matter-of-factly as if he were relaying a movie plot. "Obviously there were people with coke and stuff, but they found, like, a million other health code violations."

"Like what?" Rachel asked, leaning over Jamie's back (and unconsciously digging her nails into Jamie's shoulder).

The guy looked at them as if they'd just asked him something they totally should have known, like the details of human reproduction. "Nothing you don't find in every share house," he said, with a shrug. "They were all like, 'You have fifty people sleeping in thirty beds, and twenty cars in the driveway,' and all these other things they claimed were fire hazards. Also the house was in pretty bad shape—"

"Bad shape?" challenged the redhead buried inside the sleeping bag. Sitting upright, she turned toward Jamie defensively, as if all she needed to vindicate herself was Jamie's approval. "These idiots thought they were such hot shit! They dragged a couch outside, threw all the chairs into the pool, and tore *off* the patio door! Plus, there were so many beer bottles lying everywhere, you would have thought it was a recycling plant!"

"Yeah, but what did us in was the basement," a sullen brunette sitting next to her pointed out, in not much more than a whisper.

"The basement?" Rachel asked, horrified. (Jamie shook her shoulders free of Rachel's hand.)

The chatty redhead elaborated. "Our house managers had the brilliant idea to stack mattresses down there back-to-back—you know, makeshift bedrooms? The cops *flipped* when they found like twenty people down there."

"That's when they started taking down our IDs," the brunette added with a sigh. "They said if the owner doesn't pay the fine and shut the house down, they're going to take us all to court."

"Wait, *court*?" Rachel gasped. "What could they take you to court for?"

Craig, who was standing off to the side with Mark, now sought to nip this kind of panic before it grew contagious. "Nothing will happen to any of you—it's the owner's neck on the line," he said. "Owning share houses in New York State is illegal."

"You keep saying that. But why?" Jamie asked, glancing in Craig and Mark's direction (though making it obvious that her inquiry was addressed only to the former).

"You're not allowed to have more than five unrelated people living under one roof, according to these brothel laws from like the 1900s."

"Well, that's ridiculous! How can you tell someone how many people they can have in their own house?" Rachel said. Though Jamie was puzzling over something else.

"I don't get it. *Everyone* has shares in the Hamptons," she said, scrutinizing the sea of frazzled faces. "What made them target their house of all places?"

"It was the cars," the redhead answered gravely. And as the word reverberated throughout the sudden silence, something in Jamie's stomach tightened. "The reason the cops came in the first place was because we had too many cars parked in the driveway. That's when they found everything else."

From across the room, Jamie could feel Mark's eyes on her. She refused to look up and confirm it.

"That's why we give you guys such a hard time about things," Craig said, as if this fact could justify his gruff personality as well. "Noise, trash, not having more than one car per bedroom plus one extra in the driveway. Things have definitely calmed down since Josh Sagman's day, but this town is still out to get us."

"Who's Josh Sagman?" Jamie asked, thinking it an innocent question (and directing it equally to Mark, whom her eyes engaged pacifistically).

Alarmed, Craig and Mark exchanged uncertain glances. When Craig finally opened his mouth, he reminded Jamie of a kid at a slumber party—at the part when they'd turn off the lights and gather around and someone would freak them out with a ghost story.

"You guys were probably still in college, but it started the summer of 2002," Craig began.

"No, what about Rosebud Lane?" Mark cut in.

"Okay, fine, there was this one house they shut down in 2001. That wasn't such a big deal—they tried to set an example and fined the owners twenty G's. But the summer of 2002 was really when everything changed."

"Oh wait, was this the ABC special?" Rachel interjected. "Because Dana once told me—"

"So this couple moves into East Quogue," Craig continued, shushing her. "And they think they're buying their dream house in this nice quiet neighborhood, when really they're sandwiched in between like ten share houses."

"Our house was right around there, but the worst ones by far were on Jeffrey Lane and Laura Court," Mark added, at which Jamie looked up at him earnestly, any trace of her anger having given way to curiosity.

Craig went on. "Anyway, the minute they discover this, they immediately get the police involved—complaining about the noise, and the garbage, and the nudity, and how people are drinking outside and peeing on their lawn and stuff. They started this huge campaign, but when the police came, the only thing they'd do was give out tickets. They weren't all about shutting down share houses yet."

When Craig paused to regroup, he noticed he'd captured the entire room's attention, and thus continued more animatedly.

"Then out comes this ABC documentary that Barbara

Kopple did on the Hamptons, and one of the characters is this guy Josh Sagman. Great guy, but they depict him as being the stereotypical party animal. They show scenes of him in hot tubs, drinking with packs of people on his porch, and having wild parties with huge speakers at the share house he owns—which just so happens to be right next door to that couple's. So the couple sees it and recognizes him, and takes the tape to the police, and that's when Southampton starts this huge crackdown."

"Yeah, do you remember that night?" Mark exclaimed, shaking it off like a cramp. "All these police and fire marshals and town officials came to bust Josh's house—ten times worse than what happened tonight," he reassured the petrified onlookers.

"Did they arrest his ass?" the boy with the mop of hair asked.

"No, but they charged him with tons of safety violations and fined him like fifty grand," Craig said, defending the severity of the story. "I think he settled because it was selective prosecution, that they only targeted him because he was on TV. But after that, the town shut down like ten other houses that year, and started all these crazy new fines." He paused reminiscently, then added, "Thank God things have calmed down again since that show."

But, as if she'd just been told of a local murder, Rachel hadn't calmed down at all. "So what if that happens again?" she burst. "Like what if the police decide to crack down all over again? Would every share house in the Hamptons be doomed?"

With good reason, the death of his enterprise was a thought Mark didn't want to entertain. "Well, we can only hope for the best," he said.

Craig took a more affirmative stance. "This town would be

nothing without the young people coming out every summer. Just think of all the revenue we bring in!" he huffed, the vehemence of such a large guy a largely scary thing. "If you ask me, by cracking down on the share houses, the town of Southampton is only hurting itself."

"Yeah, but they're never going to learn," Mark said, his eyes grazing against Jamie's as they lapped across the room. "All they're doing is biting the hand that feeds them."

Jamie peered around at the displaced shareholders, who might have been her own shareholders had she not listened to Mark—had he not been persistent when she tried to bite his hand. She flashed him an optimistic smile. "You never know—they might learn."

Chapter Fifteen

Labeling, Allison taught her students, is one of the most fundamental survival mechanisms in nature.

Female songbirds label potential mates based upon the quality of their song. North American skunks wear a distinctive black-and-white-striped pelt as a warning label to predators. And dogs speak to one another's olfactory senses, labeling their territory with strategically placed drops of urine.

Similarly, as Allison learned from the start, labeling in a share house was just as intrinsic a survival mechanism.

There was the labeling of other shareholders (brought about by the proven effectiveness of nicknames, more so than actual ones, as a means to keep track of over fifty rotating roommates). Some with particular resonance:

The "Pale Riders" were three scrawny brunettes who spent a surprising amount of time out by the pool and somehow maintained a deathly white color.

"Turtle Girl" (and "Turtle Girl's Clan"—for anyone associated) was the girl whose face bore an uncanny resemblance to that of said reptile (which comparison Brian had made, and everyone had nodded in instant recognition). Allison might have found this epithet particularly cruel, save for the fact every word out of Turtle Girl's mouth was the snap of an angry tortoise.

"The Dud" was that guy who always seemed to be in the

room (who actually wasn't that bad looking, should he ever surpass the hurdle of speaking).

"Knees" was one of the two Midwesterners, inclined to dance on club benches by opening and closing the knees she kept bent to balance herself. And on the topic of body parts, it's perhaps no great mystery where "Tush" derived from.

Allison's other favorites included "Movado Boy," who was unfortunate enough to lose a Movado watch the very first weekend (yet the real misfortune was that he incessantly revisited the subject); "the Moaner," the girl who emitted foolishly loud moans while hooking up (in a room with upward of five other witnesses); and "the Tenants" (the antisocial girls who lived on their own time clock, whom people only saw in passing, and for whom the house was little other than boarding).

While Allison wasn't responsible for the creation of these catchphrases—that was mostly Brian—she often worried what others had taken to calling her.

Of course, in addition to the labeling of people, there was also the labeling of things.

Not just the labels that are instantly disregarded (like who sleeps where, or whose snacks/toiletries/cigarettes are whose, or which person's towel is intended to save a lounge chair that will immediately be derobed). Although Allison imagined these were all prime instances of labeling as well.

She was thinking of the labeling of things, like canoodles.

What were canoodles? The long, noodle-like flotation devices were initially used in the pool, but it wasn't long before they doubled as weapons in the season's most massive cock-fight (where the guys hoisted the girls on their shoulders to battle). After giving rise to such a sexually charged activity, *ca-noodles* appeared the more fitting description for them.

Then there was the labeling of things, like vodka.

Or better yet, the mislabeling. For once, right before a pre-drink, Mark was caught pouring cheap no-name vodka into empty Ketel One bottles. And because the free top-shelf alcohol was an integral part of the share house package, this was quite a considerable offense. When people requested a refund, this never happened again.

And most ridiculously of all, there was the labeling of a certain slang-like saying as "the replacement game."

Here's how it worked. Make a broad statement ("Can *everyone* stop throwing themselves at me?"), then clarify it by using the phrase "And by ___, I mean ___." ("And by *everyone,* I mean Dave.") Fine, definitely the by-product of endless hours in the sun. But a few weeks into the summer, Allison noticed everyone doing it. (And by *everyone,* she meant only the cool people.)

However, more offensive than the labeling of people, more offensive than the labeling of things...was the labeling of people as if they were things. (Things belonging to other people.)

Now, up until this point, Allison had been far removed from the Hamptons' meat-market scene (she and Brian having excused themselves since establishing their *relationship* title weeks ago). So really, it was only upon the arrival of Brian's friend Zach that Allison learned of the territory labeling that is "calling dibs."

It was the third weekend in July that Zach's visit took place. And it was the moment he pulled up in his brand-new Mercedes convertible (and refused to park it—even momentarily—where dust could dull its shiny exterior) that Allison realized she didn't like him.

After her initial alarm because, well, birds of a feather flocked together, a whole slew of realizations followed on Allison's part, all pertaining to Brian. All pertaining to the fact that, despite having been thrilled to finally seal their status

("Are we together?" he'd proposed one night out of the blue. "Yeah...I think we're together," she'd agreed, without missing a beat), Allison barely knew him at all.

"This is Allison, my *girlfriend*," Brian introduced after greeting his former fraternity brother with a cordial slap on the back.

Allison beamed—less at the prospect of meeting the Mercedes owner (who was anxiously glancing around as if a carjacker might jump out of the bushes) than at hearing the word *girlfriend* spoken aloud. This was—almost—enough to give Zach the benefit of the doubt.

But whether Zach would give her the benefit of the doubt was unclear. Tearing himself away from his vehicle, he unapologetically looked her up and down, though his eyes were masked by dark-tinted Ray-Bans.

While awaiting the verdict he was so blatantly formulating, Allison studied him as well. She could tell his short brown hair had been recently cut, given the perfect square his hairline formed on the back of his neck. And his toned, medium build was accentuated by a fitted navy polo shirt so crisp, it looked like his mother had ironed it. Apparently, clothes were on Zach's mind as well.

"Theory?" he said, chomping loudly on mint-smelling gum.

"Excuse me?" Allison asked, expecting his first word to her to be something more like...hello.

"Your shirt. Theory?" he expounded before giving a quick glance to the Mercedes.

"Oh. I don't think so," she answered, of the tank top she'd purchased years ago at someplace like Macy's. Instantly self-conscious, she pushed the hair she wished she'd blown-dry back behind her ear.

"Looks like it. I dated a girl who worked there," he said. He turned to Brian before adding "Jackie" and flashing a grin so scandalous, Allison believed whatever story was tied to the name was one she was better off not knowing. Afterward, his face held a residual smile, broadcasting a row of perfectly straight white teeth (albeit a bit too big for his face, like someone had replaced his real ones with tooth-colored Chiclets). Then, as if Allison had simply vanished into the background, Zach began to talk to Brian about people she didn't know, in contexts she didn't understand.

As she stood there feeling both uncomfortable and extraneous, she reflected for a moment how, despite his numerous flaws, Josh had always been considerate enough to include her in all conversations. She was relieved to hear the front door slam and to see Aaron and Steve trudging down the steps.

"Hey," she said, approaching them perhaps more enthusiastically than she ever had before. Unfazed, they halted and exchanged polite conversation the way she'd known they would. They were the first two people she'd met at the pre-drink back in May, and whether they recognized it or not, she felt they all shared something of a bond because of it.

While Aaron ran off to bring around his car, Steve stood waiting beside her, probably because he could tell she wanted him to. And as they spoke, Allison recalled exactly how much she liked him. A short, broad-shouldered, yet un-athletic-seeming guy with a noble face, Steve always looked a little too run-down and a lot too tired (he was a banker, after all), and—on account of the BlackBerry he clutched like an atom bomb—like he was often afraid of his own shadow. But there was also a reserved maturity to him, and his manners reminded Allison of an Old World gentleman—the kind of guy who would hold doors open on dates or help an old lady cross the street; who'd really listen and never repeat whatever you told him. The kind of guy you could never imagine breaking a girl's heart for fun.

In the house there was an unofficial rivalry between the state-school frat guys like Brian and crew and the Ivy League investment bankers like Steve and his friends. The state-school guys were older and louder and larger in both size and number, but also resentful of the bankers, who were five years their junior and making double their salaries. As a result, the bankers were quieter and more vigilant, most often scene spectators rather than orchestrators.

This rivalry was something Allison suspected was a factor in Brian's pulling her over as soon as Zach drove off in search of a less threatening parking option.

"What were you talking about with him?" he demanded.

At this, Allison was startled. "Who? Steve?"

"Sure, *Steve*," Brian repeated, as if to humor her with his name. "You know, I just introduced you to one of my best friends as my girlfriend"—he paused conspicuously to heighten the label—"and then you wander away to talk to, like, the *coolest* guy in the house. Nice."

"Sorry," Allison said, caught off-guard by the foreignness of his jealousy. "It looked like you guys were catching up."

Shrugging it off with an insincere "whatever," Brian seemed to dismiss the matter entirely. But it remained on Allison's mind all afternoon.

On Zach's mind, however, was something far more transparent. And the moment they walked through the door (actually, even while ascending the front steps), he got right down to business.

"So, do you have any hot friends?" he asked Allison, opting again to acknowledge her existence.

"Definitely," she answered—the way you always answer

when a guy asks you that, if only out of loyalty. Though whether the housemates were hot or not didn't matter as much as their romantic status, and Zach was soon brought up to speed on an outsider's boundaries.

He first took an interest in Jamie. Fighting the urge to intercept, Allison watched as he bombarded her with the bland sequence of preliminary questions most people asked—you know, where you're from, what you do, at which of the twenty or so popular universities you squandered away your parents' money. But as Jamie answered, the wheels in Zach's mind appeared still hard at work—as if he was running her qualifications through his head and deliberating whether or not she was worthy of his attention. Apparently she was, because the profound interrogation continued.

"Who makes that skirt?" he asked Jamie, and Allison again cringed at his question. But Jamie showed no reserve in answering, "It's Alice and Olivia." Frustrated, Allison was awaiting the moment Jamie would just shoot him down already. Only that's when it hit her. Jamie may have been clearly involving herself with Jeff, but there was no easy way she could label it ("I don't have a boyfriend...but I do have a recurrent Hamptons-hookup situation you should know about"?). And so Allison advised Brian he should probably clue Zach in.

"Dude, she's already hooking up with someone in this house," Brian said as they escorted him upstairs to put down his things. "That guy Jeff you met."

Letting out a hearty chuckle, Zach seemed to find his friend's warning particularly amusing. "And by *hooking up,* you mean 'kissed once'?"

"No, by *hooking up* I mean done. Off-limits. In-house territory."

Naturally, Zach wasn't thrilled to hear it. But aware that the early bird makes out with the worm, and assuming the week-end would bring plenty of other opportunities, Zach hardly minded this one restriction.

He was only first learning the laws of the jungle.

Later, when they were basking on lounge chairs during the guys' brief volleyball interlude (Allison to Brian's right, and Zach, Dave, and Rob sprawled out in a line to his left), Allison followed Zach's gaze all the way to Tara/Jocelyn (whichever one was currently hooking up with Josh). This time, however, Zach knew to preface his interest with inquiry.

"What's her story?"

Brian, Dave, and Rob all exchanged glances, as if drawing straws over who had to tell Zach the news.

"In house," Brian said. And, rather unnecessarily, he jerked his head upward and gestured to Josh with his chin. "She's hooking up with that loser."

Not wasting any time, Zach transferred his gaze to a blonde in a black cutout bikini. "Blonde, ten o'clock?" As he said this, the girl they called Tush got up and exposed her hefty rear end. "Screw that. Her?" He pointed to one of the Turtle Clan.

Alarmed, Rob rose up in his chair. "That's the girl I've been talking to on Friendster."

"Damn," Zach exclaimed, with a hostility Allison thought warranted only by car damage. But then he jokingly raised an eyebrow at the three Pale Riders, playing (unseductively) at the pool's edge with the canoodles. "Don't tell me they're off-limits, too?"

"Nope," Dave decreed, flipping open his palm in presenta-tion. "All yours."

Unfortunately, Dave's generosity didn't exactly extend to Star Room that evening. Walking in, at first Zach seemed relieved by the plethora of (unmarked) possibilities. And, drunk as a skunk off the abundance of Ketel One vodka he'd consumed during the pre-game, he soon worked up the nerve to approach a girl in a—Dolce & Gabbana?—floral wrap top. But after he rejoined the group following a lengthy conversation, Dave was quick to set him straight.

"You can't go there," he said. "That's the girl I hooked up with at Marquee two months ago. I've been meaning to hit that up again."

"Bullshit," Zach said, his patience growing thin.

Dave scrolled furiously through his phone, working himself up into a noticeable frenzy. "See? I have her right here. Jenn Marquee, two stars."

Though she'd attempted to stay out of the conversation, this was enough to make Allison break her silence. "Two stars?" she gasped, and even though it rang out like a question, the only item in question was his nerve.

"Relax, two stars is good," Dave assured her, defending the rating more so than the necessity to assign one. "I only give three stars to, like, models or celebrities." Remembering the conflict, he turned abrasively to Zach. "Anyway, I've got dibs."

"Fuck that," Zach said. "You can't call dibs on every girl in the Hamptons." As if a happiness spell had just washed over him, he smiled that scandalous, big-toothed smile. "I'm going to hook up with her."

Before Dave could react, Zach ran off. Outraged, Dave bolted behind him.

Now left alone with Brian, Allison couldn't shake her disgust. She felt almost as if she'd intruded on something inherently male that no girl should have to observe.

"Calling dibs? Do you guys really do that?" Allison confronted her boyfriend, whose gaze seemed to be stuck in the direction his friends had disappeared. "How can guys stake claims without considering what the girls want? Don't they realize girls will like who they're going to like, no matter who called dibs?"

Brian simply shrugged as if to say *What are you gonna do?* Then, excusing himself, he promptly sprinted off so as not to miss another minute of the pissing contest.

Allison wandered back over to find her friends, who were stationed around the communal house table. Though it wasn't long before she found herself in conversation with Steve.

This wasn't all that surprising, as talking to Steve was practically effortless. True, she didn't feel the same excitement she felt when speaking to other guys, but none of the nervousness, either. As if he'd been a psychotherapist in another lifetime, Steve lacked any inclination to be judgmental, prompting her to freely let her guard down. Prompting her to feel—undilutedly—like herself. And as she spoke, he received her words with an attentiveness she found refreshing—highly contrary to Brian, who was often more preoccupied with what he planned to say next.

Though at one point Allison was startled to look up and discover Brian glaring at her from across the room. Angrily, he about-faced and retreated off in a juvenile huff. However, this time, Allison felt not guilt but indignation, deciding they would have to later discuss exactly what a relationship entailed.

And even though Brian was the one overreacting, so as not to be held culpable, Allison wanted to make sure Steve knew where he stood. Awkward as it was, she laid it all out there.

"I'm not sure if you knew this. But Brian"—she pointed to the spot where he'd been standing—"is my boyfriend."

"Yeah, I know," he said even-temperedly. "He made that pretty clear at the meet and greet."

"What do you mean?" she asked, assuming that Steve had observed their chemistry even then.

Steve hesitated, then proceeded anyway. "He called dibs on you at DIP that night. Said you two had something, and told all the other guys who might have been interested to back off." Color rushed to his face, and he flashed her a shy smile.

"*What?*" Allison spat, not sure if she was flattered or stunned. Perhaps she was a bit of both. "I had no idea." Then she added, "And people just listen? What if I wasn't into him?"

Steve shrugged. "Apparently he was right."

But was he? Allison wondered. Now recalling what she'd said about "dibs" moments ago, she felt like a fool. Instantly, she flashed back to that initial meet-and-greet night—to every subsequent night. Come to think of it, had Brian really chosen her, and not vice versa? Had it really been about him, or had he just so happened to be in the right place at the right time? And as everyone kept suggesting to her, had they really needed to rush into a relationship so fast?

Still, when Brian found her again, wrapping his arms around her shoulders in an offering of truce, every last reservation melted away. And as he relayed how Zach had triumphed and escorted the girl home, she was reminded how grateful she was to no longer be on a wild goose chase.

This was enough to dismiss Steve's shocking comment, and the immature way Brian had acted. The former she'd relegated to a compliment, and the latter was merely in the nature of the beast: jealousy in a relationship was just something she should expect.

So Allison put it all behind her—until back at the house that night, when she discovered something she absolutely *didn't* expect. Lounging on Brian's bed while he was changing, she leaned her arm back and onto a piece of clothing. Uncrumpling it, she saw it was a navy blue polo shirt. "Is this yours?" she called out to him.

Brian stuck his head out of the closet. "No, I think that's Zach's."

Laying it out to fold, on closer inspection, Allison noticed that a corner of the John Varvatos label was becoming detached. Taking it upon herself to peel it (in the way a label shouldn't peel), she revealed—lo and behold—an Old Navy one beneath it. Speechless, she held the shirt far from her body like some kind of explosive.

What was this? To think that someone so morbidly fascinated with designers was himself an impostor!

Snapping alert as Brian joined her on the bed, she stood up momentarily so he could pull back the sheets. "Coming? Or are you planning to bunk with some dork down the hall? And by *dork*, I mean *Steve*."

Ignoring his comment, Allison debated showing her discovery to Brian. She decided not to, as it wasn't her style to mock someone's designer deficiency, and instead left it to nature to take its course.

Still mystified, Allison tossed the shirt onto Zach's luggage. And as she climbed into bed with Brian—the guy she wasn't sure she was in love with, yet who held the title of her boyfriend—Allison couldn't imagine why anyone would be so desperate for a label.

Chapter
Sixteen

When the lights go out, when the sun goes down, there is a dark side to the Hamptons share house. A mysterious side, an illegitimate side, a scary side. A side no one dared acknowledge, but that Rachel knew existed all the same: at night, in private, behind closed doors.

For such reasons, she'd learned at the summer's onset to close—and lock—her own prior to falling sleep. On occasions it escaped her—occasions like tonight. And that meant she was guaranteed a visit from a certain uninvited guest.

"Dave, *get out*!" she shrieked, pushing his face away from her neck and rolling his body forcefully over the bed's edge. It hit the floor solidly, with one loud thump: the signature thump of the notorious late-night bed-hopper.

Renowned for preying on girls in their sleep, Dave—fueled by both his intoxication level and his unruly hormones—would slip silently into shareholders' beds and rouse them for some last-minute late-night action. More shocking than the significant number who thrust him violently to the floor was the 50 percent whom Dave alleged did not reject his efforts.

Rachel never had been, and never would be, one of them.

"Get out!" she screamed again when he rose from the ground only to creep back in her direction. "Go try some other girl's bed!"

She was only kidding, but as he slammed the door shut and stumbled noisily down the hall, Rachel imagined that was his exact intention. Wiping her neck clean of his saliva, it never failed to repulse her how, after *normal* people had surrendered all hopes of a romantic connection and retired for the evening, the bed-hopper's hunt for chemistry was only beginning.

And as a result, Rachel's night's sleep had been brought to a premature end. She grabbed her cell phone, nestled in its charger beside her, and was outraged to see that it was 4:58 AM. But quickly her anger gave way to an entirely different emotion: fear.

More accurately, 5 AM fear. Fear, incited by the very hour in a share house that unnerved Rachel the most. The hour she'd seldom actually experienced, but—on account of others' horrific tales—preferred to pass in her bed, fast asleep. The hour when nothing good ever happened, and everything unkosher (sexual, illegal, or belligerent) always seemed to. The wheeling-and-dealing Hamptons witching hour, now upon her.

Peering around the dark, silent room did nothing to calm her fears when she found herself alone. This wasn't exactly a shocking development; she presumed Jamie was sleeping in another room with Jeff, and Allison in yet another one with Brian. But, as uncomfortable as bunking with a couple had always made her, it was even worse not to have at least one of her friends beside her. In fact, even at a loss for bed-deprived drunken strangers, Rachel found sleeping alone in a room in the Hamptons to be much like getting a great table in an empty restaurant: in theory you should like it, but something about the vacancy weirds you out.

Not to mention the fact that it was freezing. And not just throw-on-a-sweatshirt-for-the-summer-breeze freezing—more like middle-of-the-winter-in-Alaska freezing. But it was just the luck of the draw that they'd gotten a room with exceptional air-conditioning (the central air was pumped extra

high, to make up for rooms like Craig's, in which it supposedly "barely pumped at all"). And so, rolling her body into a
ball and huddling under her nonexistent sheet (which she'd
brought instead of a comforter, because it was easier to pack),
Rachel longed for the big poufy bedding back at her room
in the city. That, in addition to a winter coat, scarf, hat, and
gloves. Maybe she shouldn't have spurned the bed-hopper's
efforts, if only for sake of body heat!

But she and Dave weren't the only two awake. As Rachel
lay there shivering, she felt like a spy eavesdropping on the
sounds the door didn't stifle, the voices of gung-ho partiers
attempting to fend off morning. Oddly, she'd never wanted
to be among them, but somehow, being without her friends
in this scenario made her suddenly fearful of being discovered—as if she were hiding. As if they were the cool kids
who stayed up at night doing cool things, and she was an
uptight loser whose true prudish nature would be revealed
when they opened the door. Finding her there, alone.

Dana would never be alone if she were here, Rachel instantly
thought, turning over. Dana simply wasn't the "lonely" type.
Rather, she was the type who'd likely be off with some guy,
who would rise late the next day after a roguishly sleepless
night and relay the details of all that had transpired in the
interim to some Rachel type—the type who would pop up
first thing with the sun, feeling (shamefully) rested. Why
couldn't she be more like Dana? Rachel wondered. Why did
she have to be lonely? But of course, Rachel knew why. It
was because, in a share house, the opposite of loneliness was
promiscuity.

But even that she was beginning to reconsider. What was
the big deal with hooking up anyway? she now wondered.
Why *hadn't* she just paired off with someone—perhaps even
Aaron, who'd recently almost redeemed himself. Conjuring up

his schoolboy face, Rachel tried to envision what it would be like sleeping in his bed with him, and (considering the alternative) wasn't all that opposed to the idea. At that moment, Rachel wished she were anywhere rather than here—with anybody rather than nobody. Why, any body at all.

Unable to fall back asleep for what felt like a lifetime, Rachel waited until her bladder was nearly ready to burst (and the voices outside had practically quieted) before venturing to the bathroom. Raising her head from the tiny square throw pillow she'd grabbed from the couch (only fractionally as comfortable as the one she should have brought from her bed at home), Rachel rose to her feet. Poking her head outside her door, she was surprised to find not a single other person. Assuming she was in the clear, she rounded the bend and glanced down the long narrow hallway, only to spot the figures. Well, the backs of the shirts of the figures. She recognized those shirts from earlier that night at the pre-drink, as well as the door they were standing in front of. Then she watched as Aaron and Steve (who'd broken off from the group that night) led two stylish brunettes inside their room and closed the door.

The sound of the door clicking shut sent a chill throughout Rachel's already arctic body. She scurried the rest of the way to the bathroom, feeling her pulse race as she locked herself inside it. Letting out the breath she didn't realize she'd been holding, Rachel stared questioningly back at her reflection (which really wasn't so repulsive?). Her mind flashed back to the disturbing scene she'd just witnessed. *Who were those girls?* she asked the face in the mirror gazing back at her. And what were they doing—what was Aaron doing—behind that closed door?

Surely he was hooking up, she told herself. (The way you tell yourself you flunked an exam so your B− doesn't feel that bad.) It would have been foolish of her to assume otherwise (though they honestly could have just been friends, in dire need of a place to crash...she really couldn't know for sure). Or maybe he hooked up all the time, maybe he more than just hooked up, maybe there was more than just one bed-hopper in this share house. And maybe it was now entirely too late for Rachel to care.

Moving aside no fewer than five used beer cups, Rachel washed her hands and face in the sink. Still, the girl in the glass remained just as mystified. This was ridiculous! She could have hooked up with him weeks ago if that's what she wanted...*was* that what she wanted? He had clearly liked her, and she was the one who shut that door, who forced him to pick a different door—a wrong one—and to do behind it...well, that was the question.

Deciding she couldn't mull this over in the bathroom all night, Rachel slowly retreated to her room. With each step, her bare sole against the wood produced a soft rhythmic creak—one that was instantly drowned out by an obscenely loud knocking. And once more, Rachel found herself stopped in her tracks.

The knocking clearly emanated from downstairs, clearly from the front door. This was disconcerting, because it immediately told Rachel this wasn't someone who belonged. The fact that the door was always left unlocked was something the impostor had yet to discover, but in a matter of minutes probably would.

Ignore it, Rachel thought, taking another step forward. As if the knocker could sense this, the pounding (of a varied pitch) sounded this time from the window—its instigator having cleverly shifted a significant two feet over. That's around when Rachel realized this person wasn't going anywhere.

Fleeing to the stairwell and draping herself over the banister,

Rachel could see the door quake as the knocker returned. It grew louder and louder from neglect, to the point it sounded violent. But as if her feet were superglued to the floor and her hands to the railing, Rachel couldn't move.

It was now abundantly clear that in the event of a real emergency, rather than being that person who springs heroically to action, Rachel would be one of the dopes on the sidelines paralyzed by hysteria. But why should she open it? She wasn't expecting any 5 AM visitors! Who the hell came over a share house at 5 AM anyway? And—as she turned her body frantically from left to right—where on earth were the dozens of other people she knew were staying here?

But her soliloquy was cut short by the sound of the doorknob jiggling, succeeded by that ear-piercing squeak—not unlike that of sneakers against a gym floor—of the door cracking open.

It was the longest moment of her twenty-four years so far, and Rachel never had again such a near-death sensation. For, from the top of the banister, she silently watched as the interloper traipsed in: not a twentysomething kid, as she'd until now been expecting, but rather a man. A ruggedly clothed, wild-haired bear of a man who, stepping inside and glaring around bewilderedly, pinned his gaze on her like a hunter registering his target.

But Rachel breathed a sigh of relief when the man extended his right arm, his right hand, revealing two (of four) chubby fingers.

"Chuck!" she exclaimed, sauntering fearlessly down to greet him. She'd made it about halfway when she regretted letting her guard down.

Flailing his unintended peace sign in the air haphazardly, he was nothing (short of a finger loss) at all reminiscent of their beloved cabdriver. His words did little to better his case.

"I need *two boys!*" he wailed, like a monster needing to be fed.

Maintaining her distance, Rachel fearfully studied his inflamed face and roaming eyes. Though, rather than thinking him possessed, or the victim of a raging werewolf, Rachel's first impulse was gratitude—that she wasn't a boy.

"*Two boys!*" he bellowed again, roaming the room. He dragged out the endings of his syllables the way a megaphone might. "I need *two boooys* for *Quooogue!*"

Rachel imagined that, even if there had been two boys in this house with the intention of going to Quogue, hearing this frightening call would most certainly dissuade them.

But as he locked his gaze on her again and wiped his perpetually wet forehead, Rachel felt compelled to respond. "Uh, okay...two boys for Quogue?" she repeated.

Chuck nodded in creepy slow motion.

"Well, um, I don't think anyone called for a cab here. But I can go check." Not waiting to hear his response, she darted back upstairs as if she almost expected him to chase after her.

He didn't, but that didn't stop her from bolting frantically down the hall anyway. "Anyone order a cab?" she cried to no one in particular. Her words rang out unanswered.

Shuffling through the dining room (scattered with sleeping people), Rachel stomped her feet conspicuously in the hope she might rouse someone. Approaching the row of bedrooms, she searched for any signs of life.

Fortunately, she discerned the sounds of people behind one. Tapping the door gently, she grabbed the doorknob. For better or worse, it wasn't locked.

"Ohmigod!" Rachel shrieked, and slammed it right shut again. Without a doubt, it was the wrong door. Clearly neither of the two naked couples (one positioned on one bed, the second on the other)—who were simultaneously and unselfconsciously engaged in intercourse—were in need of a cab at that particular moment. And clearly Rachel had been unaware that this dark dank double, devoid of windows or its assigned occupants, functioned as the unofficial f...ooling around...room.

She would be sure to keep that in mind for future reference.

Continuing on down the hallway in less a frenzy than a daze, Rachel debated waking Mark—whose own door was always locked from the mysteriously early hour he'd disappear from the clubs—when she saw the light. Seeping through the cracks of a doorway, it was something she'd moments ago have considered a good sign...back before she was inclined to presume the worst. So she gave a hard knock, and (having learned her lesson) waited.

"Come in," someone yelled. (Good sign number two?)

Nevertheless envisioning naked debauchery as she opened it, an inch at a time, Rachel was relieved to find just four people, hanging out—rather than copulating.

"Oh good!" Taking a bold step forward, Rachel examined the four familiar faces: two girls with too much color to whom she'd never formally been introduced, and two frat guys who often idled away the day playing the horseshoe game Mark set up by the pool for money. "Do you guys know if anyone ordered a cab to Quogue? Chuck is downstairs...only he's acting really crazy, like he's on crack or something!"

But no sooner had she said this than out of the corner of her eye she spotted a rolled-up five-dollar bill on the floor. Her first instinct was to pick it up, until she realized it was tightly, deliberately rolled. Rachel was rather naive about drugs, having never even smoked anything other than a cigarette or two, so this was about as scary as spotting a revolver on the floor. Then as she noted the powder-tinged glass mirror on the nightstand five feet from them, she had an all-too-delayed epiphany.

"Want some?" one of the guys asked her, as if a bribe to keep his secret.

"I'm okay, thanks," Rachel said, making her way out (and sounding nowhere near as casual as she had intended). While she knew certain share houses were notorious for their open-door drug policy, Rachel had never suspected people did them in this house. Ashamed at her ignorance, she supposed that, like in college dorms, Mark simply couldn't control what people did behind closed doors. But for tonight, she was through trying to find out.

Emboldened by having made one too many unsavory discoveries (what had she expected to find at 5 AM anyway?), Rachel hung herself over the stairwell.

"I'm sorry, there aren't...*two boys for Quogue* here," she called down to Chuck, whose eerie voice she still heard in her head. "You must have the wrong house," she concluded before turning her back to him and starting away. Afraid he wasn't going to leave, when she peeked around again she was pleased (and genuinely surprised) to find him doing just that.

Though, returning to her room, her pulse still racing, she discovered Dave sprawled out on her bed.

"Get out!" she shrieked, pounding the mattress with her arm (and wondering where—or in whose bed—Dave had until this point been hiding).

As she locked the door behind him, Rachel assumed this to be the last of the bed-hopper's mischief—the last of the night's mischief. But as soon as she settled down again beneath her sheet, the silence was punctuated by a resounding howl. And it wasn't until the next morning that Rachel (and everyone else) learned why.

Determined not to admit defeat, Dave apparently stumbled

down the hall, testing out several doorknobs before discovering an unlocked one.

Undetected, he slipped inside the room belonging to the Turtle Girl's Clan, aware that Melissa, the only attractive one, slept in the bed closest to the window.

Every night but tonight.

Dave tiptoed over and lifted the covers, preparing to climb into bed beside her. He was astonished at what he found.

Not Melissa (who was hooking up with Movado Boy downstairs), nor her other two roommates (sleeping in their correct beds), but instead Aaron. Aaron, who'd moved over to Melissa's bed so the *friend* of the girl Steve was hooking up with could have her own bed.

Aaron, whom Rachel once again saw in a good light.

It was the last door opened by the bed-hopper, that night. But on nights henceforth, *both* male and female shareholders took to locking their doors more diligently. Well, shareholders other than Rachel, who began to wonder if hers had been locked too tightly.

For, true, picking the wrong door is a scary prospect—especially when you have no idea what lies behind it. But rather than close a door, Rachel was ready to open a new one.

Chapter Seventeen

In the self-contained ecosystem that is a Hamptons share house, the need seldom exists to venture past a few basic locations: the bagel store, the twenty-four-hour diner, the stand where you can buy cigarettes for only three dollars a pack, and the handful of popular nightclubs (which themselves serve as each town's most pivotal landmark).

These reference points any shareholder could navigate blindfolded; these reference points any shareholder was *expected* to know. But everything else, everything unfamiliar, fell into a gray area.

Thus, come the first weekend in August (when Jamie realized their weekend excursions to "the beach" had yet to include an actual trip to one), she set about redefining life beyond 1088 Montauk.

"Does anyone know where there's a beach around here?" she asked one Sunday morning, to the sea of motionless bodies draped lazily around the pool.

As if she'd just proposed *Who wants to run a lap around the town?* nobody budged. They were too busy offering their skin to the sun, or rehydrating with gargantuan bottles of Poland Spring or VitaminWater, and speaking proved entirely too taxing.

Throwing her head back in frustration, Jamie looked to her friends, who'd by now joined her on the patio. Allison crept over to Brian, who was sprawled out facedown on one of the lounge chairs. "Want to come with us to the beach?" she said sweetly, massaging his shoulders with her hands.

But, as if unable to move any other part of his body, he slowly shook his head from right to left. Would no one help them?

Shifting the weight of her beach bag, Jamie surveyed the idleness a share house was only capable of in the AM. This was harder than rousing the attention of a guy during a sporting event! "No one knows where there's a beach in the Hamptons?" she called out again, louder.

"Shh! What do you need to go to a beach for?" Rob finally responded, pushing his cap to the brim of his head.

"Because I'm sick of looking at your navy-blue bathing suit every single weekend," she joked. Noticing she was standing dangerously close to the edge of the pool to be making such a comment, Jamie hurried to qualify it. "It's just, we *always* lie out by the pool."

Rob merely yawned, repositioning his hat to cover his face. "Oh, stop complaining," came his muffled voice through the fabric.

Jamie seethed, because really, she hadn't been. *Complaining* would have been pointing out how it was beyond hot, or how there was virtually no breeze, or how this musty, fly-ridden pool area reeked of dirty, sweaty bodies and a weekend's worth of tequila. (Again, that was only *if* she were complaining.)

But just as she was about to...comment...on how preposterous it was that not a single person could so much as point them in the right direction...

"You're looking for a beach?" Dave called out from a lounge chair a few rows away. When she nodded eagerly, he waved her over.

This unfortunately involved circumventing Ilana and the

Tara/Jocelyns, whose iPod earphones (with lowered volume) did little to disguise their insatiable hunger for gossip. But it was just as well, for Jamie's feigned indifference did little to disguise her raging hatred.

When she negotiated her way through the maze, Dave made this big show of raising himself upright and shifting his legs so she could squeeze on the end of his lounge chair.

"Okay, ready?" Opening his eyes wide, he engaged hers intently, as if he was about to tell her a secret. "First, when you come out of the driveway, make a right."

"Wait!" Jamie turned to her friends, lingering in limbo behind her. "You guys, come here. I'm not going to remember this."

Once Dave had commanded all three girls' attention, he continued. "So, you make that first right, then continue all the way down Montauk Highway to the 7-Eleven."

7-Eleven, 7-Eleven, Jamie tried to remember.

"Then make a left, cross the train tracks, then another left." He paused and looked up at them. "Did you get all that?"

They nodded simultaneously.

"Well, actually"—he gazed off into the distance, as if suddenly recalling a better route—"actually...I'm just messing around." His serious face broke into a devilish smile (one no one else cared to reciprocate).

Smacking him on the shoulder, Jamie rose to her feet. "Does anyone here *really* know how to get to a beach?" She flashed him a reproachful look.

"Aaask Maaark," Brian droned in a nasally voice.

Upon this suggestion, Jamie scanned the twenty or so people. "Where *is* Mark?"

"Oh, I heard him leave the house at like nine this morning to run errands," said Rachel, who slept less than anyone Jamie knew.

Jamie raised an eyebrow. "And by *running errands,* you mean driving home his girl from last night?"

"I have no idea. I think Craig was with him, though." Rachel shrugged.

"Shady!" Jamie exclaimed. It was the word they most often used to describe Mark.

But just as she was debating which local store would be able to give the best directions, one of the Tenants (the girls who scarcely made an effort to interact with the rest of the house) glanced up from her *Life&Style Weekly.*

"You know, I think there's a beach on Dune Road," she said, as if just now registering Jamie's request.

Jamie pounced. "Wait, where?"

Scurrying over, for the first time all summer Jamie was afforded a close-up of her face (which, perhaps due to her slightly older age or dauntingly even tan or flashy designer sunglasses, carried an innate credibility). Though as she spoke, Jamie was conscious of little other than the ostentatious double C's staring back at her (which she supposed, was the whole point of wearing Chanel). "Do you know where the Saks is?" she began.

"There's a *Saks* here?" Jamie shrieked. This was more exciting a prospect than the beach!

"Yeah, right by the movie theater." Movie theater? "Haven't you ever driven to town?" the girl asked, noting Jamie's bewildered expression.

Jamie shook her head. She was happy when they made it to the share house without a problem.

"Well, don't quote me because I've never been there," the Tenant said, gathering her honey-blond curls into a ponytail only to shake them out again, "but I'm pretty sure if you follow Montauk Highway east and turn right on First Neck Lane, there's a beach on the end of that road. *Dune* Road. At least, I always see the signs."

"Okay, cool. Thanks." Satisfied, Jamie turned toward her friends with new conviction. "So we should probably bring a blanket. And let's stop at Goldberg's for food…"

"Wait, are you seriously going?" Rob called, flipping up his hat again.

Seeing she'd piqued his interest, Jamie couldn't resist a smirk. "I thought you liked the pool?"

But from the chair next to him, Brian rose slowly, dismissing his whole "languid" act like a kid caught pretending to be sick who instantly snaps to. "Fine, I'll go."

"Well, if you're going, I'm going," Rob joked, jumping to his feet. He began to collect his things.

Observing this mass exodus from their horseshoe game a few yards away, a trio of frat-type guys clonked down some metal pieces and headed toward them. "Yo, where are you going?" they yelled as they approached, presumably fearful of missing a food run.

Rob yanked a T-shirt over his head. "Beach."

Confused expressions all around. "What beach?"

And from the inquisitive girls lying next to them: "*Where* is there a beach?"

And from a pack across the pool: "*Who's* going to the beach?"

And one by one, the dominoes fell. When one person in a share house had an idea, it spread through the group faster than cold germs. Until—by virtue of no one wanting to be left behind—it gained enough momentum to qualify as a field trip.

This being the case, Jamie hurried inside to wake Jeff (whose bed she'd left not even an hour ago). But when she discovered only his crumpled sheets, she wandered back out again.

It always impressed her how, no matter what the time of

day, no matter what he was wearing (which was usually either a white or gray T-shirt), Jeff always seemed to be the model of male attractiveness. The one who would easily (though not unknowingly) outshine every other guy unfortunate enough to be in a room beside him. And it wasn't just his clear blue eyes or straight white teeth; it was the overall flawlessness of his package that made it impossible not to stare at him. It was as if you'd spotted a movie star in person, searched for imperfections, and realized in awe that the camera wasn't hiding anything.

But what didn't impress Jamie was that she found him standing with none other than her least favorite person. Jeff had stopped talking to Ilana for, like, a second following the hot tub incident—but now held her in even higher esteem because of it, since to the males in the house he'd become a celebrity.

Jamie, on the other hand, continued to ignore her—what earned a guy the reputation of pimp made a girl come across as a slut. "Guess what. We're all going to the beach," she informed him, smiling as she crossed the evacuated patio.

Furrowing his brow, he stared at her as if she'd just presented him with some complicated math problem. "Where is there a beach?"

Glancing over at the Tenant, Jamie found her positioning unaltered. "Well, we're not exactly sure. But she"—Jamie gestured to the girl whose name she still didn't know and realistically probably never would—"said there's one on Dune Road, not that far from here."

"I think," the girl called out.

"She thinks," Jamie corrected.

"Who's going?" He fixated his gaze on her in a way that suddenly made her conscious of it. She hoped he couldn't notice this.

"Everyone," she said, secretly wondering why the fact that *she was* wasn't enough. "It started out like three of us, now it's more like thirty."

"Cool." Jeff turned to Ilana and company, to whom Jamie expected he would promptly excuse himself. "Beach?"

Looking about as stunned as Jamie felt, Ilana wound down her (already low) iPod volume. "Where are you going?" she asked, even though someone would've had to be deaf to have missed the commotion before.

"Beach."

Flattered to receive a formal invitation, Ilana turned and consulted the (similarly brightly bandeau'd, equally prissy) brunette stick figures poised next to her. "Yeah, okay," she agreed, despite the fact Jamie had been silently willing her to say no.

"Great," Jamie coughed up. Let the games begin!

Which they did, only not quite yet. For also in the way of field trips, anything involving masses of people required extensive packing and changing and stopping for food at a variety of places, and consequently missing, like, two hours of sun. But at long last a huge lineup of cars (because no one wanted to have to stay at the beach a minute longer than desired) followed Jamie, Allison, and Rachel down the consistently clogged Montauk Highway. Having insisted on leading the pack (it was her idea, after all), Jamie did exactly as she was instructed: she turned off Montauk Highway onto First Neck Lane, and took the road all the way down. Until, believe it or not (and only upon discovering a sign bearing the aforementioned name did she), they made it to Dune Road. Following the traffic flow into a busy parking lot, Jamie pulled up to the gate and triumphantly rolled down her window.

That's when the gray cloud settled over their party.

"Do you have a permit?" the gruff older woman manning the entrance barked after bending over to glance at her (sticker-deprived) windshield.

"No, how do I get one?" Jamie said.

The thick lines around her jaw hardened, and the woman began muttering to herself as if it wasn't her job to inform people of these things. "Dune Beach is private," she said, as calmly as she had in her. "It's restricted to residents."

"We have a house here."

"But do you have a seasonal pass from the Town of Southampton? You have to apply for them with proof of ownership at the beginning of the summer. For a hundred and fifty dollars."

"Oh, no." Peering through the rearview mirror, Jamie noticed the cars piling up behind her. She leaned in closer. "Do you know where there's a public beach around here we can go to?"

"A *public* beach?" The woman wrinkled her sun-damaged nose in disgust, like Jamie had just told her they wanted to lick the ground. But falling deep into thought, her disgust quickly gave way to confusion. "I guess Fowler?"

"And...where's that?" This was like pulling teeth.

She spouted out elaborate instructions, throwing around street names like "Toylsome" and "Wickapogue" (which, unnervingly foreign, did nothing to instill confidence). And though Allison diligently took notes from her shotgun position, when Jamie pulled away and off to the side she'd obviously lost her previous sense of adventure. "This sounds too complicated. I vote you just call Mark."

Hearing his name made Jamie cringe. Though they'd since come to coexist in the house peacefully, Jamie found him as haughty and insensitive as ever. But as the train of shareholders' cars veered expectantly to the side behind her, Jamie imagined that this was no time for pride. And so, while

Allison called Brian to start the explanatory phone chain, Jamie reluctantly dialed Mark's number.

He sounded pretty surprised to hear from her, which only prompted her to describe her problem (really, it could have befallen anyone) that much more quickly and professionally. She explained how they'd mistakenly wound up at a private beach, and wondered if perhaps he knew of a quicker way to get to Fowler?

"Fowler? Never heard of it," he said. "The only beach anyone goes to in South is Cooper's." He paused pensively. "Actually, you're really close to it. Go back down First Neck Lane, make a left on Great Plains, and another left on Cooper Neck Road, and you should be good."

"Thanks," she spit out, eager to curtail the conversation.

"One more thing. Is it just one car of you?"

Jamie sighed. "No...why?"

"Because they charge daily rates for parking, thirty dollars a car. How many cars are you?"

She counted quickly, and in a small voice answered, "Eight."

He let out an amused chuckle. "Let me guess. This was all your idea?" But before she could protest, he added, "I'm going to tell you how to get to a church around there with free parking on Sundays. Leave as many cars as you can."

"Great, thanks."

"Also"—was he trying to make her feel as retarded as possible?—"you should know that no beach in the Hamptons is really off-limits, even the *private* ones. That's the big trick. Only the parking is restricted, so anyone can go to any beach if they walk or get a ride there." His superiority clearly intact, he went on to give her directions.

Though she had to give him credit. Heeding his (however pompous) advice, they were soon parked, paid, and heading happily in the direction of the ocean.

"Look, Dave. You're not allowed in from nine to six PM," Jamie exclaimed. "It says NO DOGS."

"Or alcohol or glass?" Rob said, pausing before the sign and hugging their rule-infringing cooler closer to his body. "Yeah, I can see why we left the house now."

But once they made it to the sand, they actually did.

Spreading out on her towel and reveling in the breeze, Jamie decided that going to the beach was much like joining a gym: once you finally hauled your ass there and set yourself up, you wondered why you hadn't done it a long time ago.

And unlike their overcrowded pool area—where you lived in constant fear of being thrown into the water, or having your lounge chair stolen in your absence—this was surprisingly peaceful.

Until something disrupted the peace. When the guys had made a beeline for the ocean the moment they arrived, Jeff asked if she would keep an eye on his wallet and cell phone (the latter of which was now ringing its unfamiliar ring off the hook).

Naturally Jamie fought the urge to look at it...at first. But when it stopped ringing only to start again, she dug the perpetrator out of her beach bag. Holding it far from her body, as if it could spontaneously pick up, she wondered, was it too much of a stretch that STACY was a guy? (And, after peeking at his call history, that Jessica, Alyssa, and Stephanie were, too?)

Jamie kept this to herself as her friends began babbling, conscious that she was no longer an active participant in the conversation. But this new piece of information bothered her. Obviously she had no right to be annoyed: they'd never defined their relationship, and while they hooked up exclusively with each other in the house, barring scattered calls and e-mails, none of that had translated outside the Hamptons. (Though Jamie wondered when he even had time to see anyone else, what with continually running out east every weekend!) Besides, hadn't this always been her ideal situation? The kind of situation her words and body language unconsciously solicited? *She* was the one who hated ground rules! *She* was the one who'd never wanted any.

The funny thing was...later, when Jeff picked her up and carried her kicking and screaming toward the ocean—which she'd always been a bit afraid of—she didn't mind his leading her into unknown waters.

Well, until the whole crab situation came about.

They were having this perfectly good time dodging the waves when Dave cupped some water in his hand and pointed out how, if you looked really closely, there were tiny baby crabs floating in it.

Horrified, Jamie shook her body free of invisible crustaceans (the way you immediately start to scratch when someone says they have the chicken pox). But Rob's response to Dave's discovery was far more...gastronomic.

"Eat one," he said, looking Dave dead in the eye. "Fifty bucks."

"I'll eat one," Brian said, shrugging. And in a fluid motion he scooped one up and swallowed it whole. Her stomach writhing in sympathy, Jamie wondered if Allison had yet witnessed Brian's juvenile side.

But Rob was not to be outdone. On their way back through the sand, they stumbled upon a bigger, meatier crab, around the size of a silver dollar. Rob dove for it and clutched it ravenously.

"I'm begging you. Do *not* eat that," Jamie pleaded.

"What, haven't you eaten crab before?" He dangled his prey before her eyes.

"Are you crazy? You can get diseases from eating raw animals straight from the ocean!"

"I didn't realize you were a marine biologist." And despite her pleas (in fact, probably *because* of them), he popped the little sucker right into his mouth, shell and all.

"That is the grossest thing I've ever seen!" she shrieked, listening to the vivid crunching sounds and watching him gag it down. "Let's see how much ass you get once every girl in the city hears about this."

"Hey!" he garbled, locking his elbow around her neck, then setting her free once he'd swallowed. He flashed her a cautionary look. "What happens in the Hamptons, stays in the Hamptons."

And stay in the Hamptons they did, at least until later on a Sunday than they ever had before. Pretending they all didn't have work the next day, a big group of them decided to stick around after the beach and go out for dinner at Indian Cove, where Mark claimed you could get cheap (and yet still sanitary) seafood.

But speaking of cheap . . .

Jamie still wasn't sure how this happened, but somehow Ilana wound up sitting next to Jeff on one side of the table while she was stuck sandwiched between the Dud and Mark—who'd met them there—on the other.

(Okay, fine, she sort of knew how it happened. It was because she'd insisted on stopping at a drugstore for a nail file—her chipped nail was getting caught on *everything*—and once they'd arrived everyone had already filled up one side of the table. But come on now, she was the one hooking up with him, wasn't it obvious that *she* should be sitting there?)

Having no other conversation options (each of her friends had attempted to talk to the Dud at some point this summer, and each in turn had failed miserably), Jamie struck up some small talk with Mark. And—who would have thought—he was actually funny.

Actually, he was really funny. His brown eyes lit up conta-
giously as he relayed tales of shareholders past. For instance,
the guy who'd invited twenty Resort strippers back to their
house to party late-night. Or the one who'd borrowed a
button-down shirt to wear out, only to turn around and sell
it for a hundred bucks to some meathead the Jet door guy
wouldn't let in with his wifebeater. Overcome by laughter,
Jamie was unsure whether the humor lay in the stories or
their animated storyteller.

"That's so funny!" she found herself saying again and again.
And while that was often the phrase she used when she didn't
know what else to say, as she blinked back the tears, now she
genuinely meant it.

Still, every time she heard Ilana's trademark cackle, again
and again, Jamie glanced over in annoyance. She tried to
be discreet about it, but Mark eventually called her out.

"I know you don't like her very much."

"Who, Ilana? I like her just fine," Jamie lied, taking some
more shrimp from the seafood sampler.

Mark didn't buy it. "She can come off kind of loud, like
she needs to be the center of attention. But you should cut
her some slack. I've known her a while, and she used to have
serious self-esteem issues."

Jamie watched as, in conversation, Ilana jovially placed her
hand on Jeff's shoulder. "Apparently." Though just as she was
going to change the subject (Ilana's personal life was one area
in which Jamie desired no further clarity), Mark went on.

"Her freshman year at Penn, she dropped thirty pounds
because of an eating disorder and had to be hospitalized for
a month. But don't say anything," he added quickly, "no one
really knows about it."

Jamie wasn't sure if Mark liked her enough to entrust her
with this information, or liked Ilana enough to want to defend

her. But from the flirtatious way he'd been engaging her, she had a hunch it wasn't the latter. "So what about you?"

"What *about* me?" He had this way of looking at her like he knew something about her no one else did. Or like he was constantly amused by a joke that only he was privy to. Perhaps that joke was life itself, something others in comparison took way too seriously (his work was just as lucrative even though he had a lax, entrepreneurial approach). Either way, there was a lot more going on behind his unkempt, beach-bronzed, unassuming exterior than she'd previously given him credit for.

"I just mean, no one knows a lot about you, either." She took a sip from her glass and met his gaze head-on. "Like, is it the same girl you bring back to your room every weekend, or do you grant different members of your fan club the honor?"

"I wish. I haven't brought a girl back to my room once this summer."

Jamie stared at him incredulously. "So what is it you run home to do after you deposit us at the clubs?"

"Sleep." He laughed, pausing to glance out the window at the spectacular seaside view. "I've already done the whole partying-till-five-AM thing. Plus, running a house is so much more work than you think. While you were at the beach all day, I had a ton of shit to take care of."

Jamie didn't mean to snort derisively, but this she didn't entirely believe. "Like what?"

Turning defensive, he sat up straight. "Like deal with the cleaning people and the lawn cutters, and stock up on alcohol and food, and stuff for the Labor Day White Party, and repair that chair Rob broke the other week…"

"Sounds annoying."

He attacked a lobster with a loud crack. "Try expensive."

Unmoved, Jamie let out a theatrical sigh. "So now you'll only walk away from the summer with fifty grand of our money instead of an even hundred."

"Right," he joked, strangely compelled to set her straight. "Listen, it's not that black and white. With all this summer's expenses, I'll be happy if I come out on top."

Jamie pushed the sexual reference from her mind. She rested her chin on her hands. "You could still throw us a comp once in a while. You know, just for good measure."

Stunned, he merely looked at her—really truly looked at her. "Why do you think you're so special?"

Jamie grinned. "Why are you in such denial of it?"

Proving to be a smart guy, Mark quickly surrendered. "You"—he pointed his fork at her—"are a handful."

"*Me?* I'm like, the easiest-going girl ever," she said, with a flip of her two-hundred-dollar-cut, blow-dried locks. "You just don't know me that well."

But as Jeff's phone loudly beckoned from across the way, Jamie realized there was a lot at that table left unknown.

Was it Stacy? she thought. Or perhaps Jessica or Alyssa or Stephanie? She never did find out, even after the meal when she said good-bye to Jeff, setting him loose to do whatever it was he did during the week. But as she, Rachel, and Allison headed back toward Route 27—past the bagel store, the cigarette stand, the share house, and all the clarity that came with it—Jamie's demystification effort was far from complete.

For things are all well and good when you're hooking up with someone in the Hamptons. But once 1088 Montauk is left behind on Sunday night, what happens in the Hamptons sometimes really does stay there.

And anything else, everything else, falls into a gray area.

Chapter Eighteen

Every population in statistics has a mean: an average, expected value. All other samples in this population are then measured in relation to this mean—specifically, by exactly how many standard deviations away from it that sample lies. It follows that the margin of error, the deviance from this decided benchmark, comes to assume more importance than even the sample itself.

Thus, when Mark couldn't make it out to the house one weekend, appointing his trusty second in command to stand in, Rachel supposed it only natural to compare Craig's management reign with life as they knew it. To rank just how well he measured up against what was expected.

Not that comparisons didn't run continuously throughout the minds of summer shareholders. Even before the season's start, when first selecting a house amid the flurry of promoter e-mails (each boasting different-size "mansions," in different locations, for different price packages), Rachel found comparisons to be both easy to draw and, later, difficult to forget.

Should she have done that house in ritzy, old-money-heavy East (which had been all over "Page Six" lately) rather than physically closer, younger/hipper South? And on days her butt felt glued to the pool, how about those free bagels one house promised every morning, and barbecues (not just burgers and hot dogs, we're talking chicken and sides) thrown every afternoon? And, tiring quickly of her prospects, how much better *was* the crowd at the house professing hotter guys/"all girls"? (Surely you must have seen last summer's photo album conveniently attached to the promotional e-mail? And *of course* all those beautiful bikini-clad people did actual shares in the house, and didn't just stop by once for a cameo!)

At night was when the comparisons truly ran wild, as each house manager had a preconfigured weekly lineup that he was paid to follow (Mark's being Pink Elephant on Fridays and Star Room on Saturdays). Friday was the less crowded night in general, and for this reason it left the nightclub owners more share-house-dependent. (Saturday brought with it a new spurt of scenesters, locals, and a less coveted hit-and-run crowd—who'd come out just for the night, only to sober up at the Hampton Bays Diner, then drive back at dawn.) But on those particular Fridays when Rachel found herself at Pink Elephant—congregated around the same booth with the same people, for what felt like the gazillionth time—she couldn't help but envision the classier crowds, ample investment bankers, and either more or less crowded venues (each preferable in the face of its opposite) she was being deprived of.

Though, as Rachel abruptly learned, being deprived of a "good night out" would be far from this upcoming weekend's paramount concern. Any of the share house's inherent shortcomings—even the unnerving fact that Craig would be steering their ship solo—paled in comparison with the monumental source of worry that hit her all at once. Well, that actually serenaded her.

"Guess *wha-aaat*?" her sister had chimed over the phone line the previous Thursday.

"What?" Rachel humored her, restoring the word's monosyllabic correctness, and all the while holding her breath. It wasn't so much that she disliked hearing from Dana as the fact that Dana only called her when she needed something.

"Guess where we're going for my non-bachelorette par-tyyy?" her song continued.

Rachel, regretfully, interrupted the melody. "What are you talking about? We already had your bachelorette party." It was true—they (in fact, *she*) had orchestrated an elaborate night out in the city weeks back, complete with dinner at Le Souk besides belly dancers, tickets to the drag-queen-themed *Donkey Show,* and late-night dancing at Tenjune. And Rachel didn't want to be petty, but belly dancers and donkeys these days didn't come cheap.

"You're not listening. I said my *non*-bachelorette party!"

Rachel gave in. "What," she asked calmly, "is a *non*-bachelorette party?"

"Weeell," Dana drew out, as if getting Rachel to ask hadn't been her objective all along, "this is the weekend Gregg's going to Vegas with like ten guys for his bachelor party, and they're going *all*-out. They're staying at THEhotel at Mandalay Bay, hired a limo, and already have reservations at Tao, Pure, Tryst, all the best clubs. Obviously I can't let him have more fun than me!"

Obviously. But Rachel still wasn't following. "So?"

"So...I planned this little weekend excursion for just the bridal party, to keep myself occupied. But come on, you haven't guessed *where*!"

Rachel didn't want to guess. And she most certainly didn't want to go. "Montreal?" she tried.

"To the *Hamptons*!"

Oddly, Rachel was not expecting this. "Seriously?"

"Seriously! What could be more perfect? It's where Gregg and I met, and no one's been back there in ages." *No one* meant none of Dana's friends, which in her mind constituted the entire population.

"I guess," Rachel said. Though once she'd mentally digested

the idea, she decided that maybe it wouldn't be so bad...it was her weekend to be out there anyway. And it might actually be fun to sneak away from the house and seek refuge at whatever swanky hotel they'd be staying in.

"Good, it's already a done deal," Dana continued. "I just got off the phone with Mark, and he practically insisted that me, Amy, Shari, and Danielle take his room in the house this weekend."

"Wait, you're coming to *my* house?" Rachel was glad Dana couldn't see her jaw drop.

"How quickly we forget," Dana said, the first of her words she didn't sing. "It was *my* house first."

And it was merely a means to an end, Rachel concluded, after spending the bulk of the night dissecting why this prospect was even remotely appealing to Dana. Surely it had to be about the money! Didn't hotels out there rape you for something like three or four hundred dollars a night, with two-night minimums? (Not that she'd ever before known her sister to act in the interest of finances.) Still, even Rachel had to admit (to herself, not out loud) that she was beyond impressed to see Mark let her sister and three friends stay for free (a favor she had yet to see him bestow upon anyone else), and in his room no less (an unprecedented second). But then again, never in her life had Dana been "just anyone."

Yet she did want to know about *everyone*—as did each of her friends. And so, during the lengthy drive out on Saturday morning, Rachel (smushed in the back with two of the zeros and the entire Louis Vuitton luggage collection) was thoroughly interrogated for share house gossip. They wanted to know every detail about the house, about the people, about their hookup statuses, and most uncomfortably, about Rachel's own love life.

"So who have *you* been hooking up with?" Dana asked her nonchalantly after Rachel had just finished outlining the romantic links among everyone else.

Rachel peered distractedly out the window, like the prominent red deer sculpture along the route was suddenly fascinating to her. "No one."

Just as she feared, though, Dana wouldn't let it drop. "Oh, come on! Why won't you ever tell me anything?"

If only that were the problem! "No honestly, no one," Rachel pronounced again, less certainly but with more volume.

Despite the fact that she was driving, Dana twisted her whole body around. She pushed her Fendi aviators on top of her head and looked Rachel right in the eye. "Let me get this straight. You're out there practically every weekend, and there's not *one guy* you've been involved with?"

Rachel felt herself blush. Why was her nonpromiscuity so hard to believe? And why did Dana always make her feel so inferior, so subpar? Under the familiar scrutiny of her sister's similarly crafted yet somehow perfected face, Rachel experienced painful flashbacks to the dorky teenager she was in high school: the one with braces and untweezed eyebrows and unstraightened hair, who wasn't selected for Dana's old cheerleading squad despite having been a legacy, and who instead was forced to join the math team by her calculus teacher. Years later Rachel hated that Dana had the power to instantly turn her back into this girl—a girl she'd hoped would forever lie dormant inside her—with one judgmental look.

Dana finally turned to face forward, but gazed back at her through the rearview mirror. "Okay, what about a guy you have your sights set on, at least? Just give us something!"

Rachel's resolve finally broke. "Fine, there's this one guy." And, picturing Aaron, Rachel actually cheered up a bit.

"Who?" The zeros pounced with a hunger they'd never shown for food.

"No one that you—that any of you—probably know," she answered. Then, since she didn't want to mislead them, she added, "And nothing's really happened yet. I just mean, I think he has potential."

"Well, if you're thinking wedding date potential, you realize I have to meet him first," Dana said, raising a dainty eyebrow she'd never had to wax.

"You'll definitely meet him," Rachel said, definitely hoping it wouldn't come to this. But, working up the nerve to disclose her crush (and the fact he and Dana were already acquainted) became a less immediate concern the moment they arrived and lugged their things up the steps, because Craig was apparently worked up enough for them all.

"I need you to move your car. *Stat!*" came the recognizable sound of his gruff voice from inside. Rachel, Dana, and the zeros paused on the front steps by the window to see what the drama was. Seconds later they heard him add, "You're going to throw out that Slurpee cup, right?"—as if at any minute the cup in question would spontaneously combust.

"Just chill out!" Rob's agitated voice hollered back. But no sooner had they cracked open the door, causing each head in the common room to reflexively turn, than was it clear that no one (particularly no one male) was still thinking about a Slurpee cup. "Well, well, well!" Rob said, verbalizing the unspoken sentiment.

There is nothing like fresh meat in a Hamptons share house. And it isn't just a one-sided scenario—there is nothing like being fresh meat. All at once every guy made a beeline to help the girls with their luggage (a chivalrous gesture they'd aborted with the other girls after pretty much the first weekend), while Dana stepped into the house so boldly you'd have suspected she owned it.

"Levy!" she cried, hugging Rob as if she knew him better than anyone else. This had once intimidated Rachel—until she'd realized that Dana always acted like she knew someone better than everyone else, be it friend, family member, or mailman.

But as Ilana and Jeff and Craig and lots of randoms (whom Rachel didn't even know) rushed forward to greet her, there was no denying Dana really did know a lot of people—or at least knew someone who knew someone who did. Even the few people Dana didn't know seemed magnetically drawn to her. And for the second time that day, for the umpteenth time in her life, Rachel could have been in high school.

Sadly, though she'd tried to observe and learn in her youth, Rachel simply couldn't command a room the way her older sister could; it just wasn't a formula that could be taught. No matter how friendly or forthcoming her presence, Rachel knew she lacked the same high-on-life magnetism, the same confidence, the same allure. But it hit closest to home when Dana stood overshadowingly beside her. Rachel believed it begged people to compare them.

"You guys look so much alike," Jamie noted, as she previously had, even though Rachel was certain it was only their similar coloring. In fact, observing them in a room together, Rachel supposed *Jamie* and her sister to be a lot more alike—not so much in appearance as in overall effect. They were beautiful in different ways: Jamie had a more urban, New York City trendiness to her, and with her funky, model-like outfits emanated glamour from every pore. But Dana could have stepped out of a Cover Girl ad, with her iridescent blue eyes and perfect hair and skin, always appearing impeccably polished, department-store friendly, and expensive. Still, both girls carried themselves with a sense of entitlement you believed in mostly because of how much they did, and summoned attention in a way they always expected yet seldom seemed conscious of.

It would have made much more sense if Jamie were Dana's sister, Rachel thought, supposing what everyone in the room must really be thinking: that in relation to her sister, in the family of Bursteins, Rachel stuck out like an outcast.

She was almost grateful for the distraction of Craig. Minutes later he bothered them again, about a pile of duffel bags someone had left a considerable distance from the stairwell. He'd decided they were a life-endangering obstacle.

"Whose stuff is this? I can't have it out here," he sputtered, his focus shifting nonsensically to random points about the common room. Perhaps because he juggled so much, it always seemed to Rachel like his eyes were one step ahead of his brain.

"Oh, that's mine," Dave called, taking a swig from a Heineken bottle out of the family of them multiplying on the coffee table. "I'll get it later."

"*No!* I need you to get it now," Craig barked. "*I'm* the one responsible for the house this weekend, and *I'm* not rushing someone to the hospital if they trip and break their ankle!"

After this unwarranted frenzy, silence uncharacteristically overcame the room, and for a moment Rachel wondered if Dave would argue back. For a moment, it seemed like Dave was wondering this same thing. But, rolling his eyes, he took a long swig from his beer, then placed the bottle back down on the coffee table. Hard. "I'll move it. But I'm telling you, you better relax." He lifted his finger in admonition. "Just because Mark leaves one weekend, you don't have to treat us like we're infants."

"Just get it out of my sight," Craig snapped, opting to ignore the second part of what Dave said. With that, he sped off on another rampage, like a windup doll that had been wound too many times.

Similarly eager to escape the drama, Rachel decided to lead Dana and her friends on a grand tour of the house—which was impressive at the weekend's start, and incrementally less so each day it was further trashed. Just as Rachel had been anxiously expecting, in the course of their rounds she came upon Aaron stationed around the kitchen table with Steve and the Dud.

"Hey," she said, returning the smile he instantly flashed her. Though just as she was about to initiate introductions, Dana brushed past the trio as if the kitchen were otherwise empty.

"So, Rach, is your guy here?" she blurted out, with a typical lack of discretion.

Everyone (including "her guy") glanced up at her.

"No," Rachel muttered softly, both horrified and irritated—that Dana had unconsciously filtered Aaron out through her "important person" radar. If there were ever a moment to 'fess up to her feelings, it was so far from this one. "I'm sure that—everyone—will be at Star Room tonight," she answered instead. Determinedly, she turned back toward the guys. "Dana, I think you know Aaron, right? And this is Steve, and Evan."

"Hi," Dana said, smiling politically. Her sister could turn her charm on and off like a light switch. She turned to face her friends. "Let's go bring our stuff upstairs." This replacing a farewell, they marched right up the steps.

Predictably, the girls gushed over Mark's gargantuan room, beyond ecstatic he'd gone away for the weekend. However, everyone else in the house was considerably less ecstatic, as their list of grievances against Craig began to grow.

Some of his requests were actually reasonable (and had they not been accustomed to doing things Mark's way, they might never have been the wiser). And everyone did try to appease him…at first. Moving the cars the moment they walked in was utterly loathsome, but something they knew had to be done. Cleaning up every trace of their food and confining all their belongings to their rooms wasn't exactly the norm, but it was a reasonable enough request. Though when Craig announced they'd be leaving for the club at 10 PM sharp (rather than post-flip-cup at around eleven), and that every single beer bottle had to be removed *prior* to departure (this was always done afterward—if at all), people couldn't take it anymore. They couldn't take *him* anymore. So what they took was him, down.

"Now!" Rob cried.

Evidently previously orchestrated, on this cue all the guys in the house charged at Craig at once. And sure, Craig was a hefty guy, but what is one guy compared with twenty (riled-up) ones? Standing back to avoid the shuffle—the way you did in a bar when a fight broke out—Rachel watched them lift him up off his feet and high into the air, like a float in a parade. She supposed they were merely going to throw him in the pool (always the default solution in a share house). Instead the throng of guys clamored toward the front door.

They stopped slightly short of it, threw open the adjacent door to the hall closet, and dumped Craig inside. Then, before he could resist, they slammed the door shut and twisted the lock. At first Craig began pounding his fists and spouting obscenities, but he gave this up shortly, perhaps wary he might be in there for the long haul.

Though it was a tempting prospect, no one really intended to hold him captive beyond an initial scare. So after twenty or so minutes, Rob graciously unlocked the closet (it then took another ten for Craig to realize this and open the door). But to everyone's amazement, when Craig stepped out, he didn't try to avenge himself. He didn't seize his offenders in fury. What he did—what he said—was absolutely nothing at all. As if he'd retreated into the closet of his own volition, he wore a solemn, poker-like expression from the instant of his liberation, all the way to Star Room, where the night proceeded in a similarly atypical way.

By this point in the summer, two weeks shy of Labor Day, Rachel had been to Star Room countless times. But truth be told (and to her sister, it never would), Rachel had never seen Star Room like this.

In the way she always did, Dana knew everyone. And not just everyone—Dana knew everyone who mattered. Within minutes of their arrival, the doormen Pete and Tony comped her entire party and whisked them in ahead of the masses. Once inside, barely inches beyond the door, front man Charles Ferri and the longtime owners (two jovial men both named Scott) came over to bid their hellos, and photographer extraordinaire Rob Rich instantly accosted them for a cameo. Then, when the beret-adorned bottle-service host Bey learned it was Dana's "non-bachelorette" party, he set Dana up with a free bottle inside the celeb-filled Hip Hop room (which Rachel usually just passed in laps—the crew of people most like her were mostly stationed outside this VIP area). There, lining the rim of a central table with Heather Graham across from them, the Gottis to their left, and Macy Gray to their right, they could relish the ambiance a comfortable distance from the bustling crowd below—the crowd of which, until now, Rachel had always been a member.

They still took intermittent strolls through this crowd, Dana insisting on leading the line so as to toss out over-enthusiastic salutations (to casual acquaintances, no doubt).

And despite her engagement ring (or more likely, because of it), Dana flounced about and basked in being the center of attention—making Rachel, at least in her mind, the object of comparison. Of course, the sisterly comments were always laudatory, but people's true sentiments were transparent: Why could Dana throw back the shots while Rachel nursed just one drink? Why was Dana's wardrobe so stylish and colorful, Rachel's so muted and black? How was it that Dana was such an exceptional dancer while Rachel could barely sway to the beat? And most conclusively: Wasn't Dana simply the life of the party—and Rachel the death of it? It was no wonder Dana was the one getting married!

If this was Dana's "non-bachelorette" party, you couldn't get any more "non-Dana" than Rachel.

Strangely, despite the night she was having (the kind of night Dana felt entitled to, but that Rachel always considered as beyond her means), the Hamptons still weren't good enough for Dana. Like the prom dress you rewear only to discover it can never live up to that original night, the reality of the East End just couldn't measure up to her memories of it.

"This sucks. The Hamptons have gone so downhill," Dana complained at one point to the zeros. (Rachel opted not to confess this had been one of the most impressive nights she'd ever had.) "I remember things so differently."

"Me too! We had the *best* summer of our lives here," one of her friends agreed. "Now it feels like everything's changed."

As if a testament to exactly how much, Dana jumped down off their table. "I'm going to go call Gregg," she said, leaving the pumping hip-hop music and thriving party behind her.

Also slipping away, on her way to the bathroom, Rachel spotted Craig's frenzied figure through the crowd. In his usual manner, he was huffing around as if charged with executing something exceedingly important. As she approached him, his rage erupted, like the air from a punctured balloon.

"Why should I put up with this shit?" he bellowed, a rhetorical question Rachel imagined was directed at the guys. "I've been running this house for five years, and *they* think they know better than me?"

Rachel didn't say anything. Instead, she merely watched as Craig's eyes flared angrily around the room—as if debating exactly what belligerent move should come next. Then, surprisingly, he gazed at her in a timid, almost vulnerable way she'd have never thought him capable of. "Do you think I was bossy?"

Rachel thought *bossy* was an understatement! "Well, yeah," she admitted quickly. "You were definitely bossier than usual. Like, with the beer bottles, and wanting to go out at ten."

She stopped, expecting the expulsion of more hot air. But rather than get defensive, Craig sounded deflated. "Did you know that last week, this guy Parry's share house got here at eleven, and Star Room was so packed they couldn't get in? He had to take his entire house to the Foggy Goggle!" He chuckled a bit at the image. "Can you picture your sister at some dive bar?"

Rachel shook her head.

"And how two weeks ago, these other share house managers, the Zinns, had to rush some girl to the hospital because glass from a beer bottle went into her foot?"

Um, *ow*! Rachel shook her head again.

"This house is a lawsuit waiting to happen, and this weekend, it's my lawsuit. If you don't put your foot down, people will walk all over you." Fiddling with his hands, Craig suddenly paused, his harsh demeanor melting further. And with finally stationary eyes, eyes whose fervor had disappeared, he added, "Mark has it easy—he just rents the house and hires a sucker like me to do all the grunt work. Well, you know what?

They like the way Mark runs things so much? They can have him. I'm done."

Oddly, as annoying and scary and control-freakish as Craig could sometimes be, Rachel couldn't seem to picture the house without his colorful presence. And, maybe in light of these new realizations, maybe in light of the sensitivity surprisingly hiding behind his coarse exterior, Rachel now saw Craig for what he really was: a big guy carrying an ever-bigger responsibility on his shoulders, and doing so in the only way he knew how. A way that just didn't happen to be Mark's.

At that moment all Rachel could feel was pity. "Honestly, who cares if you run the house a different way than Mark? I think you're doing a great job," she said, hoping she wouldn't later regret these words. She went one further, now seeing Craig as not just the house outcast but someone who was constantly living in another person's shadow—something to which Rachel could wholeheartedly relate. "If other people don't like how you do things, it's not your problem."

Nor, did she realize, was it *her* problem if her sister wasn't Aaron's biggest fan. Besides, all it was at this point was a crush. Thus, even though her sister had paid Aaron as much mind tonight as, say, the cement, Rachel decided to satisfy her curiosity.

"Okay, so, remember how I told you there's a guy I like?" she began, when they were all gathered together on the patio, waiting for the group to depart.

"Yeah?" Despite her moments-ago tiredness, Dana whirled around curiously. "Is he here?"

Rachel directed her body toward Aaron. "Actually, he's right there. By that table."

Dana followed her gaze and, despite the 2 AM darkness, squinted. "You mean next to that guy Aaron?"

Rachel clenched the muscles in her stomach. "It sort of is that guy Aaron."

Awaiting the punch line that never followed, her sister looked back at her in horror. "Aaron Nash? You can't mean Aaron Nash!"

"Well, I already told you, nothing's happened yet," Rachel said. "But he's a really great guy. And I know you two were never friends, but—"

"Never *friends*?" Dana pronounced the term like it was suddenly pejorative. "No offense, but he is hands-down the biggest dork I know."

Why would Rachel possibly take offense?

Getting increasingly worked up, her sister continued. "And just so you know, Aaron Nash is *not* coming to my wedding. So I hope that's not what you were thinking."

Rachel wasn't, but of course she certainly was now.

Interrupting the silence, one of the zeros standing next to them conveniently chimed in. "You know, I actually grew up with Aaron—in Livingston, New Jersey."

Rachel turned, wondering if the girl might come to her defense. "And?"

The girl narrowed her eyes. "And he hasn't *existed* since the fourth grade."

Rachel couldn't even see how this was possible! But she did see how naive she'd been for thinking anyone would dare defy her sister, who kept going on and on.

"Rach, just trust me, you can do *so much better*. Please, for all our sakes!" She peered around frantically. "Not that I blame you—none of the guys here can even hold a candle to Gregg! How about when we get back to the city, I'll set you up with one of Gregg's friends…" Dana continued rambling, but Rachel had already stopped listening.

Was Aaron really not up to par? Was it like those times

Rachel tried on a shirt she liked, but Dana convinced her to leave it at the department store, claiming it was nothing special? Just because Aaron wasn't some carbon copy of Gregg didn't mean he wasn't good enough! Rachel was sick of everything in life being measured against *Dana's* ideal—she was sick of being measured against Dana herself.

Her sister's dismissal of Aaron as not measuring up was perhaps intended to be helpful. It was—though Rachel had yet to determine this for herself—perhaps even accurate. But accurate or well intended, either way, it was just...mean.

Take two rats of the opposite sex, confine them in a box together, and sooner or later they will mate.

This trapped-in-a-box theory has been used to explain why men and women confined in houses together for shows like *The Real World* eventually become intimate. Can't be with the one you love? Simple! Learn to love the one you're with.

As the summer drew to an end, Allison thus began to wonder exactly how much of her romance was share-house-stimulated.

However, her reservations might never have surfaced had it not been for the rain.

Now, an unpromising forecast from the Internet weather sites (which the group religiously consulted, despite the fact they were frequently incorrect) was nothing new. The response to typing in "Southampton, NY" was invariably a 60 percent chance of precipitation. But by some miracle, in the Hamptons, the sun always seemed to shine.

Until now.

Allison knew they were in for a rude awakening that last weekend in August when a thundercloud seemed to have planted itself in Manhattan for two weeks. These perpetual downpours induced the kind of all-encompassing depression that painted the town gray, that zapped your zeal for everything from working out to going out, and that made you forget what the sun even felt like.

Rain in a share house wasn't something Allison imagined

to be much different. Foreseeing a whole weekend of lying around in sweats, dozing intermittently, downing junk food, and replaying the same movie over and over again until they could recite every word—in short, doing the same "nothing" they usually did, only more of it, and for longer stretches— she was all for staying in the city and cutting their losses.

But the thing about rain—or rather, the thing about guys and rain—is that they just don't give a damn.

Isn't it just as easy to get hammered and get laid in torrential thunderstorms as it is in brilliant sunshine? they seemed to think. But the truth was, deep down, no one honestly believed it would rain. Rain in the Hamptons seemed about as unlikely as, say, sobriety in the Hamptons. And so, against any reasonable logic, everyone was still expecting to find the Hamptons as sunny and idyllic as ever.

What they found instead was themselves, trapped in a box.

And boy, did it get old quick.

Allison didn't just feel this way because Brian had yet to arrive (he, Rob, and Dave had made a stop at his house on Long Island). She felt this way because, honestly, there wasn't a single constructive thing to do.

Dinner might have been an option, had they not just consumed half of 7-Eleven (with junk-food wrappers littering each countertop to prove it). Going out might have been a second one, were the girls willing to wear T-shirts and flip-flops to someplace like Surf Club and just "slum it" (a phrase Jamie claimed she'd never before even heard). And the movie idea had actually gone over quite well—until they called Southampton's sole theater to reserve a block of seats. Apparently some drunken driver had plowed into it the night before, forcing them to shut the entire place down.

Only in the Hamptons, kids. Only in the Hamptons.

Fortunately, just as the normally productive lawyers and

bankers and movers and shakers were lying around in boredom, it was Brian, Dave, and Rob (and their endless stream of shopping bags) to the rescue.

Allison realized something right then: An unmarried thirty-something man with a senior-rank salary and a teenage mentality is a dangerous thing. Or—maybe that was unfair. The unmarried thirtysomething men with senior-rank salaries and teenage mentalities residing at 1088 Montauk were dangerous things. For, having finally earned their place in the sun, rather than contribute their impressive incomes toward the typical priorities of their same-age counterparts (such as graduate school, real estate, or racking up interest for future families), the guys in the share house discovered a much more practical place to invest their paychecks: KB Toys.

And—as with most of their profligate splurges—when it rained, it poured.

"You guys are insane!" numerous girls cried out, but they gathered around and observed the spectacle anyway.

Unloading bag after bag bearing the toy-store emblem, the guys confessed to making a "minor" (read: thousand-dollar) pit stop, and, well, time flies when you're playing with toys. Watching them pull out everything from childhood board games to talking stuffed animals, Allison could vividly picture the trio running around the toy store like children. It was the kind of thing that was so utterly juvenile, you couldn't *not* smile. Which was sort of how Allison thought of Brian himself. Though when they afterward arranged a group tournament in a charades-type game called Gestures (doubly entertaining when accompanied by alcohol), Allison had to applaud the guys' efforts to think outside the box.

But the game proved harder than it looked, and gesture-ability was apparently not one of Dave's strong suits. So after describing at least three different clues by flapping his arms wildly with the same bird-like motion and being officially declared worst player of the bunch, he rose indignantly to his feet and resigned from Gestures.

Then, ironically, using nothing but gestures, he opened up a Connect Four game and jerked his head invitingly toward Turtle Girl—perched on the couch arm only inches from him. Because she wasn't participating in the game, either (which was just as well, for Allison feared someone would yell *Turtle?* the moment she stood up to enact a clue), she turned to face him. And with still no verbal exchange whatsoever, the two began silently placing chips into the plastic yellow game board.

Allison was surprised to discover herself a decently good Gestures player (due to her fear of public forums, she was also perhaps taking the game more seriously than most). Though as the alcohol took effect, both the guessing and the gesturing grew that much more ridiculous. Ridiculous, and sexual.

But oddly, as X-rated as the Gestures game quickly became, the playful innuendos thrown about were no match for the bona fide sexual tension mounting across the Connect Four board. Allison wasn't exactly sure how or when this came about, but judging from their hungry looks, each chip dropped seemed to be about a whole lot more than simply winning a game. Maybe it was because Dave and Turtle Girl had clearly reached the state of drunkenness (was that his ninth beer he was pounding? No, it had to be his tenth!). Maybe it was because they'd secretly harbored feelings for each other all along (doubtful!). Or maybe (and this was what Allison's money was on) it was merely the product of two people with raging hormones sitting conveniently across from each other. Brushing each other's hands. Trapped inside a box.

Watching her flirty, forthright motions, his propositioning glare, the color rushing helplessly to her (turtle-like) face, Allison could feel the moment happening. The moment you knew—in the pit of your stomach, you just knew—things were going to happen.

And sure enough, they did. One minute the two of them were sitting there thrusting black and red circular chips into empty spaces, and the next the spaces they'd been occupying themselves were suspiciously empty. It was a logical move on the part of Dave—surely uneager to broadcast the fact that he was hooking up with the girl whose resemblance to a reptile was something of a house joke. Earlier in the summer (back before she'd learned the share house mantra, *Ugly ass trumps no ass*), Allison might have been surprised by his lack of discretion. But now the only thing that surprised her about this particular scenario was the guys' cruel reaction to it. The guys' cruelty, in general.

Following Rob's head as he belatedly registered the couple's disappearance, Allison knew he was about to make this discovery public. Especially since Turtle Girl's friends weren't present to defend her. And so, grabbing the talking stuffed parrot they'd just purchased, he spoke into it in his best cartoon voice, "I'm a *tuuurtle!*"

Recording his sentence, the animal chirped back, "I'm a *tuuurtle!*"

Again. And again.

And in response to this infantile stunt, the entire room erupted with sudden laughter—Brian's louder than anyone else's. But beneath her forced smile, Allison felt as if she'd been laughing at these immature stunts for too long.

Still, these reservations might never have surfaced had it not been for the rain.

When the storm showed no signs of letting up, the guys retreated to the kitchen for a single-sex game of poker, adopting such brutal concentration that even a *Playboy* model wouldn't have distracted them.

Left downstairs in the face of this isolation, Allison's friends joined in the assembling Twister game. But having already worked up the nerve to participate in one thirty-person group activity, she felt safe in concluding she'd done her part to be social. Thus, positioning herself on the circle's outskirts to (at least pretend to) watch the game, she also realized herself the kind of drunk where you're strangely contented just sitting and staring.

Which was probably why she was so startled when Steve broke her intoxicated trance. He did so with a tap on her shoulder that was so light, she wondered if she had imagined it even as she turned around.

Though she had to admit, she was pleased she hadn't.

"Want to play?" he asked, holding out a deck of cards, then flipping them around in some elaborate shuffling move.

"Sure," she said, mostly because she was flattered he'd asked. "What game?"

He stared at her intently for a moment, as if she hadn't been speaking English (or maybe she had something stuck on her face?). Then he suddenly snapped into comprehension, the way you do when you're caught staring at someone on the subway, and smiled faintly. "Your call."

Of course, under the hasty pressure of being asked, Allison instantly forgot every card game she ever knew. Then, in a move that was surprisingly bold for her (her default response was typically *Whatever you want*), she sat up on her knees and recalled her favorite childhood card game. "Spit?"

Just as she was wondering if guys even played Spit, he grinned. "I have to warn you, I'm a kick-ass Spit player."

She smiled gratefully (if only because he actually knew the game). "You're on."

As it turned out, Steve really was a kick-ass Spit player.

They played three times, and he beat her easily every one. Embarrassed, Allison suspected the fact that she was drunk wasn't helping matters. Though as she watched his hands flying and his mind turning (an unfamiliar observer with nothing else to go by might have deemed Spit a match of wits), Allison imagined Steve probably brought an intelligent approach to most things.

What Brian brought, on the other hand, was the complete opposite.

In the midst of their second session (well, Allison's second ass whupping), he reappeared from his poker game looking far from thrilled with Steve—and more than satiated with Patrón. Kneeling beside Allison, he began massaging her shoulders territorially.

We're playing Spit, not swapping Spit! she wanted to say. But before she could open that Pandora's box, they were doused with a shower of poker chips.

"Ass!" Brian yelled at Rob's sprinting back.

Then, grabbing a handful of chips from the Connect Four game, Brian darted off after him.

Finding themselves alone again, Allison and Steve exchanged a glance, tacitly scolding such childish behavior. She immediately felt guilty. However, there was no denying that Brian was far too immature for her—that this immaturity had plagued their relationship from Day One, back when he'd called dibs on her at DIP like love was some kind of schoolyard game. By knowing this and staying with him, all she was doing was allowing herself to remain trapped.

Still, after all the games had finished (or so Allison had then believed), she passed out next to Brian in his room as she usually did. She wasn't at first sure what woke her up again. But it didn't take long to figure it out.

Judging from the light coming through the window, it was definitely five or six in the morning. And judging from the sound in the room, Dave and Turtle Girl were definitely having sex. Loudly. Uninhibitedly. In the bed directly next to her. But this wasn't even the shocking part.

When she glanced to her left, she was surprised to discover that Brian was also awake.

Not just awake, but lucid, captivated, and reaching for his cell phone.

Watching him unplug it from the nightstand, she held her breath, hoping he wasn't about to do the thing she was dreading he would. As if she could stop him, she honestly held it tight.

But he nevertheless flipped it open and, using the video feature, began to record the action.

Turtle Girl was on top, facing down, and for this reason wasn't the wiser. But when Dave discovered he was in the spotlight (and his sexual escapades would later be subject to share-house-wide scrutiny), he did the only thing an unmarried thirty-year-old guy with a teenage mentality could do.

He pulled the covers completely off them, so Brian's footage would capture more of the action.

Panicked by this whole outrageous scenario, Allison immediately rolled over and squeezed her eyes shut. She could barely believe what Brian was doing. And even as she tried to make sense of it, Allison could feel the moment happening. The moment when you knew—in the pit of your stomach, you just knew—things were going to end.

Brian would probably try to explain himself. How, in the context of share house world, he was only trying to be funny. But in Allison's world—in the real world—this kind of humor just wasn't acceptable.

Perhaps it was naive to think a relationship with someone so wrong for her could have remained sunny and bright forever. Perhaps the rain was necessary to finally see the light. But it was now obvious beyond all doubt that she was trapped in this tiny box of a room, with rats.

Her little experiment with Brian was now officially over.

Chapter Twenty

In English heraldry, white...signified brightness, purity, virtue, and innocence. (*The American Girls Handy Book,* 1887, page 369)

One cardinal rule governs every Labor Day White Party. Yet somehow, within the first five minutes, Rachel Burstein was already contemplating breaking it.

Not that she'd ever been one to break the rules. Especially where social etiquette was concerned. But to someone who wore black about as religiously as other people wore...shoes, say, wearing head-to-toe white felt no less preposterous than wearing head-to-toe polka dots. White wasn't just a departure from her preferred wardrobe palette, it was a departure from her comfort zone. And upon the very first opportunity she was afforded, she had every intention of slipping away and changing out of it.

"Well, why not?" she'd challenged her friends after stepping onto the pool patio like a disoriented sophomore stepping into her first high school prom. Though, rather than having swapped street garb for fancy evening attire, they'd tonight exchanged swimsuits and cover-ups for any combination of the following: flouncy white skirts (the BCBG sequined model a perennial fave), tight white tank tops, solid white dresses, or calf-length white capris—with differentiation attempted through various belt and jewelry accents (all courtesy of the same West Village street vendors).

Aside from surrendering her routine going-out color, what made Rachel even more uncomfortable was that wearing all-white outfits necessitated wearing absolutely no underwear. *No* exceptions. It was the kind of thing Rachel couldn't stop thinking about for even a minute, creating a state of constant paranoia that her practically knee-length skirt left far too little to the imagination. She knew remaining in this clothing for the next few hours just wouldn't feel right.

Jamie was hardly sympathetic.

"Are you serious? You can't change yet! You're supposed to wear white for the *entire* White Party!" protested the girl who rarely wore black—or for that matter, underwear—out at night, anyway. Rachel should have anticipated this; they always *had* found themselves at odds about practically everything. "Besides," Jamie continued, "we haven't even taken pictures yet! If you change, you'll have to spend the whole rest of the party avoiding everyone—or having everyone else avoid you, because you'll ruin their white pictures. Is it really worth it?"

"I guess not," Rachel had agreed, and—picturing her sister's framed photographs of tanned, glowing girls sporting goddess-like white ensembles for this annual occasion, which was known to be the "affair of the summer" and actually the invention of shareholders her sister's year—she was temporarily convinced. Convinced, and commando.

"And anyway," Jamie added, prompting them all to walk down the pool steps (the attention-summoning equivalent of a model walking down a runway), "white is like, the symbol of purity. Virginity. If there ever was someone I'd think would feel comfortable in the color, it'd be you."

"Not funny," Rachel said, pulling down her skirt like it made a difference and instantly growing self-conscious again. Though, catching sight of Aaron stationed opposite them on the deck in what was practically the male uniform—white polo shirt and white pants (khakis were prohibited)—the thoughts she proceeded to entertain were anything but pure.

And her reaction to them was anything but characteristic. Aaron was standing around talking to Steve—the two seeming as approachable as any two guys in blaring white outfits possibly could seem. However, as if alongside her black clothes she'd shed her confidence (or as if she'd suddenly morphed back into a twelve-year-old who froze in the face of her crush), Rachel couldn't seem to approach them.

Instead, assuming a more mature approach (pretending not to notice his presence), she stayed tight in the huddle of her friends, mimicking their steps through the crowd on the patio. Which, she had to admit, was transportingly beautiful.

The White Party (initially modeled after Diddy's annual event) was a longtime Labor Day tradition in Mark's house and nothing short of a share-house-wide effort: from the moment they woke up until the three-hour mark when, naturally, they needed to start getting ready, they'd decorated the place with streamers and balloons and special-order white roses (the majority of which wound up in all the girls' hair). Even more impressively, they'd set up a bar station (Craig revealed himself to be a skillful mixologist), hired a DJ (some guy with his own equipment who'd been a shareholder years back), and invited every single person in the Hamptons any of them knew. Still, while everyone indeed expected this built-up party to be great, nothing could prepare Rachel for the sight of a hundred people cloaking the pool area in a blanket of white, the setting sun casting a postcard-like pink gleam in the background.

Lost in a sea of monochromatic fusing fabric, Rachel looked around for people she recognized, and succeeded in spotting a few (those girls from the Midwest, that lawyer Dan who'd at one point seemed promising). But something about being dressed in spanking white costume-like attire made them feel like strangers all over again. Maybe it was because, at six in the evening, they all still felt the burden of sobriety. Maybe it was because there actually *were* so many strangers here. Or maybe she had merely forgotten what it was like to go out in Manhattan—as three girls alone in a sea of strangers—back before they'd grown accustomed to traveling in a pack of forty housemates. Maybe this was all just an unwelcome foreshadowing of how things would shortly be again.

Thinking about it, Rachel felt the pang in her stomach that far too often preceded tears. Everyone knew Labor Day was synonymous with the end, like the last day of camp or school, when you honestly believe you'll see each other again but sometimes never do. What's more, she wondered where everyone would be *next* weekend—when the weather was virtually the same, though someone somewhere had appointed summer officially over. Well, next weekend *she'd* be at Dana's wedding, but would they all still hang out a week from now? A month from now? Would there be a reason for e-mails other than soliciting rides or swapping photo albums? Or (and this was the part she hated thinking about most) was their only common ground their shared roof and collective interest in summertime debauchery? If so, she'd discover this soon enough.

"Wow, where did the summer go?" Allison said, reading Rachel's mind (yet peering around as if she'd meant to ask, *Where did Brian go?*).

"I know!" Jamie sang, probably feeling her tan fading already. "Doesn't it feel like forever ago that we met everyone at DIP?"

Rachel nodded, but then decided it did and it didn't. A lot had transpired since that night in May when their now tight-knit group came together awkwardly for the very first time. In fact, she felt like she'd done more and made more memories in three short months than she'd done and made in the entire last year! Now spotting Rob and Dave over by the bar, trying to rile up Craig as usual, Rachel smiled. In this way an outsider could never fully understand, doing a summer share is like pledging a fraternity—subjecting yourself to the epitome of randomness, revelry, intimacy, and fear, learning more about yourself, and sharing with others a secret life. It's both nothing and yet everything you expect it to be, for it's those things you think you'll hate that wind up winning you over most. Also like pledging, seeing your companions at all times of day, reacting to all types of situations, wearing all types of clothing (and sometimes, inevitably, none at all) is like pressing the fast-forward button on a relationship. Although catching Aaron's eye and then glancing away purely as a reflex, Rachel was reminded of one relationship she hadn't forwarded fast enough.

But she wasn't going to dwell on it. She'd even (sort of) come to terms with it, like any goal she'd happened to mistakenly overshoot (scoring the perfect wedding date, dropping a full bridesmaid's dress size). Summer shares might serve as an additional social avenue, but they certainly weren't magic! You couldn't expect to walk into a share house and walk out with a boyfriend any more than you could expect to walk into a bar and walk out with one. Well, maybe you could, maybe some people could, but the alternative wasn't necessarily walking away empty-handed. And boyfriend status aside, Rachel was actually walking away with plenty: new friends, new experiences, new exposure (or—given her present lack of underwear—decidedly *more* exposure). In fact, with everything she had to show for the summer, who could possibly care about a stupid label like...

"Patrón?" Brian said, coming up from behind clenching two shot glasses and a bottle of his favorite tequila.

Instinctively Rachel shook her head, glancing away for a moment as (she imagined) he was going to pour. But turning back, she was surprised to discover Brian, Jamie, and Allison staring at her conspiratorially.

"No!" she said.

"Come on! It's the *last* weekend. Just do one!" Jamie pleaded.

"It's not as bad as you think," added Allison.

"Do it for ol' Ten Eighty-eight Montauk!" chimed in Brian.

Rachel paused. It must have been because she'd just been so emotional before that she was even considering this. But no—what was she thinking? She'd never done a shot. Shots were for sloppy drunk girls! And besides, she'd gone this far in her life without ever trying it—just like not smoking pot or not pumping her own gas—what reason was there to start now? "You don't even have another glass," she protested, realizing it was a lame excuse as Brian tilted back the bottle.

Seeing the fright in her friend's eyes, Jamie quickly offered her own glass, but Rachel pushed away her hand. Her mind was already made up.

"If I throw up all night, you're holding back my hair!" Rachel warned, bending her neck and opening her mouth into an O. At this, Jamie's eyes lit up.

"To a great summer!" she chanted, prompting Brian to tip the bottle.

The Patrón burned as it hit the back of her throat. But Rachel realized that sometimes getting burned was just part of the game.

"Want to go over to the bar?" Jamie suggested after Allison and Brian began arguing over something or other. Rachel nodded emphatically, perhaps more emphatically because of the Patrón, but just before they started away she snuck a peek in Aaron's direction. He was still in the same spot, chatting with Steve, more like they were at home on someone's couch than out in public at a party—and Rachel couldn't help but wonder when there'd be an occasion to see him again. After tomorrow—the final night—would they just wave and say good-bye? Would he dare attempt to call her, when she'd gone and spurned his initial text? Or would she just have to wait for some overlapping birthday party months down the line, where everyone in their scene just happened to be? What if by then it was too late?

Directing her focus back toward Jamie, Rachel stayed close on her heels as she shoved her way through the crowd. Funny, as much as she always criticized Jamie for her boldness, her friend would never be caught in such a left-to-chance situation. For better or worse (or for only one night), she just wasn't the type to leave it up to the guy to call, to ask her out, to initiate the first move. Jamie went for what she wanted—whatever it was she wanted—and would never wait around to be rescued by some white knight.

"What can I get ya?" Craig joked as she approached him—the joke being that they were serving only one thing. In special honor of the White Party, they'd created a mysterious vodka-pineapple mixture—cleverly light in color, so that if anyone spilled, they wouldn't have to worry about staining. Diligently, Craig had spent the last few hours on the deck mass-producing the stuff in a gigantic tub, and (as if he'd chosen rather than been assigned to the task) was now proudly doling it up.

"Uh…surprise us," Jamie said, before turning around to interrupt Jeff, who was standing in the center of a huddle enclosed by Ilana and ten white clones, hardly looking like he wanted to be interrupted.

Watching as Craig scooped two plastic cups into the tub, Rachel leaned over the bar. "So how does this White Party compare with past ones?" she asked him, trying to picture her sister here.

"No comparison. There are way too many people tonight," he barked, putting down the cups and wiping the sweat from his forehead.

As she'd often found herself doing with him, Rachel tried to point out the positive side. "Well, next summer you'll know to cut the guest list."

He looked her straight in the eye then, as if she should have been able to read his mind. "I'm not going to be here next summer," he said.

"*What?*" Rachel said. "Whh—why?"

"I'm running my own house," he declared, presumably trying it out on his tongue. "Actually just squared it away today. In Ocean Beach, Fire Island, in case you know anyone who's interested."

"Wow...I think that's great," she said, genuinely proud. She couldn't believe that after years of being Mark's assistant, Craig was finally taking this initiative, and secretly wondered how Mark would ever manage without him.

But that's when it happened. Turning around to pass a cup back to Jamie, she noticed that Aaron and Steve had wandered over to join their group.

Had she known, she might have prevented it. But now catching his eye from only a few short feet away, she had no choice but to go over.

"Hey," she said, overcome by a nervousness she'd never felt in speaking to him before. It was actually quite alarming, for she'd always been a pro at icebreakers and could conduct marathon conversations with everyone from doctors to lawyers to cabdrivers (of whom, this summer, she'd learned to grow wary).

Oddly, Aaron seemed just as uncomfortable. "You look great," he said, and his compliment encouraged her (though she hoped it wasn't merely what he'd been saying to girls all night).

"Thanks," she answered, now fearing the transparency of her nerves alongside her attire. The features of her face felt unnaturally loose, making it difficult to smile. "Actually, I borrowed this skirt from Dana," she said, stammering for conversation. "She wore it to her White Party, a few years back..."

But noting the weird expression he'd made at the mention of her sister, Rachel stopped herself. Perhaps old flames died hard. "Sorry if she wasn't all that friendly last weekend," she added, feeling the need to excuse her sister's overtly snobbish behavior. "She was just—"

"She was just being a bitch. As usual," he said boldly. And, judging from his alarmed expression, perhaps more boldly than he'd even intended.

All Rachel could do was stare.

"You think my sister's...a bitch?" she finally got out, thoroughly stunned.

"Well, sometimes," he said, this time more timidly, as if he were insulting her favorite band rather than her only sibling. But he suddenly looked overwhelmingly relieved. "We worked together for two whole years, and—I have to be honest with you—I never got along with her. She could be pretty selfish and condescending, and was whining all the time."

Rachel remained frozen in shock, but Aaron continued speaking.

"I actually thought you'd be the same way when I met you

at the meet-and-greet party," he added bashfully, color rushing to his face. "But then I saw how nice you were when everyone bombarded you with questions about her. And, well, fortunately you're nothing like her."

Neither of them spoke for a minute, the resultant silence long and awkward. Throughout it, Aaron's gaze shifted frenziedly all about the room, while his face remained flushed, almost regretful. To alleviate this apparent discomfort, he finally excused himself.

"Anyway, I'm going to go change out of this ridiculous stuff," he said, gesturing to his clothing. "I'll catch up with you later."

Rachel watched his white back assimilate quickly into the crowd. As if her feet were nailed to the ground, she lingered there, floored—mostly at the prospect that there existed even one guy on the planet who was impervious to her sister's spell. A guy she'd assumed the exact opposite of, no less! She imagined her face hadn't yet relinquished its expression of disbelief when Ilana and crew engulfed her.

"You guys, *this* is the girl I was telling you about!" she squealed, approaching Rachel with white counterparts flailing in all directions like tentacles. "This is *Dana Burstein's* sister! Can you believe it, they're all going to be at the wedding next week!"

Simultaneously, the girls began shrieking, as if Ilana had introduced them to the sibling of some celebrity.

"You're *Dana's* sister?" Initial pause of surprise. "I've heard *so much* about you!"

"You have to tell us *everything*—the guest list, the flowers, the dress?"

"*Wait,* wasn't it *here* that the two of them *first met*?"

Overwhelmed, Rachel merely looked from the white-clad vultures to Aaron's fleeing figure disappearing up the steps. And she realized she had to act fast.

"Yeah...but you should probably just ask Dana," she said, whipping around. "Sorry!" she called insincerely over her shoulder as she darted away.

Throwing back the remainder of her drink, and pounding the empty cup down a bit harder than she intended, she followed Aaron. She followed him through the glass patio divider, into the house, up the steps...and managed to catch up with him right as he'd entered his bedroom. And then what she threw was all rules out the window.

Turning and discovering her there, Aaron simply stared at her, his eyes wide with surprise. "Oh. I bet you want to talk about what I just said. Honestly, I didn't mean to offend you..."

"Actually"—she leaned in closer and went in for the kill— "I'm not so sure I want to talk."

It was fair to say that this was the last possible thing he was expecting. And—though this next part happened rather fast—somehow they went from not-kissing to kissing in a matter of seconds. Without a date, without a dinner mention, without a phone call at a reasonable hour. Though, once it had been initiated, it really wasn't such a big deal. And Rachel found herself loving every minute of it.

They paused only for a moment, so that Aaron could get up to close and lock the door; a door Rachel suddenly feared people would wonder what was happening behind. But as he sat back on the bed and they picked up where they'd left off, Rachel decided sometimes it was better that people be in the dark.

"I can't believe we're doing this," she giggled, semi-impressed with herself.

"You can't believe it? I was totally shocked." He ran his hand along her neck.

"Why?" she asked, clearly because she'd been drinking.

He shrugged. "I guess I thought I ruined things in the beginning, with that text." Peering out the window, he then returned his focus to her, his earnest brown eyes looking straight into hers. "I was out and didn't realize it was so late, but I know you were probably annoyed. A different girl might not have been, but..." He paused, unsure of where he was going with this. "I can see how that's not the best way to *build a relationship.*"

Upon hearing this premeditated catchphrase, she eyed him with a flirtatiousness she rarely unleashed. "What makes you think I want a relationship?" she teased.

Momentarily caught off-guard, he said, "Doesn't every girl want a relationship?"

She thought about it, ready to confess how she was exactly that girl. That girl who hated swapping pickup lines, hated long nights of partying at nightclubs, hated public (well, perhaps even private) drunkenness, and most vehemently, hated random hookups. Who hated absolutely everything that characterized a share in the Hamptons—and who, most of all, hated being single.

But Rachel stopped herself—because she wasn't "exactly" that girl anymore.

And so, playing along, she instead replied, "Sometimes all a girl wants from a summer is a good time."

It was a joke, of course, but Aaron seemed visibly disappointed, and almost immediately, Rachel feared this might preclude his taking her phone number. "So you're saying you wouldn't want to go to dinner sometime?" he asked.

Rachel smiled. "Well, I can give you my number, just in case."

"Actually, you don't have to. I still have it." Producing his cell phone from his pocket, he turned the entry around—allowing her to see not just the number, but the name he'd keyed in to precede it.

And quicker than you could say *Patrón,* Rachel felt the rush of that tequila shot all over again.

For perhaps she would watch her beautiful sister float down the aisle while she stood fittingly (and most predictably) on the sideline. Perhaps she would be unengaged, unattached, underappreciated, and alone.

For now, for tonight, though, RACHEL was the Burstein sister wearing white.

Only, as Aaron reached over and pulled off her strap, Rachel wasn't wearing white... at the White Party... for long.

But hey—maybe love wasn't so black and white. Maybe life wasn't.

And maybe where guys were concerned, cardinal rules were made to be broken.

Chapter
Twenty-one

*F*lip went Ilana's hair, tossed flirtatiously between playful words to Jeff.

Flip went Jamie's lid, as she found herself unusually bothered by this.

Slumping down onto their cushioned booth at Pink Elephant on the last night of Labor Day weekend, the music and lights pounding relentlessly around her, Jamie Kessler allowed herself a moment of frustration. How she'd ever survived a whole summer of this was beyond her.

True, Jamie hated the restrictiveness of being bound to one person. She hated going out without free rein to do whatever (with whomever) she liked. And she hated everything about the words *monotony* and *monogamy.*

But there was one thing, Jamie was discovering, she hated more than all of these elements combined.

She hated feeling insecure. Vulnerable. Threatened. Jealous.

And while she and Jeff had made no claims of exclusivity, perhaps a few ground rules were as ideal a resolution as any.

Staring around at the hordes of gyrating partygoers (who instantly became cheesy again the moment she stopped being one of them), Jamie couldn't believe *this* was how she was spending her very last night in the Hamptons. Her very last night of the entire summer. And, from the unpromising looks of things, the very last night of her and Jeff's entire...interaction (to use the word *relationship* would be overly glamorizing things). Why, Jamie might have been appalled—if first she could shatter her utter disbelief.

But what the hell was going on here? She felt as if she were trapped in a dream from which she couldn't wake up, a ghost-like spectator forced to watch a scene from the outskirts. It just didn't make any sense—unless she'd suddenly turned invisible and Ilana had suddenly turned into a different person. Because up until five minutes ago, Jamie was certain she was a million times more pretty, exuberant, interesting, and fun. Really, all Ilana was, was a whiny, generic, scowling girl!

Although, come to think of it, Ilana was currently laughing and flirting, and the only girl with a scowl on her face at this moment was Jamie.

"Are you okay?" Allison asked, her face emerging through the mass of bodies surrounding the bottle-bearing table like a defensive line.

Jamie nodded, wondering if she wore her dissatisfaction as flamboyantly as her wardrobe. Though, given that she was accustomed to either (a) standing on the benches shaking her ass for hours on end, or (b) doing lap after lap around the club and chatting with as many different people as possible, sitting down (something other people did regularly) was Jamie's equivalent of throwing in the towel.

Fearful that others were noticing this, Jamie quickly mustered all the energy she had in her to rise to her feet. Forging a smile, she resolved then and there to (at least pretend to) enjoy herself—harping on guys was to her the epitome of female weakness.

Good thing she was such a capable actress. For the drumbeats that normally took strong possession of her now sounded like a five-year-old banging haphazardly on pots. And each time she attempted to shake her body to them, this dorky guy—who was a friend of a friend of someone in their share house—began grinding up against her. Plus, as if she had up and disappeared into thin air, Jeff remained continually engrossed in Ilana (not that Jamie was continually looking). Instead, she merely peered around determinedly, attempting to locate any good-looking guys in the crowd, but couldn't spot a single one. Who were all these random holiday people anyway? How was it Pink Elephant was so uncharacteristically bad? Why, if this night weren't their final one (and Mark hadn't been so kind as to comp their entire party), Jamie hardly believed it worth it to stay out here at all! Seriously, she'd rather be...

"Shot?" Brian asked, returning from the bar with Rob in tow, and (not before receiving an annoyed looked from his girlfriend) passing out the numerous shot glasses they could barely hold in their hands.

Jamie mechanically took one, but for reasons unbeknownst to her, she just as mechanically passed it on. Surely it wasn't wise to risk a hangover when, after observing Jeff and Ilana, she already felt nauseated.

Watching her housemates pound back the shots, Jamie found it quite ironic that she was painstakingly (and unprecedently) sober—on a night she anticipated being trashed beyond belief! At least, that had been her intention some hours ago at the house, when she'd looked on sentimentally during their final game of flip cup. When she'd celebrated getting ready in a share house for the final time (it never did get any easier, even if she had gotten used to it). When she'd posed with everyone on the deck for some final group pictures (to make up for not having taken any all summer long, and to be used in the Ofoto album that would be instrumental in luring candidates for next summer).

Catching Mark's eye and feeling guilty that he'd seen her

sulking, Jamie really *did* want to be enjoying herself. Though it hardly felt that way at the moment, this would be their last time all occupying a booth together as 1088 Montauk, in the way they'd been doing for the past three months—in the way she would so fondly picture them whenever she later thought of the summer. Suddenly it all felt so fleeting, and Jamie felt like she should somehow be trying to prolong it, trying to mentally capture it like a photograph. But instead she was only letting the songs play, letting the seconds pass, letting it all slip away like sand through open fingers.

From a distance, Jamie noticed Ilana lean over and give Jeff a joking shove.

She decided to close her fingers. He wasn't gone yet.

"How's it going?" Jamie said, walking over and immediately feeling like she was interrupting something.

"Hey," Jeff said, momentarily turning but not really looking at her. In a way Jamie had never before seen—in a way alcohol couldn't entirely excuse—he appeared in some kind of trance that even her presence couldn't fully abort. Finally, in a delayed reaction of sorts, he seemed to will his eyes to meet hers, a half smile on his face. But it was the kind of smile that clearly wasn't intended for Jamie, but left over from whatever thought it was he'd just been entertaining. He was giving her Ilana's smile.

"Turns out Ilana's cousin just moved into my building," he said, as if that could possibly justify their hour-long conversation. They were flirting in a way Jamie could clearly see, but would feel stupid calling to his attention without some kind of proof.

"Oh, that's so funny," Jamie answered, her patience wearing thin. But just as she was about to suggest going over to the bar for a vodka soda...

"Wait, I forgot to tell you!" Ilana exclaimed, leaning in close to his ear like the club's noise level left her no choice (even though everyone at 1088 Montauk knew what tremendous volume Ilana's voice was capable of). And that's when Jamie'd had enough.

She knew she couldn't get upset with him—not when they hadn't set any kind of boundaries, established any kind of rules, professed to be anything other than two single shareholders seeking innocent fun. The problem was, while she couldn't put a finger on when it had happened, Jamie wasn't exactly having fun anymore. And perhaps because the summer was ending, perhaps because they were coming to a crossroads, perhaps because, for the first time in her life, she wasn't sure she could get what she wanted, Jamie found herself needing some definition. Needing to know what would come next.

Then, before she knew what she was even doing, before she really took the time to think about it, she tapped Jeff on the shoulder pointedly. "Listen, I think we need to talk," she snapped, hardly recognizing her own voice attached to the nagging, girlfriend-ish words.

To that, Jeff and Ilana exchanged a telling look. Jamie instantly hated that she had triggered it.

And in that moment, Jamie could hear it.

The sound of the tables going *flip*.

If only because he'd have looked uncooperative otherwise, Jeff followed her outside onto the patio, which was littered with partygoers and smokers and couples seeking intimacy for more scandalous reasons. In utter silence, Jamie led their way through the crowd on the narrow wooden planks, concentrating on not falling into the sand or catching her heel in a crack, and losing more of her nerve with every step. Debating how to express the sentiments she'd for weeks now been holding in. Once she'd settled on the words, and they'd settled on a bench, her mind promptly went blank.

"So," she said, gazing around shyly. (Was it just her imagination, or were those girls in the corner glaring?) "Last night
here."

"Yup. Crazy," he said, seeming more concerned with her
cleavage than with where she was going with this.

Unsure of how to broach the topic casually, she decided to
just put it out there. "Well, I was thinking. I know neither of
us was looking for anything serious"—she shot him a quick
glance to ensure his reaction corroborated this—"but maybe
when we get back to the city next week, we can step it up
a little. Like do something other than just meet up at your
apartment late-night. Like maybe...dinner." As if she'd just
hit on a buzzword, the light in his formerly iridescent eyes
extinguished. "Not that I don't like drunk text-messaging at
two AM," she quickly followed with a tense smile.

"Are you trying to tell me you don't like my texts?" he said,
presumably a joke, but pronounced with a perfectly straight
face (making it difficult to tell if he was actually joking). He
seized her then with his innocent blue eyes—eyes that, when
focused on her, could seemingly do no wrong.

"I *live* for your texts," she said, a sarcastic statement that
carried more truth than she'd have cared to admit. "It's
just...some girls might be offended if you only called them
when you're drunk and want to hook up."

And by *some girls,* she most of all meant herself.

He didn't say anything, so Jamie went on. "I have to work
a screening on Tuesday, but what are you doing Wednesday?
Or Thursday?"

He let out a long sigh, perhaps to buy himself some
time. "Next week is going to suck at work," he said, looking
strangely uncomfortable (and not looking anywhere near the
vicinity of her cleavage). "Why don't we just play things by
ear?"

Jamie frowned. She was all too familiar with the not-wanting-to-be-pinned-down-with-a-day spiel. Heck, it used to be her mantra! "Why don't you not call me again until you know when you're free?" she said, not realizing until after she said it that it sounded a hell of a lot like a rule. Like an ultimatum, even.

And she certainly didn't realize the consequences that would follow.

His eyes wandered around the pool dismissively before finally finding hers again. Though, when they did, she immediately felt a difference. A coldness. He was looking at her now not as the pretty girl—like he always had—but as the annoying one who'd just pressed him for more than he wanted to give. And as Jamie knew from her dealings with guys, a clingy person who sought a relationship instantly lost all attraction. No matter how beautiful at the outset, once this motive was exposed, the person instantly turned ugly. "Look, I would never want to hurt you or anything," he began, the word *hurt* hurting her most of all. "But I told you from the beginning. I'm only twenty-nine. I'm not really looking for anything serious right now."

Jamie was stunned—less at the prospect of being refused than at his accusation that she actually wanted something. Or perhaps at the realization that a small part of her did. That even though she'd always preferred to keep things casual and physical (between the sheets as much as during the nighttime hours), this share house had eased them involuntarily into daybreak, into being not just sexual partners but hang-out-all-day friends, into a whole new level of intimacy that Jamie met with less repugnance—less fear—than she'd initially thought. And now that it'd been forced upon her, Jamie didn't want to give it up.

But even if she was surprisingly open to a relationship, Jeff had just made it clear that he wasn't. And at this point, why should he be? Why would a guy (of *only* twenty-nine, God forbid!) want to operate in reverse? She was already giving him something for nothing—allowing him to have his cake and eat it, too! What incentive had he to pay for it now?

"*I'm* not looking for anything serious," Jamie said, mostly because it was the only thing she could get out.

"Well, either way. If you're not happy, you shouldn't have to put up with this," he continued. He put his hand on her shoulder, more the way a brother might. "Jame, I think you're a beautiful, smart girl, and I have a really good time with you. But you deserve to be with someone who can give you what you want."

Suddenly feeling the night chill, the only thing Jamie wanted at this moment was to get the hell off the patio. That, and to as quickly as possible make him eat his words (which she was nonetheless certain in an hour or so he would do). Crossing her arms around her chest, she rose to her feet. "It's freezing. I'm going back inside." And without waiting to see if he was going to follow her, she darted away from him.

Winding through the maze of people, Jamie was practically fuming. She was beyond furious at Jeff, of course, but—recalling Rachel's frequent claim that "drunken hook-ups never lead to relationships"—she couldn't help but also point the finger at herself. As much as she'd always ridiculed Rachel for her rules, her friend would never be caught in such a dead-end situation. Maybe there was something to be said for driving with directions, looking farther ahead than your headlights, following your head instead of your heart (or, worse yet, your hormones).

Or maybe that wouldn't have changed anything at all.

When Jamie finally made it back inside, Allison (who was standing as far as she could away from Brian, all the way across the table) came over to her. "You'll never believe the text message I just got," she said, turning around her phone.

```
Left with Aaron. C U at the house ;)
Rachel
              Sun, Sept 3, 1:02 am
```

Jamie had to smile. "Finally!" she said. "I knew that Patrón was the right move." She also knew it was time to put an end to her own pathetic pity party.

Climbing up top one of the benches, she grabbed Allison's hand and yanked her up onto another one. Shaking her ass (like everyone was watching), Jamie reveled in the music and attention that instantly turned her mood, and swore to herself she wasn't going down without a fight.

It took only a moment for Jeff to follow her back in, and even less time for Ilana to accost him. But Jamie remained confident her magnetism would eventually sway his hesitance, especially when she saw him intermittently watching her (prompting her to dance that much more charismatically). Like metal to a magnet, she honestly thought she had him hooked—had him following each toss of her hair, shake of her hips, desirous stare from other interested parties. She thought this—expected this—yet didn't turn around to confirm this. Rather than acknowledge him, Jamie believed flirtation was a cat-chase-mouse game. To get him, you had to ignore him. The only way to get something was to give nothing.

And just when she thought she'd won him over, the darnedest thing happened. She didn't.

But someone else did.

When Jamie finally looked his way, what she saw stung her like a whip to her face. Like everything she knew in life all at once pulled out from under her. For, in the quintessential act of betrayal, she saw Jeff and Ilana. Kissing. Embracing. Making a drunken public spectacle of themselves (and certainly not watching her moves on the platform). Repulsed, enraged, and most of all confused (Jamie was prettier, sexier, bubblier! Who chose a burger over steak?), she stood in disbelief. She simply couldn't believe her eyes and, unfortunately, wasn't watching her feet.

For in that moment, Jamie could hear it. The entire club could hear it.

The sound of the bench going *flip.*

The whole thing happened extremely quickly—the unsturdy rocking back and forth, Jamie's bending her knees in an attempt to steady it, and finally that scary unsalvageable falling. A falling that culminated with a scene-stoppingly loud crash, bringing Jamie from her high suspension in the air all the way down to the floor, taking everything (the table, the glasses, the alcohol bottles) along with her. There was the distinct shattering of glass (which summoned dramatic screams and gasps, yet fortunately landed nowhere near her) followed by a deafening silence—leaving Jamie frozen on the floor, unable to budge.

As if she were a gunshot victim, a huge crowd quickly gathered (in addition to the thirty or so housemates who'd had the privilege of witnessing her acrobatics up close). Jamie imagined she'd be a laughingstock, though rather than burst out in hysterics, the stares of the horde encircling her seemed to be inquiring, *Is that girl okay?*

Which was actually a pretty good question—one whose answer even Jamie didn't know for sure. For, despite her instant tears (triggered less by her fall than emotional distress), she was strangely impervious to the physical pain. She simply lay there on the ground, wishing she could just about die of embarrassment—wishing this night were just a really bad dream. And wishing most of all that people would just stop looking at her.

The club's cleaning crew appeared then, swiftly moving in to disperse the crowd. Jamie noticed Jeff among them, appearing earnestly concerned, but then retreating a bit too willingly per the crew's gruff instructions. It was actually Mark who offered his assistance.

"She's okay, everyone just step back," he called out with assumed authority. When they obliged, he knelt down beside her. "Are you hurt?" he asked, scanning her body for cuts.

In truth, her ankle was a bit sore and she feared her new Louboutins had taken an irreversible beating, but Jamie merely shook her head—because the kind of hurt she was, no doctor would detect.

"Well, do you want to get out of here?"

Nodding, Jamie took the hand Mark offered out to her, and hobbled around the upturned bench.

I thought you'd never ask, she said to herself.

Chapter
Twenty-two

Allison Stern had brought far too much baggage.

Not only that, she'd barely worn half of it.

But sometimes, in life as in luggage, you didn't end up needing everything you thought you would.

You couldn't have possibly known at the time—heck, having it along perhaps provided a trivial comfort—yet you could recognize all too well the moment you stopped needing it anymore.

Thus it was with newfound independence that Allison knocked on Brian's door that final morning—ready to get rid of her deadweight.

"Do you think we can talk?" she asked, entering his dark room and discovering him cramming everything (that had lived all weekend on the floor) into a small duffel bag.

Pausing, clothing in hand, he merely raised an eyebrow.

"Somewhere else maybe?" she added, noting his frustrated expression (no doubt exacerbated by his raging hangover) and wondering if now was really the best time for this. But in actuality, *when was* there a good time for this kind of conversation? (She'd learned that the *where* of the equation was certainly not in a confined vehicle.)

Abandoning the duffel without further question, Brian rose to his feet and followed her, attempting to read her body language like someone's cards in a poker match.

He halted when they'd made it up the steps to an empty

living room, though Allison continued to lead him out the door and away from the windows.

"Where are you taking me?" he whined, rubbing his eyes with his fists and squinting away the morning sunlight, whose cheerful intensity Allison suddenly resented.

She didn't answer, only dragged him on till she was satisfied they were no longer within earshot of anyone. Then she knew she was expected to start talking. But she just looked up at him, inhaling that familiar amalgamation of his cologne with last night's Patrón—which she'd imagined might repulse her, yet instead served to trigger her sympathy. The silence that followed then seemed to extend indefinitely. Despite being a phenomenal poker player, Brian had absolutely no idea what she was going to say. Allison took a deep breath.

"I feel like, lately, things between us haven't been...the same," she began, fiddling with her fingernails. She failed to say the same as what, yet this seemed to suffice in getting her point across.

"Are you serious?" Brian asked, her blunt declaration immediately sobering him. Struck by disbelief, he stared at her hard, as if searching her face for some sign that she was joking (a sign she was *this close* to giving him), before turning on the defensive. "I thought things were going great."

"Well...not exactly." She scrunched her nose as if she were telling him his shirt didn't work with his pants, rather than that they didn't work as a couple anymore.

"How so?" he challenged, kicking the driveway's pebbles as he said this, perhaps to defuse the emotion behind it.

Um...Allison racked her brain for an eloquent way to express that he was immature, insensitive, and the kind of person she could never be with...

"I just think we're two very different people," she said instead, wishing he weren't staring at her so intently, or hanging on her every word like it contained some hidden meaning. "And as much as I hate to admit it, we kind of did rush into this. I mean, the summer was amazing, and I don't regret anything—"

"But you want to *slow things down?*" he said, pronouncing the clichéd phrase with the kind of sarcastic smile people use when they really mean the exact opposite.

Growing frustratingly inarticulate, Allison glanced away.

"To be honest, I just came out of a relationship," she said, aware this trite explanation left much to be desired. But also supposing that, when it's not what you want to hear, any explanation might have. She gazed at him with an earnestness she hoped could compensate. "I think I should try being single."

In the manner she knew it would, in the manner she'd expected it to, that word rattled her every nerve. For in her head, it'd sounded right. In theory, it'd sounded necessary. But now, coming from her lips that morning, it sounded frightening. It sounded hasty. It sounded irreversibly wrong.

But unlike the last time, it sounded remarkably better than maintaining an ill-suited relationship for the mere sake of avoiding it. In comparison with what she'd been through, *single* wasn't so scary a label anymore.

"So this is it?" Brian asked, his heartfelt hazel eyes revealing a pain his words never would. And long after his voice had given up, they continued to plead his case.

Lingering there, Allison avoided his gaze. For in it she no longer saw traces of immaturity or jealousy or cruelty; she saw only softness. She saw the guy who had waited around with them at the share house for Jamie's mom to arrive, who lent Jim a pair of jeans when no one else was willing to, who escorted her home from the club when Josh was trying to make her jealous. In a dopey, desperate trance, his eyes channeled these things: maybe if they engaged her hard enough, long enough, deep enough, they could somehow change her mind. But—with a resolve she hadn't felt even at the start of their conversation—Allison's mind was made up.

"This is it," she echoed with certainty. And they remained there, motionless, until Mark's car pulled into the driveway. Jamie's SUV swerved in seconds later (simultaneously swiping the bushes).

"We hit *so much traffic!*" Jamie squealed, hopping out of the driver's seat, seemingly oblivious to the fact she was interrupting something. Then—realizing that a lot had happened since they'd gone to get Jamie's car at the train station—she and Rachel grew silent.

Brian, in a valiant effort to appear casual, raised his arm to Mark in greeting, looked Allison in the eye one final time, and walked away. Out of the driveway, out of her life.

But that was how it had to be.

When her friends requested details, Allison candidly relayed what had happened.

"Wow. Are you okay?" Jamie asked, looking at her like she shouldn't have been.

Allison nodded. In fact, she was surprised by how okay she felt. Much more okay, even, than when she'd done this the last time. Maybe it was because she'd never loved Brian the way she had Josh (who'd cowardly slipped out of the house this morning without so much as a good-bye). Maybe Brian was merely an ephemeral replacement. Or maybe Allison was just getting stronger.

"I think I will be," she said, turning around to retrieve her luggage.

As she started for her room and headed up the front steps—those same steps she'd so cautiously ascended months earlier—Allison thought about how far she'd come since the summer. How naive she'd been walking into it. How she never wanted to be that shy, sheltered, dependent girl again. And yet she highly doubted she would be.

There was no being "shy" in a Hamptons share house. When you lived alongside forty-odd other people, you had to get used to being seen at all times, speaking before a large group more often than not, watching indecent behavior happening right in front of you. Throughout the summer, Allison had been forced to get behind the wheel (literally), to handle uncomfortable situations, to exercise her own opinions, to make her voice heard. As a result, her tolerance for randomness had grown considerably stronger, and things didn't seem to shock her anymore. Life didn't seem to shock her anymore.

Still, hardened buffer or not, she dreaded the thought of being back *there*. Doing *that:* soliciting dates, commanding introductions, buying "going-out clothes" (more realistically, borrowing Jamie's), and conducting endless small talk with people she hardly knew. Allison hated being back there—she might always hate being back there—but she'd done it before, and she was nearly certain she could do it again.

Trudging back through the common room, she passed by two guys she'd never before seen stretched out on the sofa. Witnessing her futile attempt to transport her trusty rolling suitcase along with pillows and blankets and multiple shopping bags out the front door, they politely rose to their feet.

"Need a hand?" asked one, whose confident demeanor seemed highly contrary to his tall, lanky body.

"Thanks," Allison said after a momentary pause. She wasn't sure if his words were pronounced with an outer-borough accent or an international one, but either way she was willing to let them relieve her of her stuff. Then, feeling strangely uninhibited—both physically and emotionally—she paced behind them.

"That's my friend's car, over there." She pointed to Jamie's abandoned vehicle. "But you can just put that down anywhere."

Gentlemen that they were, they insisted on negotiating everything into the back (a bit of a struggle, given the full-length mirror and million other oddities already crammed in there). Once successful, the taller, more gregarious one turned to her.

"That's a lot of stuff for one weekend," he said, in what Allison was now able to identify as an Australian accent.

She immediately blushed. "Oh, no. That's all the stuff we stored here in the closets. We had a share," she explained. Eager to change the subject, she added, "What about you?"

"Same. But we didn't make it out that much. Like, ever." He shot a reprimanding glance to his friend—a shorter guy with light, spiky hair. Neither of the two said anything further, yet both continued to stand there.

"Well, thanks for your help," Allison said finally, hoping she wouldn't offend them after their benevolent deed. "What are your names again?"

"I'm Mike," said the taller one, in that accent that made anything sound fascinating. "And this is John."

Feeling a surge of recognition, Allison turned to him. "John what?" she pried.

"John...Hiscock?" he said, clearly confused by her extreme interest.

Allison could barely contain her delight. *"Hiscock?"* she cried, studying him as if some TV star had just jumped off her screen into real life. *"You're Hiscock?"*

Color rushing to his face, John grew even more uncomfortable. "Uh, yes?" he stammered—like she'd accidentally mistaken him for someone else, and was any minute going to realize it.

Unable to banish her giddy grin, Allison whipped around, wishing there were someone else here to share in her amusement. Too bad Hiscock wasn't discovered even half an hour earlier! And what was the sense in his coming now? It was the last weekend of the summer! He'd taken absolutely no part in the share house at all!

But the more Allison thought about it, the more she realized that—even in his absence—Hiscock was actually a pretty big part. Some might even say huge.

For, as the unofficial icebreaker, he'd been there when he was needed the most. In the face of distress and uncertainty, he had facilitated an uncomfortable transition. He'd served more of a purpose than he'd ever know.

And so had Brian.

Maybe down the line, Allison would reunite with him, or Josh, or even Steve, say. Maybe she wouldn't. Or maybe, without a guy, she'd always feel somewhat naked.

But Allison left the share house that day taking all her baggage with her, yet finally (finally) leaving much of her baggage behind.

And long after she'd finished (her share, that is), she was happy she came.

Epilogue

It starts with a party, unlike any they've been to before.

The time of choice: happy hour on a weeknight. The location of choice: a local bar in a neighborhood like Murray Hill, where 99 percent of the participants already coexist in adjacent doorman buildings. The crowd of choice: anyone willing to fork over upward of two (point five) grand for a single bed in a five-person bedroom on alternating summer weekends.

And newcomers will learn: anything they say, do, drink, dance on, or go home with will forever be held against them. Worse yet, it will *define* them.

Now swap one sampling of overworked, sun-deprived twentysomethings for the next, their hard-earned dough for an entrapment that is both finite (three months) and grandly paid for, and...

"Welcome to our Hamptons meet-and-greet party," boomed an authoritative voice from across the room. "Don't worry, I'll make this brief," it continued, when a collective murmur of booing ensued. "I'm Mark, the one running the house this summer. And this is my co-house-manager"—he turned and pointed—"my girlfriend, Jamie."

As nearly fifty heads whirled to face her all at once, Jamie glanced up at Mark and flashed the smile that title always seemed to precipitate. Funny, even though it'd been almost nine months since they'd gotten together, Jamie doubted she'd ever be able to hear that word attached to her name without considering it an oxymoron. Still, she had to admit she liked it.

Having captured the crowd's full attention, Mark continued. "Now, I know some of you signed on months ago, and others of you are here just to see what this is all about. But I have to caution you, there are only a *limited number of spots left…*"

"Yeah, right," whispered a snooty girl in front of Jamie, to her friends next to her.

"…so if you brought your checkbooks, a deposit is the safest way to ensure your spot in the house." Stifling her laughter, Jamie gazed around at the solemn, apprehensive faces, ingesting Mark's words the way you would a professor's on the first day of school. To think that her face had ever been one of them! "Anyway, that's it—go drink, mingle. Jamie and I are going to be walking around handing things out, if you have any questions."

Taking this cue, Jamie jumped down from her bar stool and grabbed the pile of stapled Xeroxes they'd assembled pretty much ten minutes earlier (a comprehensive listing of directions, regulations, and emergency information—updated marginally from year to year). Flipping to the rules portion, it was with particular pride that Jamie's eyes glanced over her own contributions to the list:

- In case of emergency, please bring (not one but) *two* sets of car keys.
- Stray from the house at night at your own risk!
- Before going to sleep, it is advisable—and for girls, imperative—to lock your bedroom door.
- Commitments to the house are final and nontransferable: no refunds, no weekend swapping, and (absolutely) no substitutes!

- Guests are a privilege, especially on holidays, and must be approved in advance.
- Parking spots are a privilege, especially on holidays, and allotted on a first-come, first-served basis (nothing personal).
- Baked goods are best confined to the kitchen.
- If you buy bottles at nightclubs, you're on your own to collect. (See Bottle-Service Etiquette, attached).
- There will be no drugs (cough), no pets, and *no parents*!

Her eyes fixated on the page, Jamie didn't even notice Mark had come up behind her until he draped his arm around her shoulder. "So, how do you like being on the other side of things?" he said, his dark eyes sparking with excitement.

"This is *so* weird," she answered, handing him half her stack. "It's like being on the other side of sorority rush sophomore year. Although I have to say, it kind of makes me miss everyone from last summer."

"Well, last summer we had a very special group." Holding her gaze, he then turned to survey the crowd. "But not bad, right? What do you think of this year's prospects?"

Jamie glanced about the room, whose occupants were busy scoping one another out and responding in one of two ways: by either (a) keeping to themselves, as if they were incapable of interacting and might as well have been at home on their couch; or (b) racing to move in on any desirable (and hence, overlapping) romantic candidates.

"They seem really...young," she said. "Well, except for that group over by the pool table," she corrected, pointing to a trio of guys chugging beers and conversing rowdily—a telltale sign they were trying to knock at least a decade off their age. "Don't they look too old?"

"Too old…to sign a check?" Mark joked, never one to discriminate when it came to maximizing his income. Though, upon hearing a loud shriek of laughter, their attention was simultaneously diverted to the bar, where a girl in a sequined tank top stood commanding a (mostly male) crowd. "That girl's going to be trouble," Mark predicted, shaking his head.

"Well, the guy she's talking to, in the light blue Lacoste shirt, looks like a huge player," Jamie countered. She peered around some more. "Although," she added, beginning to get into this, "the one sitting at that booth there, with all the girls around him, might give him some competition. That's Jay—he was on Season One of *The Bachelorette*."

Mark looked at her and raised an eyebrow. "I hope you're not planning on ditching me for one of these twenty-year-olds."

"No way," she said. "I mean, not unless he has prime real estate south of the highway."

She winked and went about distributing the sheets, which most people accepted readily enough. Although apparently not everyone could appreciate all her efforts.

"Rules?" she overheard one guy exclaim moments after she'd handed him a copy. "They've got to be kidding me! This is supposed to be, like, our *vacation*."

Jamie glanced back at the dissenter (who, even without his green corporate Merrill bag, seemed to scream *investment banker*). And in that fearless yet haphazard way she had perfected, she approached him.

"No, I hear you," she said, with a toss of her hair. "But the thing is, if we didn't have rules, the entire share house would fall apart. There wouldn't even be a share house to do in the first place."

"Well, I'm not sure I'm doing it yet," the guy said, shrugging and exchanging a supercilious look with his banker friend.

"Really?" Jamie exclaimed, like he'd just told her he'd forgotten to put on underwear this morning. "Have you seen the pictures from last year? Ten Eighty-eight Montauk is, hands-down, the sickest house!" Leaning in, she lowered her voice to a whisper. "Also, I'm the one doing the schedule. If you guys end up doing it, I'll make sure to put you on the good weekends."

After some minor convincing (in the form of an extensive conversation detailing where they lived, what they did, and where in the tristate area they were from), Jamie emerged with two fresh checks. It'd been a tough sell at first, but—just as many guys had done before them—they'd conceded.

Though, as Jamie was about to run off and relay the good news to Mark, she felt a tap on her shoulder. Turning, she found herself face-to-face with three skeptical-looking girls, their tiny bodies decked out in designer jeans, wedge heels, and the exact same studded Kooba bag (in three different colors).

"You were in the house last year, right?" asked one, her intonation annoying yet not unkind. "I recognize your face from the pictures."

But before Jamie could confirm or deny this, the girl went on. "So, we want you to tell us all the dirt. Like, what's the house really like?"

"What do you mean?" Jamie asked, not sure where she was going with this.

The girls exchanged dubious glances, then all started talking at once. "I heard share houses are dirty and disgusting, and there's beer and garbage *everywhere,*" the first attested.

"I heard there's *one* shower for, like, *twenty* people," her friend spoke up.

"Well, my older sister's friend Ilana did this house last year, and she said it was an absolute nightmare," said the snooty girl Jamie recognized from interrupting Mark's introduction earlier. "How they'll throw *cake* at you, and how this one guy used to climb into girls' *beds* in their *sleep.*"

At once all three of them whipped around, reexamining the room for any overlooked bed-hoppers.

Jamie had to laugh. "What happens in the Hamptons, stays in the Hamptons," she sang, with a suggestive gleam in her eye.

Although seeing as they were still unconvinced, Jamie tried her best to allay their fears. She knew any honest insight into how the *other half* Hamptons—all the drunken escapades, public nudity, hot tub hookups, hideous hangovers, explosive arguments, emotional bonding, and juvenile mischief—could send them running in the other direction. But she also knew that discovering this secret life—discovering you *liked* this secret life—was perhaps the best part.

"There's no way words could ever describe it," she told them, a reminiscent smile spreading across her face. "Just trust me—you're in for the time of your life."

About the Author

I'm pretty much a die-hard New Yorker who grew up in Park Slope, Brooklyn, always sure of two things: that I would always live in New York City and that someday I was going to become a novelist.

This isn't to say I didn't waver from this path. In high school I wrote for my school newspaper, but I was also cheerleading captain, danced in school productions, tutored math, conducted medical research, worked at the Gap on Eighth and Broadway, and was one of those "clipboard girls" at nightclubs.

I attended college at the University of Pennsylvania during a time when it was glamorous (not to mention lucrative) to go into finance. I spent summers working at Salomon Smith Barney, Goldman Sachs, and Merrill Lynch, respectively, then graduated in 2002 with a major in economics and a minor in mathematics. I worked for a few years as a financial analyst at Standard & Poor's, still dreamed of becoming a writer, and made a decision to stop wavering.

I began doing some freelance nightlife reporting and, shortly after, landed a sixteen-week column in the *New York Post*. Each Sunday I documented my share house experiences in the Hamptons—which, to someone who was accustomed to things like pavement, taxicabs, twenty-four-hour everything, and, well, sleeping in beds, proved somewhat of a culture shock.

After resigning from finance, I now do celebrity and night-life reporting alongside writing fiction. Sometimes it's shocking to think I left the business world, and other times shocking to think I ever entered it. Still, there's something to be said for the wisdom of my youth: I currently live in New York City, and am proud to say I am a novelist.

Jasmin

Five Signs You're in a Summer Share House:

1.
You've slept in a room with twice
as many people as beds.

2.
You're impressed when a bathroom
actually has toilet paper.

3.
You'd sooner spend half the day stuck in traffic on
27 than attempt to learn the "back roads."

4.
Your entire weekend wardrobe ends up covered in dirt
(though you don't actually remember seeing any dirt).

5.
You've forgotten what it feels like
to be alone.

If you liked
HOW THE OTHER HALF HAMPTONS,
here are 2 more books that will hit the SPOT

about life, love, and friendship. I loved it."—Melissa Senate, author of *See Jane Date* and *The Breakup Club*

a novel

Knitting under the influence

Claire LaZebnik

Life, love, and the pursuit of the perfect cast-on...

"**Charming... LaZebnik has created three smart, engaging characters, each of whom is complicated and real enough to be worth an entire book on her own.**"

—*Chicago Sun-Times*

Fren•e•my\frĕn´ -mĕ\noun: The friend who gives you the sweetest smile to your face, while holding the sharpest knife to your back.

"**Brilliant... hugely enjoyable... It's romantic, funny, intelligent, believable, and gripping.**"

—Marian Keyes, bestselling author of *Angels*

frenemies
a novel

MEGAN CRANE